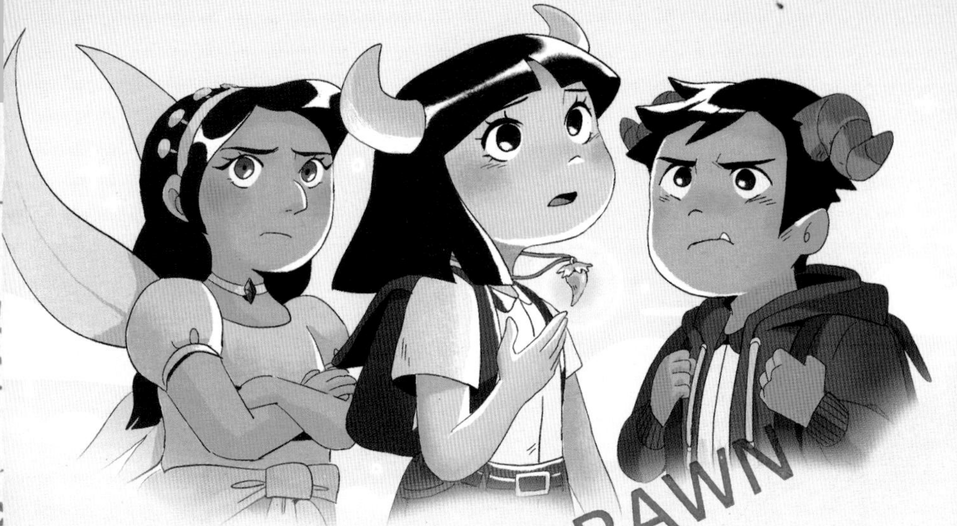

Meesh the BAD DEMON

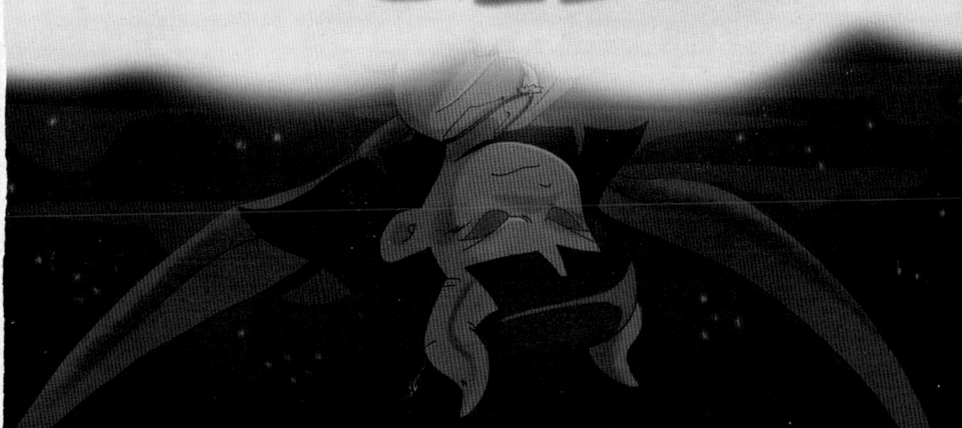

MICHELLE LAM
WITH COLORS BY LAUREN "PERRY" WHEELER

ALFRED A. KNOPF NEW YORK

THIS IS A BORZOI BOOK PUBLISHED BY ALFRED A. KNOPF

Visit us on the Web! rhcbooks.com

Educators and librarians, for a variety of teaching tools, visit us at RHTeachersLibrarians.com

Library of Congress Cataloging-in-Publication Data is available upon request.
ISBN 978-0-593-37287-6 (trade) — ISBN 978-0-593-37288-3 (lib. bdg.) —
ISBN 978-0-593-37289-0 (ebook) — ISBN 978-0-593-37286-9 (trade pbk.)

The text of this book is set in Caffe Lungo.
The illustrations were created using Photoshop.
Book design by Michelle Cunningham
With colors by Lauren "Perry" Wheeler

MANUFACTURED IN CHINA
10 9 8 7 6 5 4 3 2

First Edition

To my grandparents, Chow Yee Cheung,
Lai Cheung, Tsang Lam, and Yeung Ng Lam,
and my parents, Caren Cheung and Kenneth Lam,
for dealing with the REAL Meesh growing up.

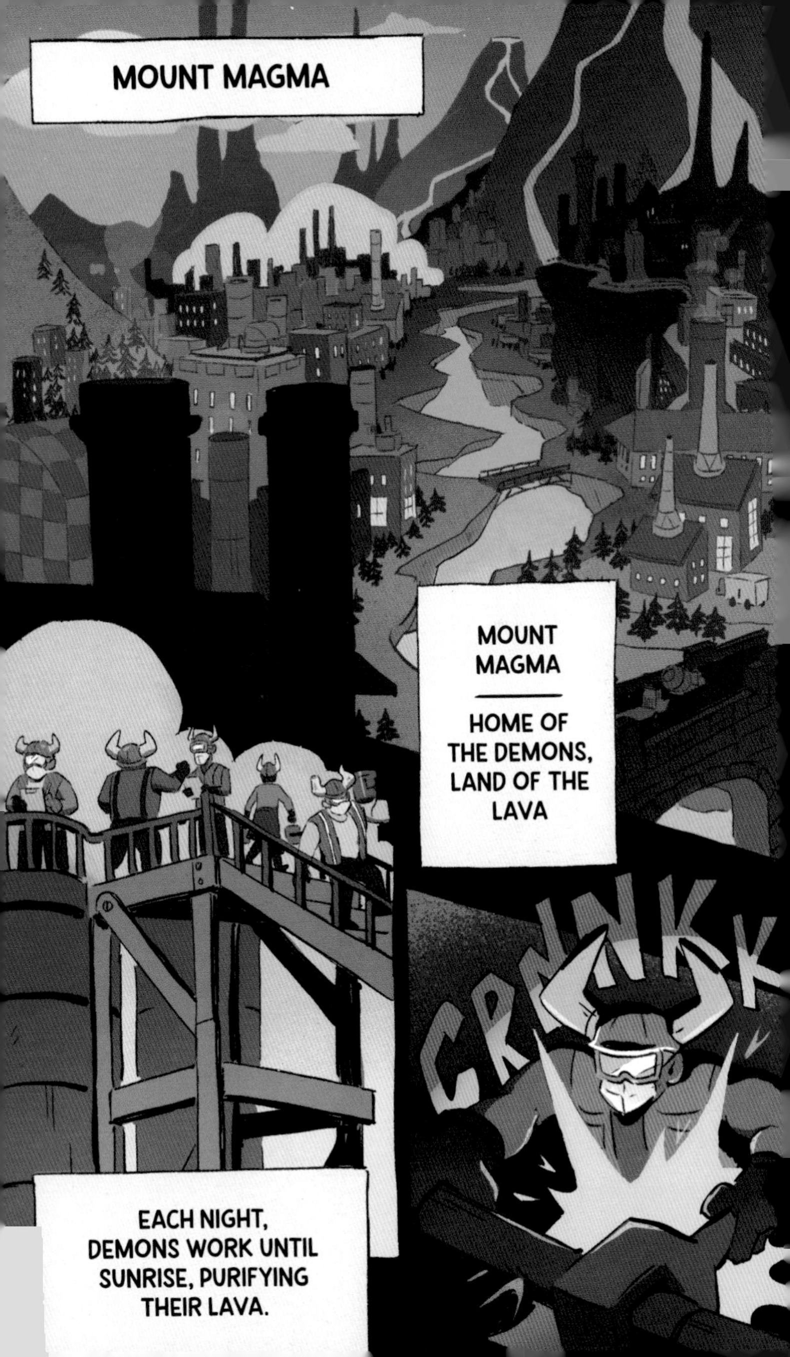
MOUNT MAGMA
MOUNT MAGMA
HOME OF THE DEMONS, LAND OF THE LAVA
EACH NIGHT, DEMONS WORK UNTIL SUNRISE, PURIFYING THEIR LAVA.
CRNNKK

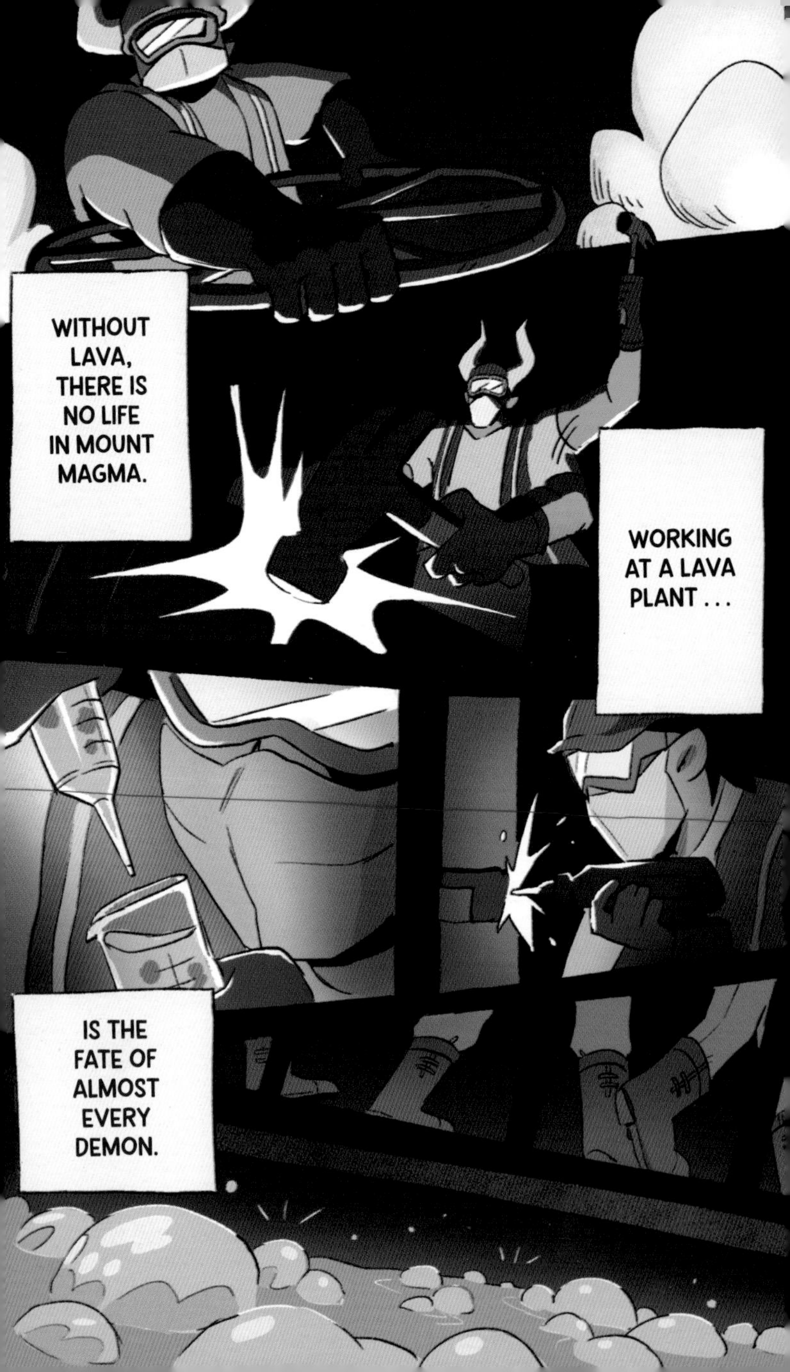
WITHOUT LAVA, THERE IS NO LIFE IN MOUNT MAGMA.
WORKING AT A LAVA PLANT . . .
IS THE FATE OF ALMOST EVERY DEMON.

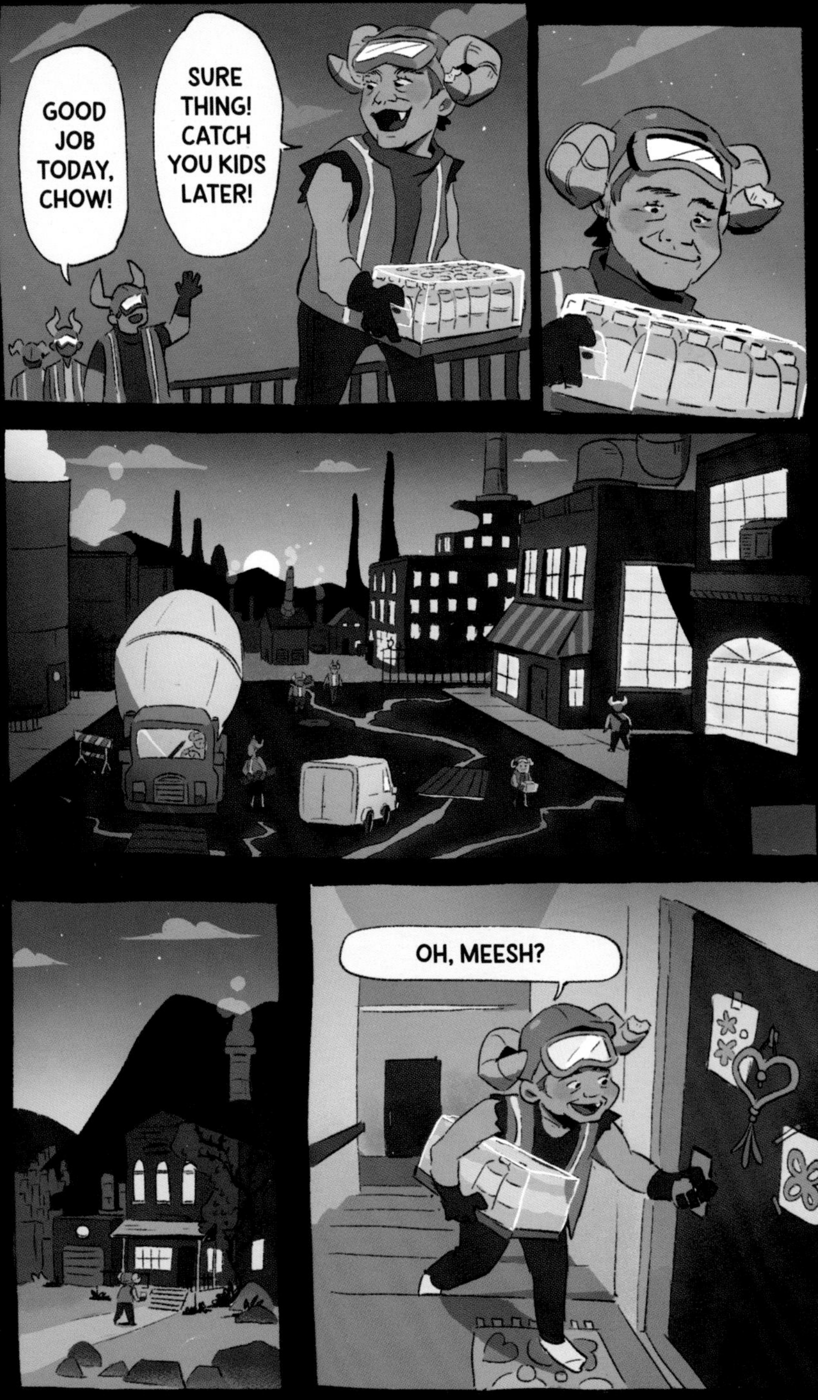
GOOD JOB TODAY, CHOW!
SURE THING! CATCH YOU KIDS LATER!
OH, MEESH?

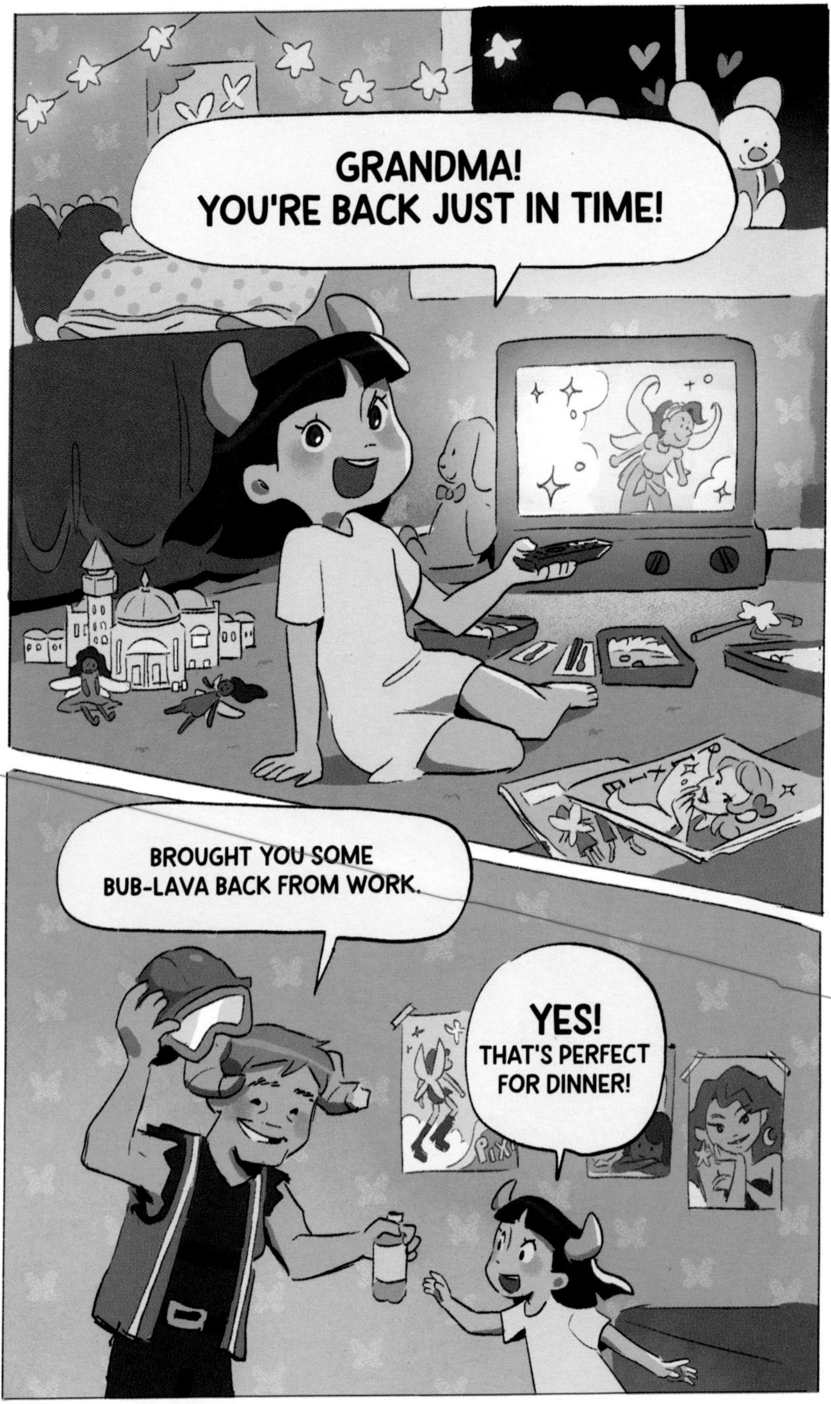
GRANDMA!
YOU'RE BACK JUST IN TIME!
BROUGHT YOU SOME
BUB-LAVA BACK FROM WORK.
YES!
THAT'S PERFECT
FOR DINNER!

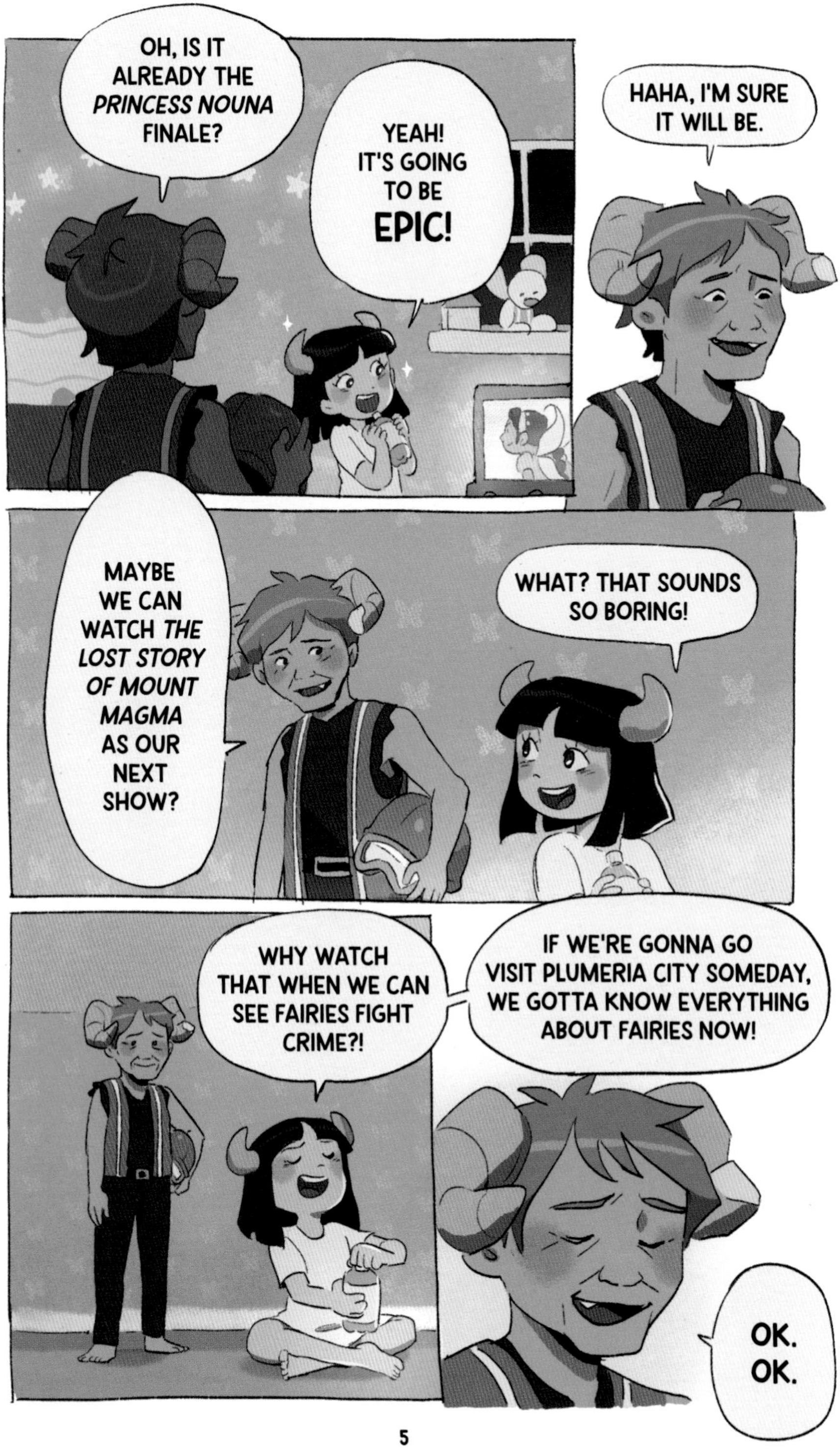
OH, IS IT ALREADY THE *PRINCESS NOUNA* FINALE?
YEAH! IT'S GOING TO BE EPIC!
HAHA, I'M SURE IT WILL BE.
MAYBE WE CAN WATCH *THE LOST STORY OF MOUNT MAGMA* AS OUR NEXT SHOW?
WHAT? THAT SOUNDS SO BORING!
WHY WATCH THAT WHEN WE CAN SEE FAIRIES FIGHT CRIME?!
IF WE'RE GONNA GO VISIT PLUMERIA CITY SOMEDAY, WE GOTTA KNOW EVERYTHING ABOUT FAIRIES NOW!
OK. OK.

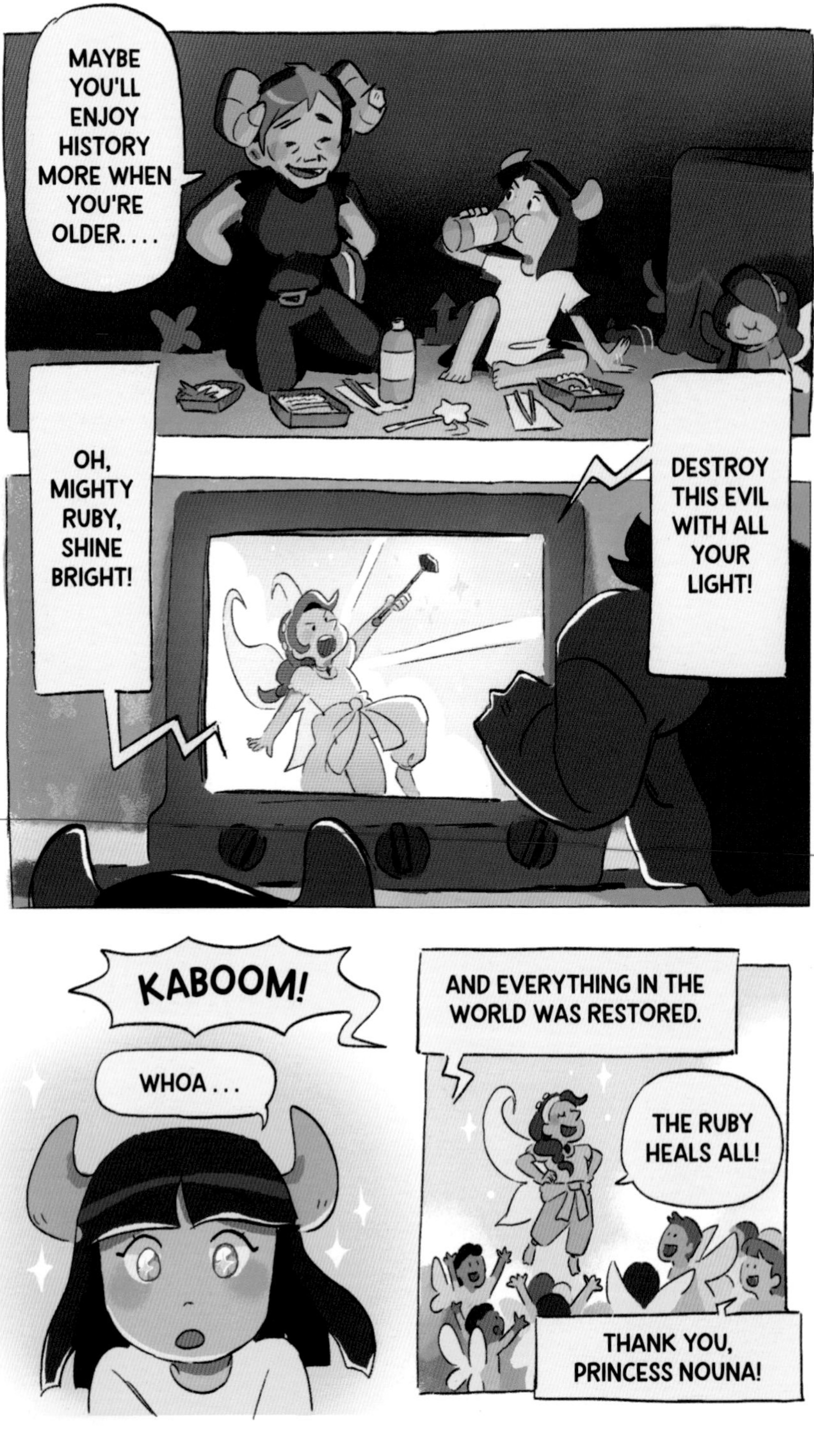
MAYBE YOU'LL ENJOY HISTORY MORE WHEN YOU'RE OLDER. . . .
OH, MIGHTY RUBY, SHINE BRIGHT!
DESTROY THIS EVIL WITH ALL YOUR LIGHT!
KABOOM!
WHOA . . .
AND EVERYTHING IN THE WORLD WAS RESTORED.
THE RUBY HEALS ALL!
THANK YOU, PRINCESS NOUNA!

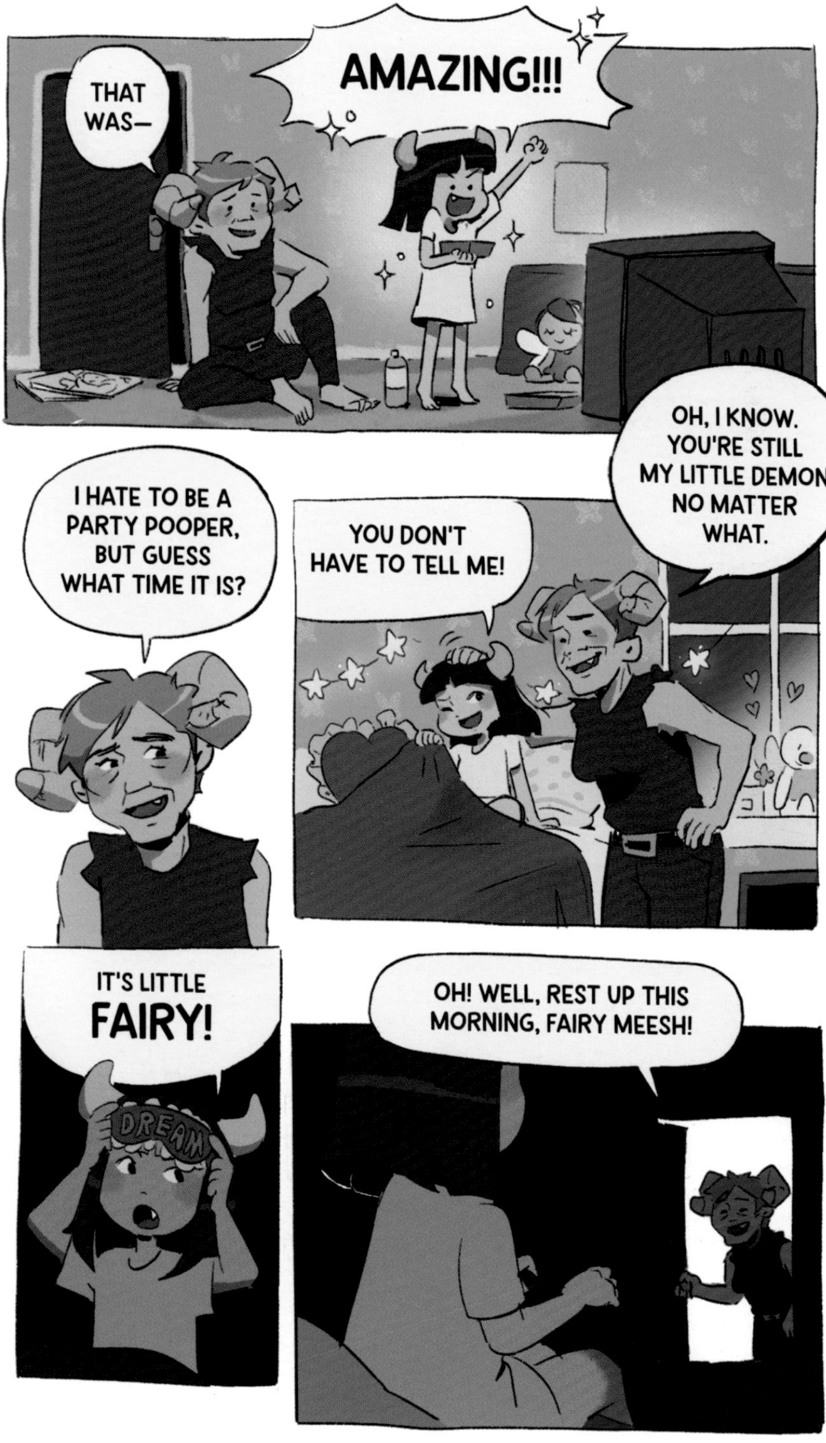
THAT WAS—
AMAZING!!!
I HATE TO BE A PARTY POOPER, BUT GUESS WHAT TIME IT IS?
YOU DON'T HAVE TO TELL ME!
OH, I KNOW. YOU'RE STILL MY LITTLE DEMON NO MATTER WHAT.
IT'S LITTLE FAIRY!
DREAM
OH! WELL, REST UP THIS MORNING, FAIRY MEESH!

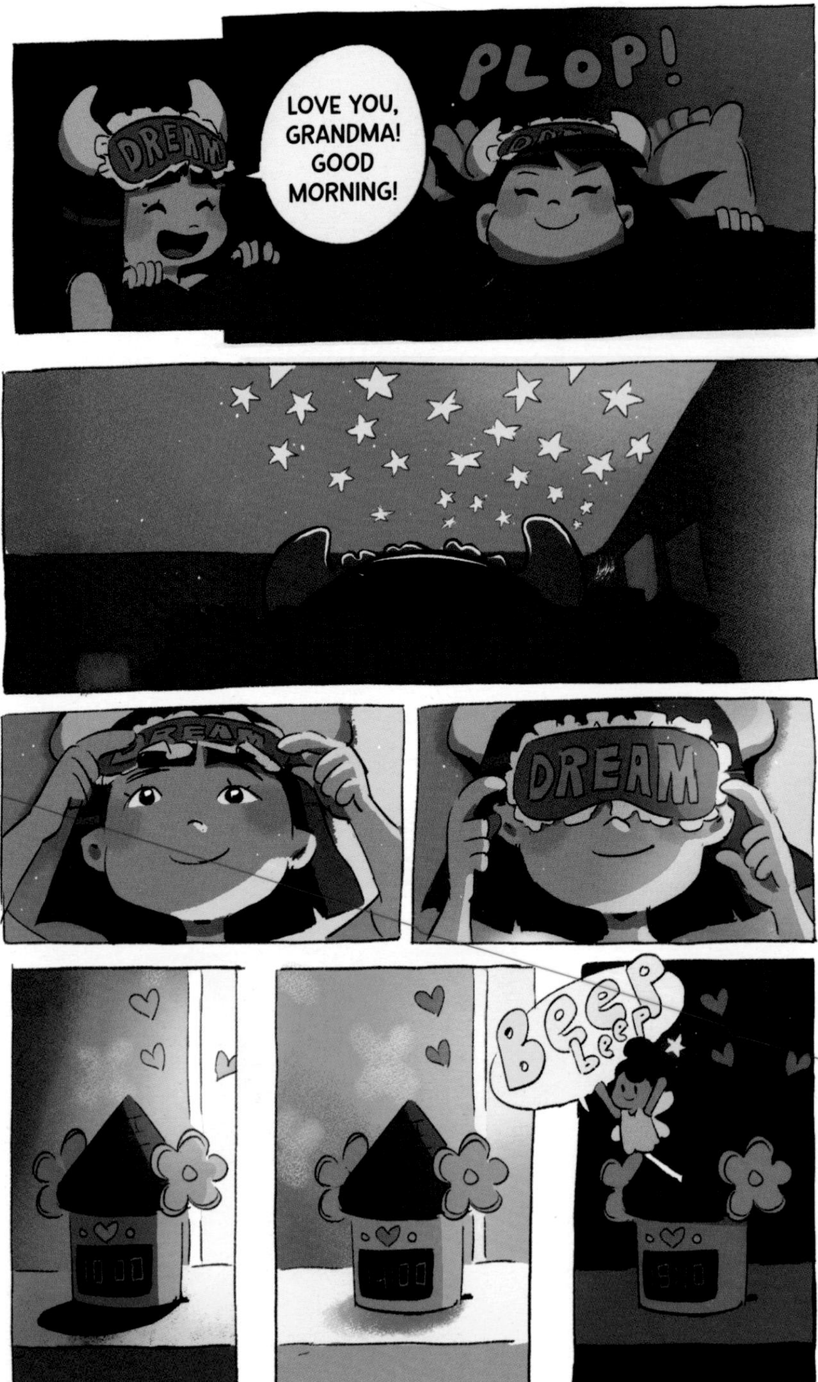
LOVE YOU, GRANDMA! GOOD MORNING!
PLOP!
DREAM
DREAM
Beep beep

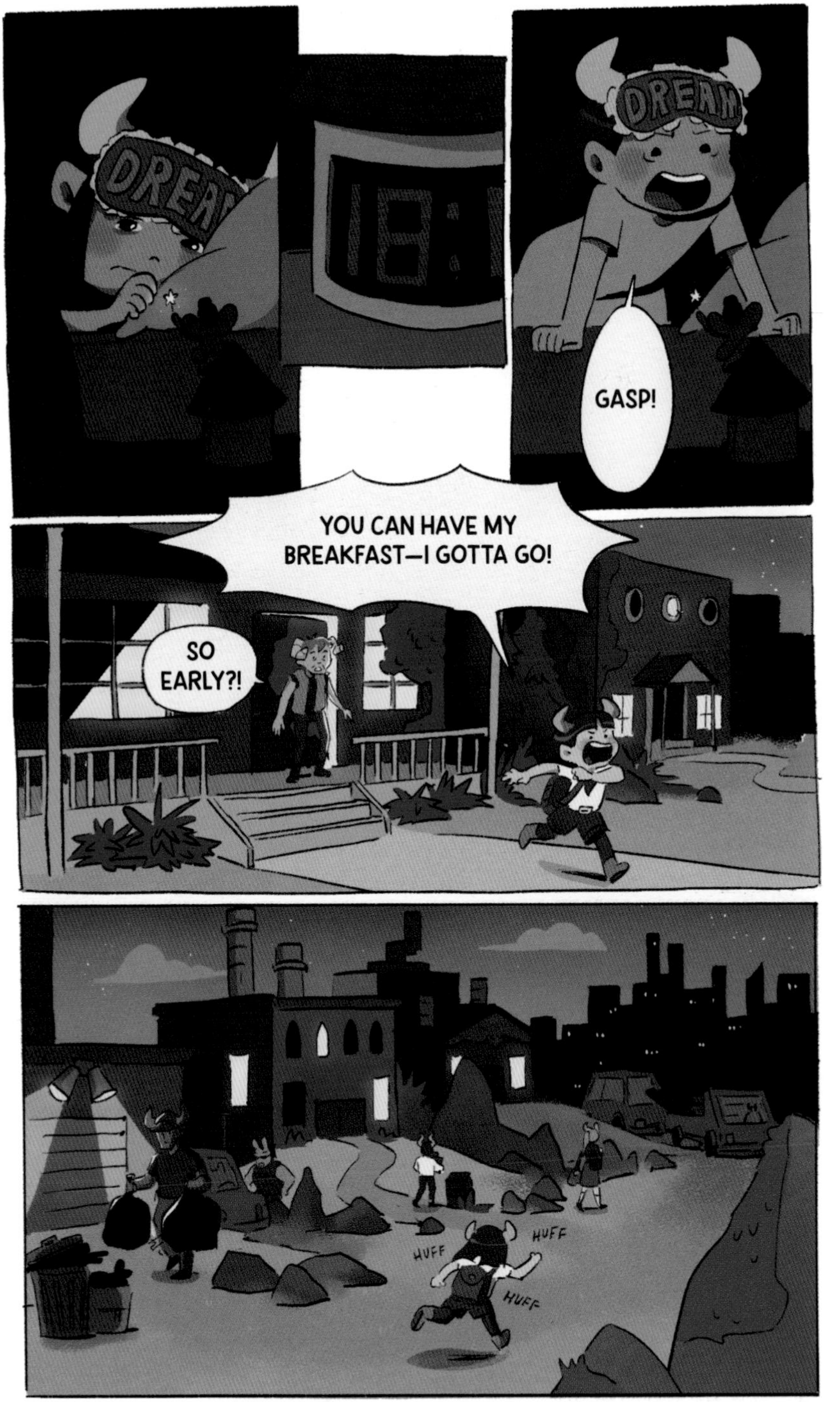
DREAM
18:
DREAM
GASP!
YOU CAN HAVE MY BREAKFAST—I GOTTA GO!
SO EARLY?!
HUFF
HUFF
HUFF

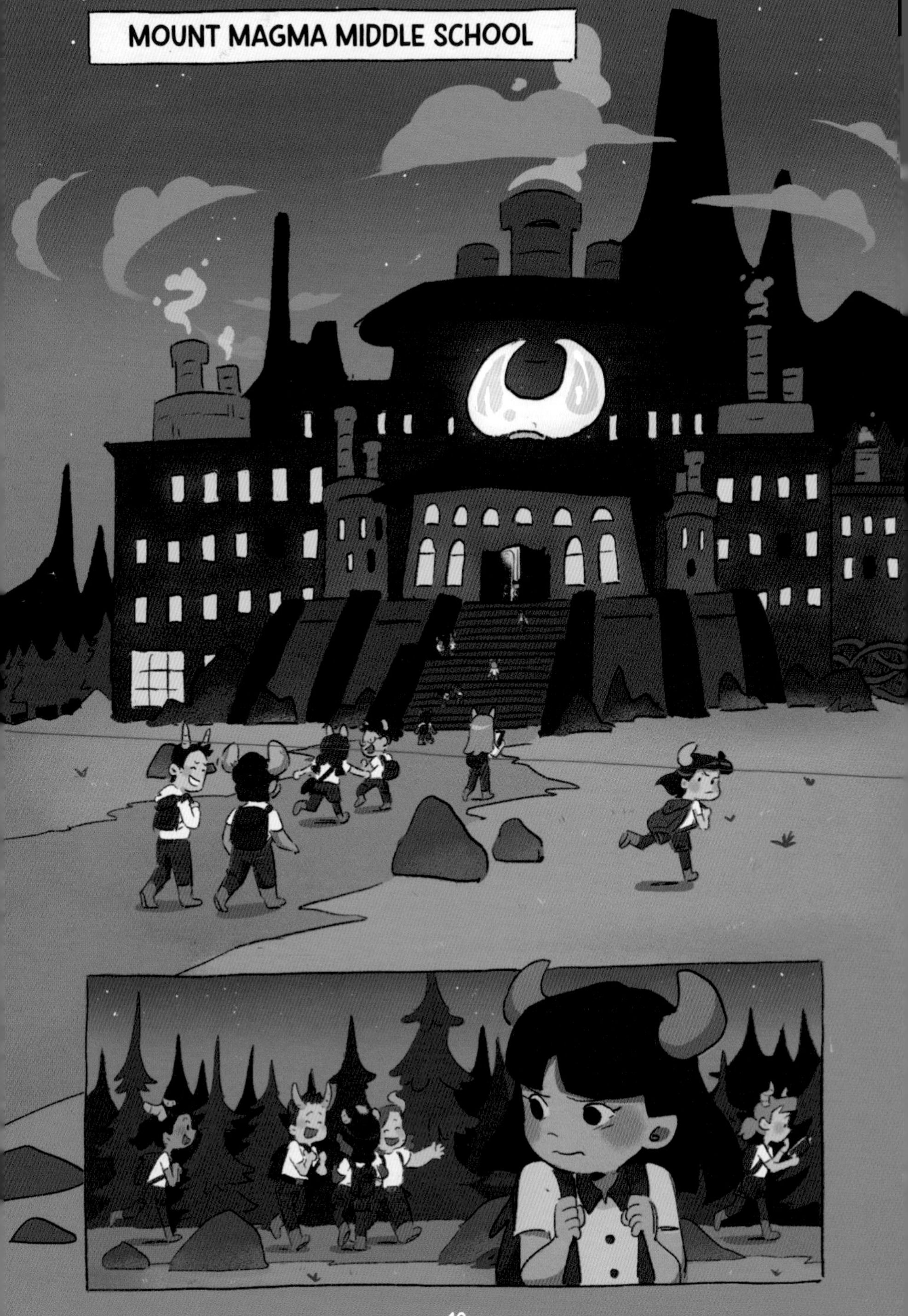
MOUNT MAGMA MIDDLE SCHOOL

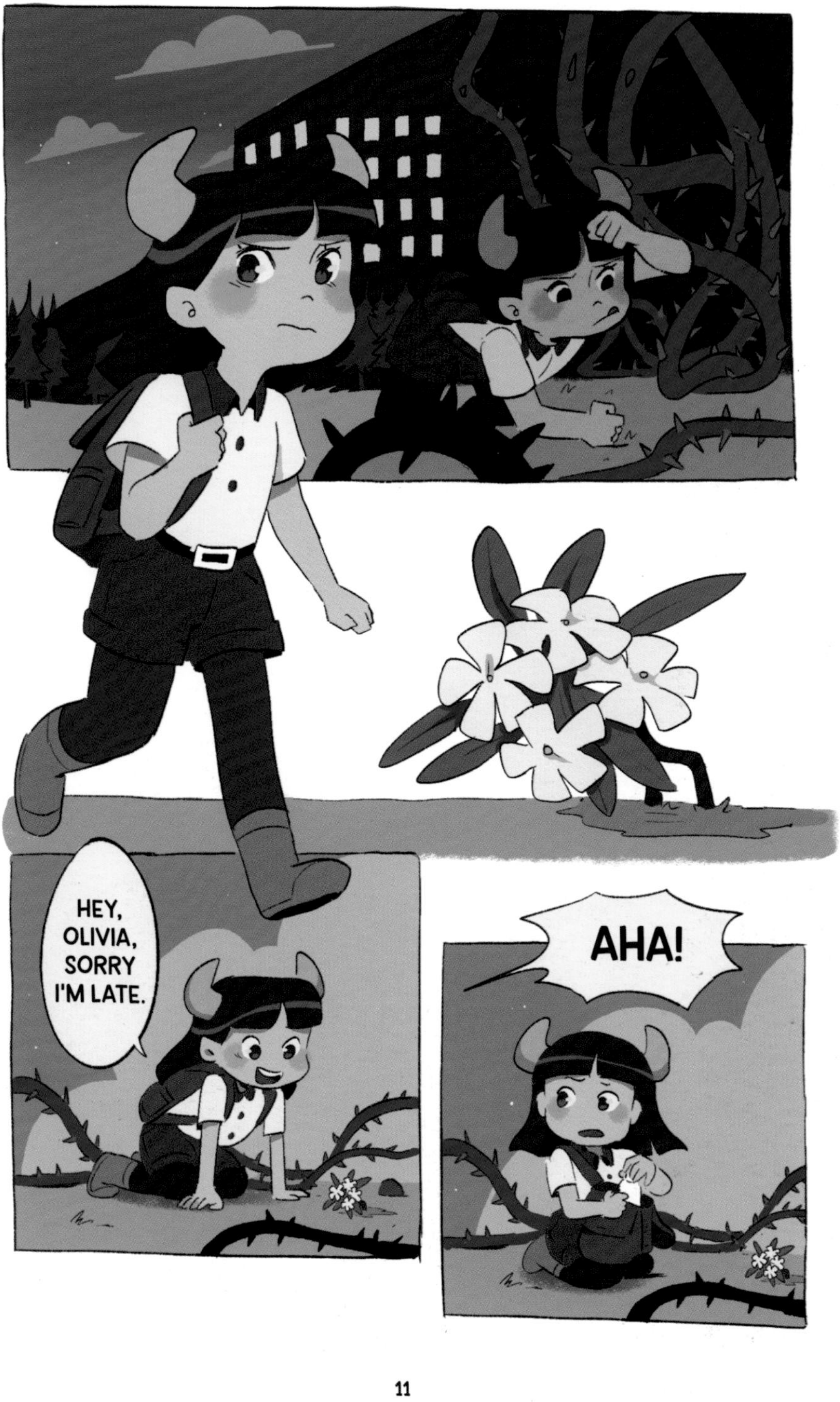
HEY, OLIVIA, SORRY I'M LATE.
AHA!

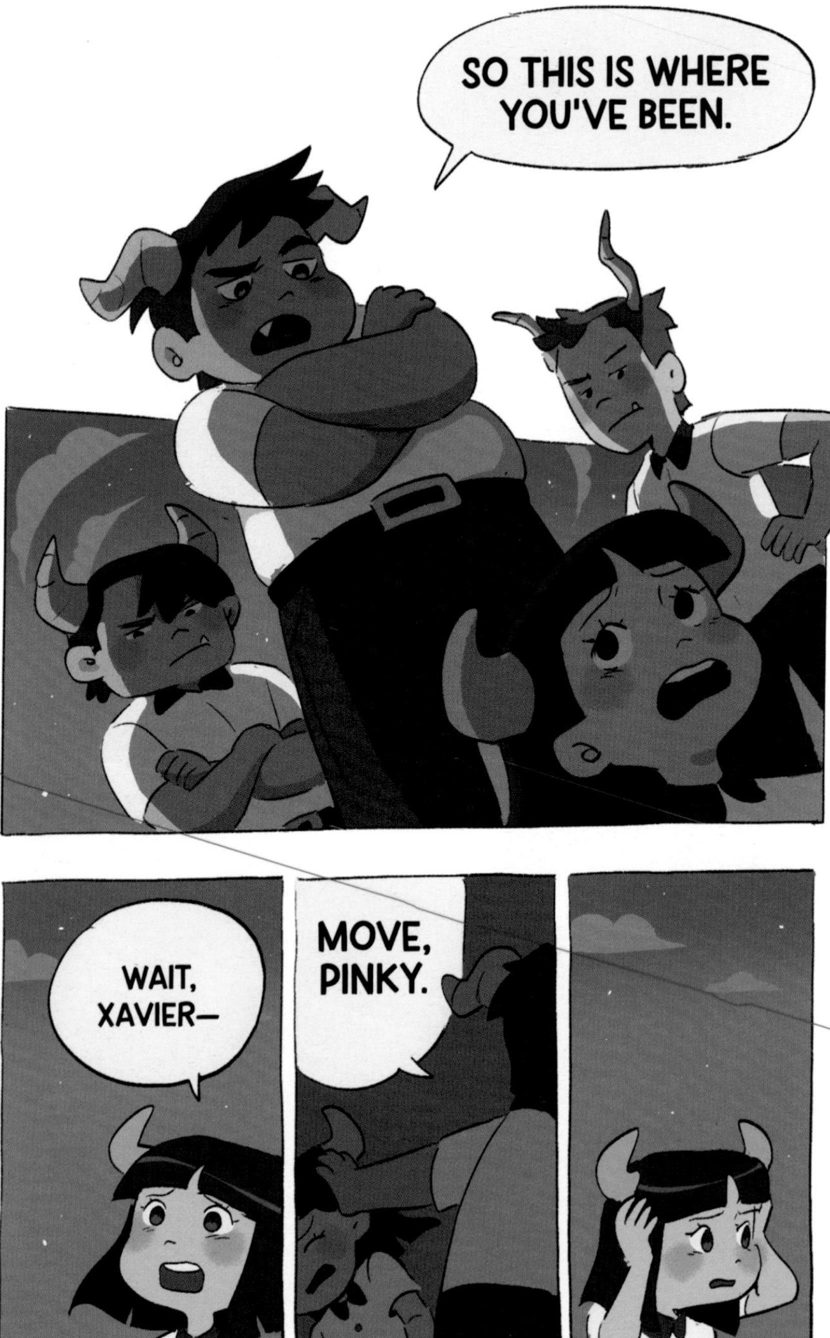
SO THIS IS WHERE YOU'VE BEEN.
WAIT, XAVIER—
MOVE, PINKY.

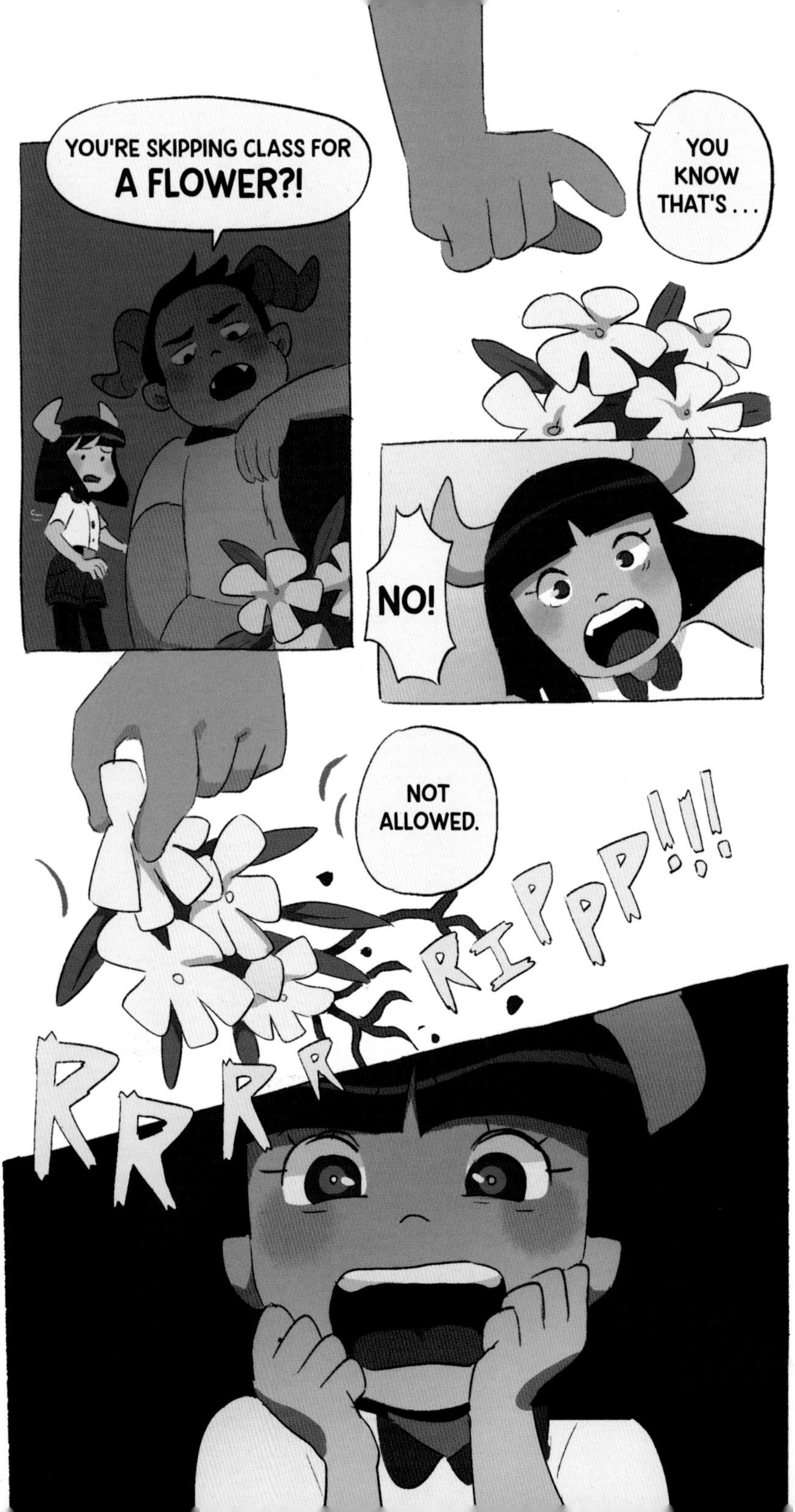
YOU'RE SKIPPING CLASS FOR A FLOWER?!
YOU KNOW THAT'S . . .
NO!
NOT ALLOWED.
RIPPP!!!
RRRR

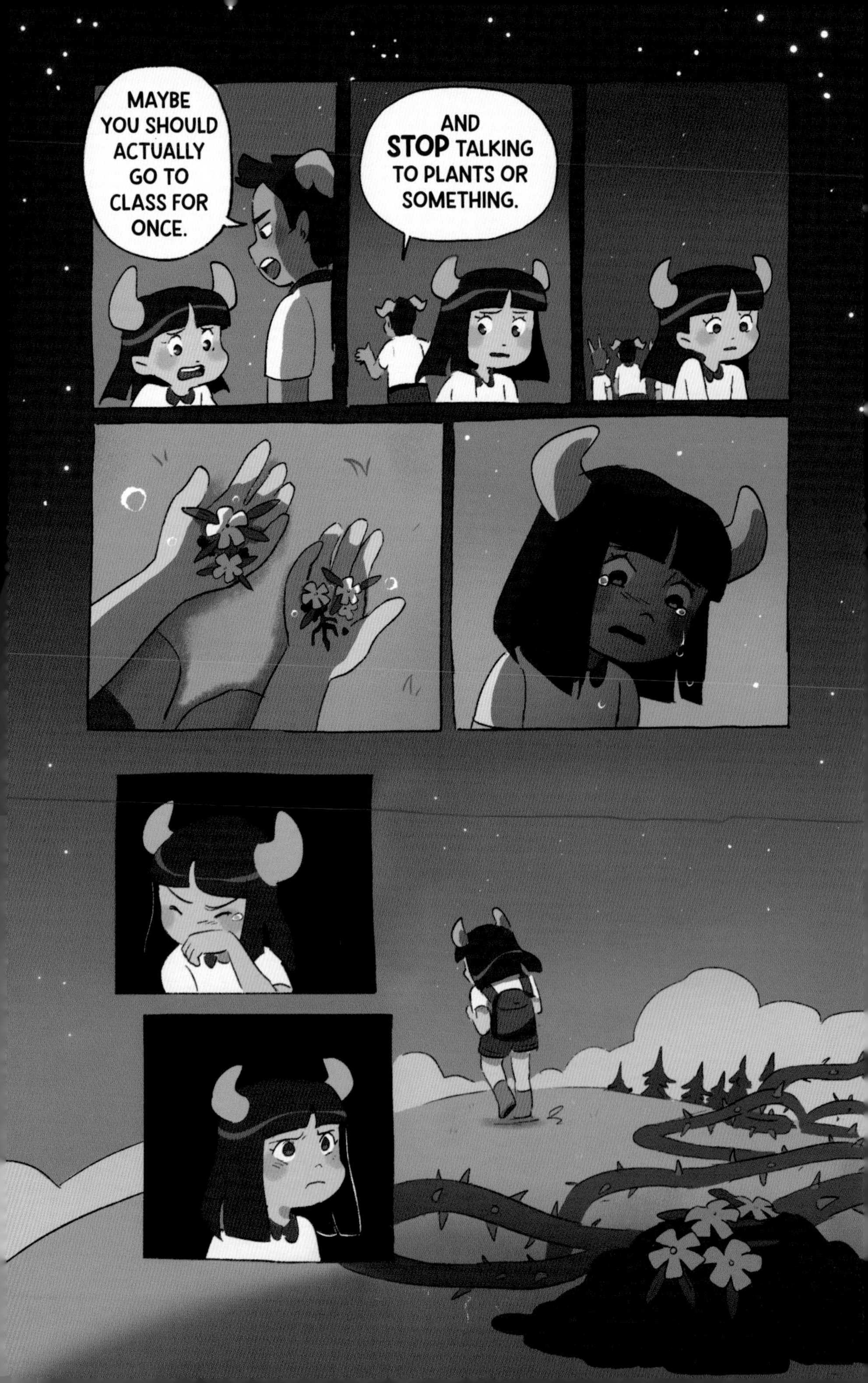
MAYBE YOU SHOULD ACTUALLY GO TO CLASS FOR ONCE.
AND STOP TALKING TO PLANTS OR SOMETHING.

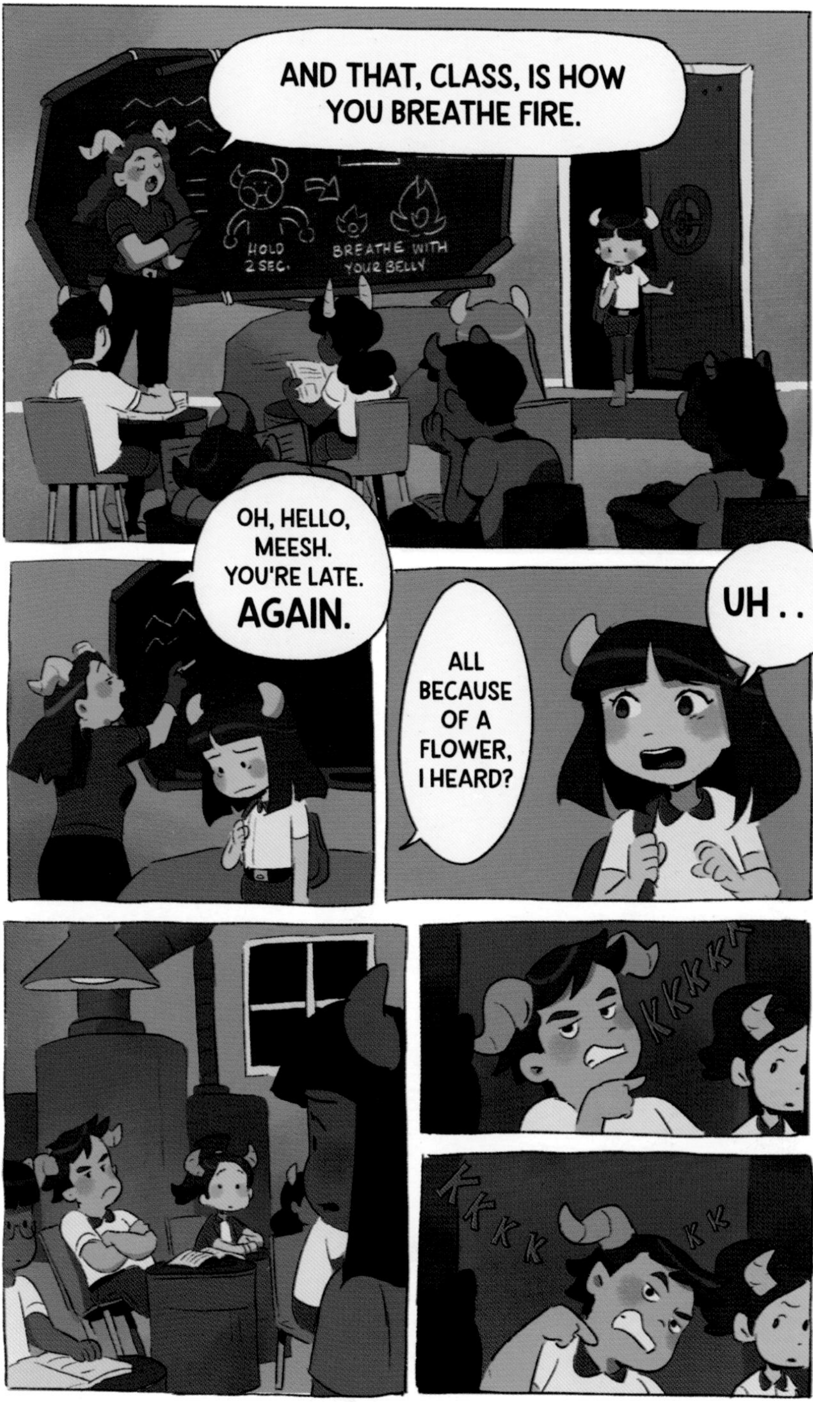
AND THAT, CLASS, IS HOW YOU BREATHE FIRE.
HOLD 2 SEC.
BREATHE WITH YOUR BELLY
OH, HELLO, MEESH. YOU'RE LATE. AGAIN.
ALL BECAUSE OF A FLOWER, I HEARD?
UH . . .
KKKKK
KKKK
KK

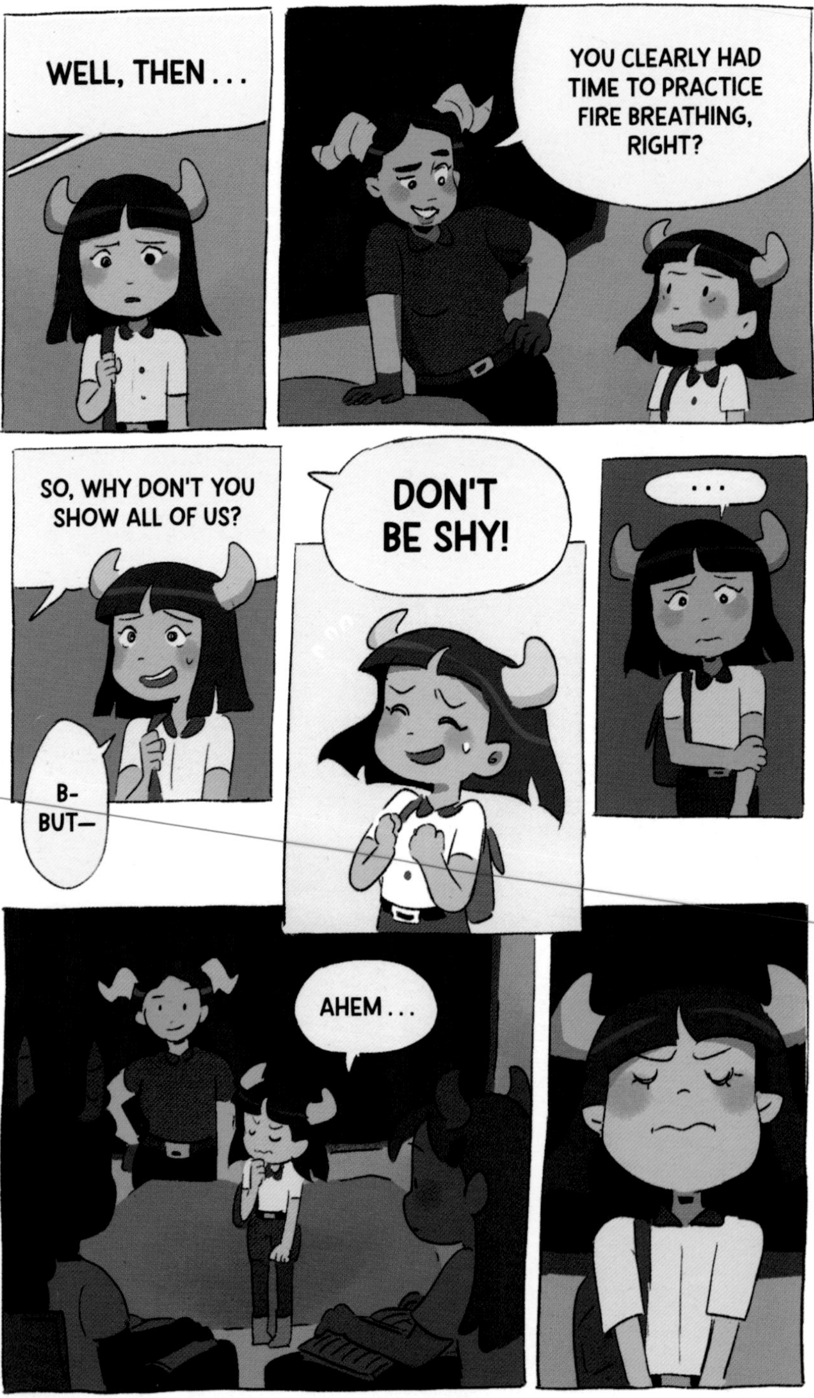
WELL, THEN . . .
YOU CLEARLY HAD TIME TO PRACTICE FIRE BREATHING, RIGHT?
SO, WHY DON'T YOU SHOW ALL OF US?
B- BUT—
DON'T BE SHY!
. . .
AHEM . . .

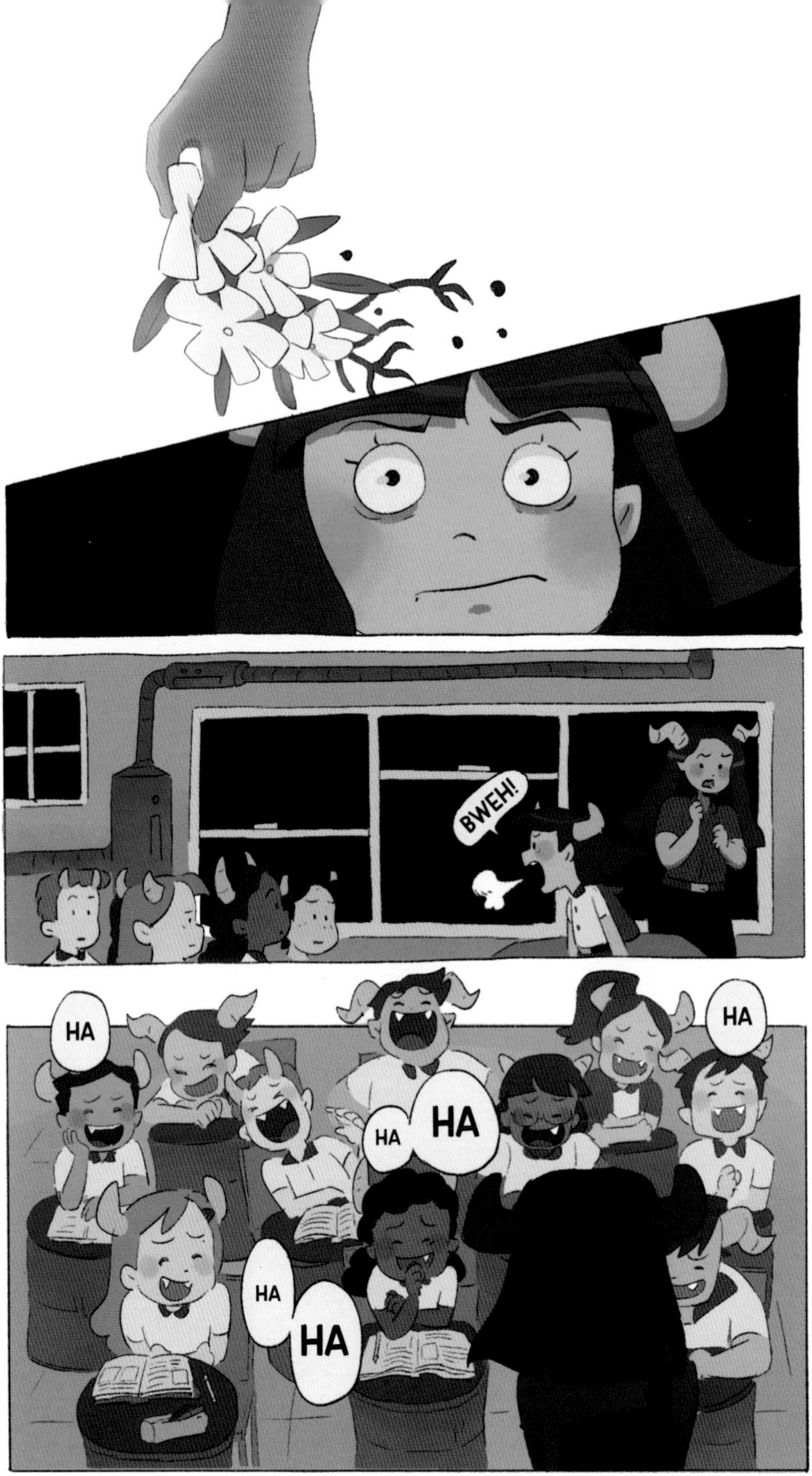
BWEH!
HA
HA
HA
HA
HA
HA

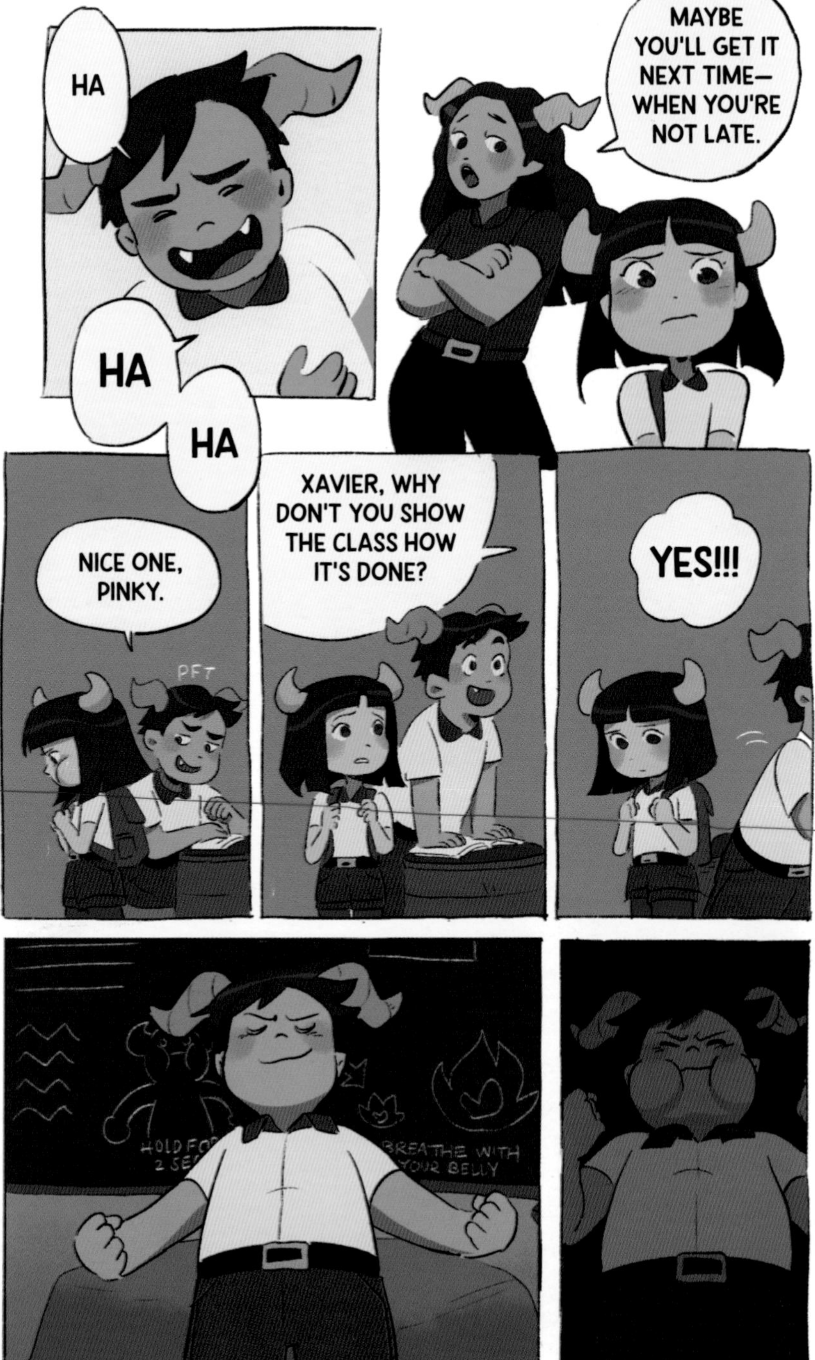
HA
HA
HA
MAYBE YOU'LL GET IT NEXT TIME— WHEN YOU'RE NOT LATE.
NICE ONE, PINKY.
PFT
XAVIER, WHY DON'T YOU SHOW THE CLASS HOW IT'S DONE?
YES!!!
HOLD FO
2 SE
BREATHE WITH YOUR BELLY

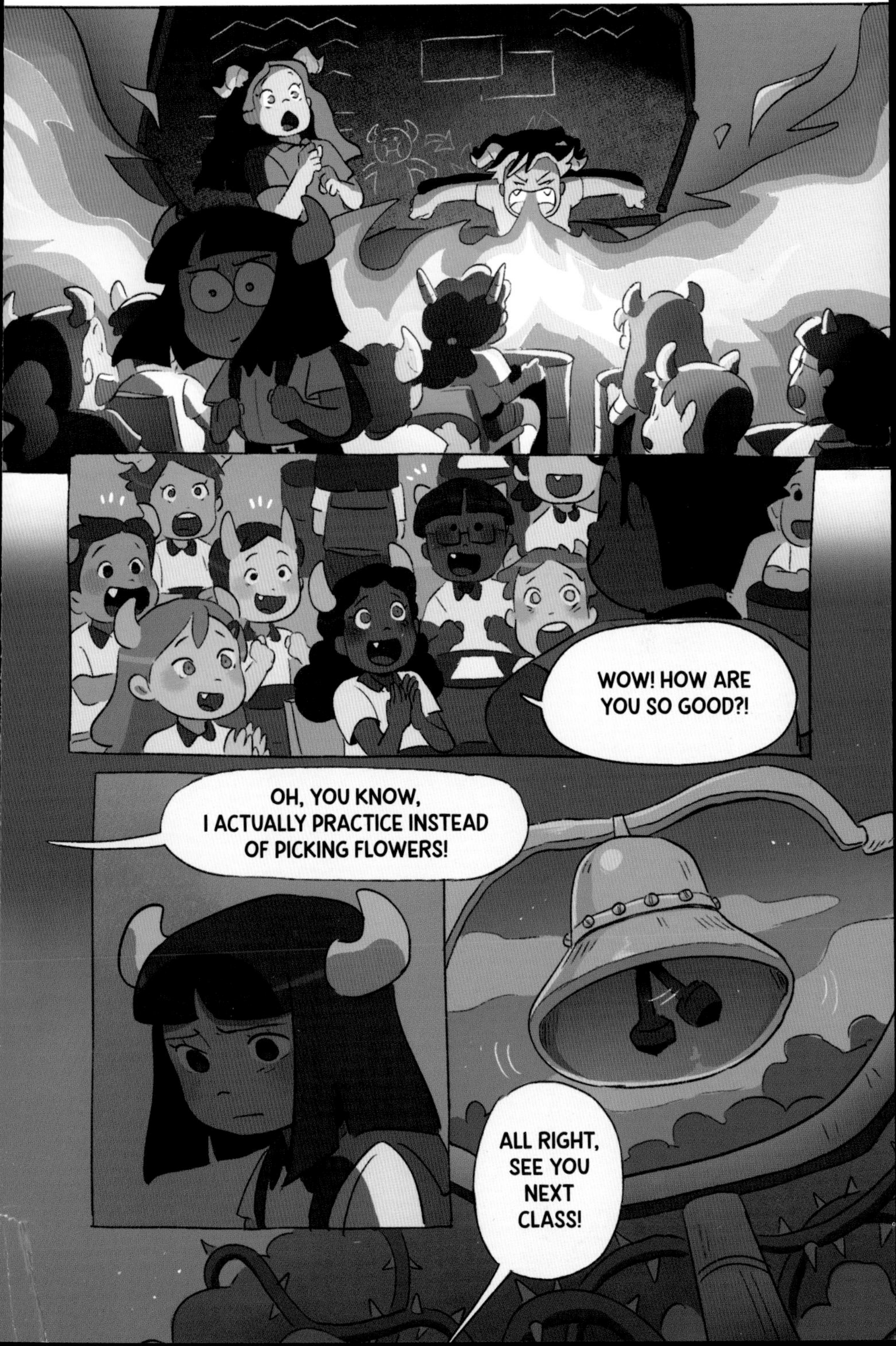
WOW! HOW ARE YOU SO GOOD?!
OH, YOU KNOW, I ACTUALLY PRACTICE INSTEAD OF PICKING FLOWERS!
ALL RIGHT, SEE YOU NEXT CLASS!

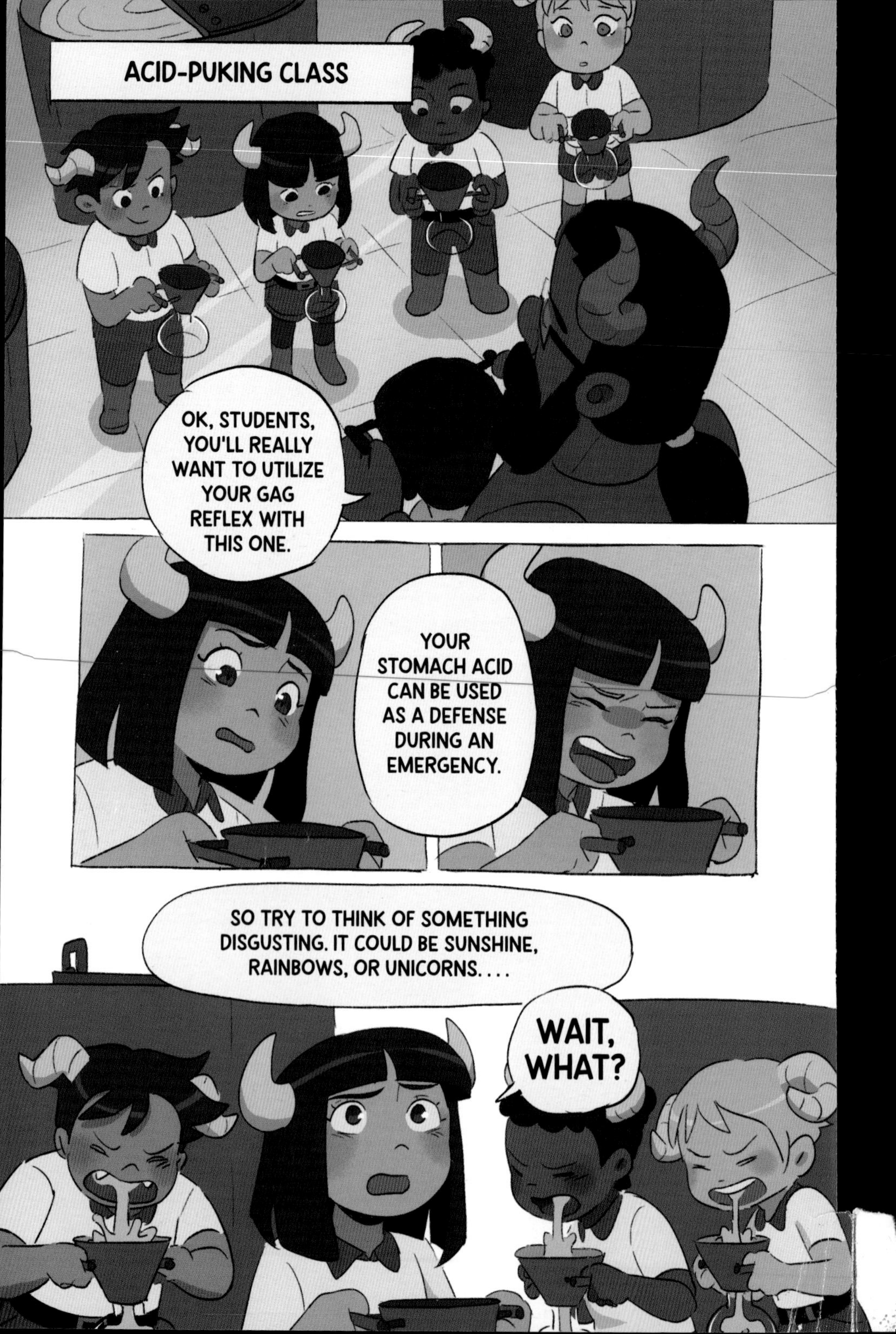
ACID-PUKING CLASS
OK, STUDENTS, YOU'LL REALLY WANT TO UTILIZE YOUR GAG REFLEX WITH THIS ONE.
YOUR STOMACH ACID CAN BE USED AS A DEFENSE DURING AN EMERGENCY.
SO TRY TO THINK OF SOMETHING DISGUSTING. IT COULD BE SUNSHINE, RAINBOWS, OR UNICORNS. . . .
WAIT, WHAT?

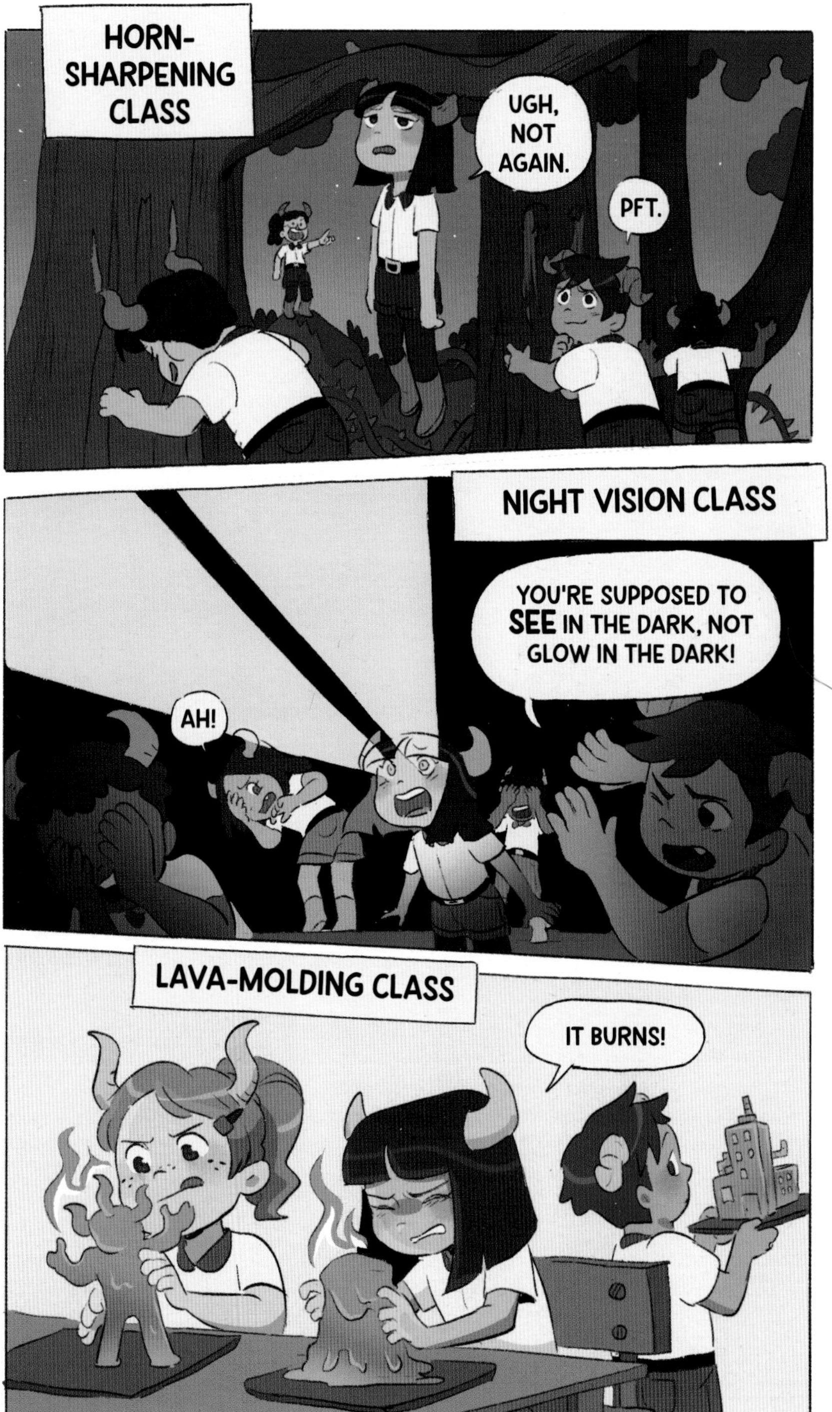
HORN-SHARPENING CLASS
UGH, NOT AGAIN.
PFT.
NIGHT VISION CLASS
YOU'RE SUPPOSED TO SEE IN THE DARK, NOT GLOW IN THE DARK!
AH!
LAVA-MOLDING CLASS
IT BURNS!

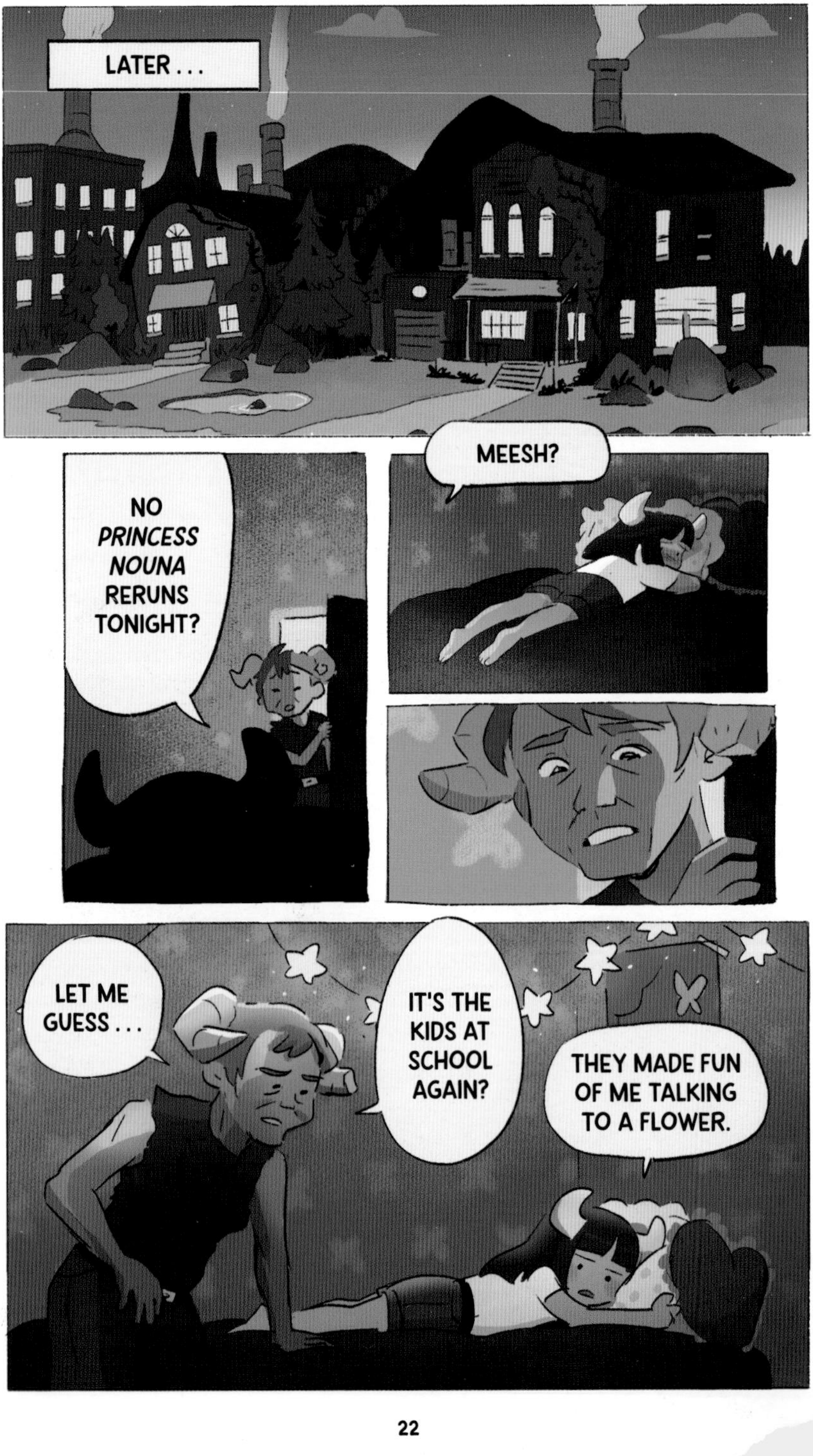
LATER . . .
NO *PRINCESS NOUNA* RERUNS TONIGHT?
MEESH?
LET ME GUESS . . .
IT'S THE KIDS AT SCHOOL AGAIN?
THEY MADE FUN OF ME TALKING TO A FLOWER.

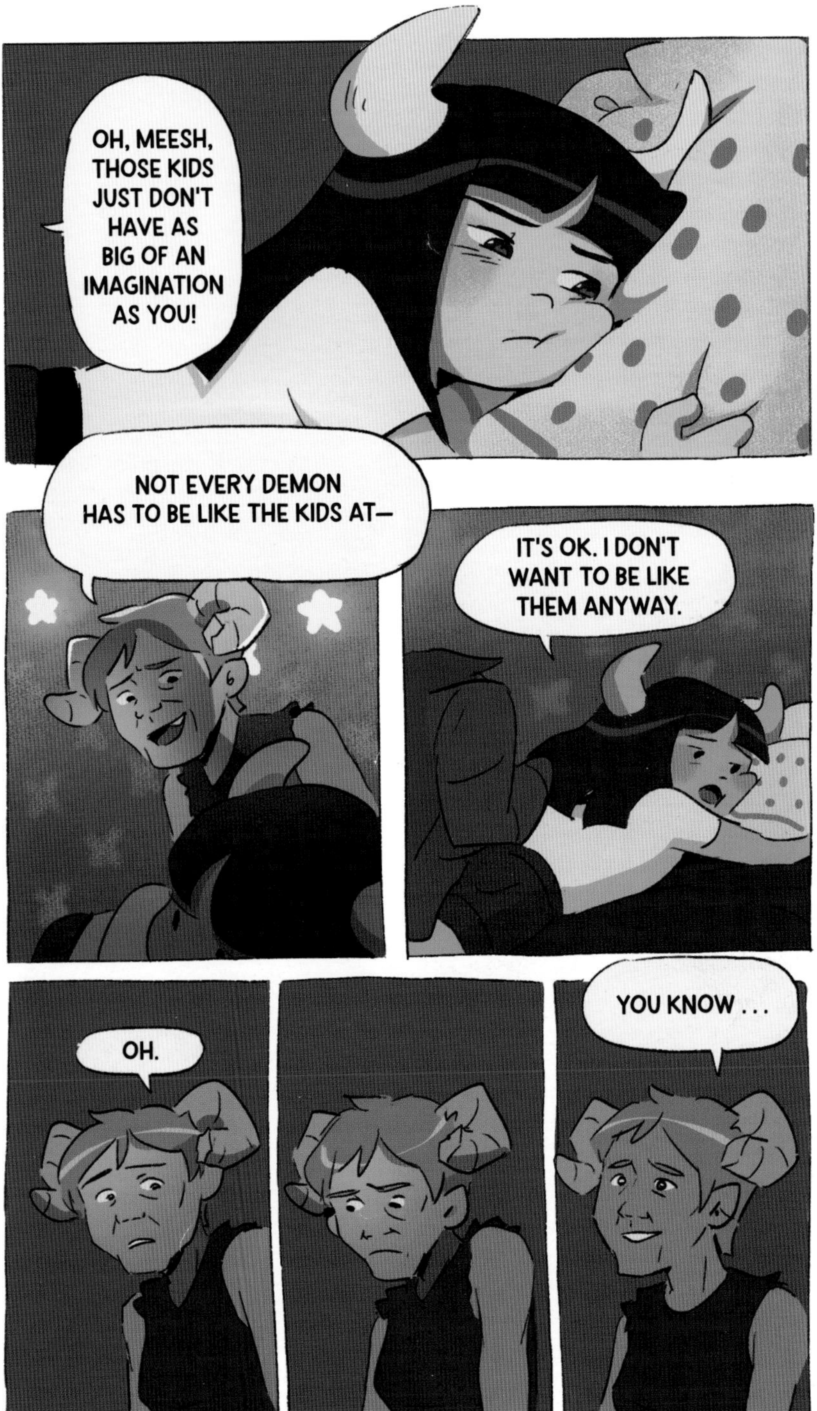
OH, MEESH, THOSE KIDS JUST DON'T HAVE AS BIG OF AN IMAGINATION AS YOU!
NOT EVERY DEMON HAS TO BE LIKE THE KIDS AT—
IT'S OK. I DON'T WANT TO BE LIKE THEM ANYWAY.
OH.
YOU KNOW . . .

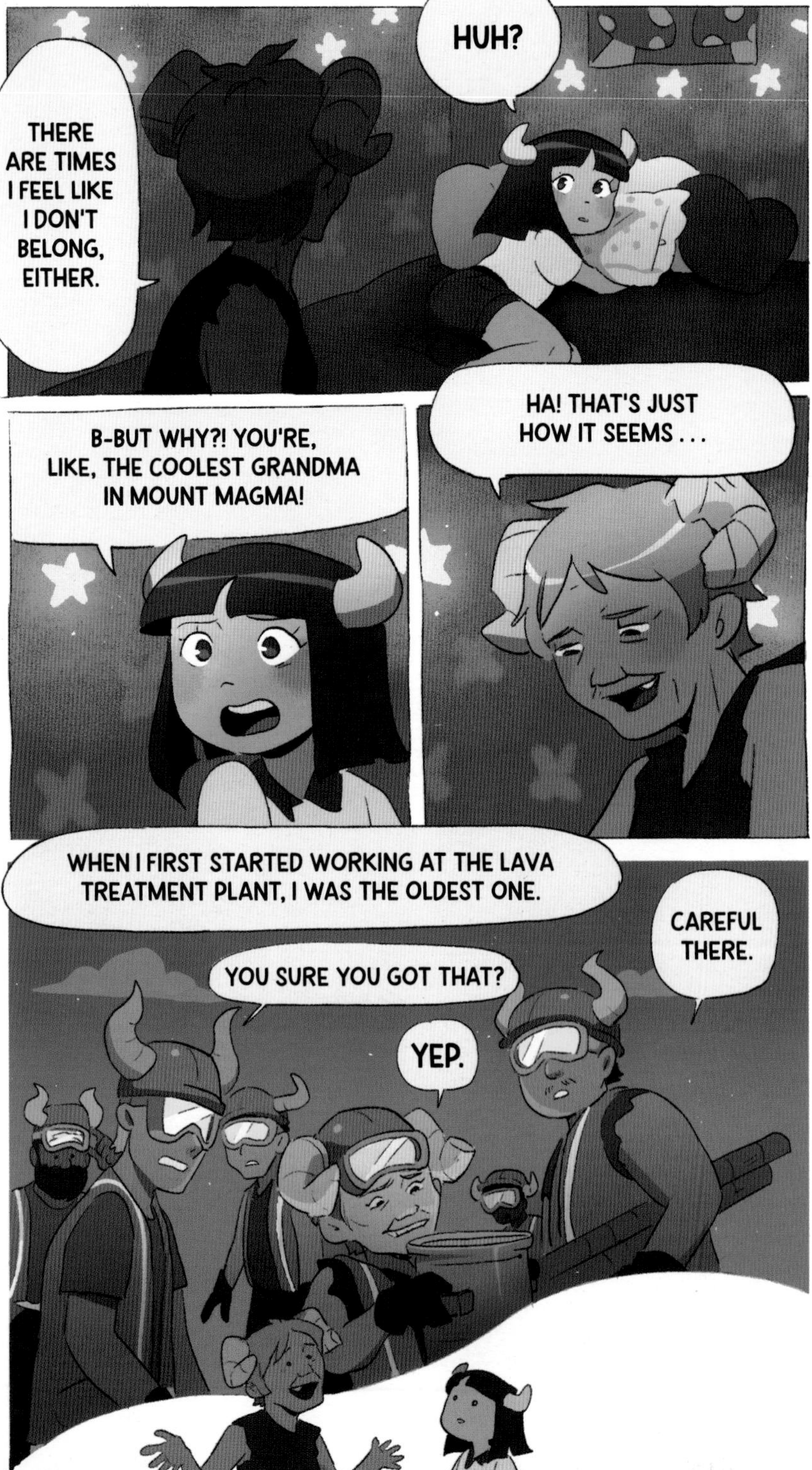
THERE ARE TIMES I FEEL LIKE I DON'T BELONG, EITHER.
HUH?
B-BUT WHY?! YOU'RE, LIKE, THE COOLEST GRANDMA IN MOUNT MAGMA!
HA! THAT'S JUST HOW IT SEEMS . . .
WHEN I FIRST STARTED WORKING AT THE LAVA TREATMENT PLANT, I WAS THE OLDEST ONE.
YOU SURE YOU GOT THAT?
CAREFUL THERE.
YEP.

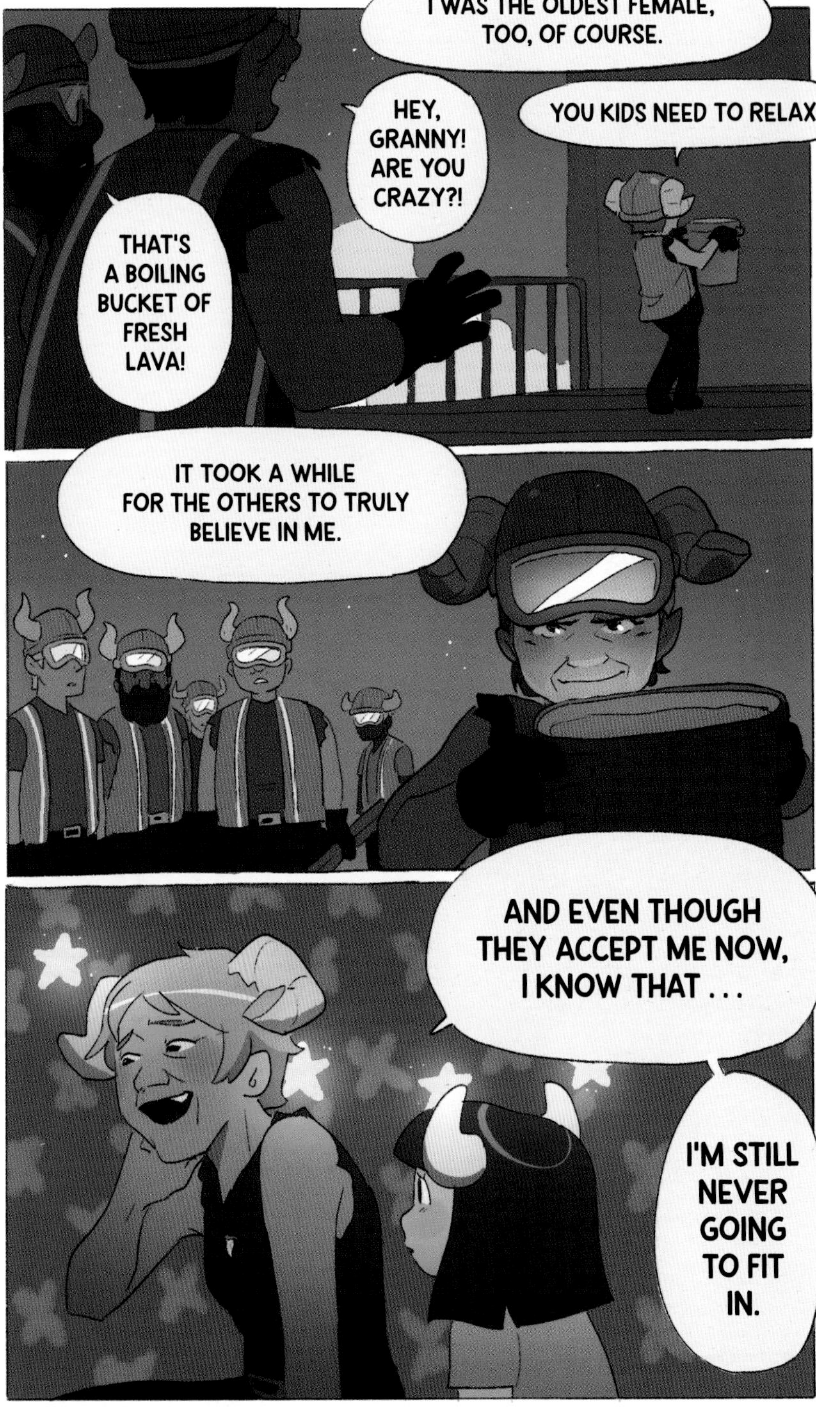
I WAS THE OLDEST FEMALE, TOO, OF COURSE.
HEY, GRANNY! ARE YOU CRAZY?!
THAT'S A BOILING BUCKET OF FRESH LAVA!
YOU KIDS NEED TO RELAX.
IT TOOK A WHILE FOR THE OTHERS TO TRULY BELIEVE IN ME.
AND EVEN THOUGH THEY ACCEPT ME NOW, I KNOW THAT . . .
I'M STILL NEVER GOING TO FIT IN.

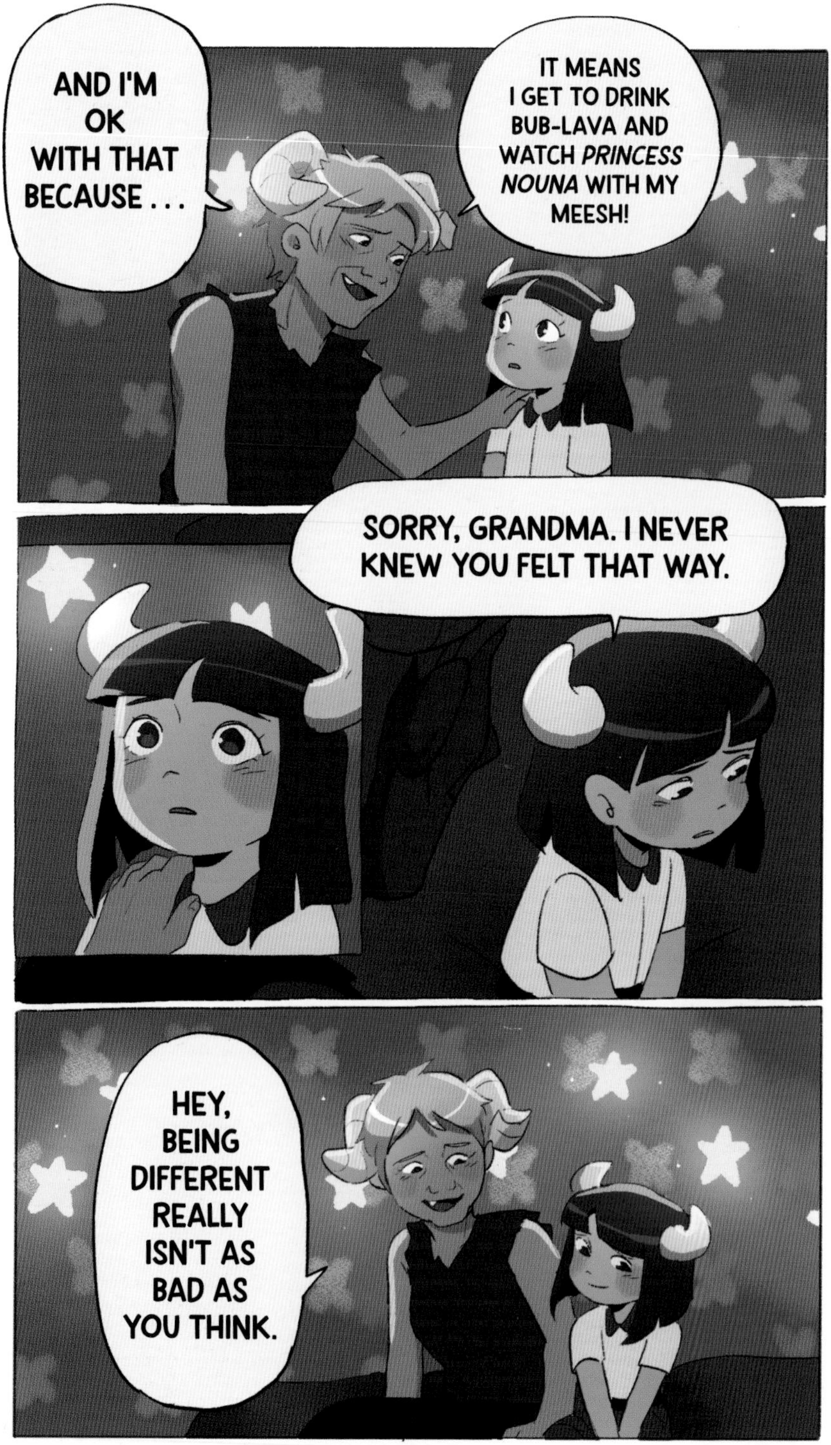
AND I'M OK WITH THAT BECAUSE . . .
IT MEANS I GET TO DRINK BUB-LAVA AND WATCH *PRINCESS NOUNA* WITH MY MEESH!
SORRY, GRANDMA. I NEVER KNEW YOU FELT THAT WAY.
HEY, BEING DIFFERENT REALLY ISN'T AS BAD AS YOU THINK.

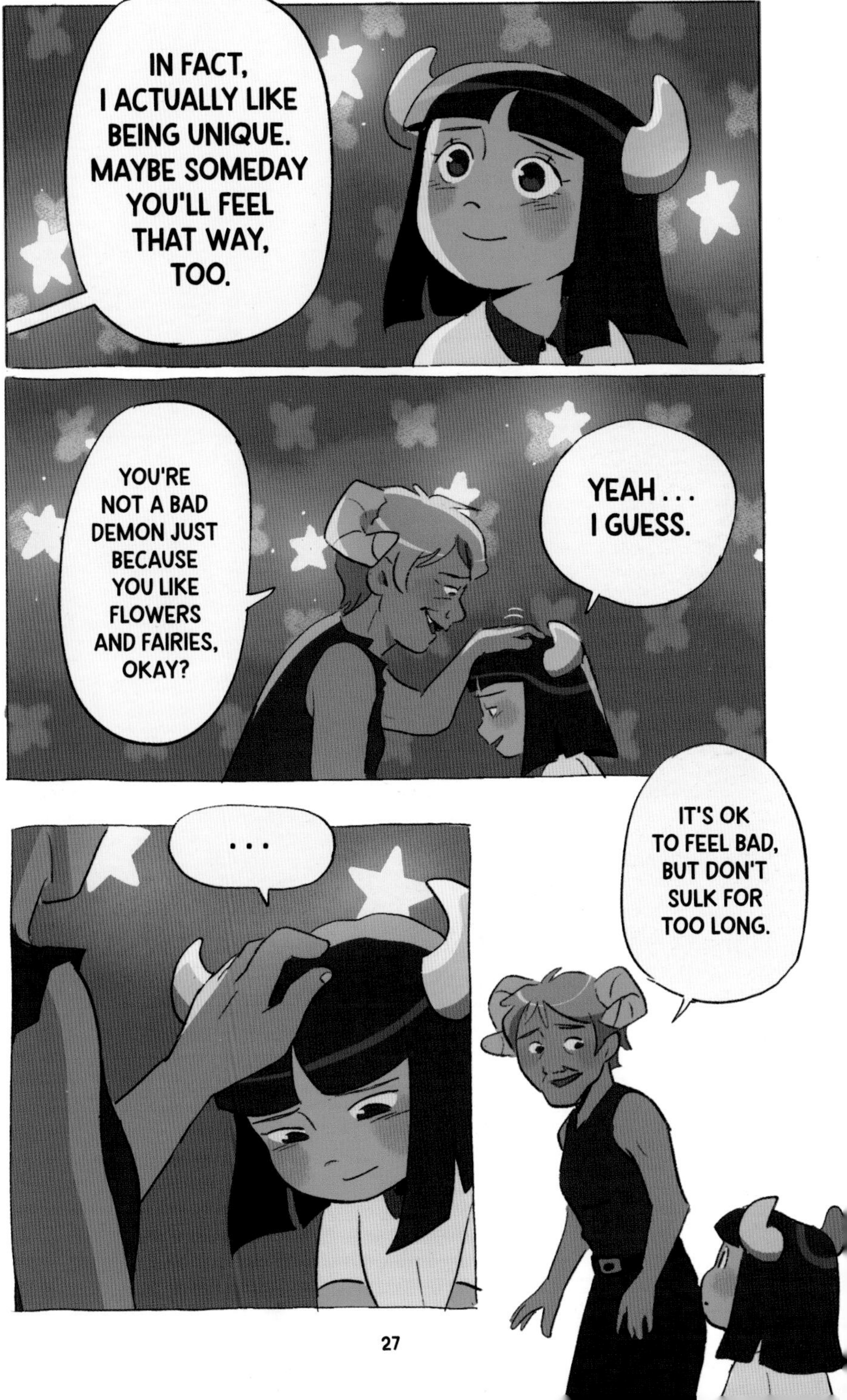
IN FACT, I ACTUALLY LIKE BEING UNIQUE. MAYBE SOMEDAY YOU'LL FEEL THAT WAY, TOO.
YOU'RE NOT A BAD DEMON JUST BECAUSE YOU LIKE FLOWERS AND FAIRIES, OKAY?
YEAH . . . I GUESS.
. . .
IT'S OK TO FEEL BAD, BUT DON'T SULK FOR TOO LONG.

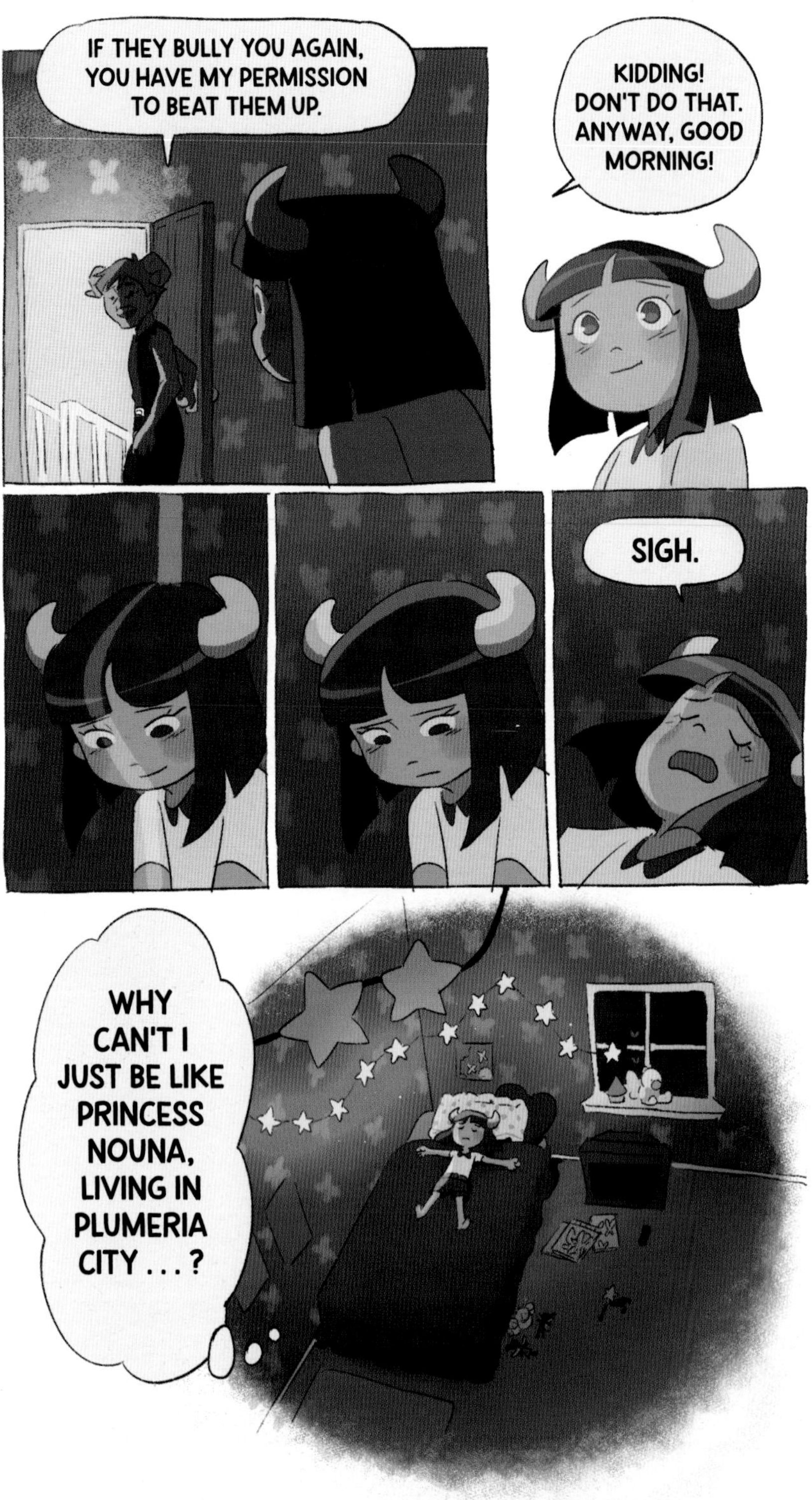
IF THEY BULLY YOU AGAIN, YOU HAVE MY PERMISSION TO BEAT THEM UP.
KIDDING! DON'T DO THAT. ANYWAY, GOOD MORNING!
SIGH.
WHY CAN'T I JUST BE LIKE PRINCESS NOUNA, LIVING IN PLUMERIA CITY . . . ?

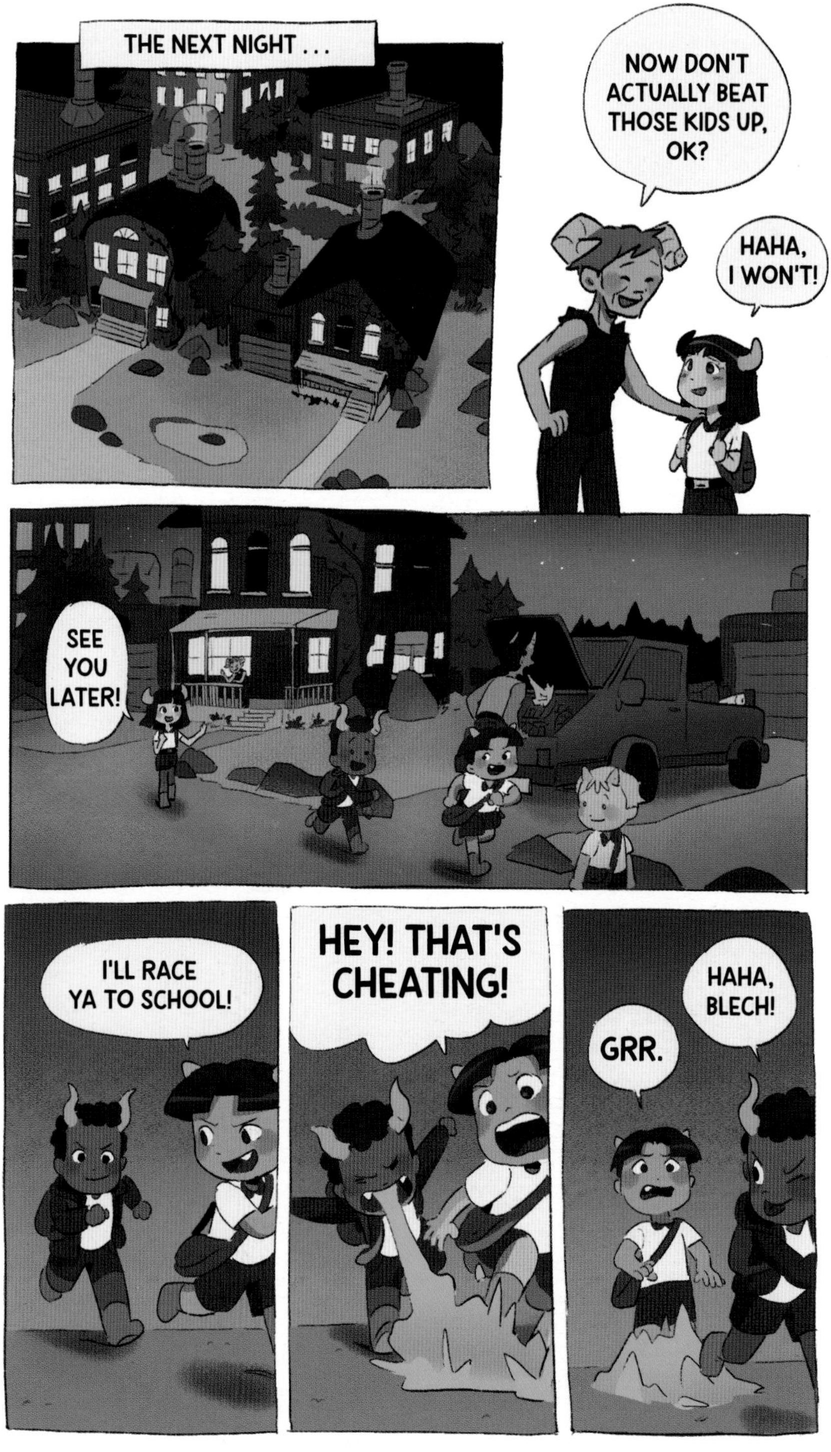
THE NEXT NIGHT . . .
NOW DON'T ACTUALLY BEAT THOSE KIDS UP, OK?
HAHA, I WON'T!
SEE YOU LATER!
I'LL RACE YA TO SCHOOL!
HEY! THAT'S CHEATING!
GRR.
HAHA, BLECH!

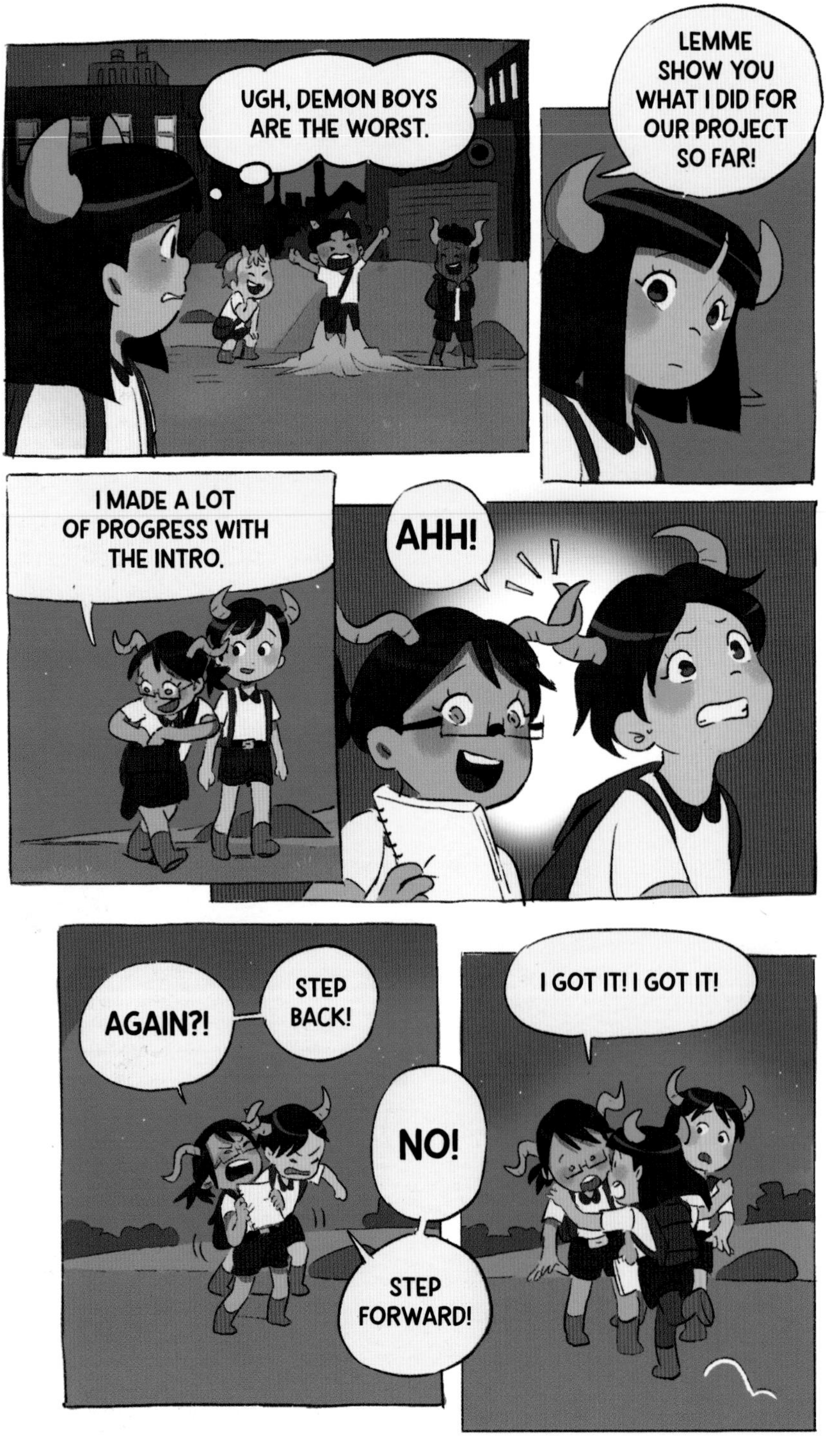
UGH, DEMON BOYS ARE THE WORST.
LEMME SHOW YOU WHAT I DID FOR OUR PROJECT SO FAR!
I MADE A LOT OF PROGRESS WITH THE INTRO.
AHH!
AGAIN?!
STEP BACK!
NO!
STEP FORWARD!
I GOT IT! I GOT IT!

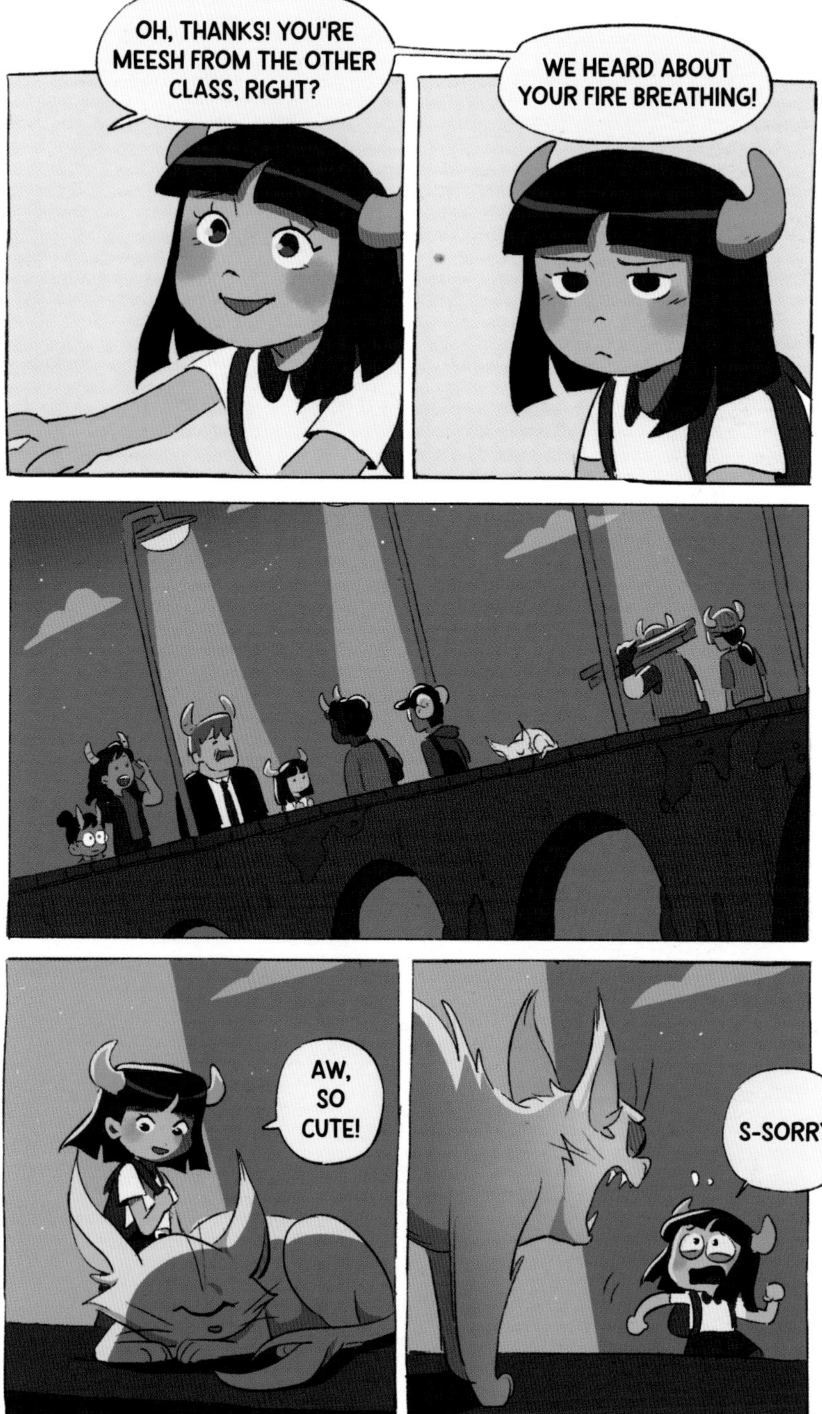
OH, THANKS! YOU'RE MEESH FROM THE OTHER CLASS, RIGHT?
WE HEARD ABOUT YOUR FIRE BREATHING!
AW, SO CUTE!
S-SORRY!

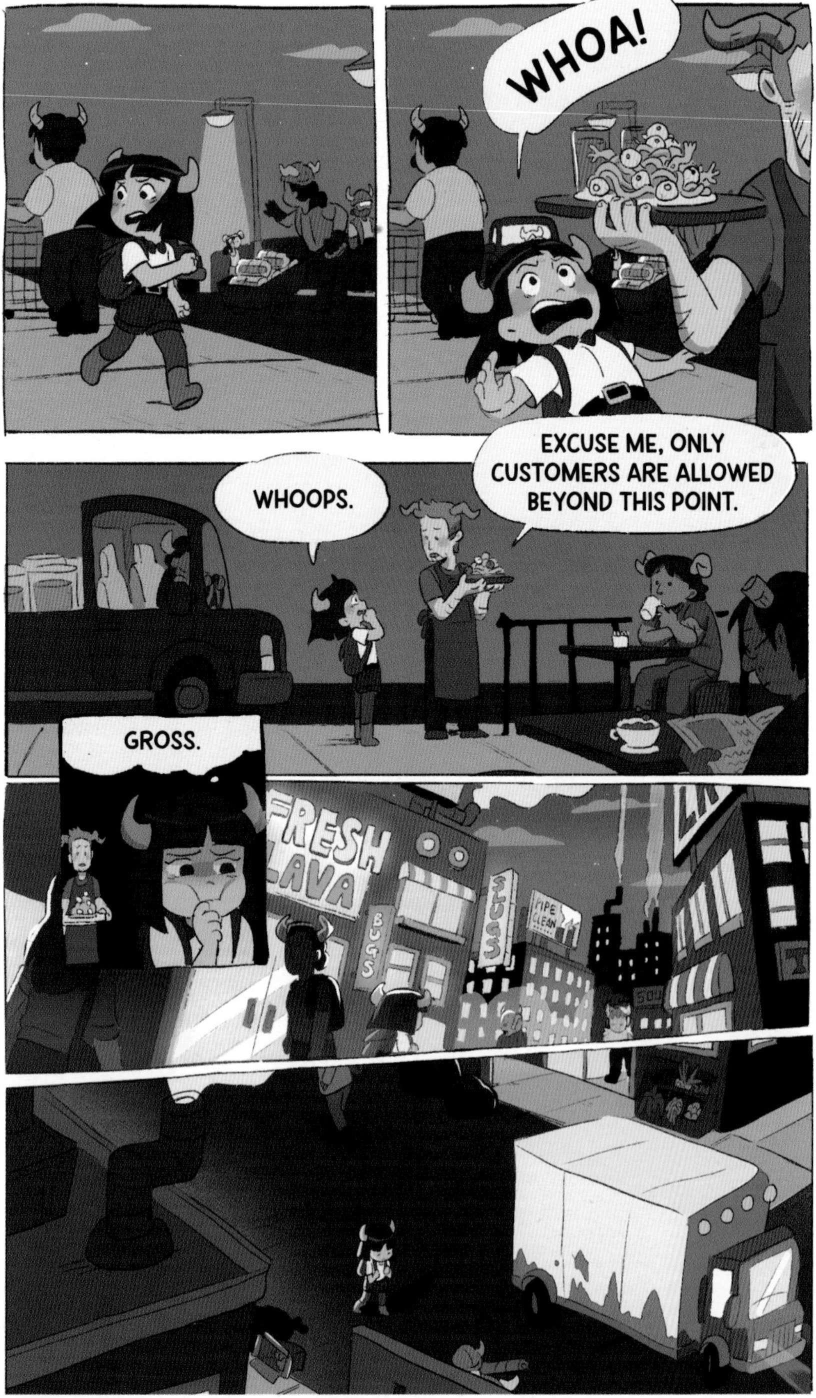
WHOA!
WHOOPS.
EXCUSE ME, ONLY CUSTOMERS ARE ALLOWED BEYOND THIS POINT.
GROSS.
FRESH LAVA
BUGS
SLUGS
PIPE CLEAN

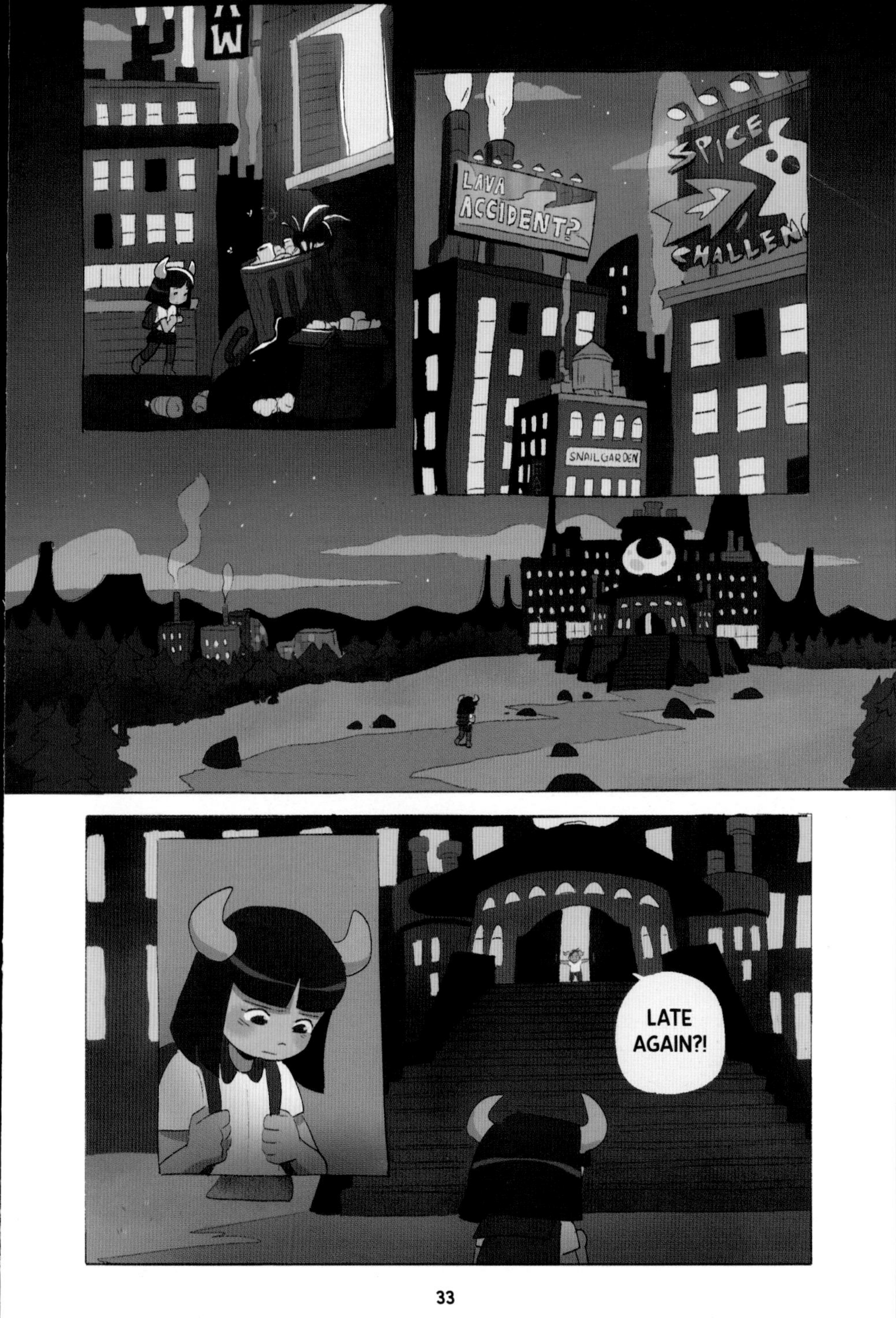
LAVA ACCIDENT?
SPICE
SNAILGARDEN
LATE AGAIN?!

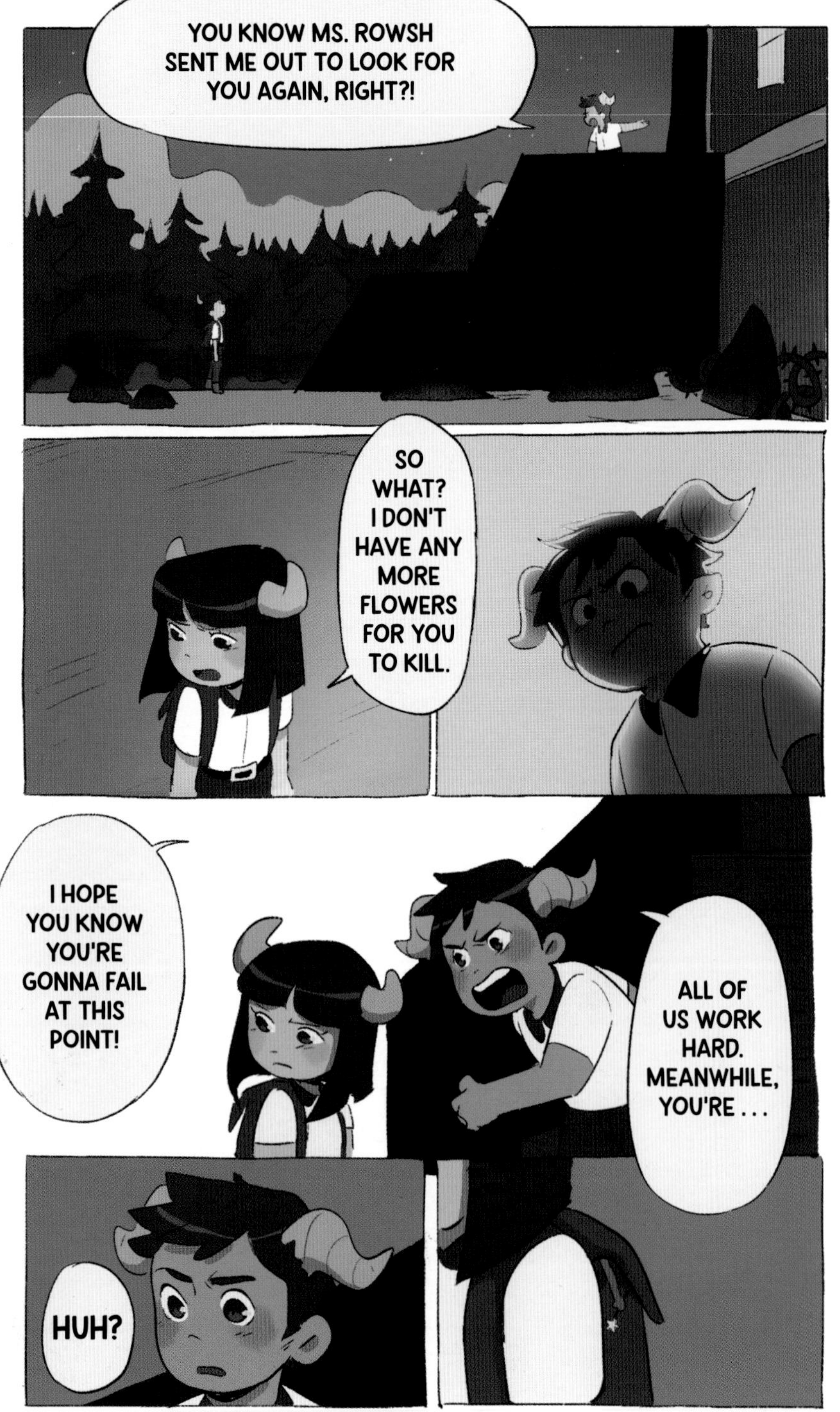
YOU KNOW MS. ROWSH SENT ME OUT TO LOOK FOR YOU AGAIN, RIGHT?!
SO WHAT? I DON'T HAVE ANY MORE FLOWERS FOR YOU TO KILL.
I HOPE YOU KNOW YOU'RE GONNA FAIL AT THIS POINT!
ALL OF US WORK HARD. MEANWHILE, YOU'RE . . .
HUH?

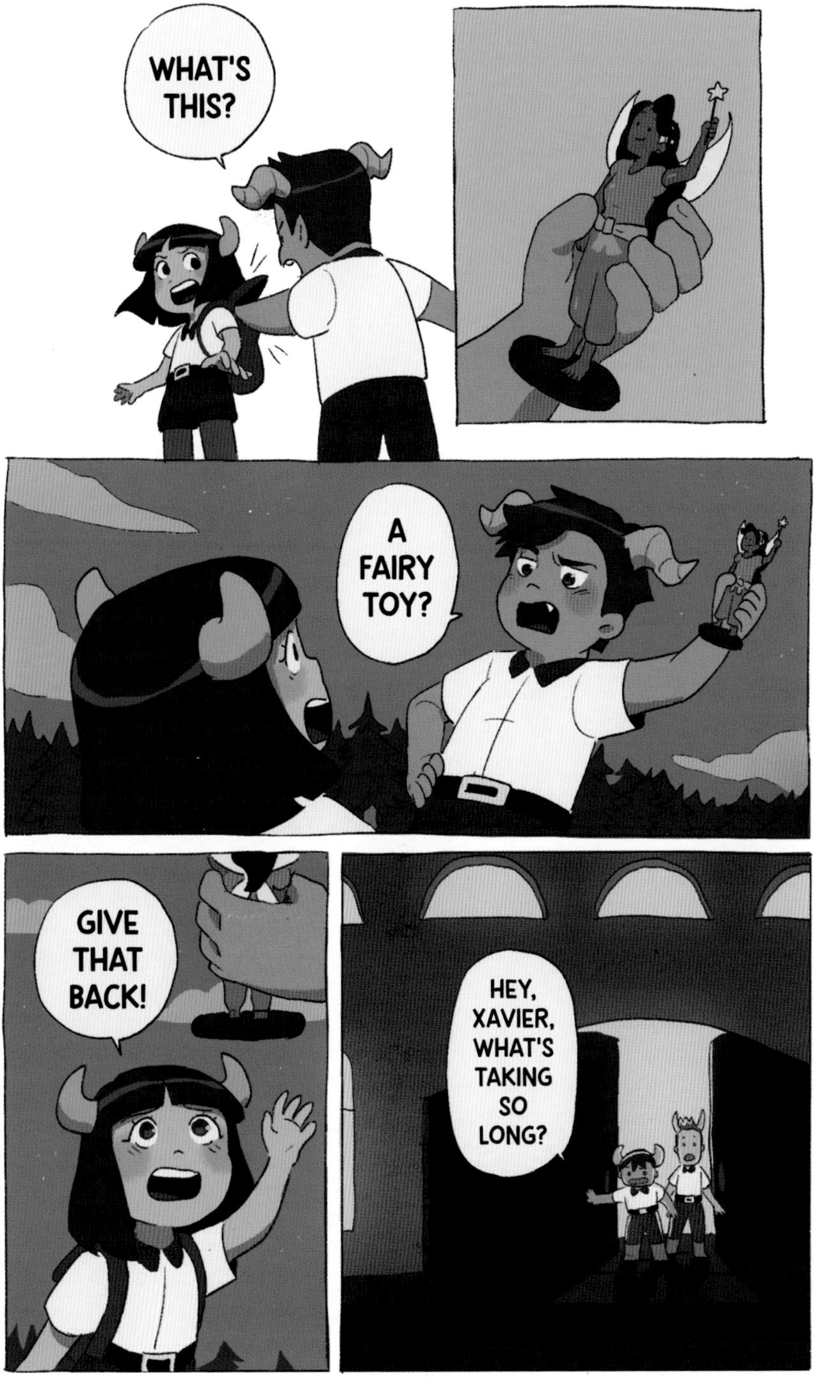
WHAT'S THIS?
A FAIRY TOY?
GIVE THAT BACK!
HEY, XAVIER, WHAT'S TAKING SO LONG?

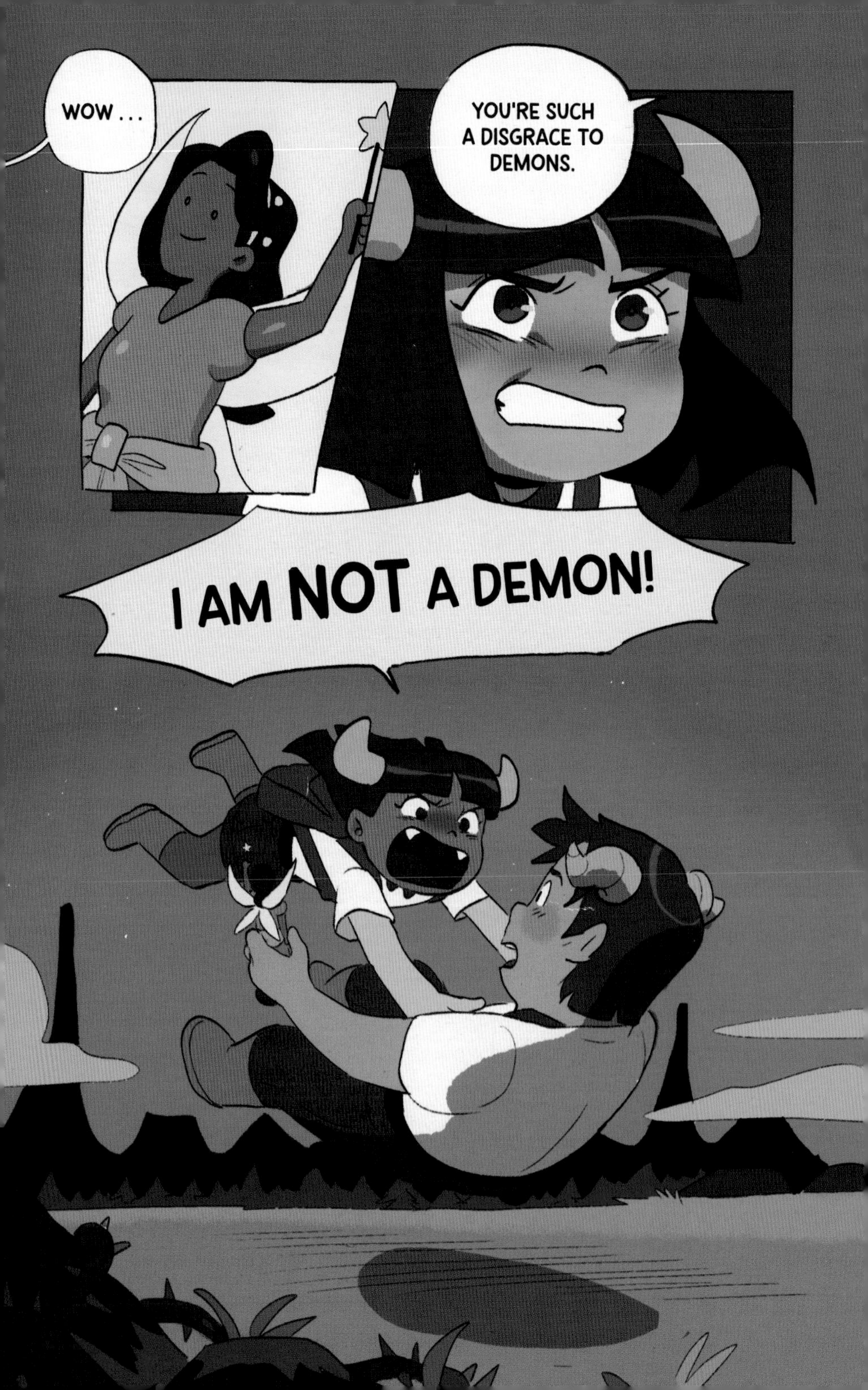
WOW . . .
YOU'RE SUCH A DISGRACE TO DEMONS.
I AM NOT A DEMON!

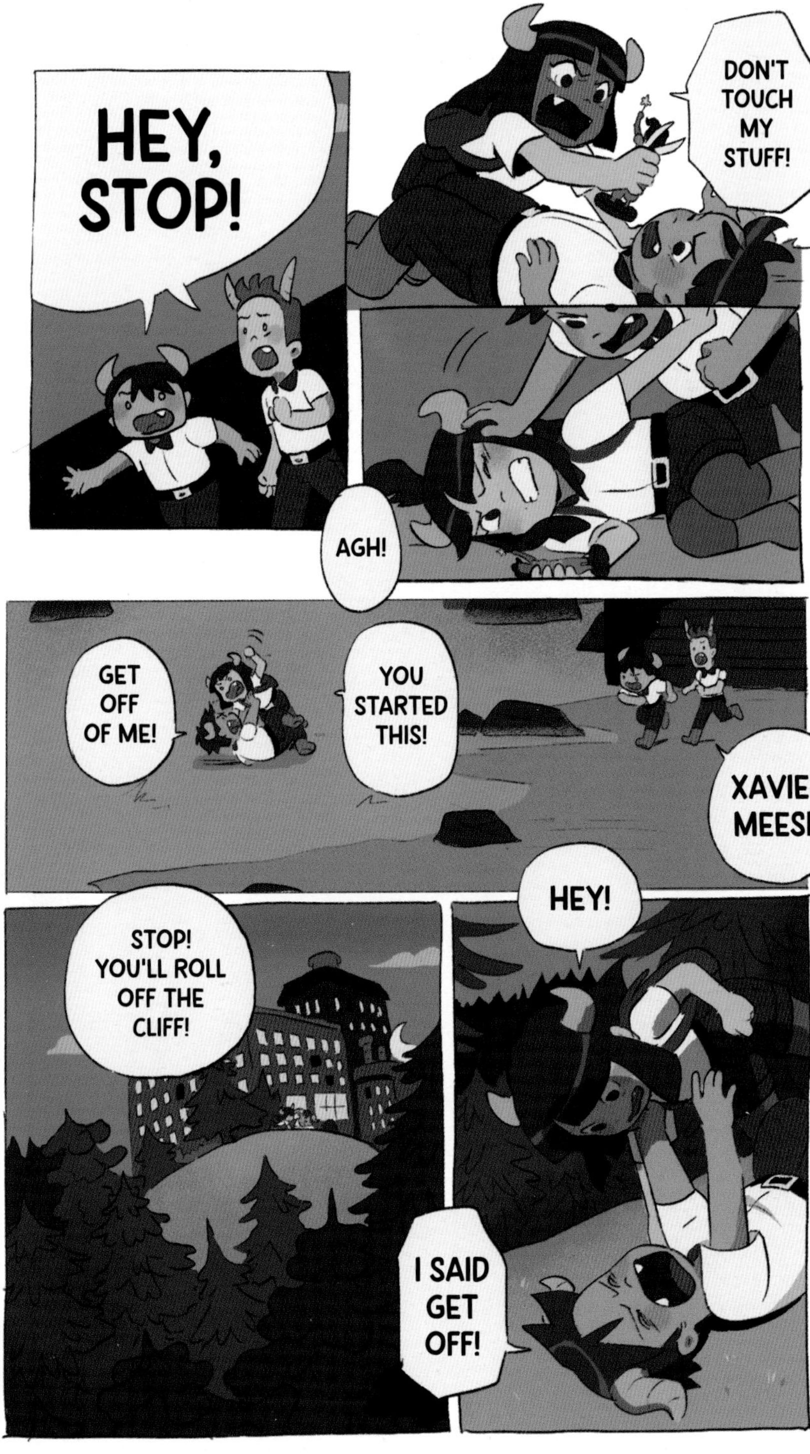
HEY, STOP!
DON'T TOUCH MY STUFF!
AGH!
GET OFF OF ME!
YOU STARTED THIS!
XAVIER! MEESH!
STOP! YOU'LL ROLL OFF THE CLIFF!
HEY!
I SAID GET OFF!

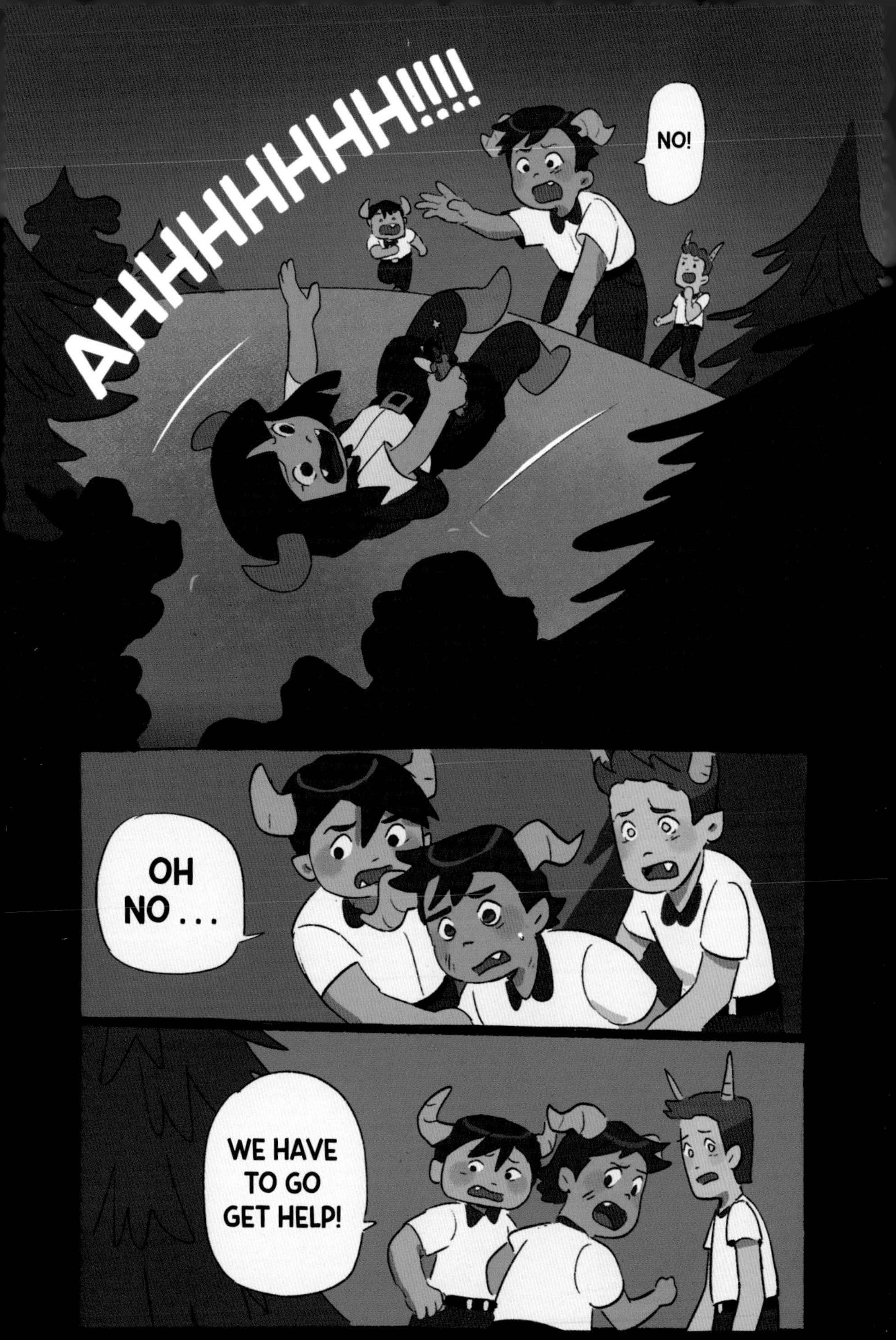
AHHHHHHH!!!!
NO!
OH NO . . .
WE HAVE TO GO GET HELP!

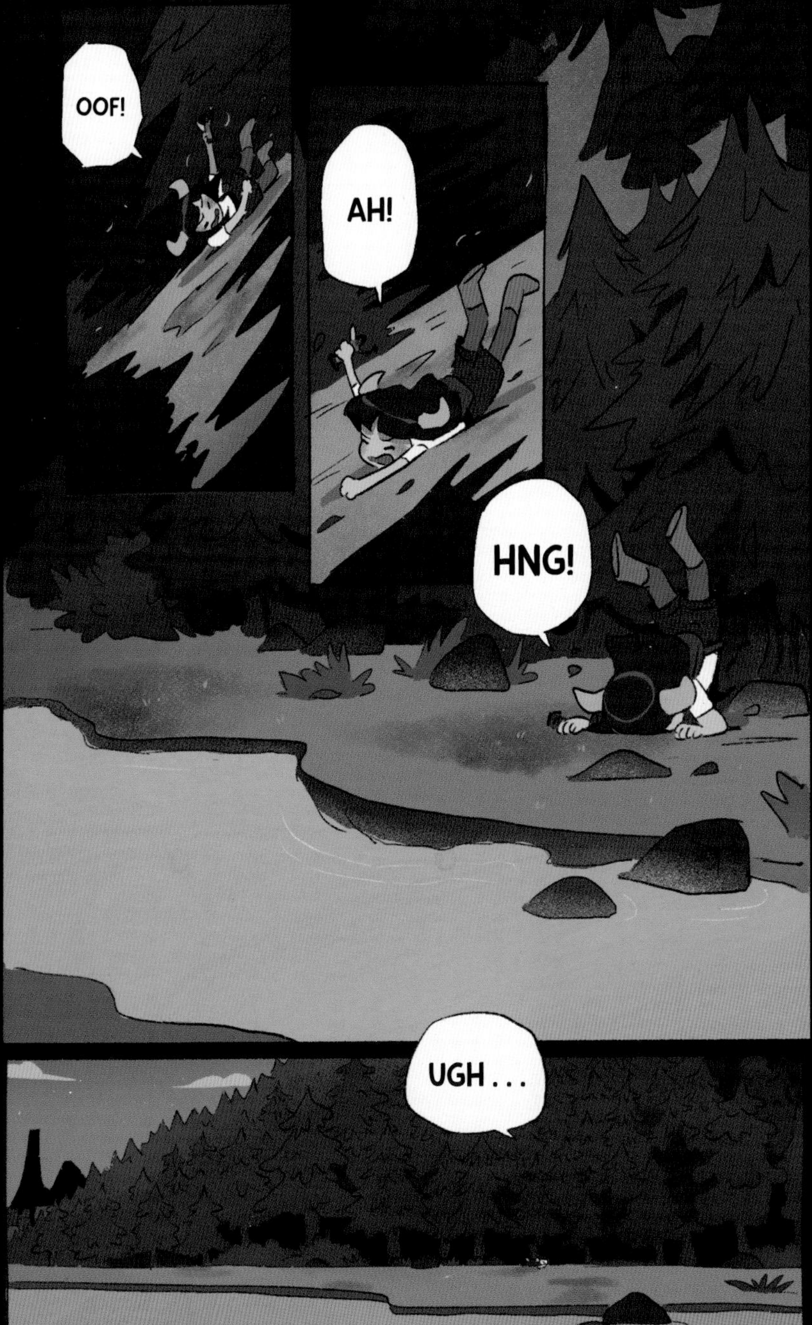
OOF!
AH!
HNG!
UGH . . .

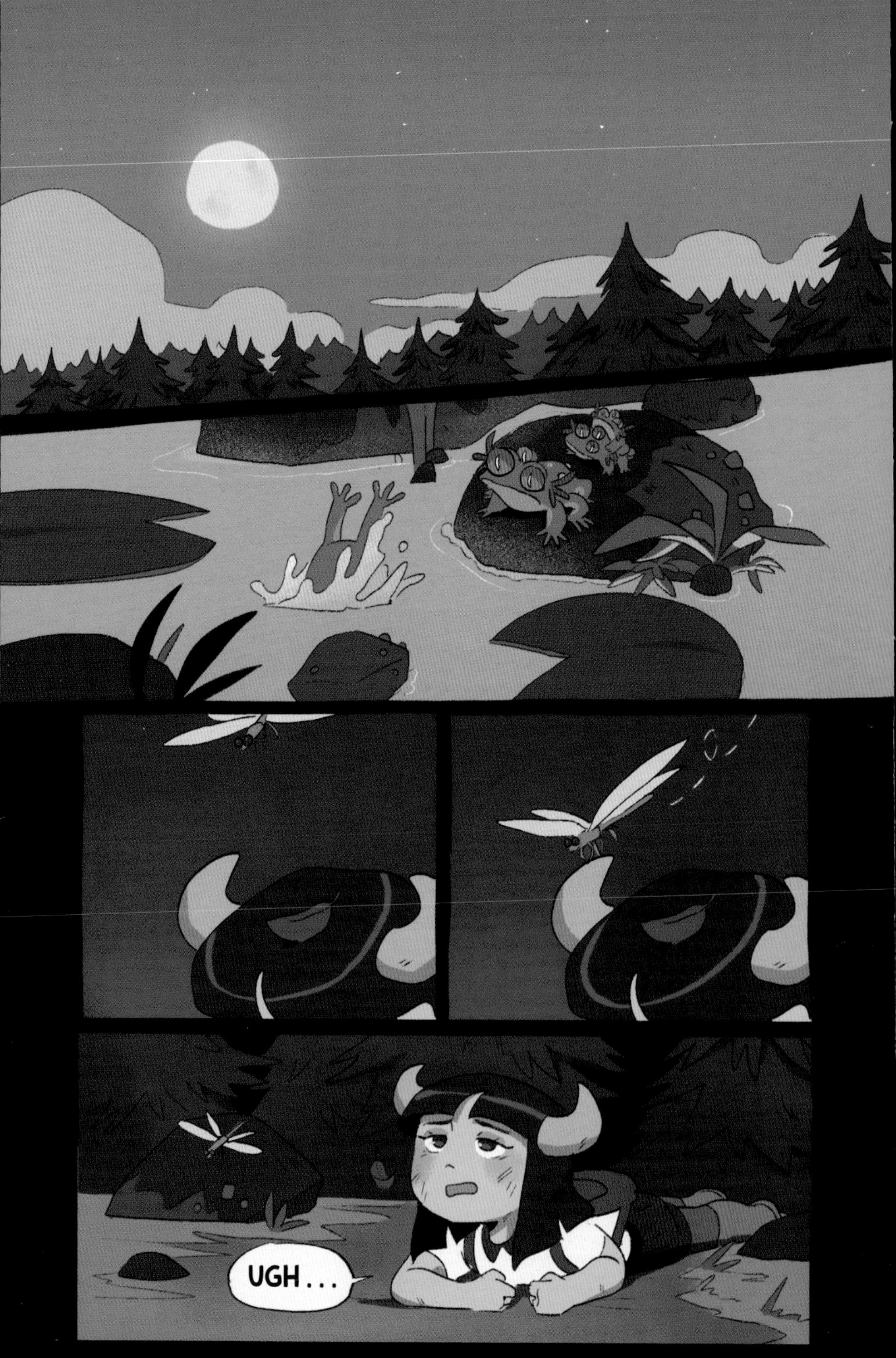
UGH . . .

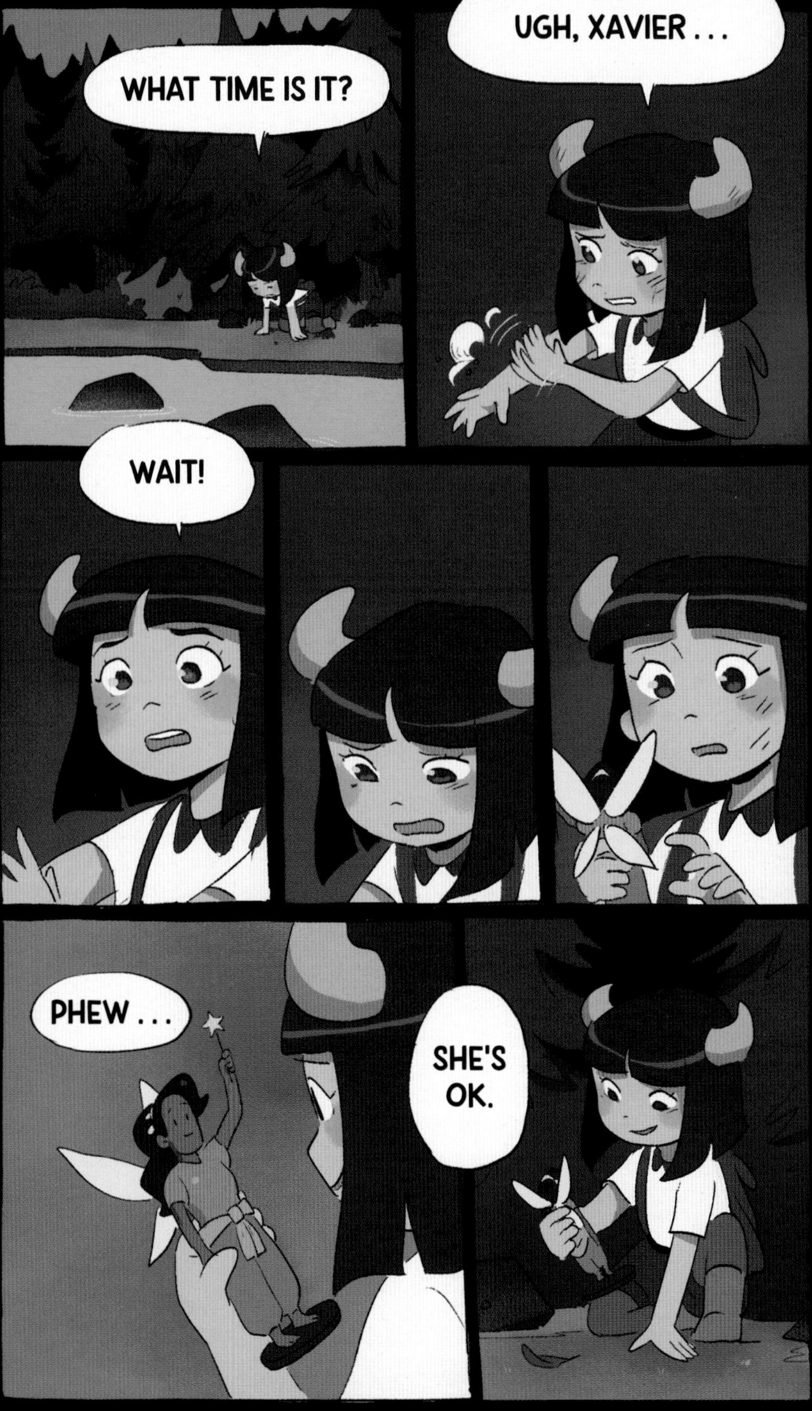
WHAT TIME IS IT?
UGH, XAVIER . . .
WAIT!
PHEW . . .
SHE'S OK.

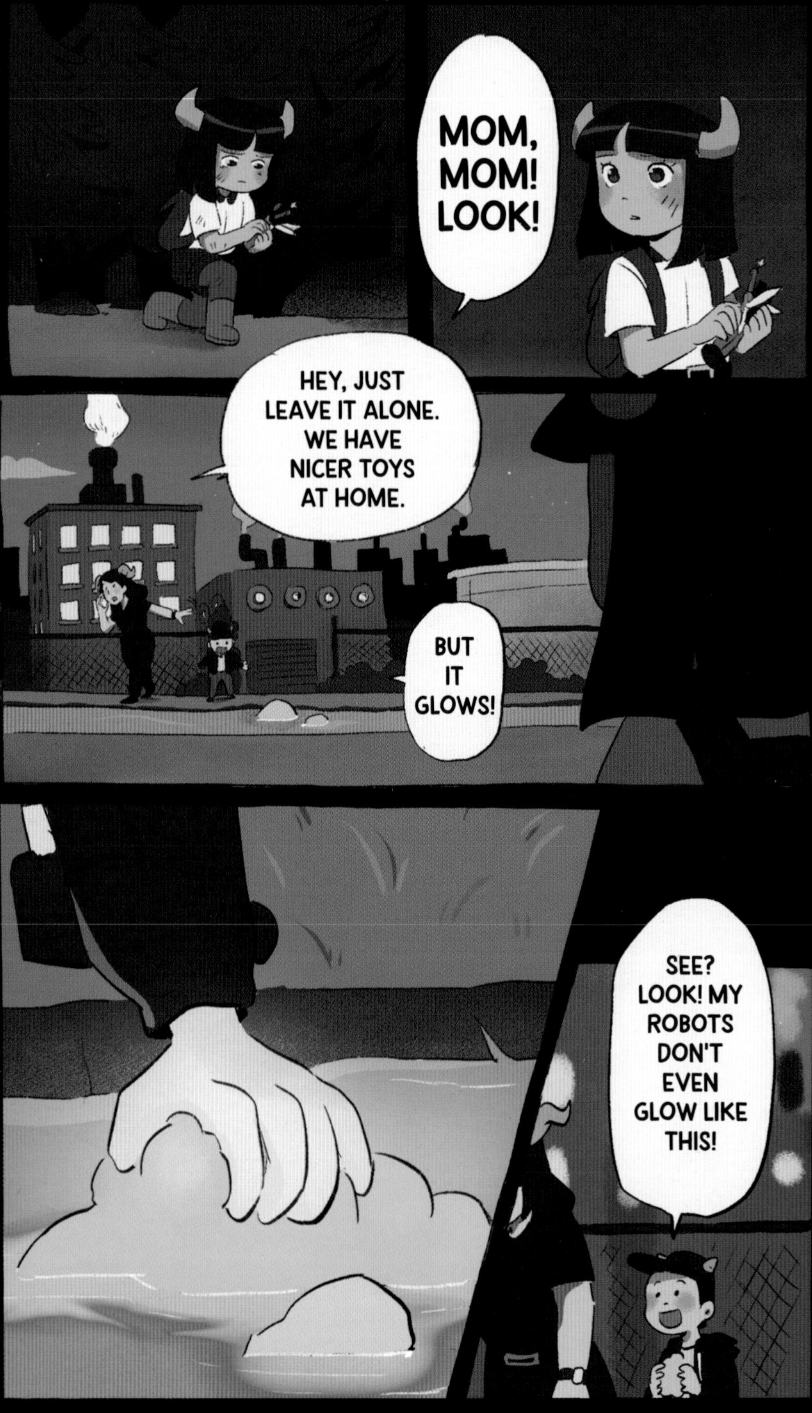
MOM, MOM! LOOK!
HEY, JUST LEAVE IT ALONE. WE HAVE NICER TOYS AT HOME.
BUT IT GLOWS!
SEE? LOOK! MY ROBOTS DON'T EVEN GLOW LIKE THIS!

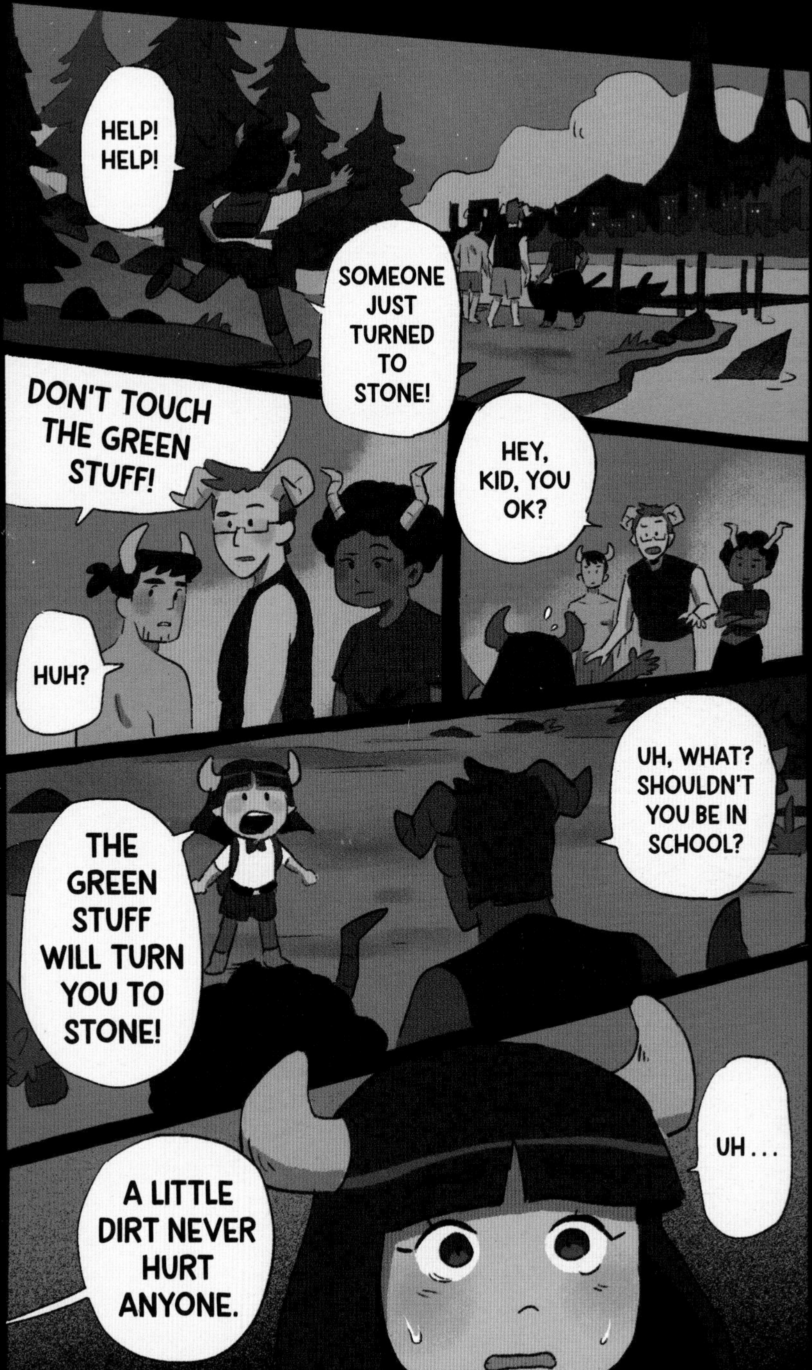
HELP! HELP!
SOMEONE JUST TURNED TO STONE!
DON'T TOUCH THE GREEN STUFF!
HUH?
HEY, KID, YOU OK?
THE GREEN STUFF WILL TURN YOU TO STONE!
UH, WHAT? SHOULDN'T YOU BE IN SCHOOL?
A LITTLE DIRT NEVER HURT ANYONE.
UH . . .

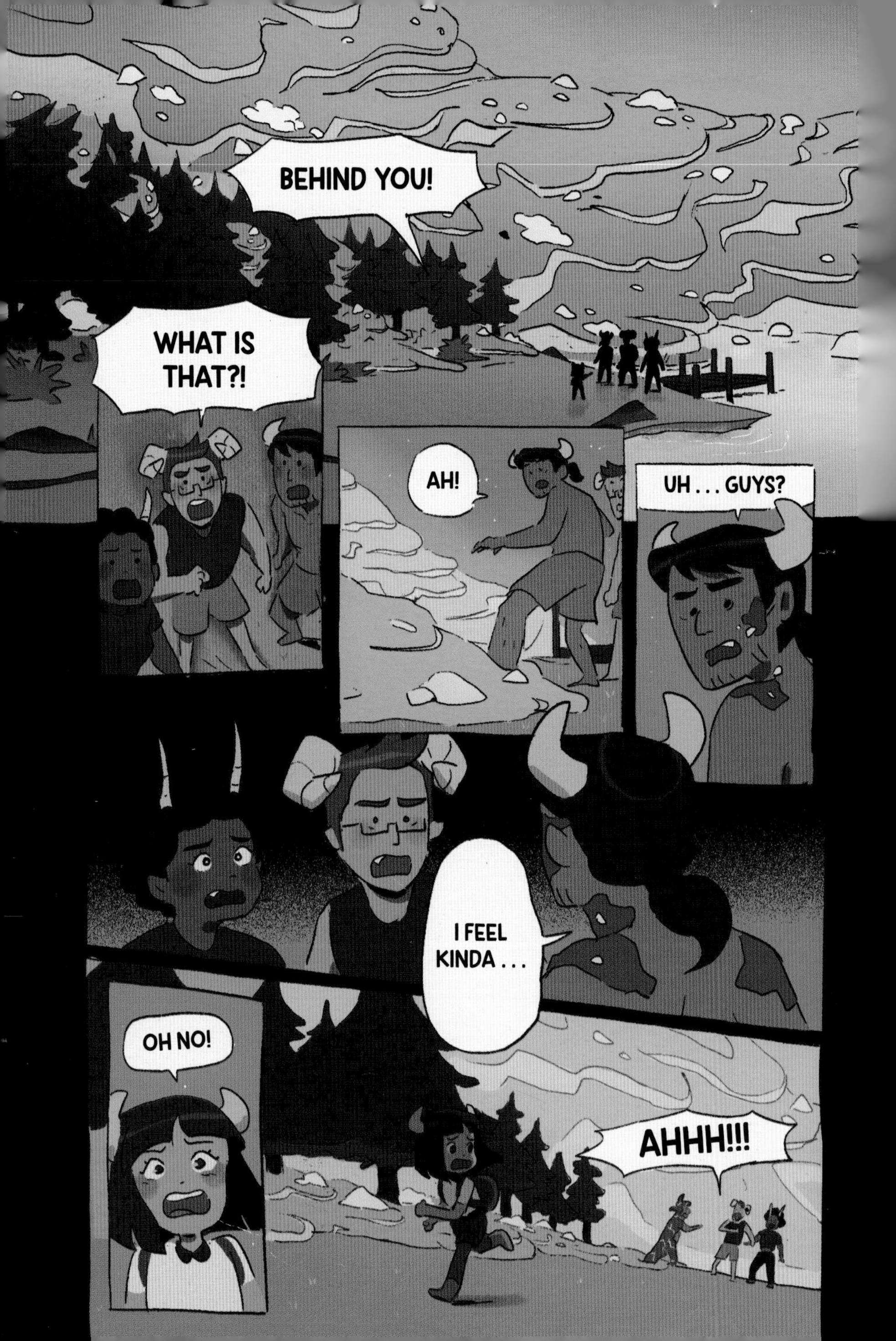
BEHIND YOU!
WHAT IS THAT?!
AH!
UH . . . GUYS?
I FEEL KINDA . . .
OH NO!
AHHH!!!

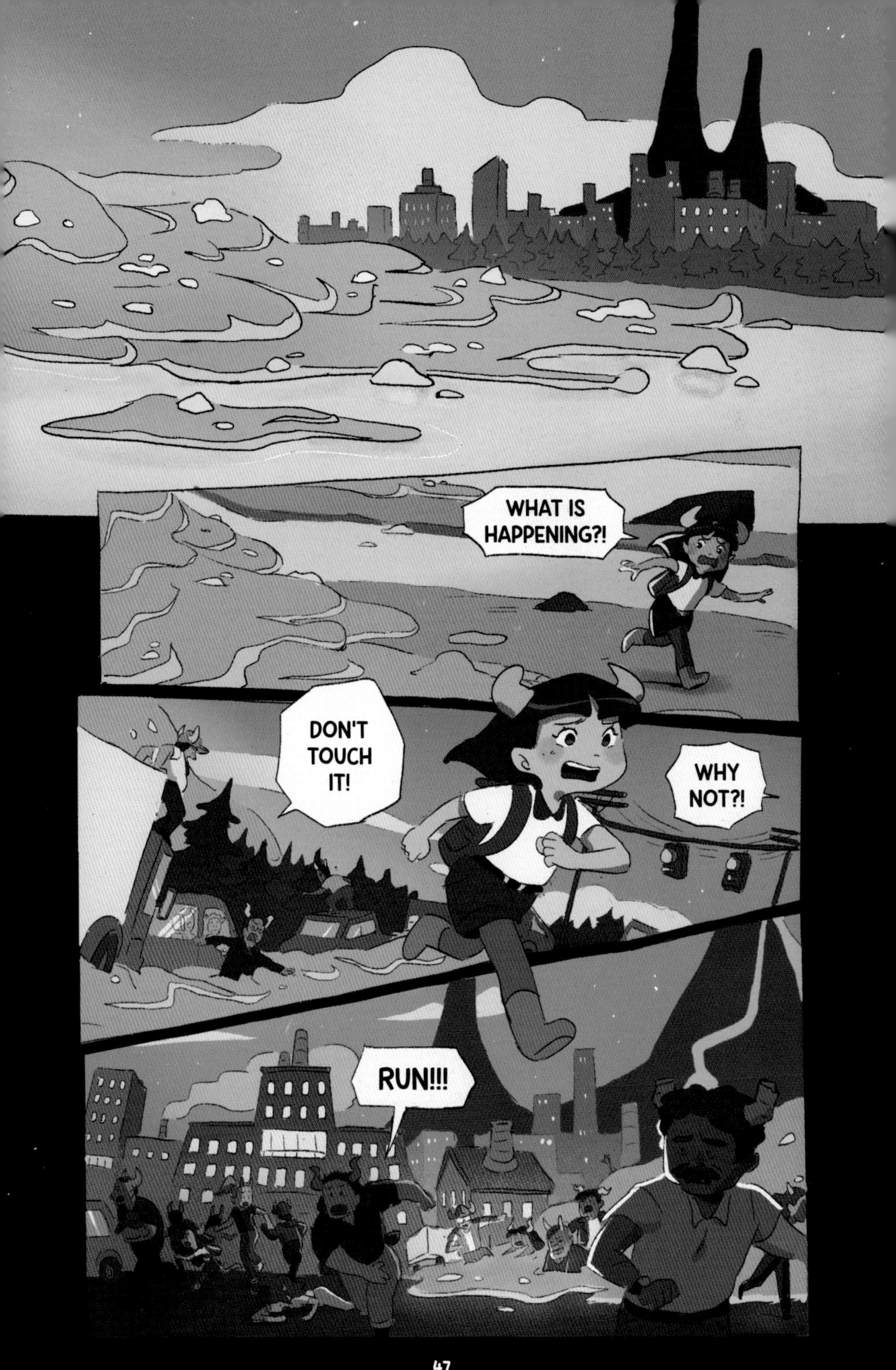
WHAT IS HAPPENING?!
DON'T TOUCH IT!
WHY NOT?!
RUN!!!

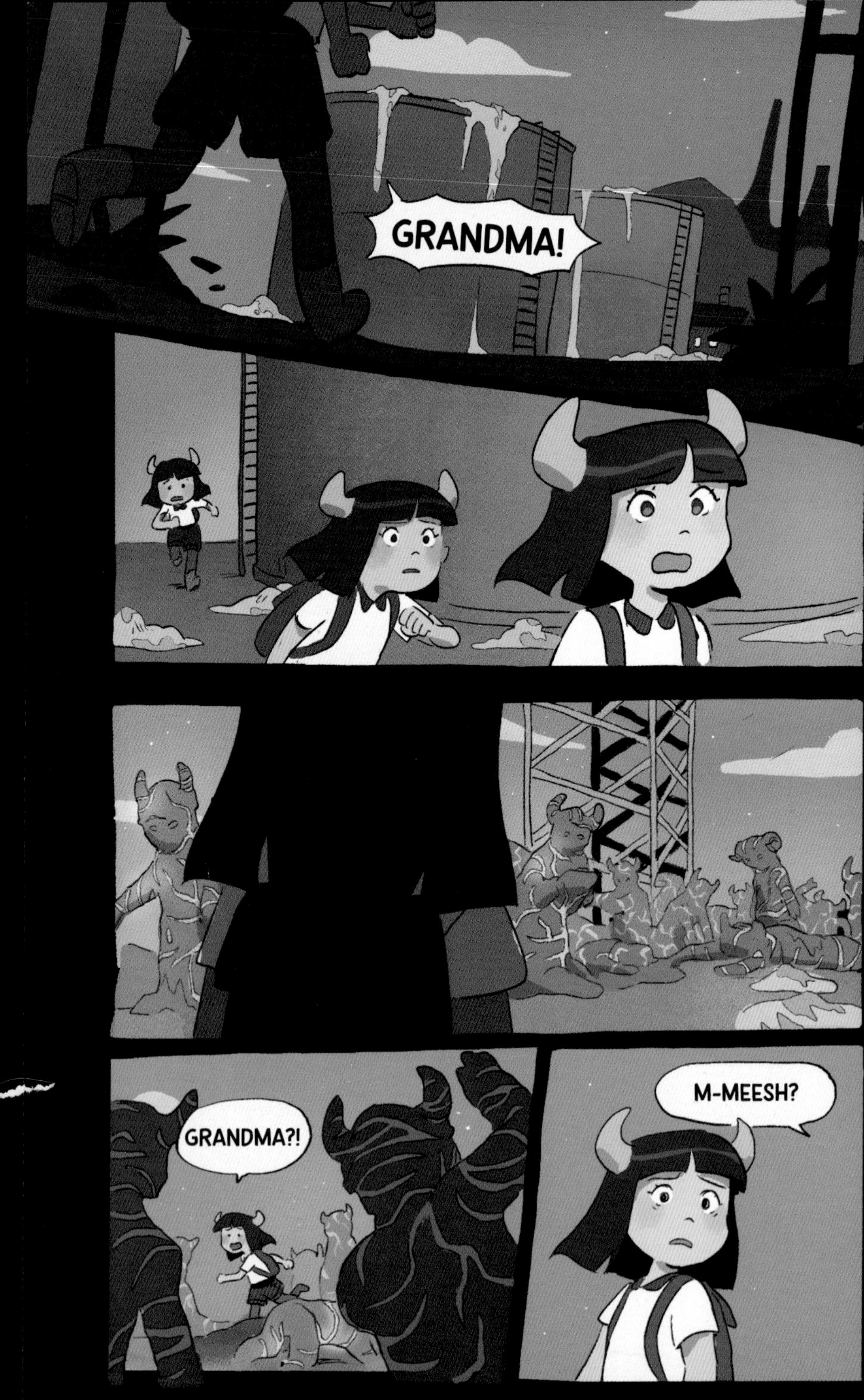
GRANDMA!
GRANDMA?!
M-MEESH?

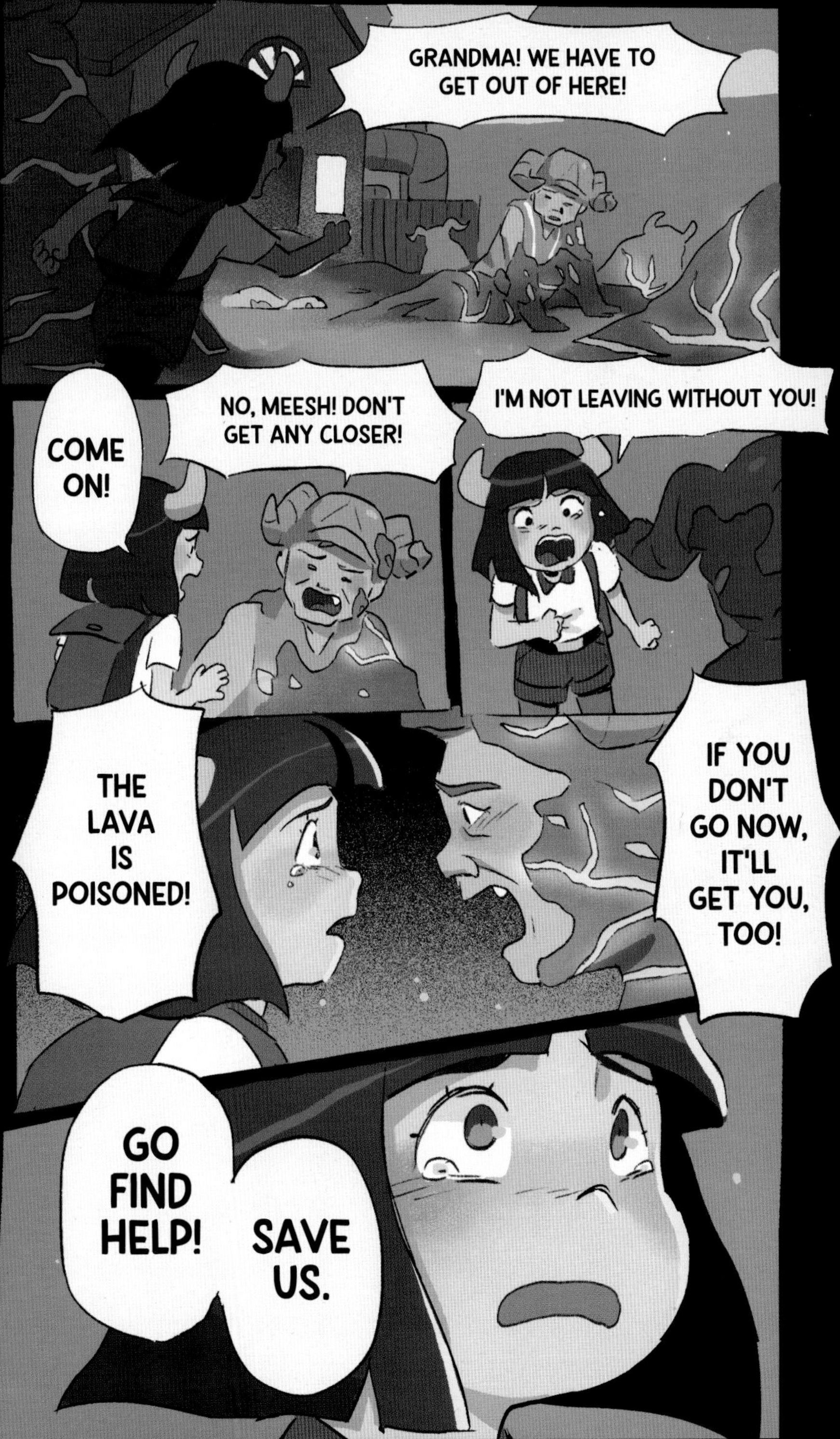
GRANDMA! WE HAVE TO GET OUT OF HERE!
COME ON!
NO, MEESH! DON'T GET ANY CLOSER!
I'M NOT LEAVING WITHOUT YOU!
THE LAVA IS POISONED!
IF YOU DON'T GO NOW, IT'LL GET YOU, TOO!
GO FIND HELP!
SAVE US.

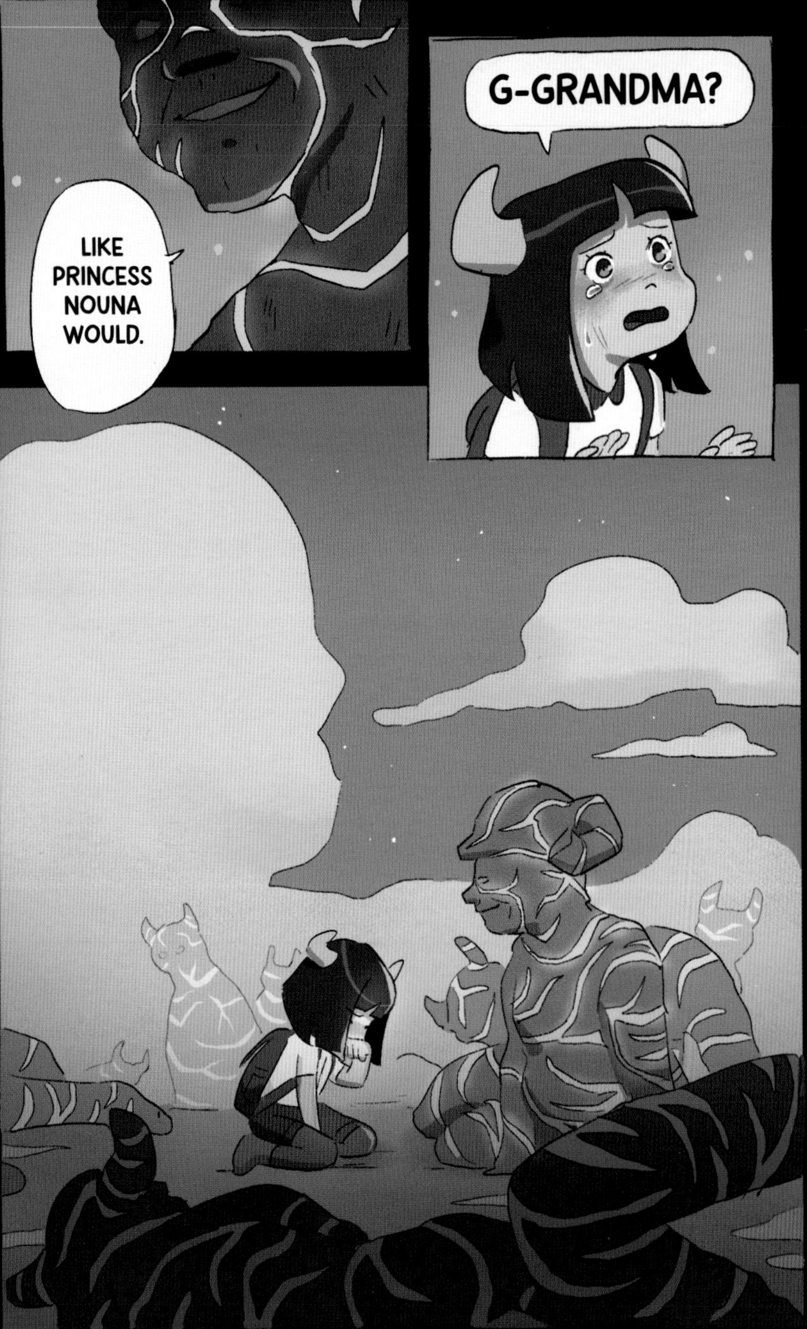
LIKE PRINCESS NOUNA WOULD.
G-GRANDMA?

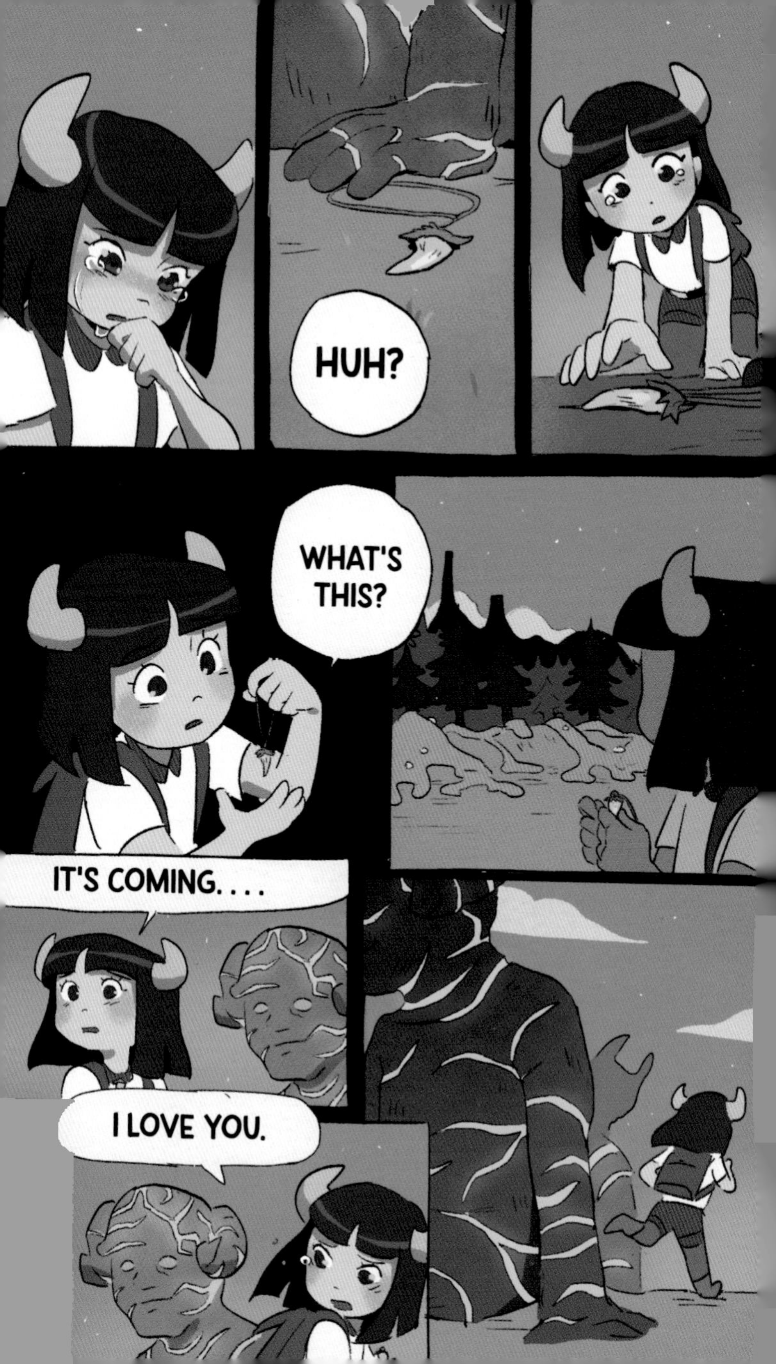
HUH?
WHAT'S THIS?
IT'S COMING. . . .
I LOVE YOU.

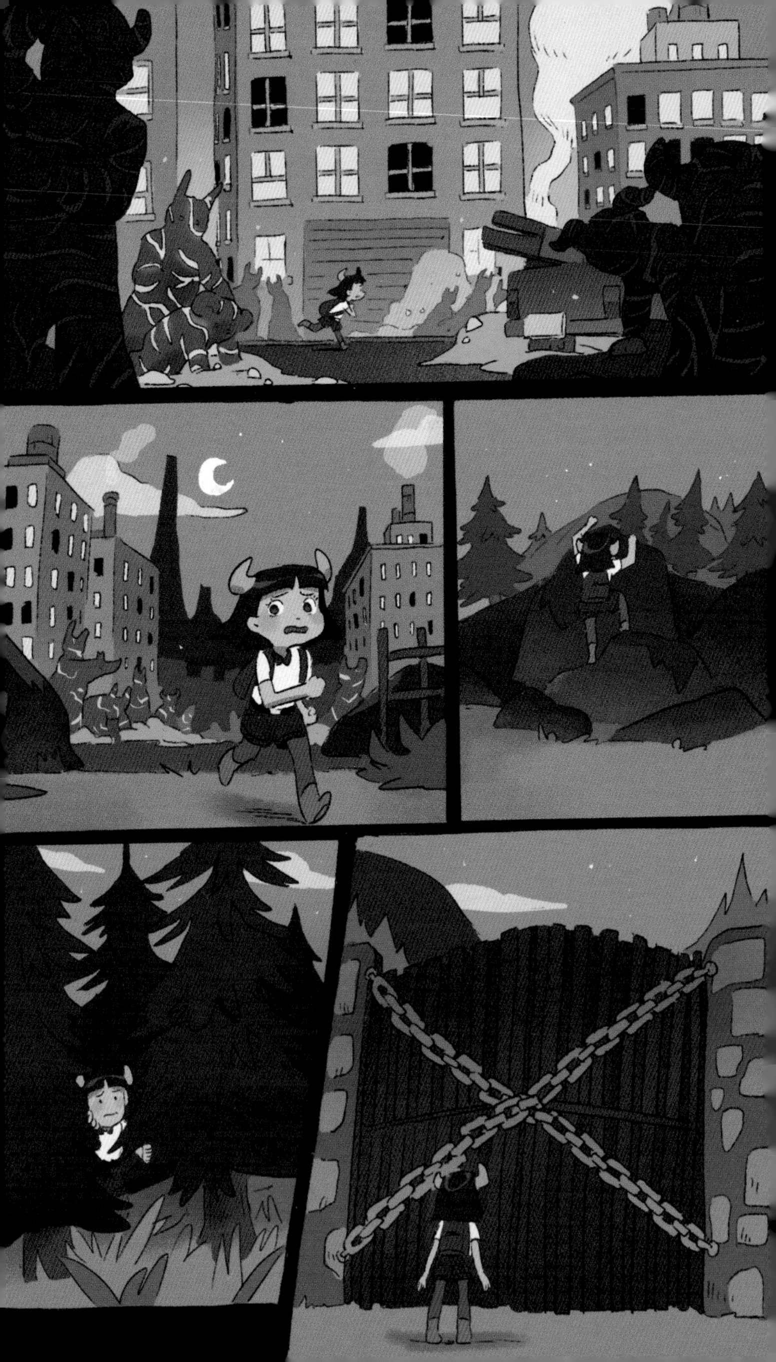

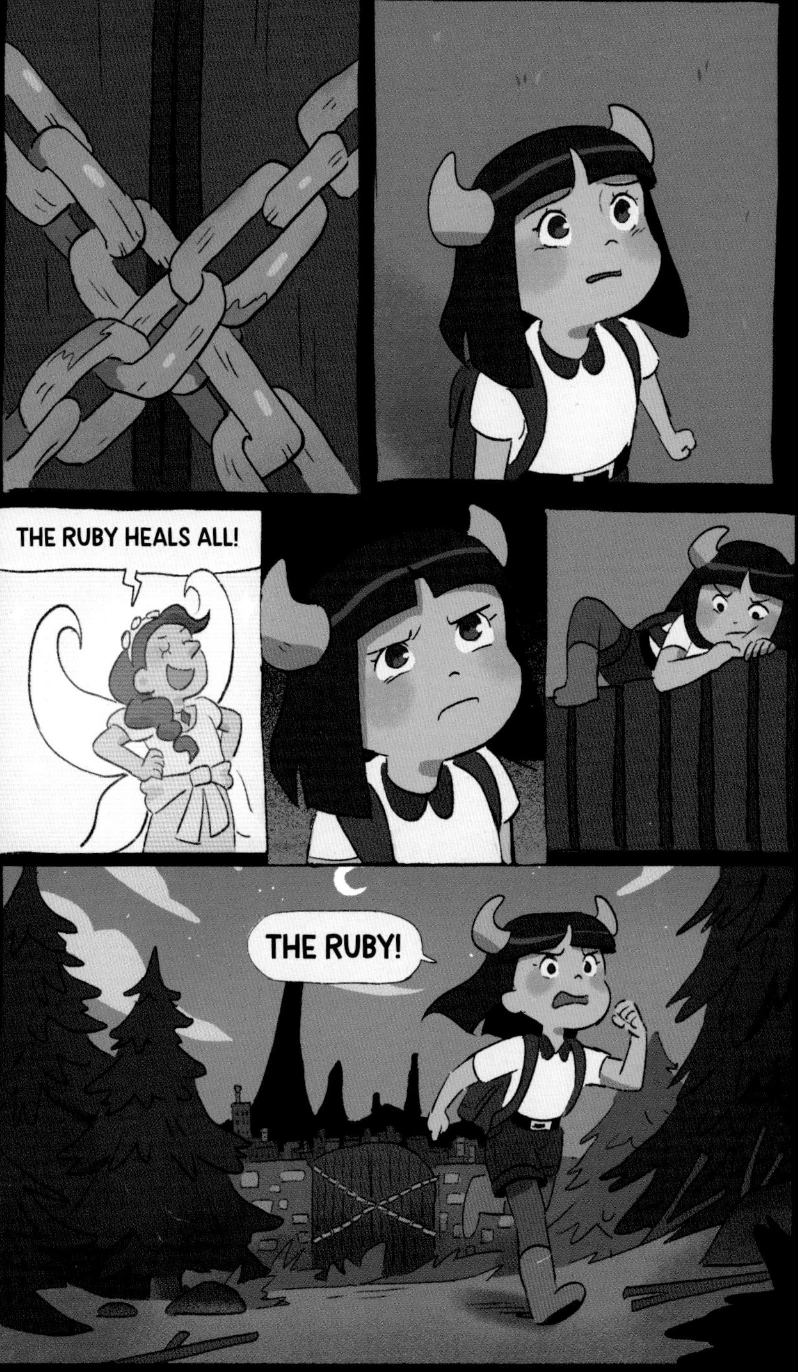
THE RUBY HEALS ALL!
THE RUBY!

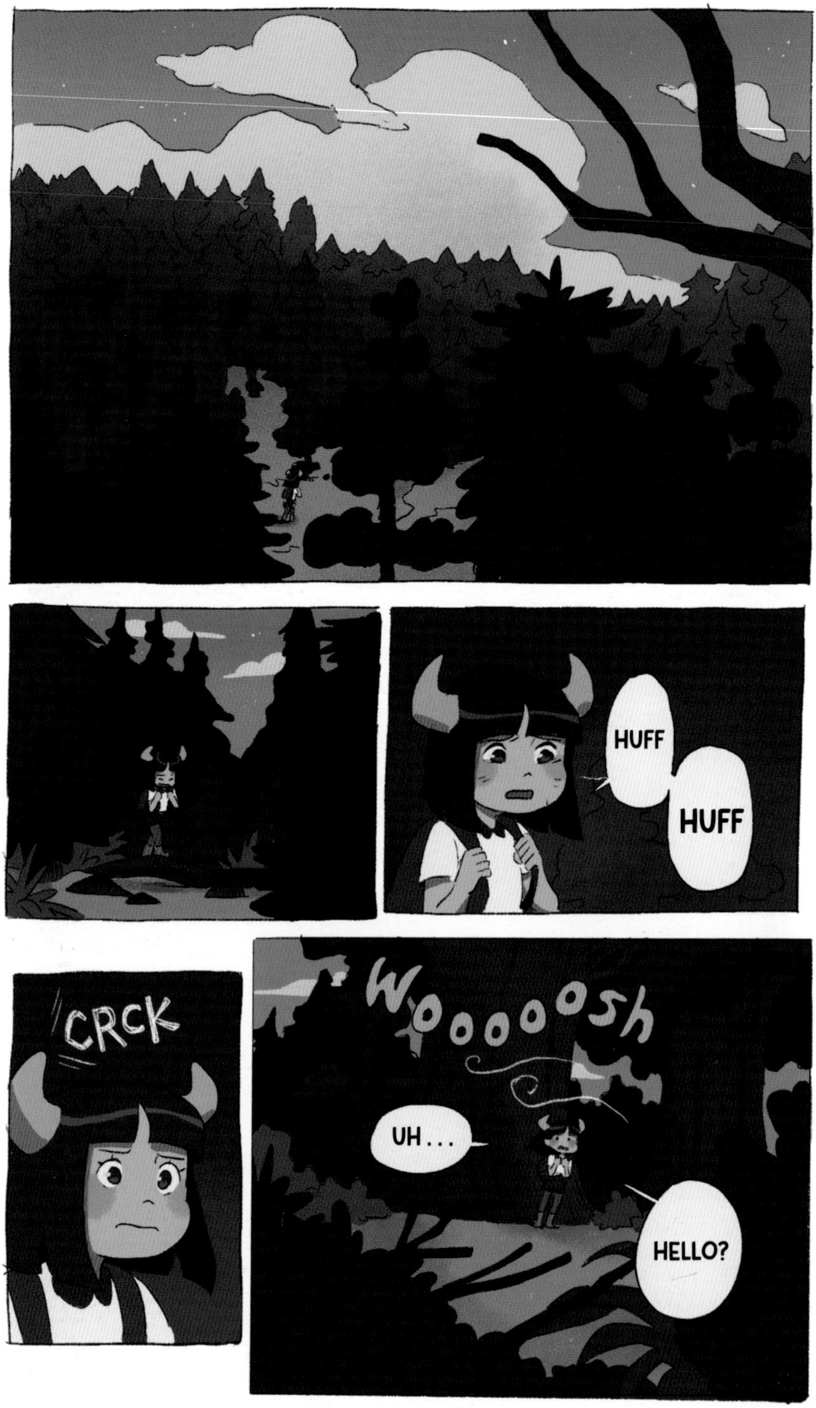
HUFF
HUFF
CRCK
WOOOOOSH
UH...
HELLO?

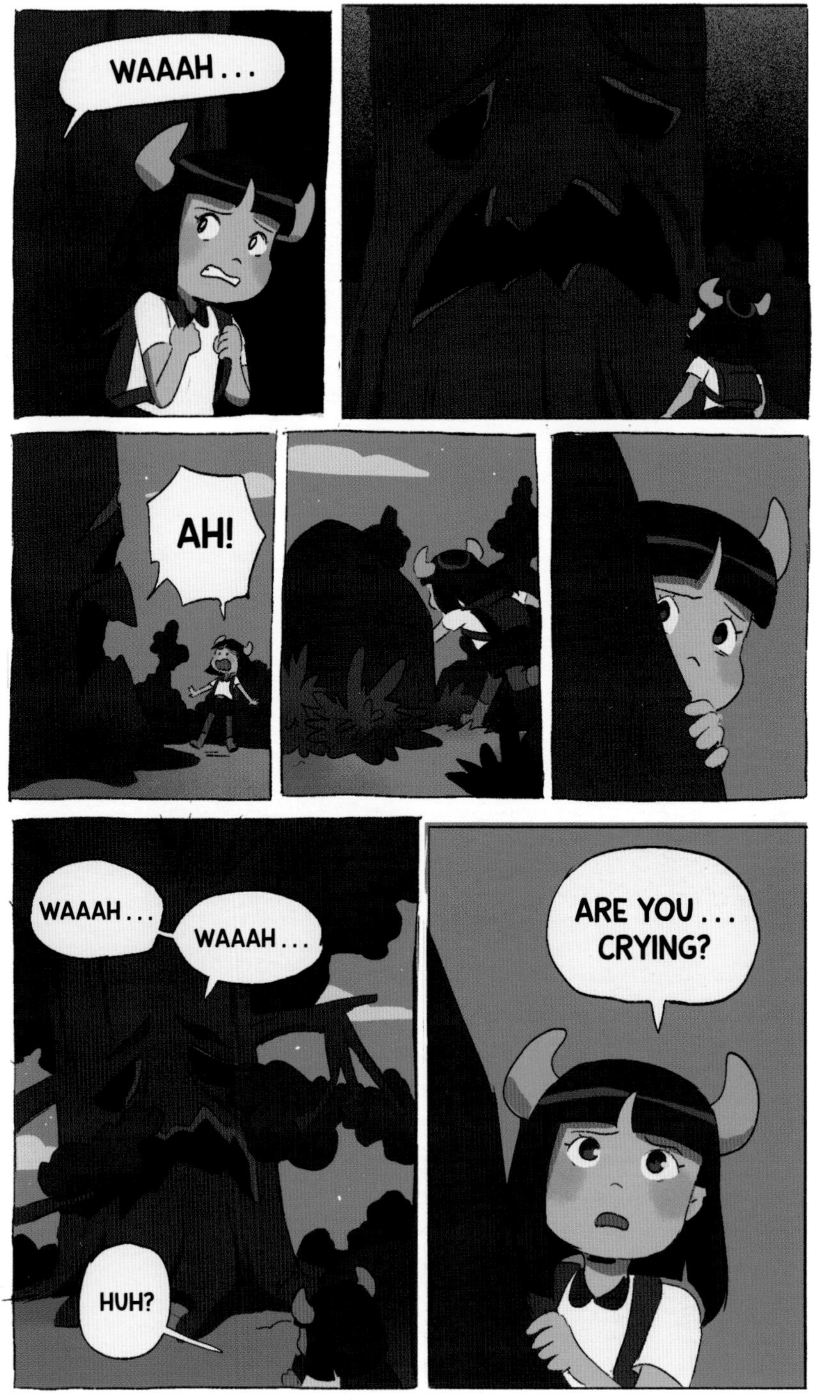
WAAAH . . .
AH!
WAAAH . . .
WAAAH . . .
HUH?
ARE YOU . . . CRYING?

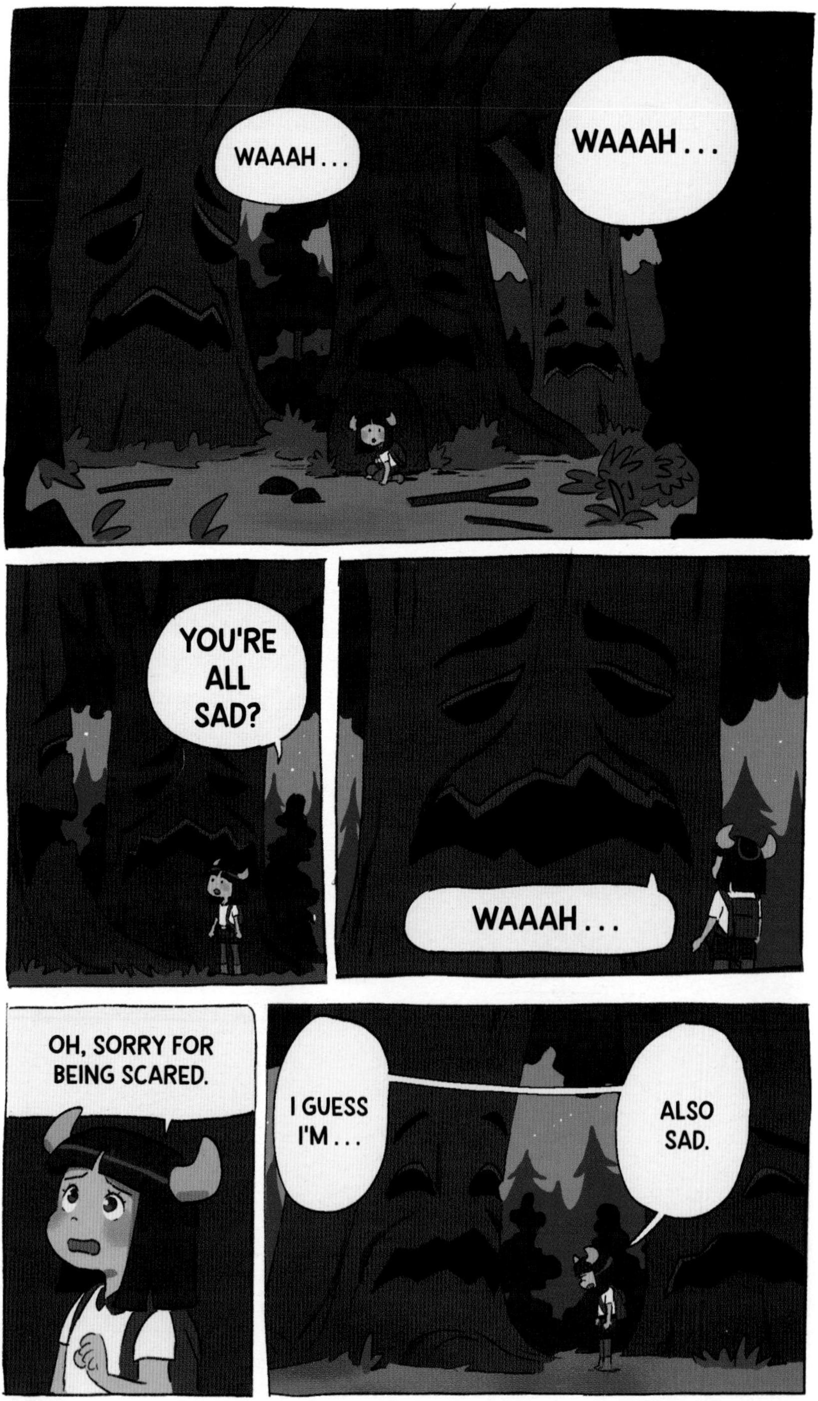
WAAAH . . .
WAAAH . . .
YOU'RE ALL SAD?
WAAAH . . .
OH, SORRY FOR BEING SCARED.
I GUESS I'M . . .
ALSO SAD.

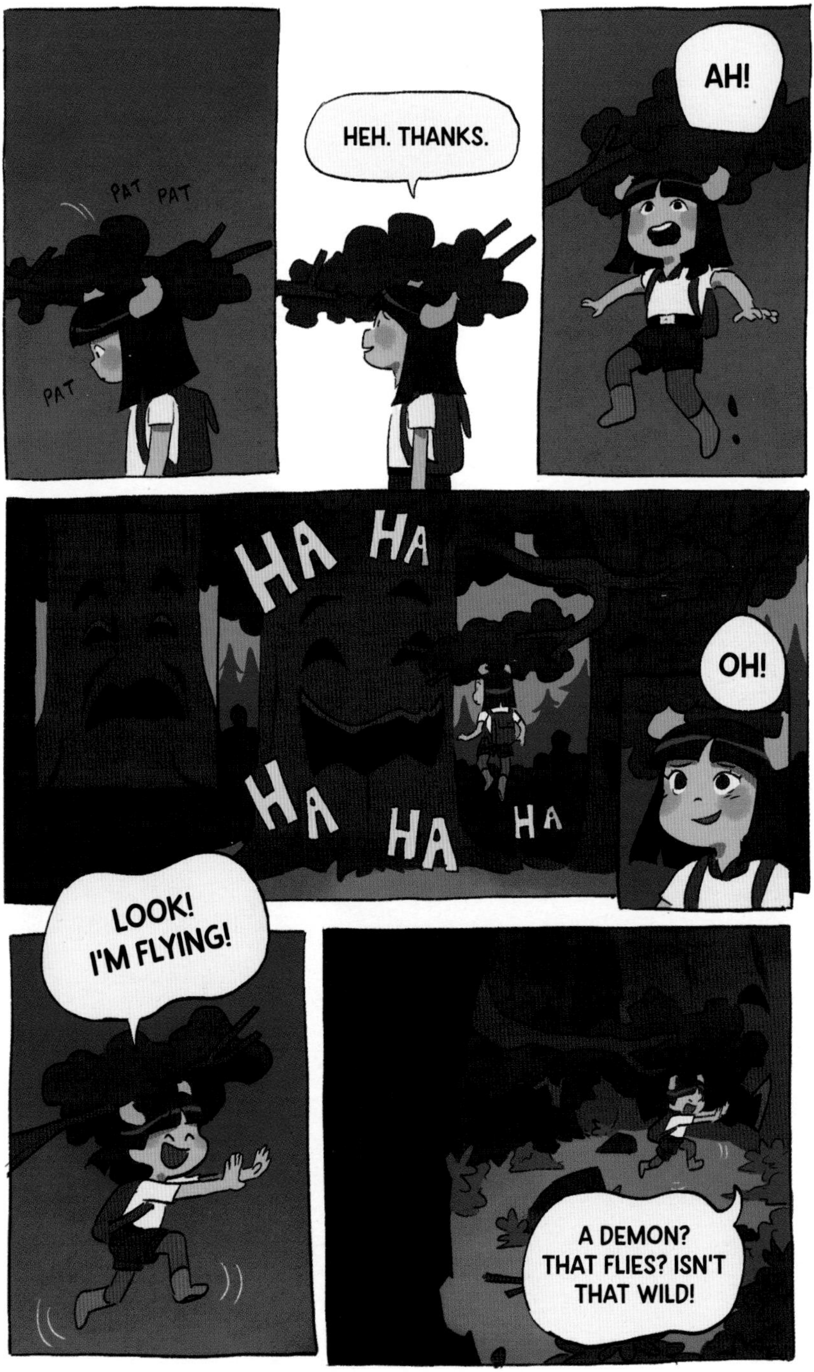
PAT PAT
PAT
HEH. THANKS.
AH!
HA HA
HA HA HA
OH!
LOOK! I'M FLYING!
A DEMON? THAT FLIES? ISN'T THAT WILD!

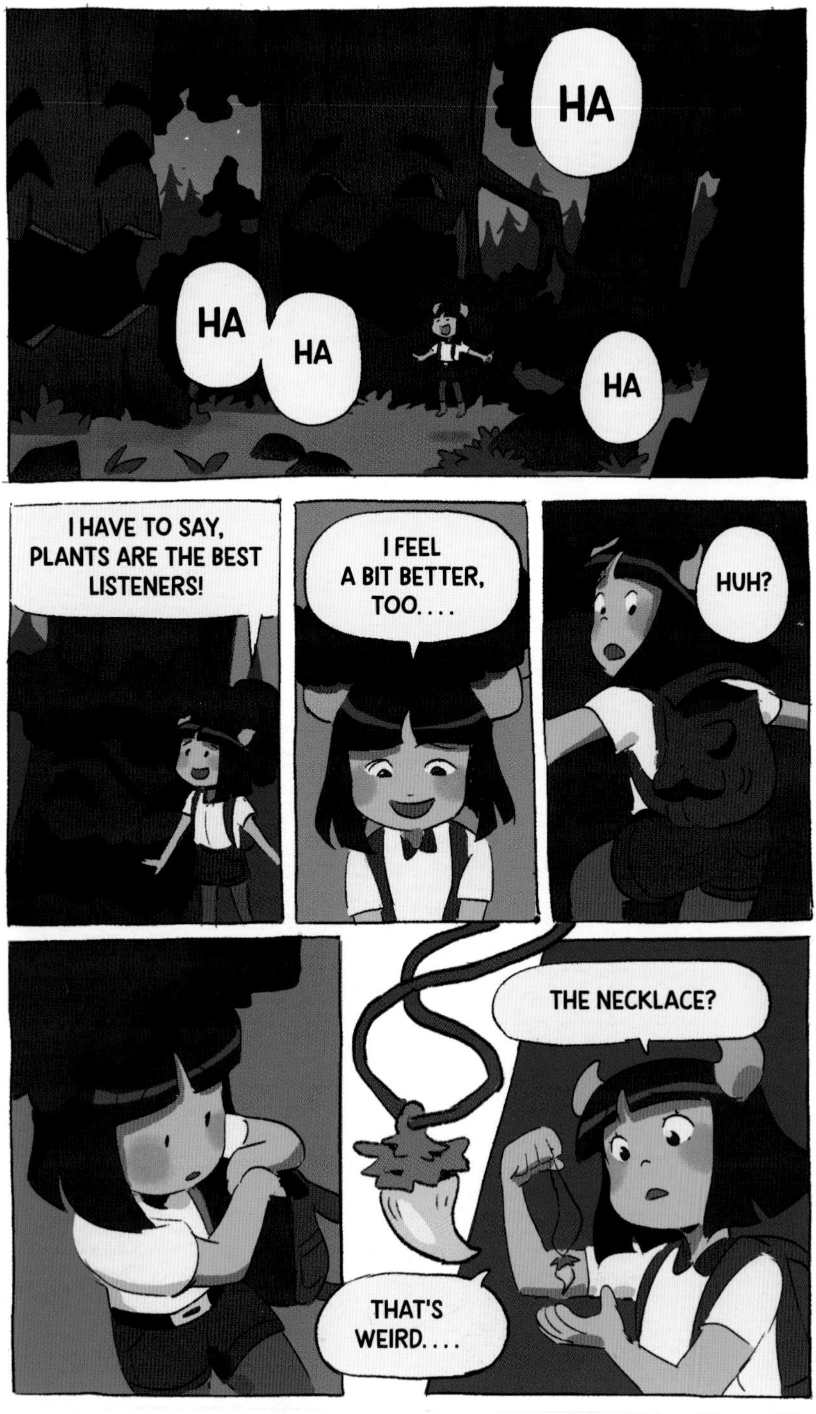
HA
HA
HA
HA
I HAVE TO SAY, PLANTS ARE THE BEST LISTENERS!
I FEEL A BIT BETTER, TOO. . . .
HUH?
THE NECKLACE?
THAT'S WEIRD. . . .

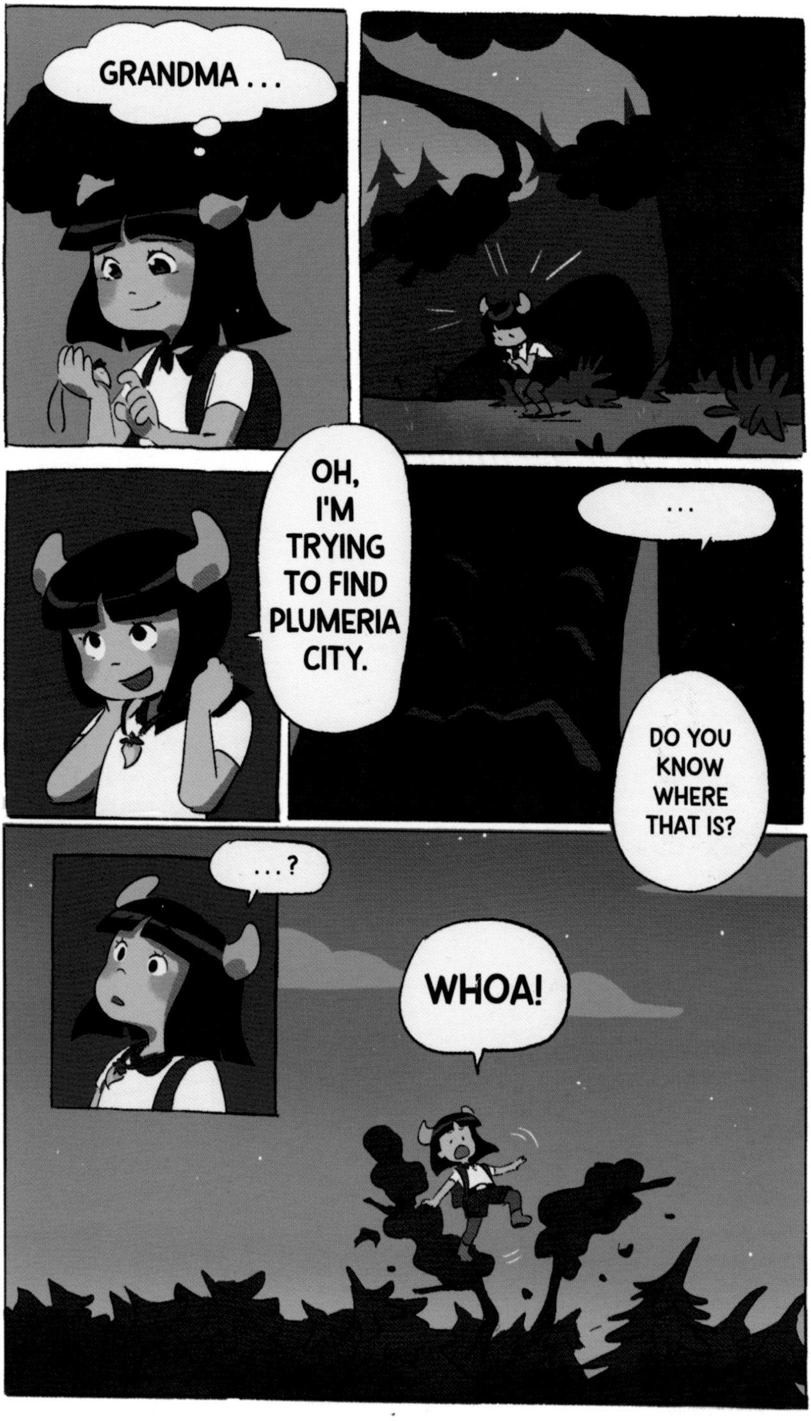
GRANDMA . . .
OH, I'M TRYING TO FIND PLUMERIA CITY.
. . .
DO YOU KNOW WHERE THAT IS?
. . . ?
WHOA!

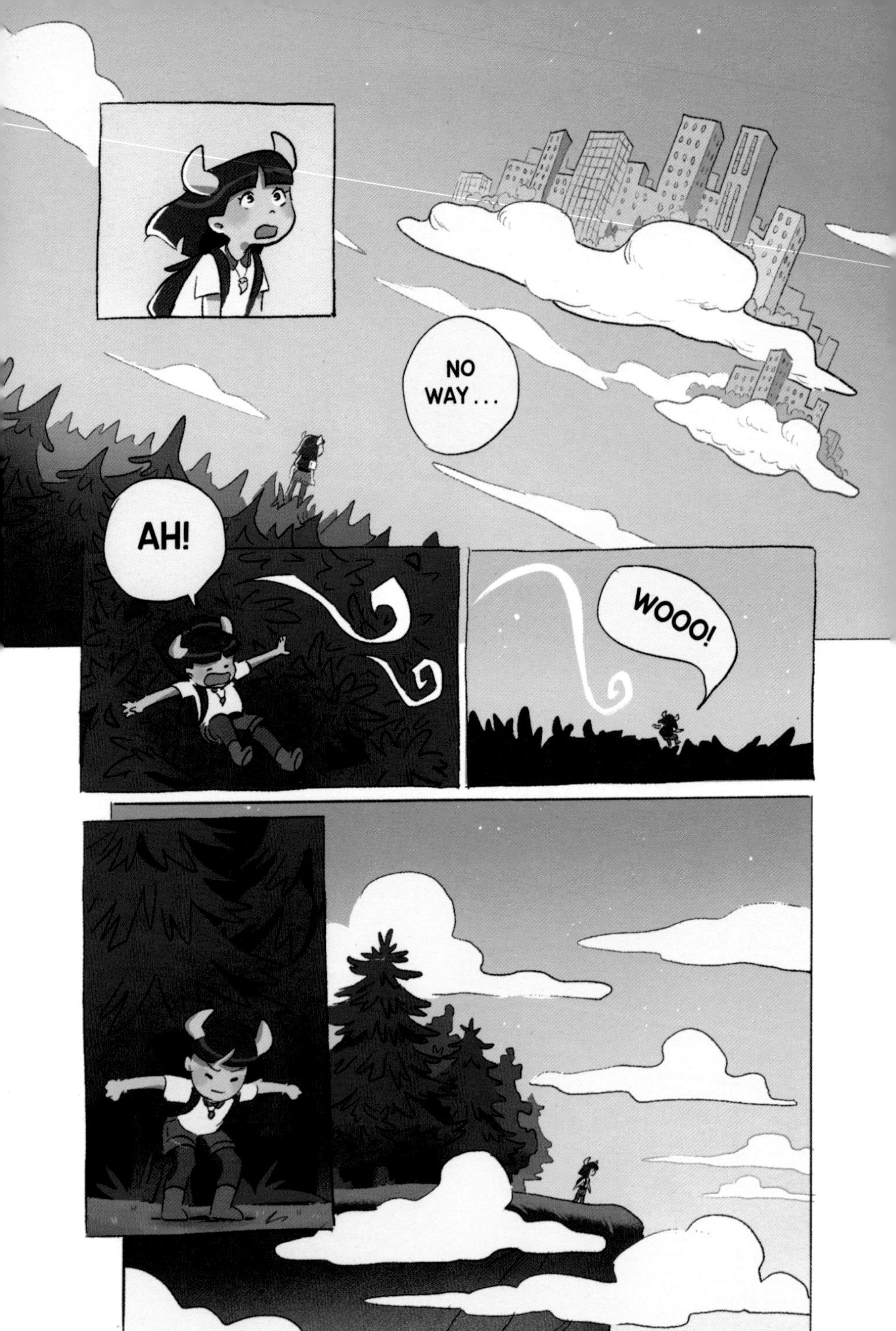
NO WAY...
AH!
WOOO!

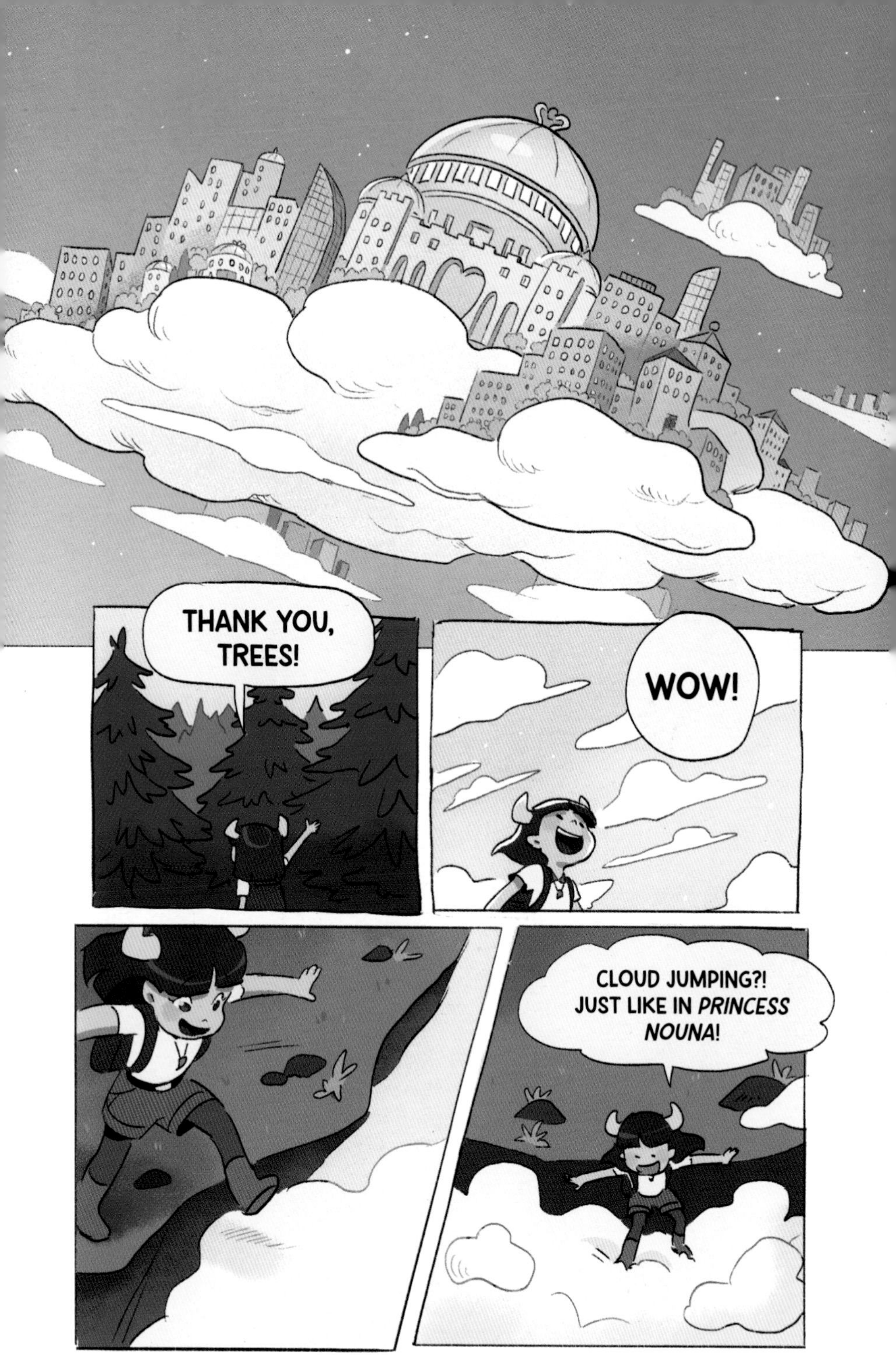
THANK YOU, TREES!
WOW!
CLOUD JUMPING?! JUST LIKE IN *PRINCESS NOUNA*!

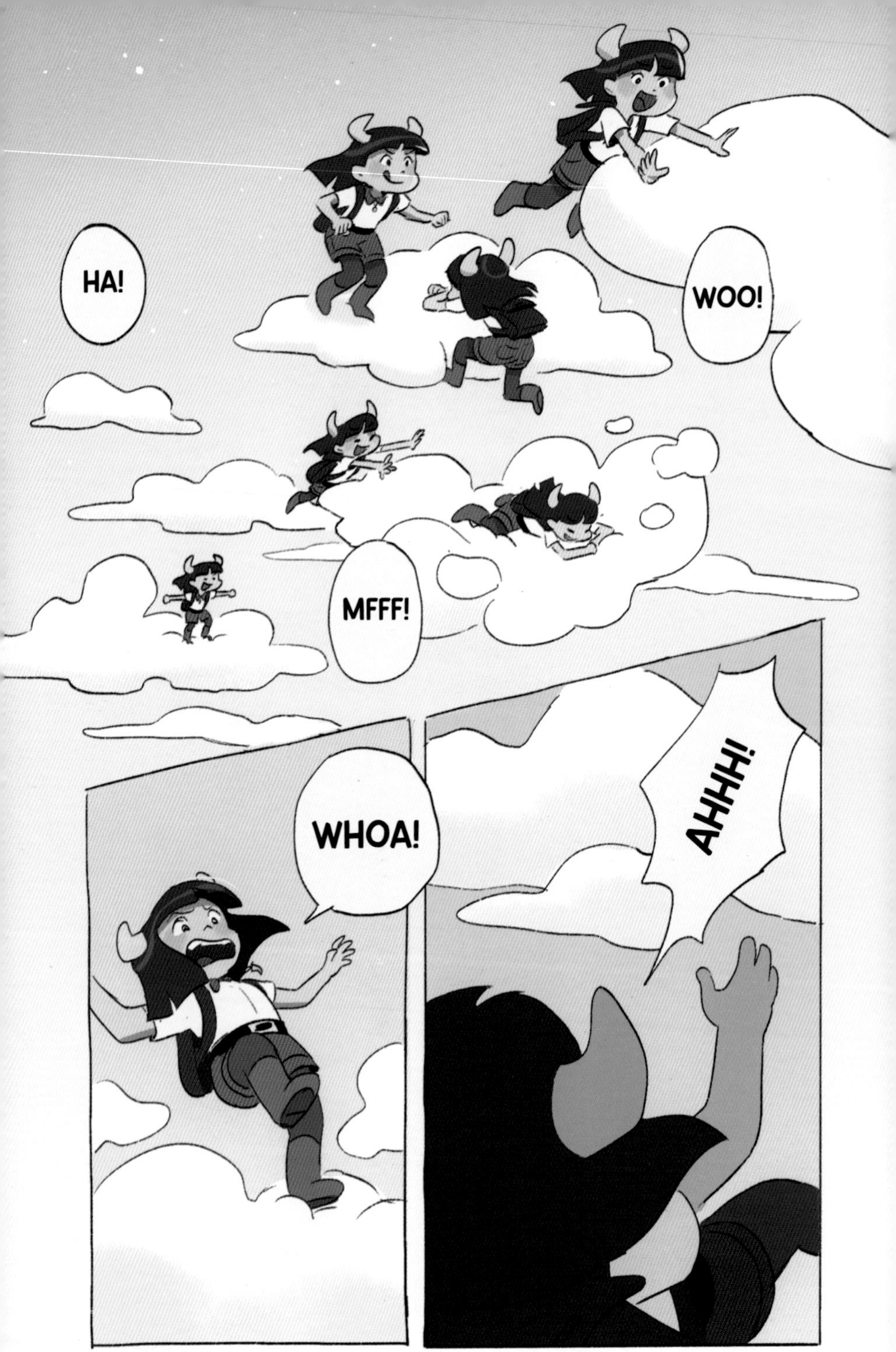
HA!
WOO!
MFFF!
WHOA!
AHHH!

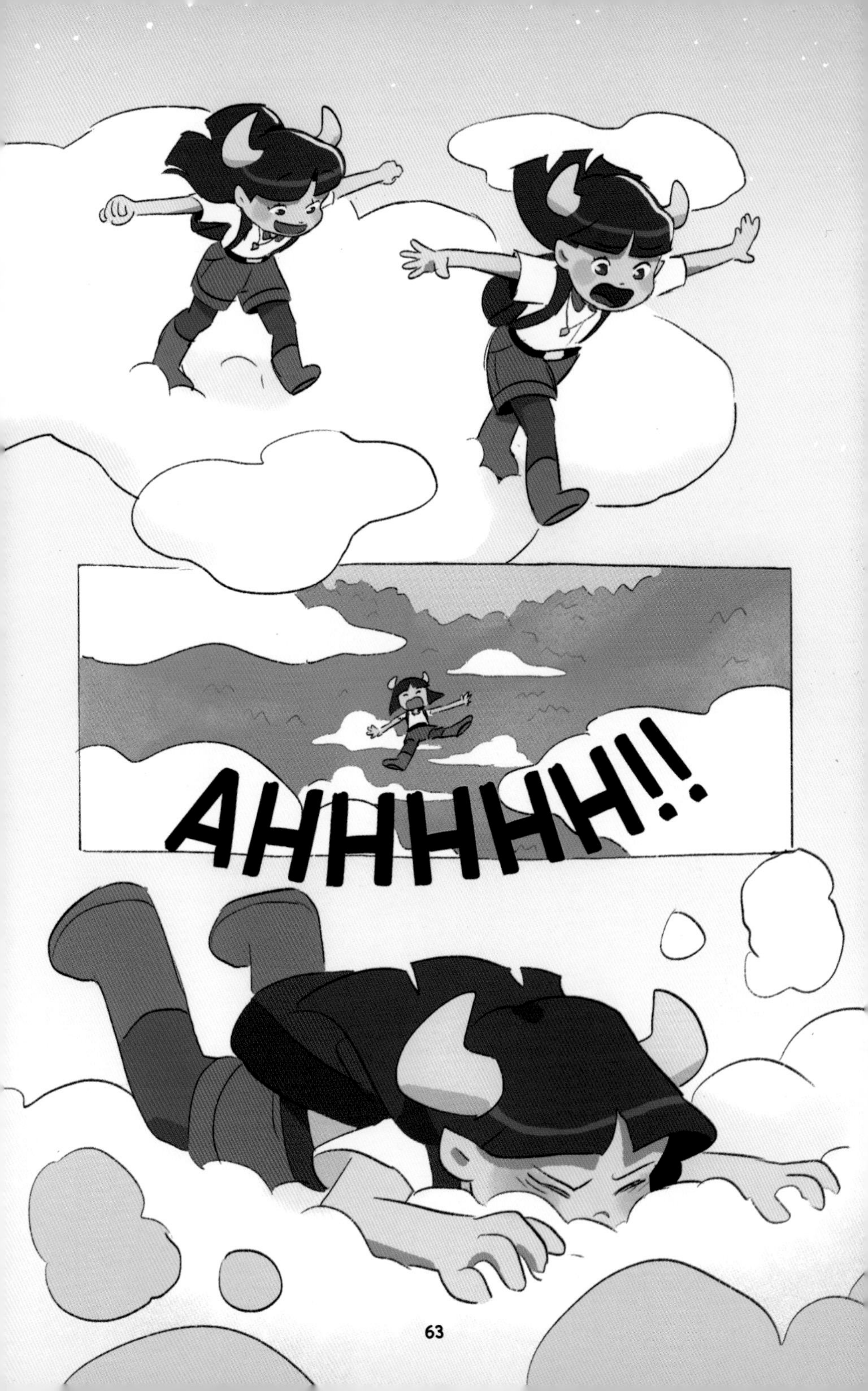
AHHHHH!!

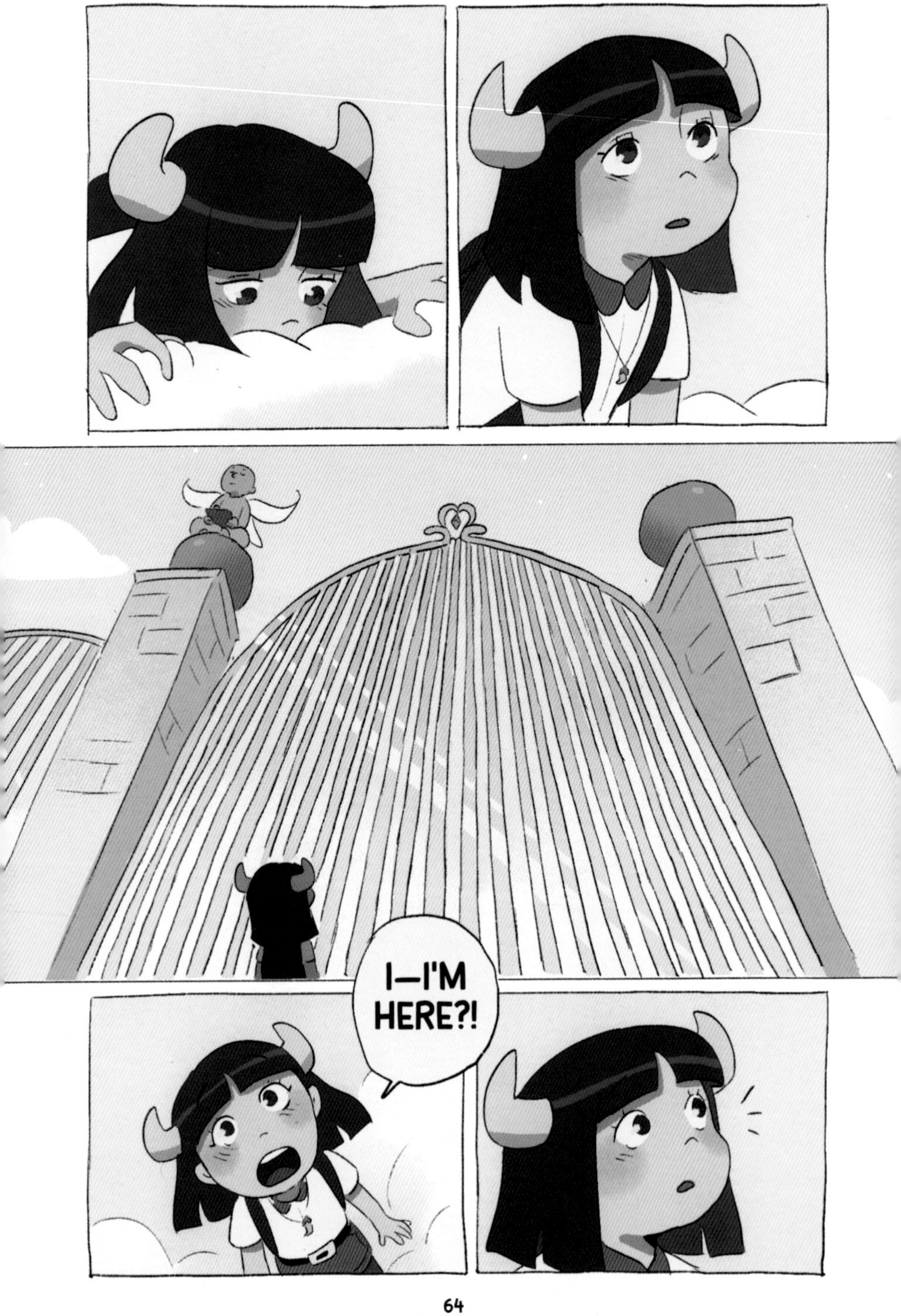
I—I'M HERE?!

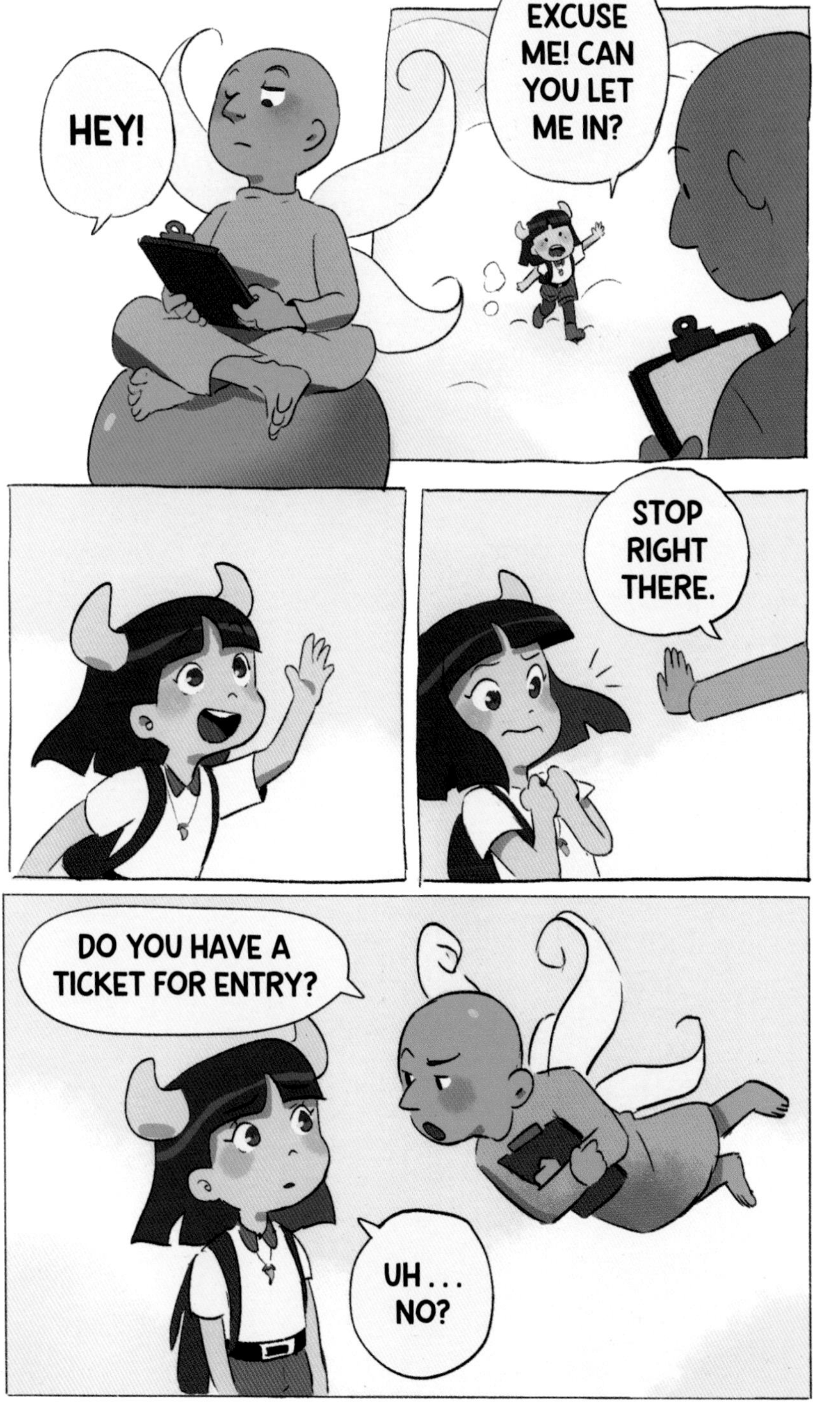
HEY!
EXCUSE ME! CAN YOU LET ME IN?
STOP RIGHT THERE.
DO YOU HAVE A TICKET FOR ENTRY?
UH . . . NO?

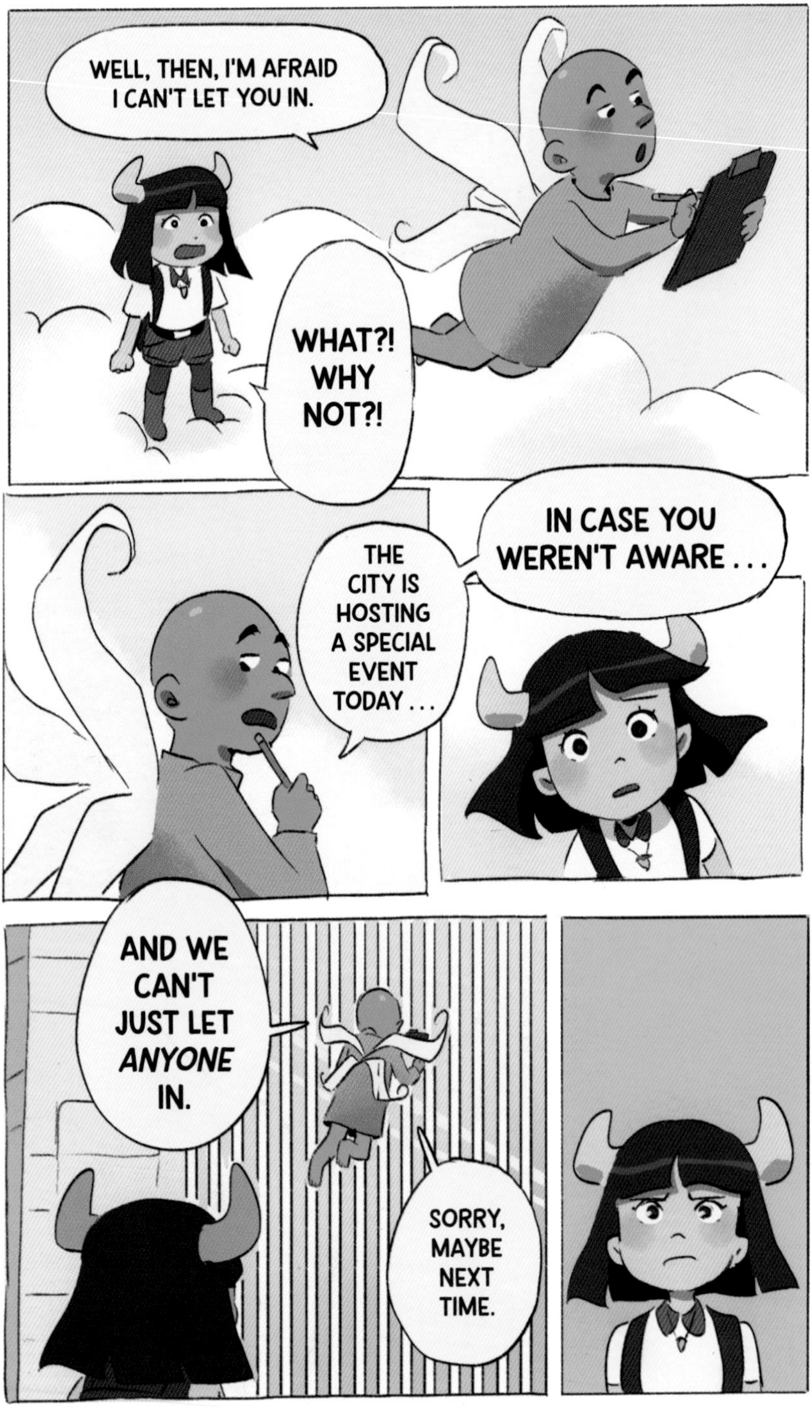
WELL, THEN, I'M AFRAID I CAN'T LET YOU IN.
WHAT?! WHY NOT?!
IN CASE YOU WEREN'T AWARE . . .
THE CITY IS HOSTING A SPECIAL EVENT TODAY . . .
AND WE CAN'T JUST LET ANYONE IN.
SORRY, MAYBE NEXT TIME.

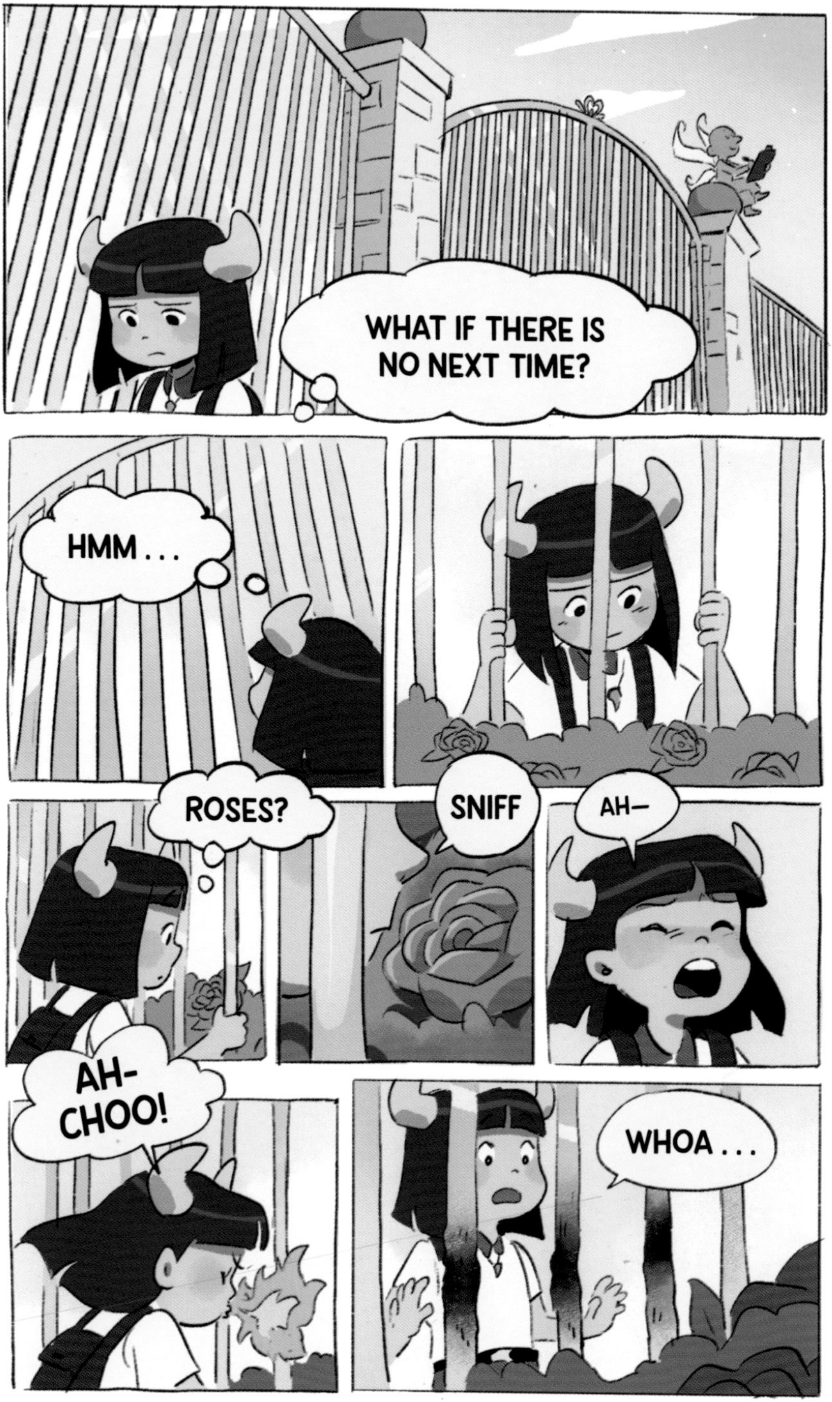
WHAT IF THERE IS NO NEXT TIME?
HMM . . .
ROSES?
SNIFF
AH—
AH-CHOO!
WHOA . . .

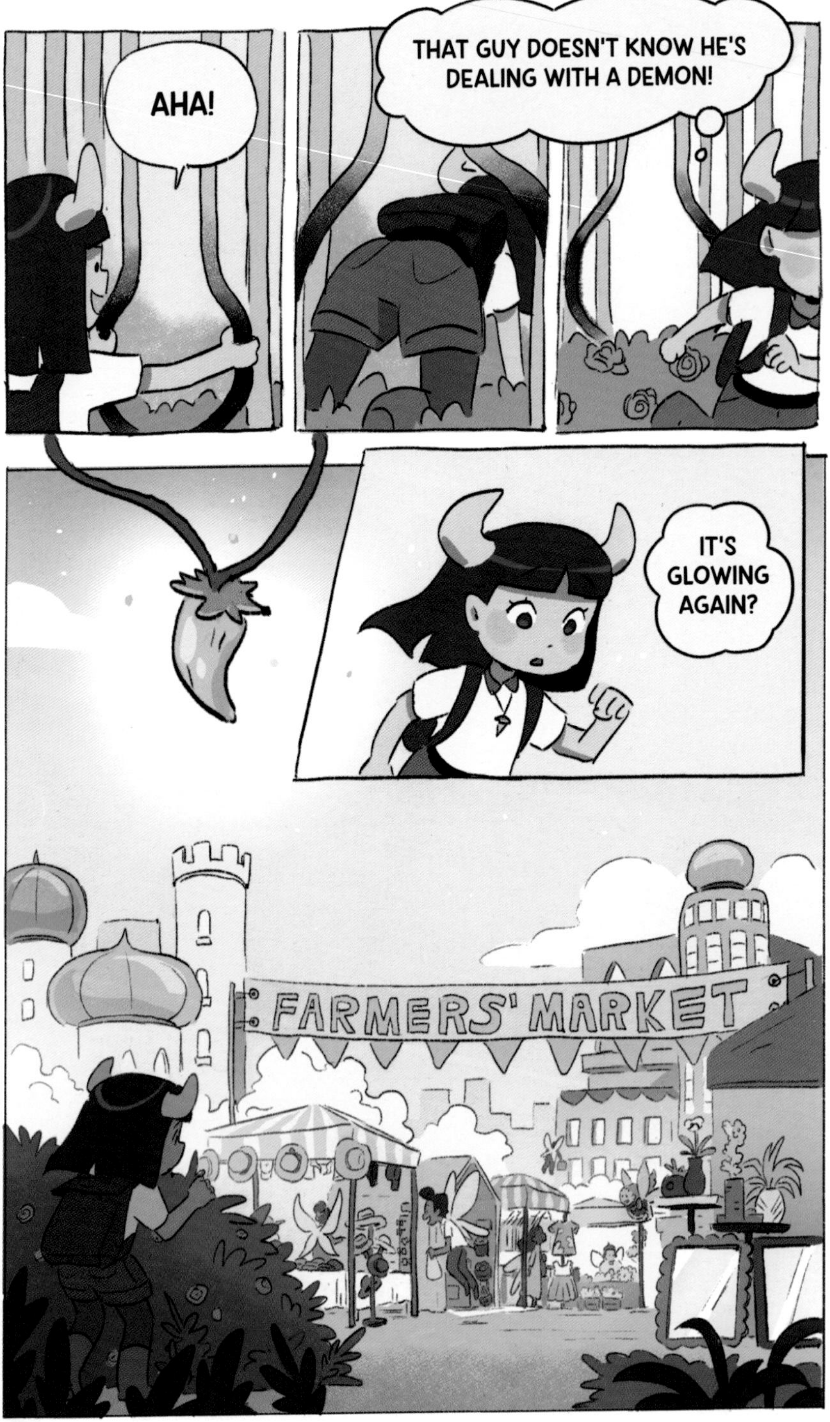
AHA!
THAT GUY DOESN'T KNOW HE'S DEALING WITH A DEMON!
IT'S GLOWING AGAIN?
FARMERS' MARKET

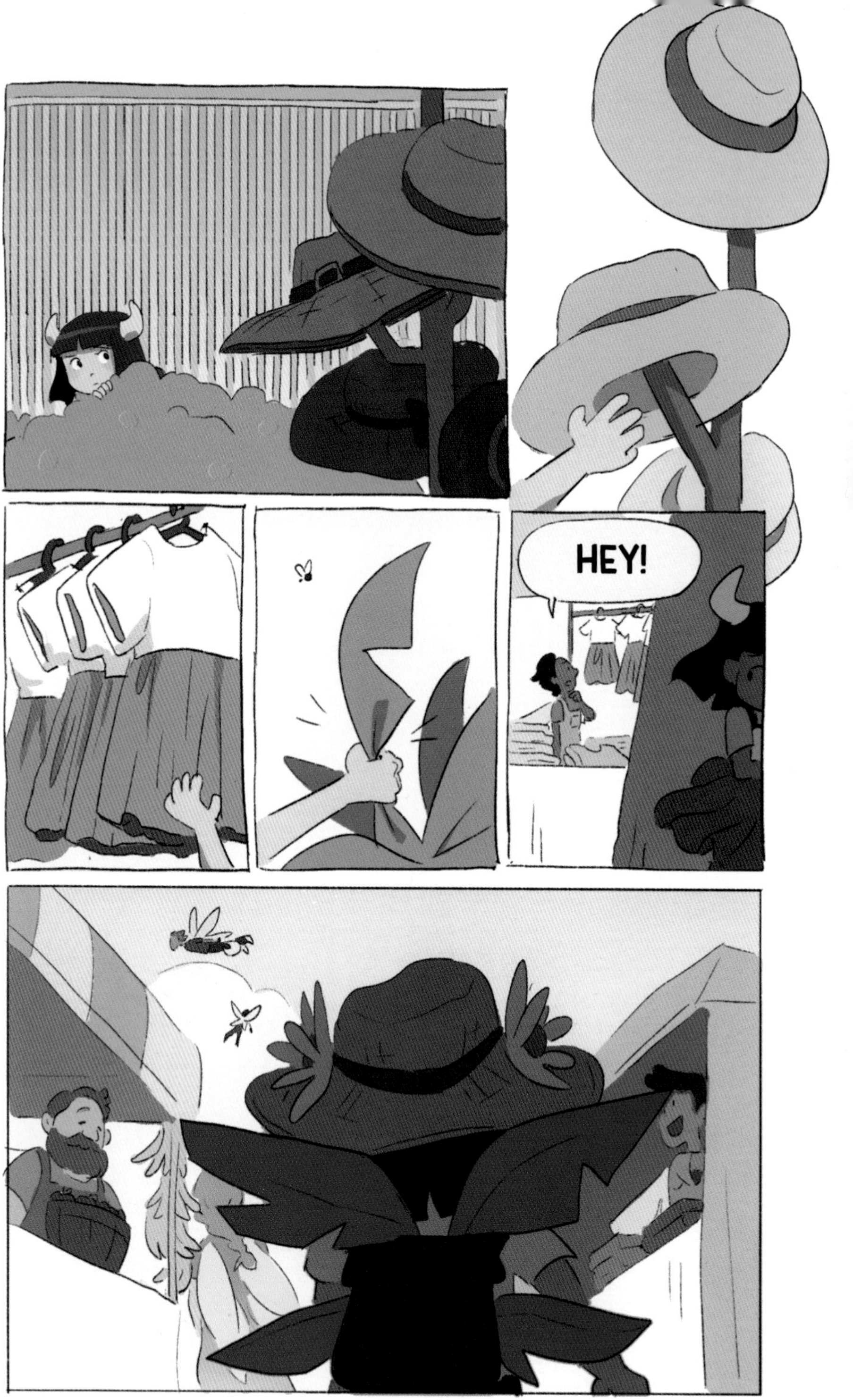
HEY!

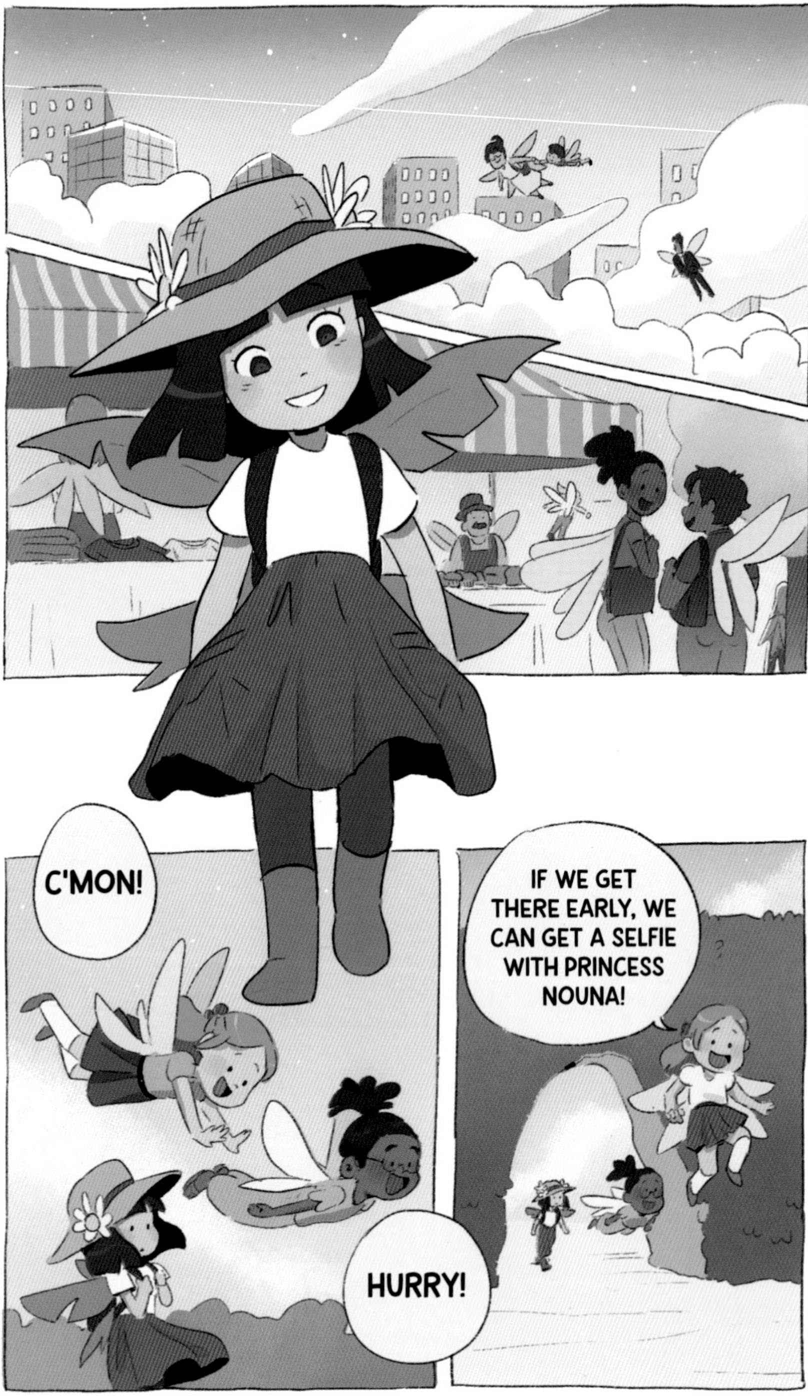
C'MON!
HURRY!
IF WE GET THERE EARLY, WE CAN GET A SELFIE WITH PRINCESS NOUNA!

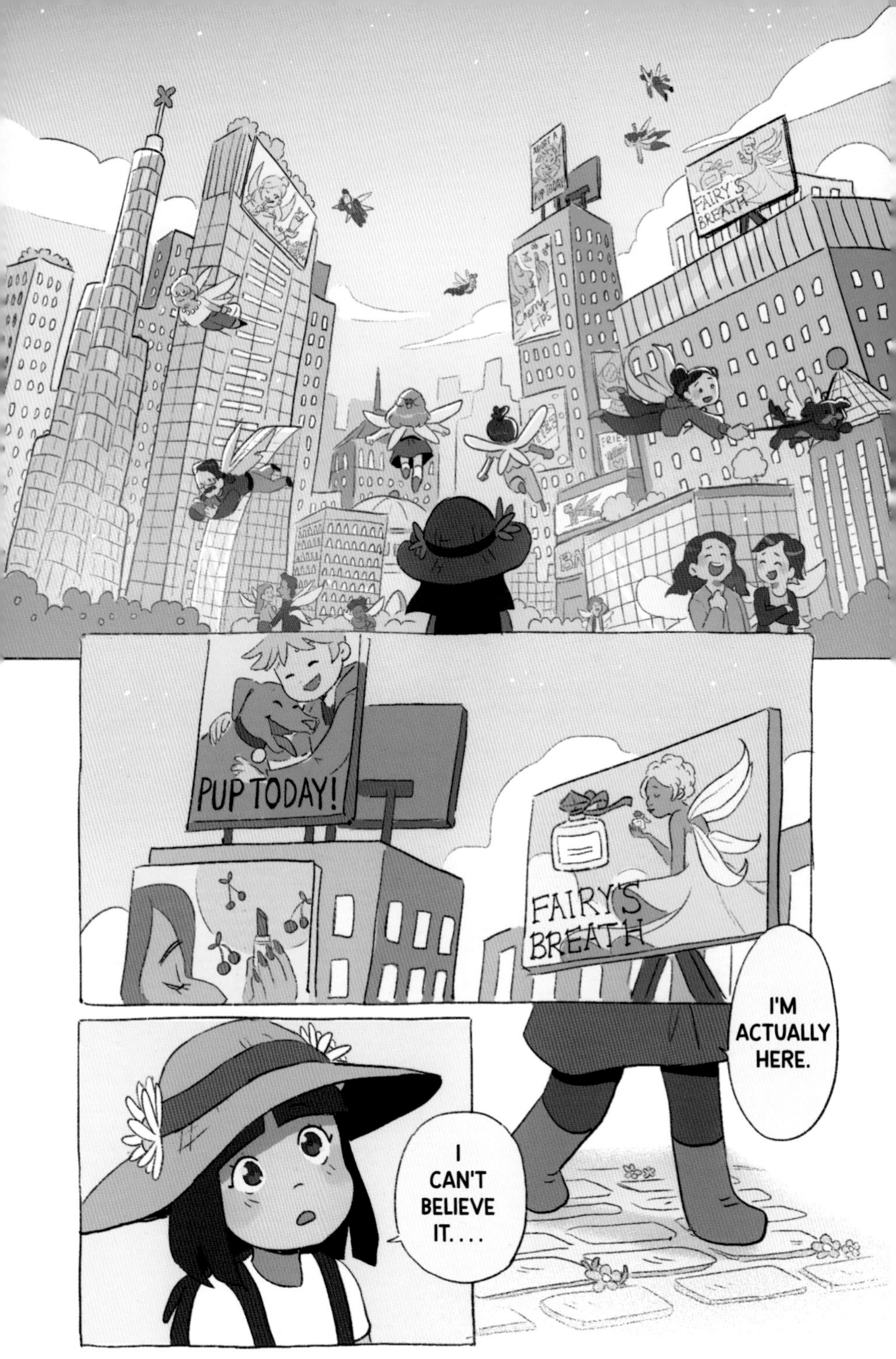
PUP TODAY!
FAIRY'S BREATH
I'M ACTUALLY HERE.
I CAN'T BELIEVE IT. . . .

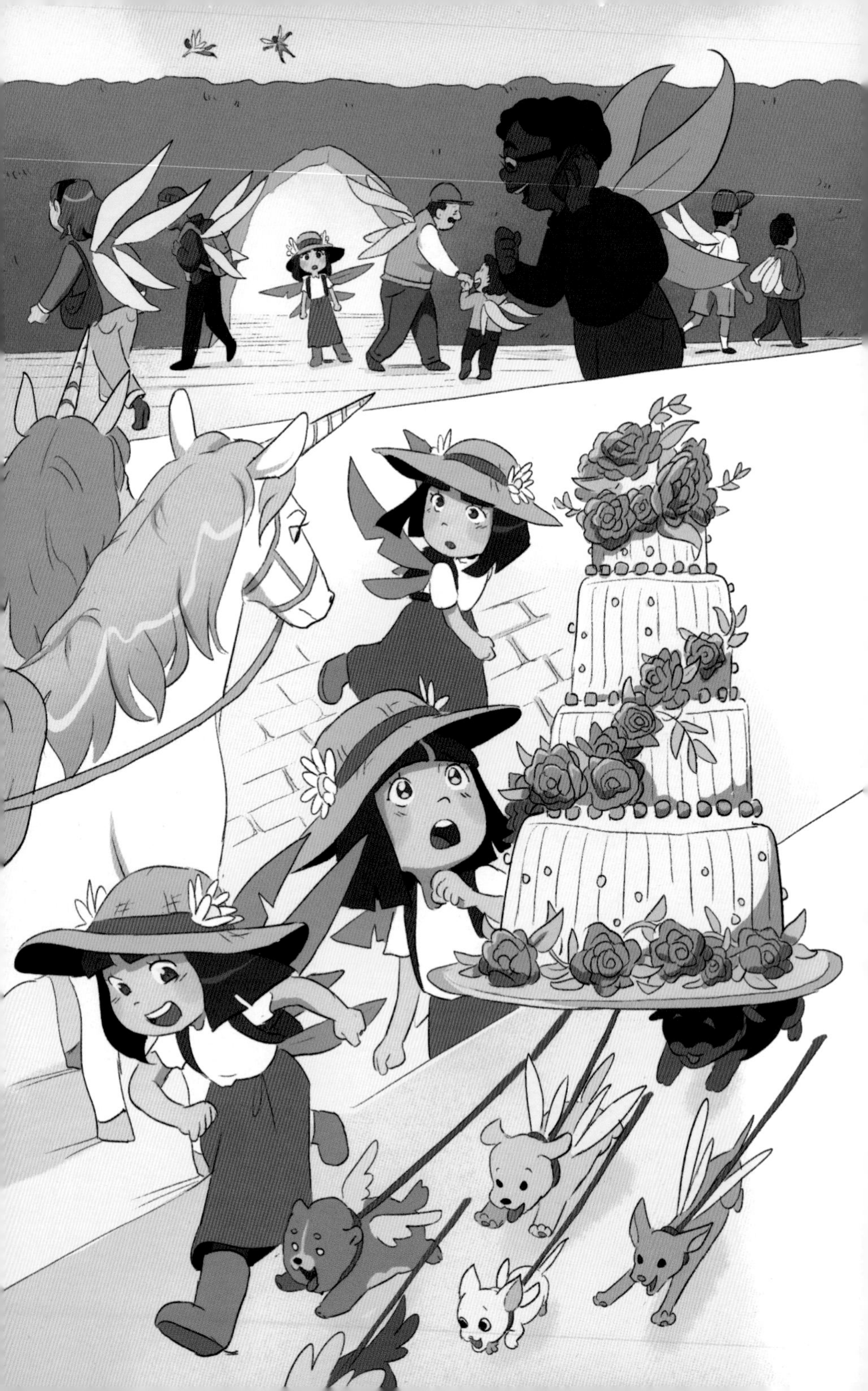

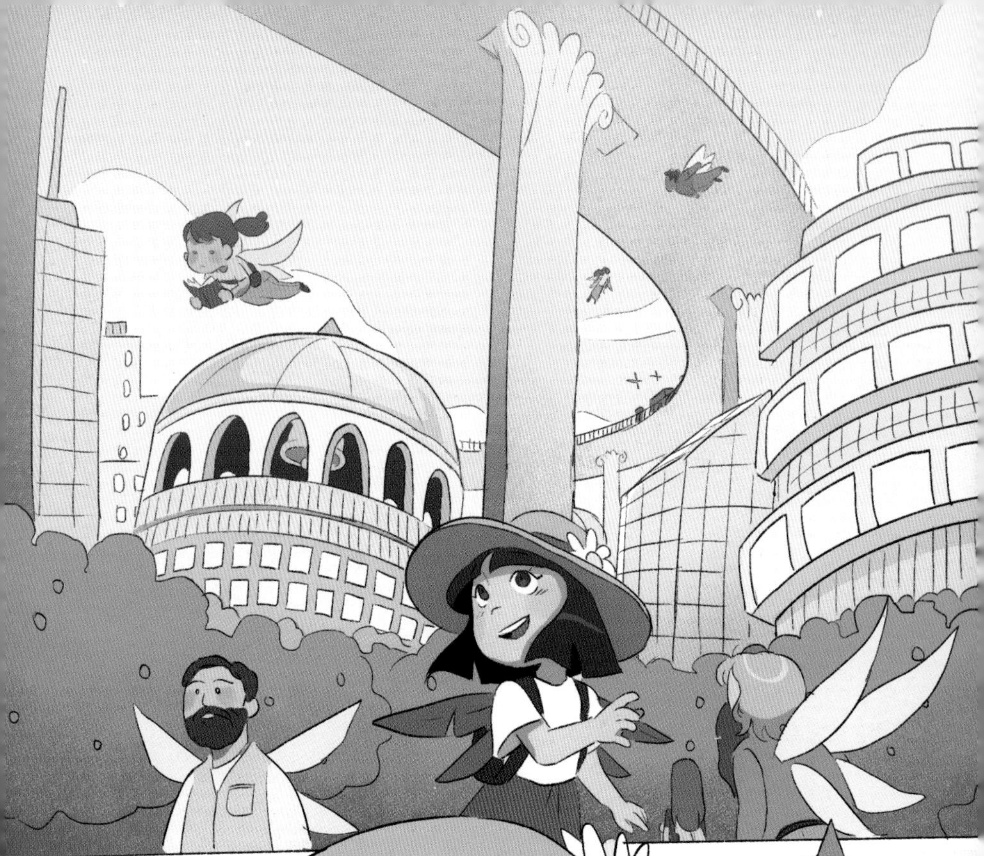

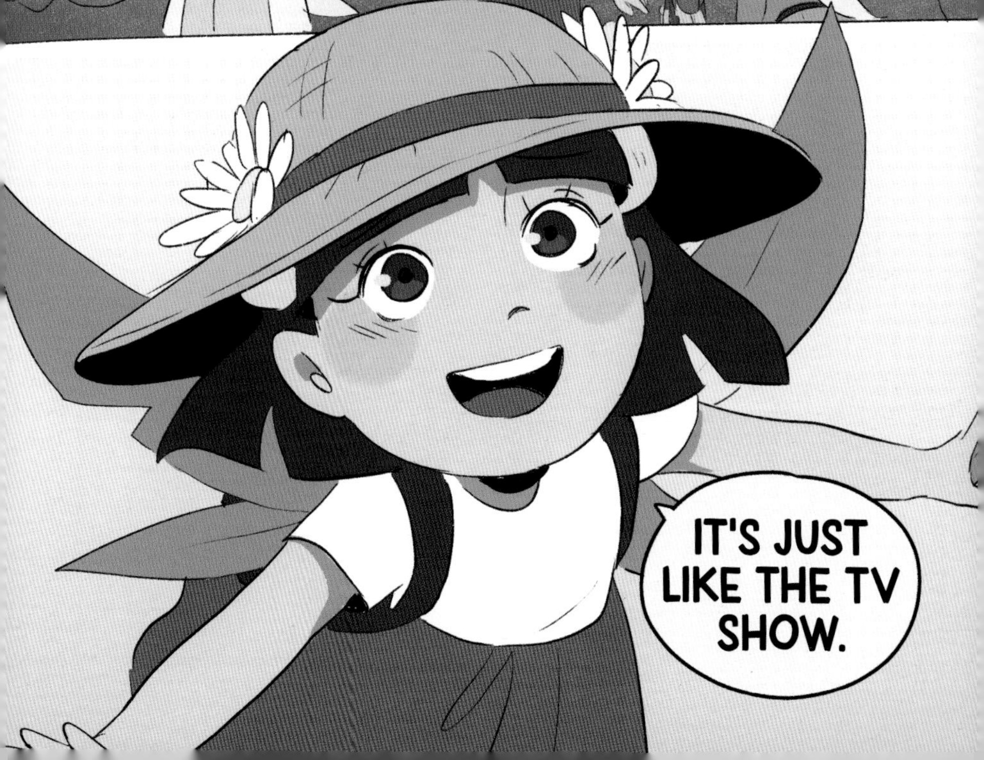
IT'S JUST LIKE THE TV SHOW.

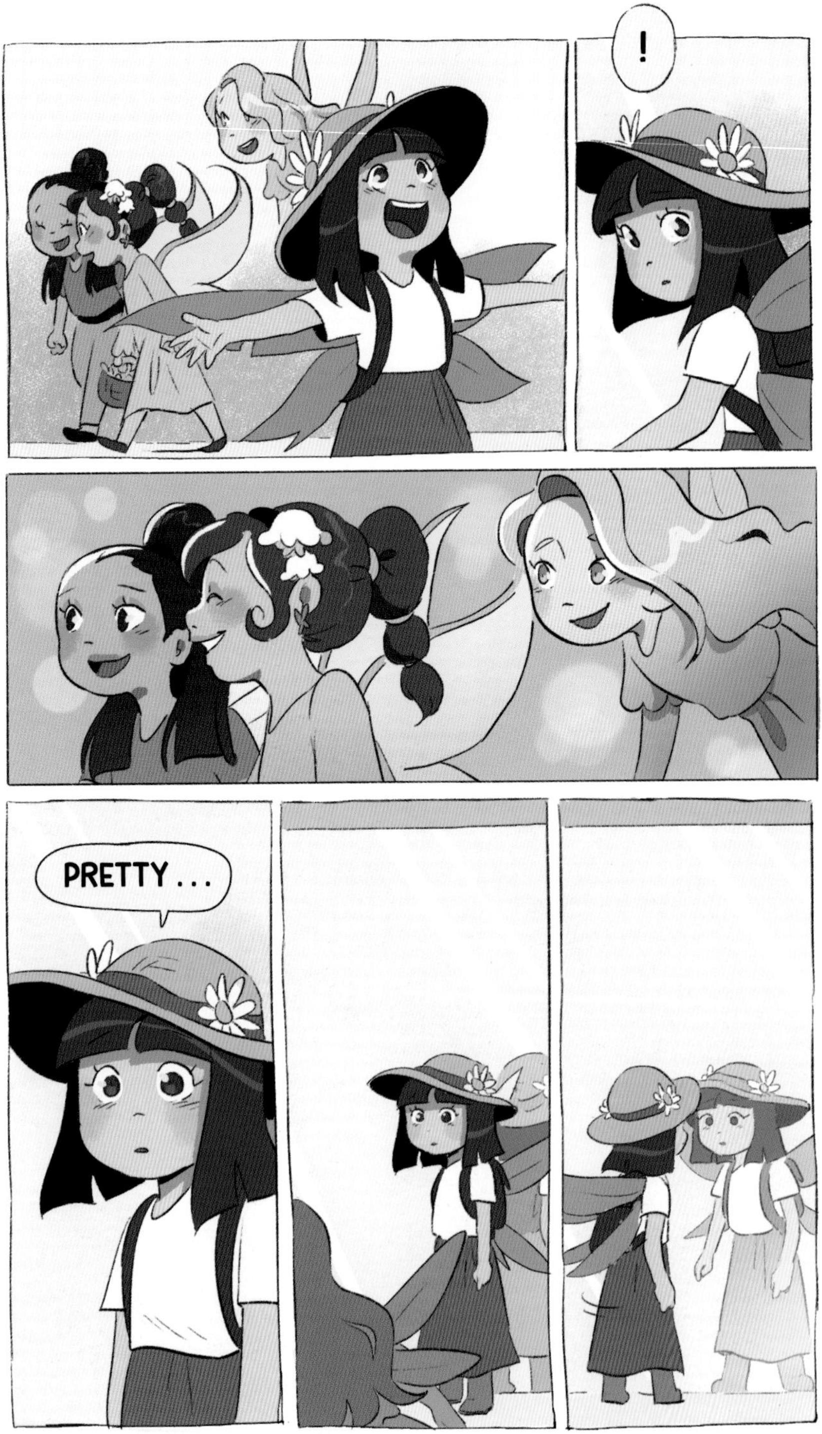
!
PRETTY . . .

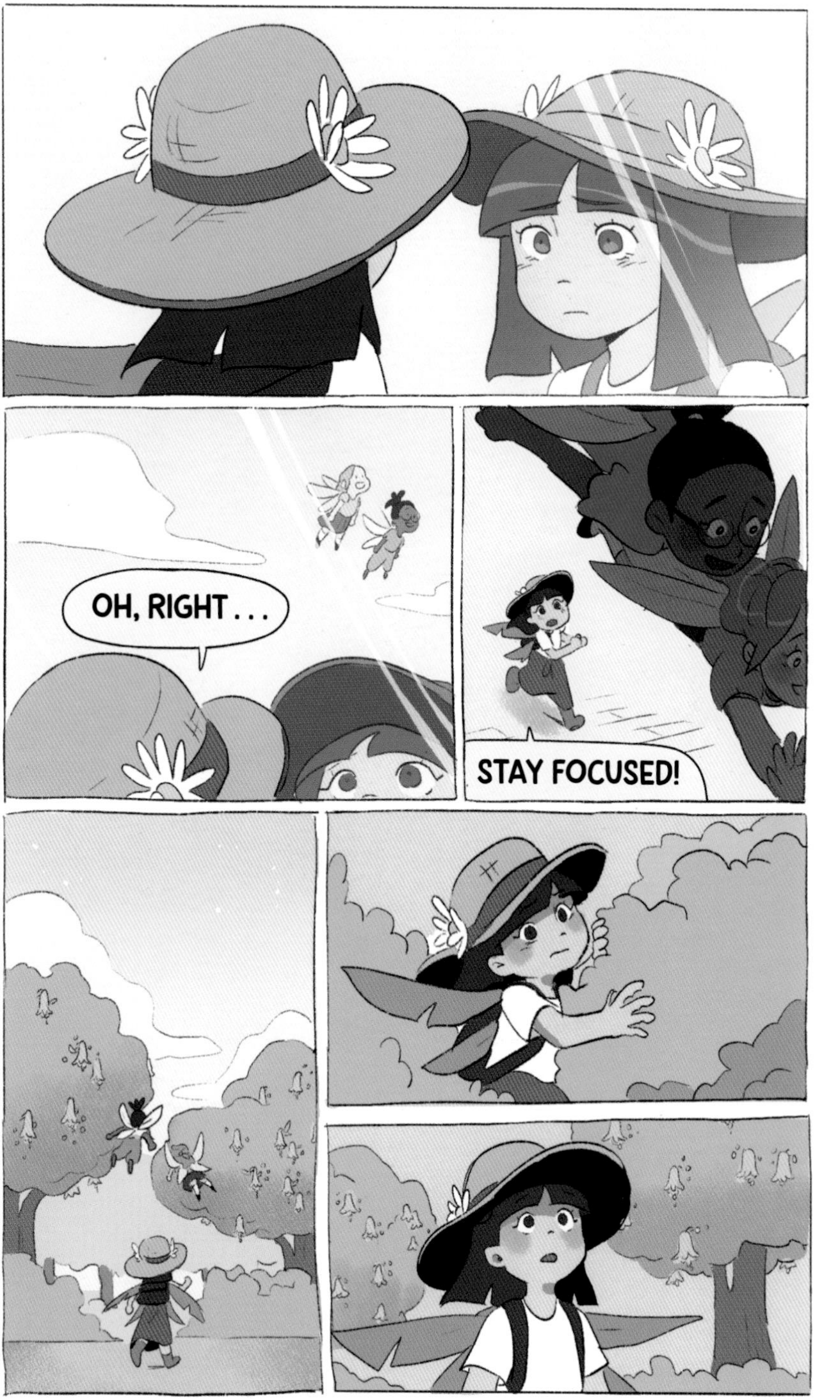
OH, RIGHT . . .
STAY FOCUSED!

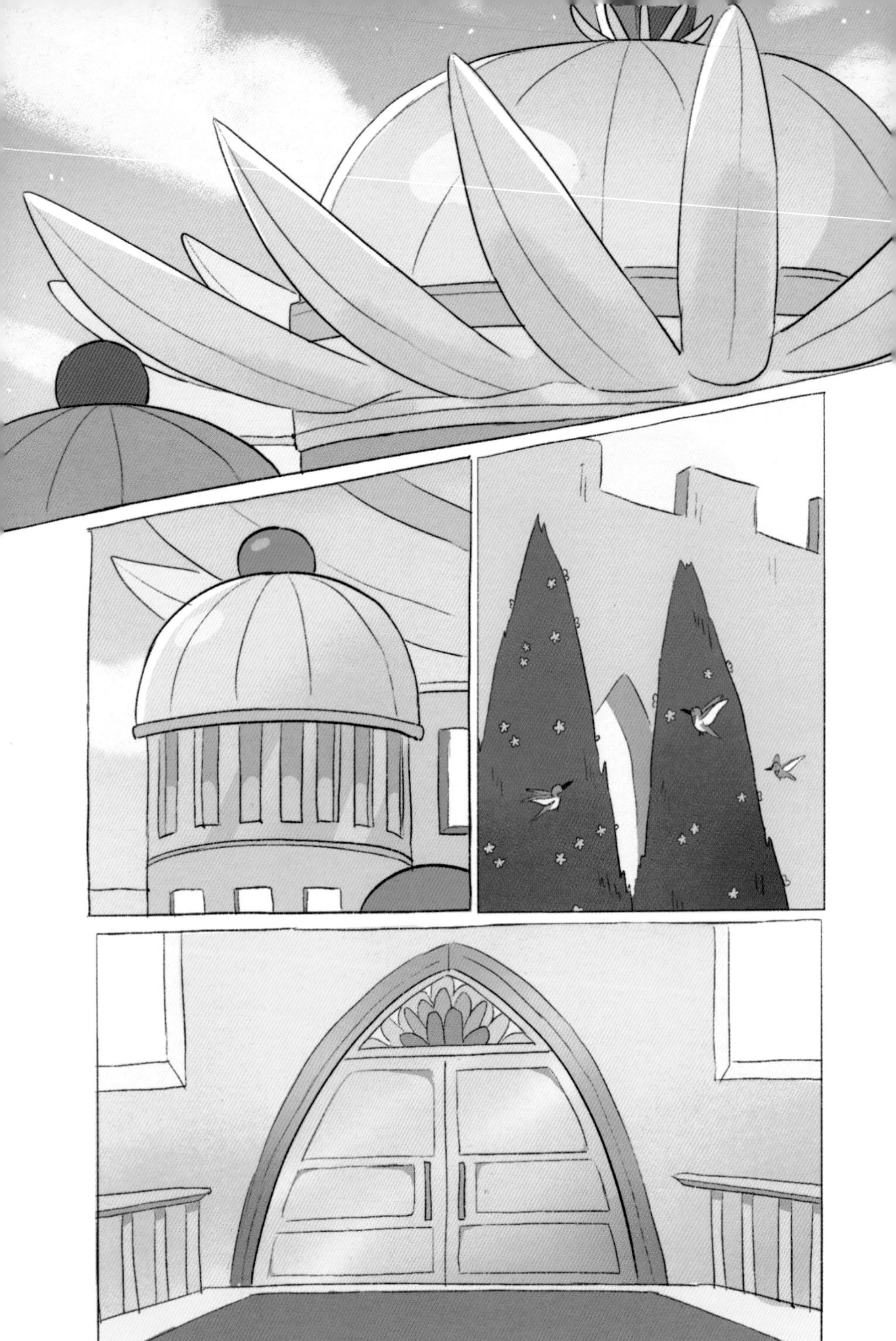

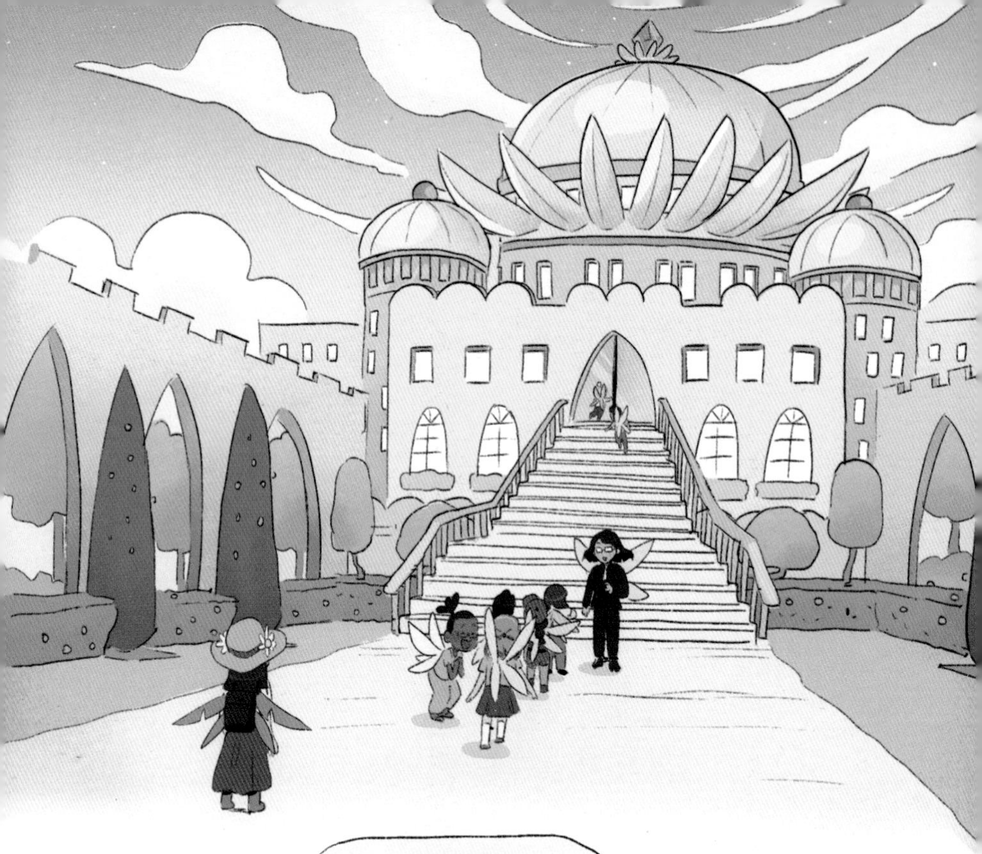

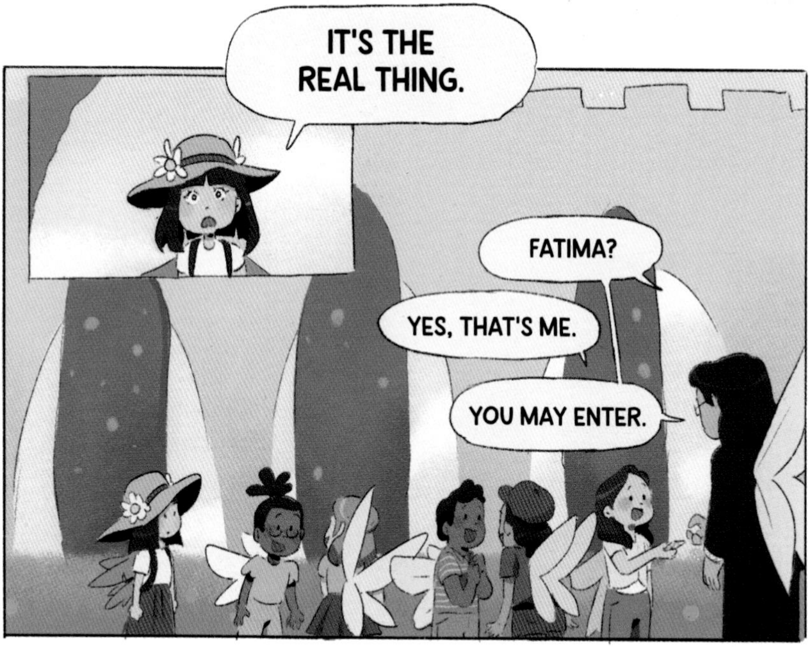
IT'S THE REAL THING.
FATIMA?
YES, THAT'S ME.
YOU MAY ENTER.

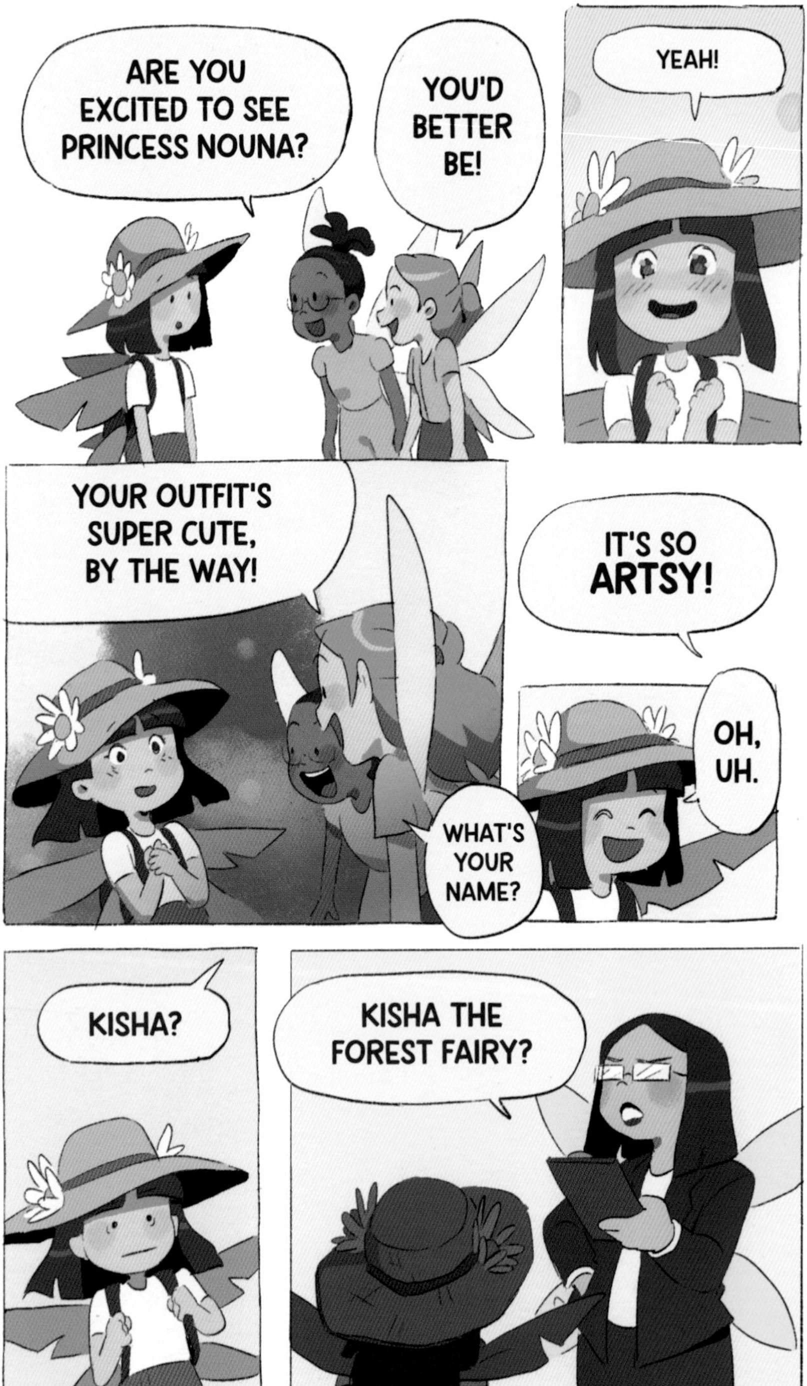
ARE YOU EXCITED TO SEE PRINCESS NOUNA?
YOU'D BETTER BE!
YEAH!
YOUR OUTFIT'S SUPER CUTE, BY THE WAY!
IT'S SO ARTSY!
OH, UH.
WHAT'S YOUR NAME?
KISHA?
KISHA THE FOREST FAIRY?

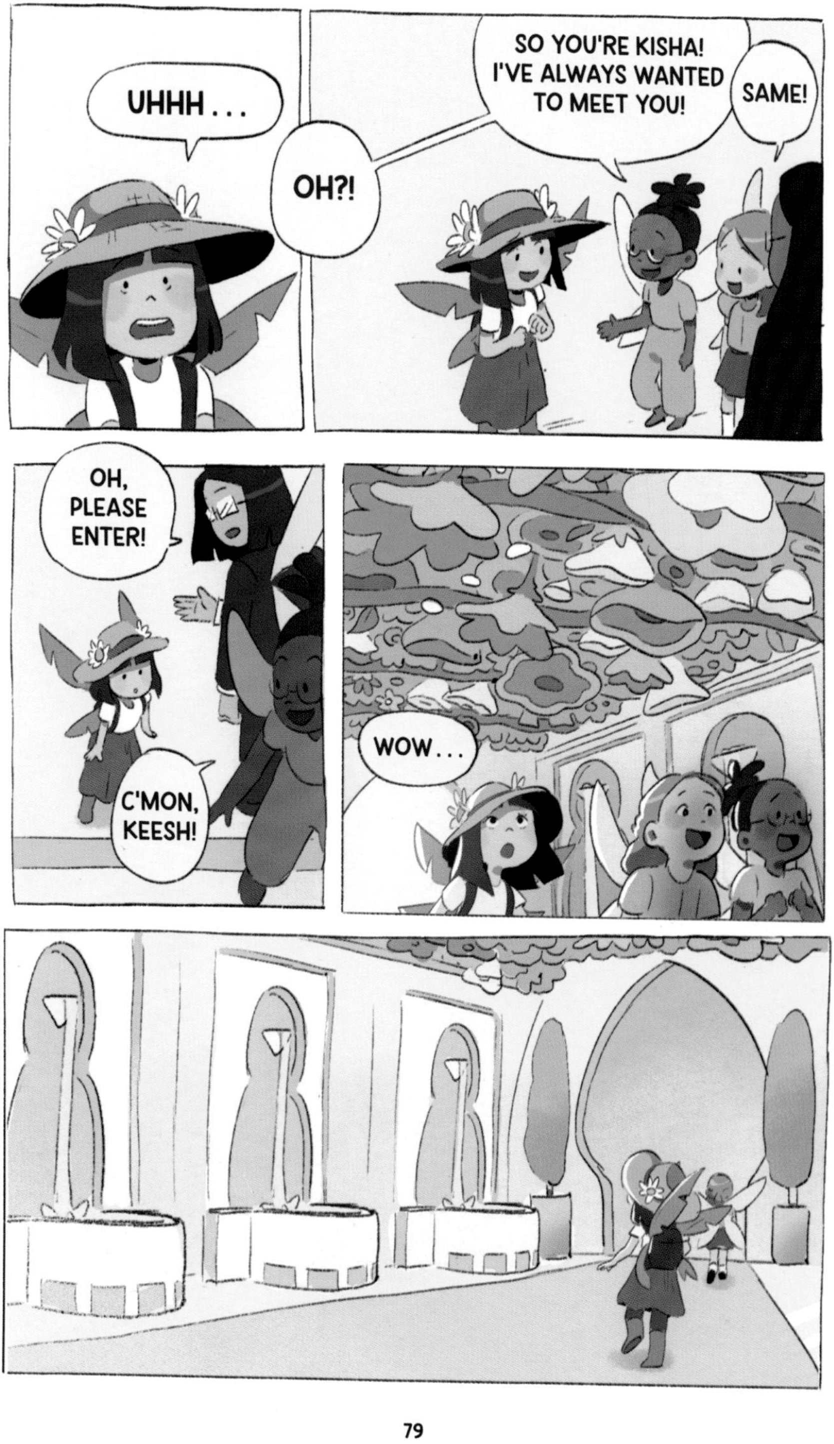
UHHH . . .
OH?!
SO YOU'RE KISHA! I'VE ALWAYS WANTED TO MEET YOU!
SAME!
OH, PLEASE ENTER!
C'MON, KEESH!
WOW . . .

THIS PLACE IS TO DIE FOR!

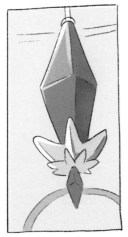

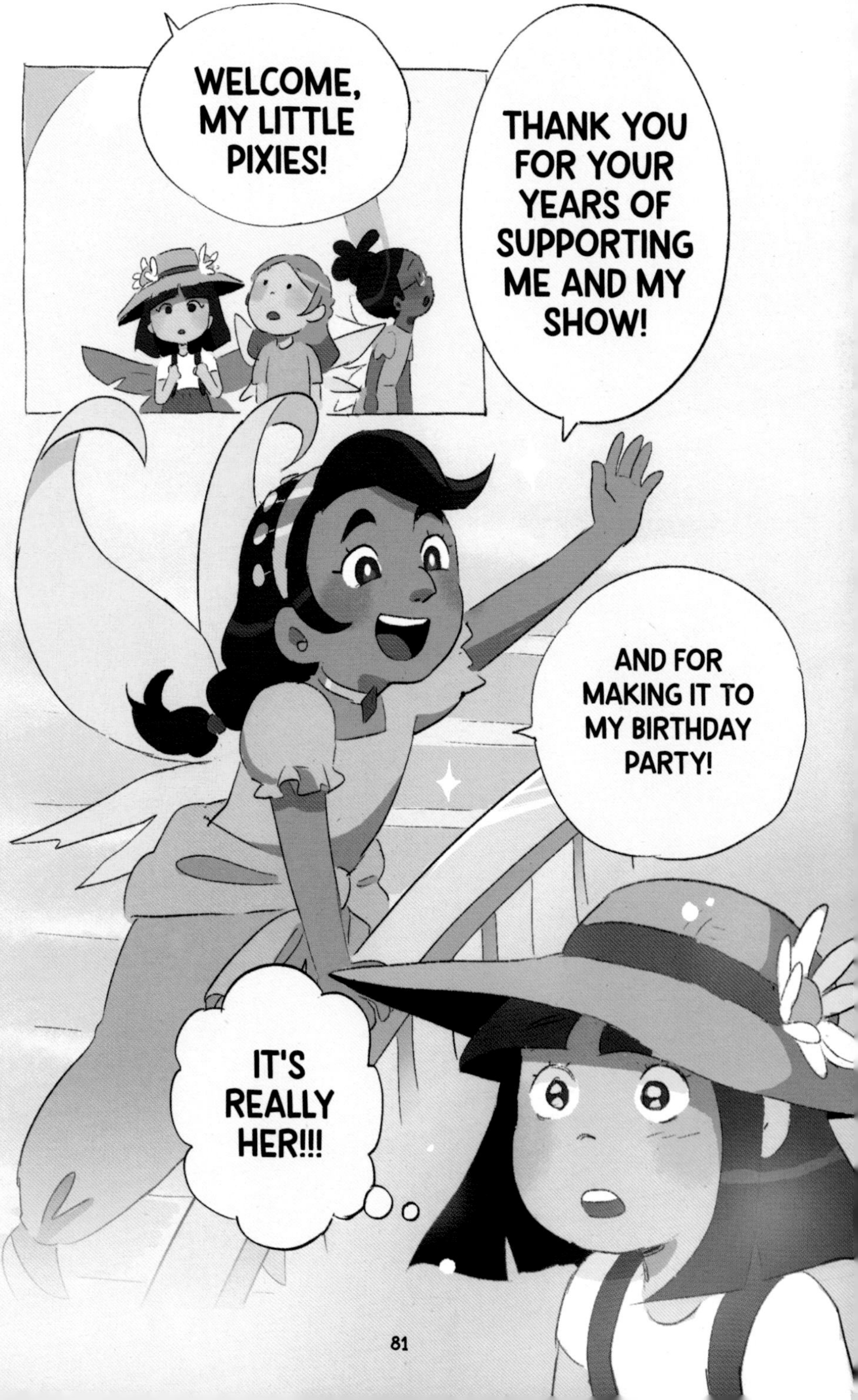
WELCOME, MY LITTLE PIXIES!
THANK YOU FOR YOUR YEARS OF SUPPORTING ME AND MY SHOW!
AND FOR MAKING IT TO MY BIRTHDAY PARTY!
IT'S REALLY HER!!!

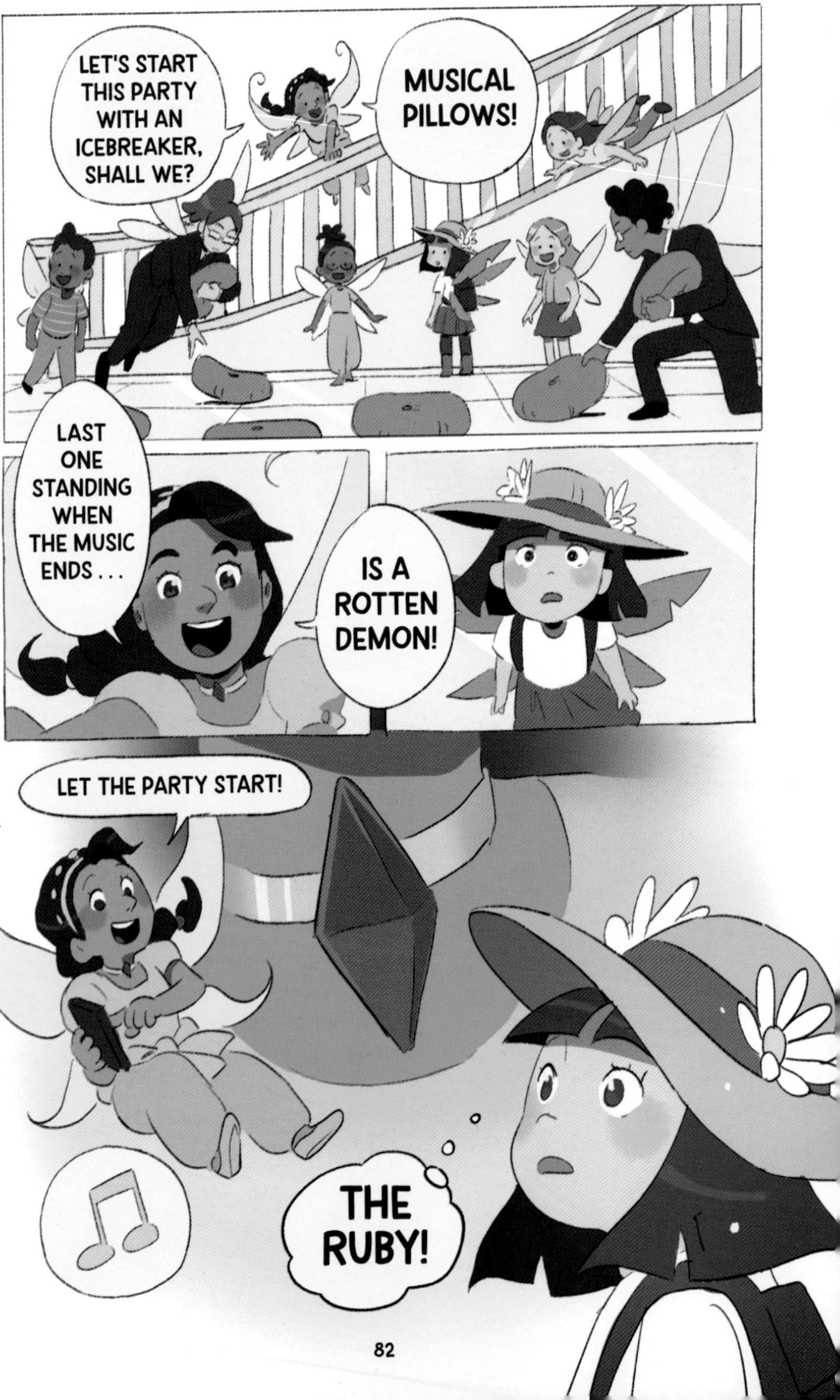
LET'S START THIS PARTY WITH AN ICEBREAKER, SHALL WE?
MUSICAL PILLOWS!
LAST ONE STANDING WHEN THE MUSIC ENDS . . .
IS A ROTTEN DEMON!
LET THE PARTY START!
THE RUBY!

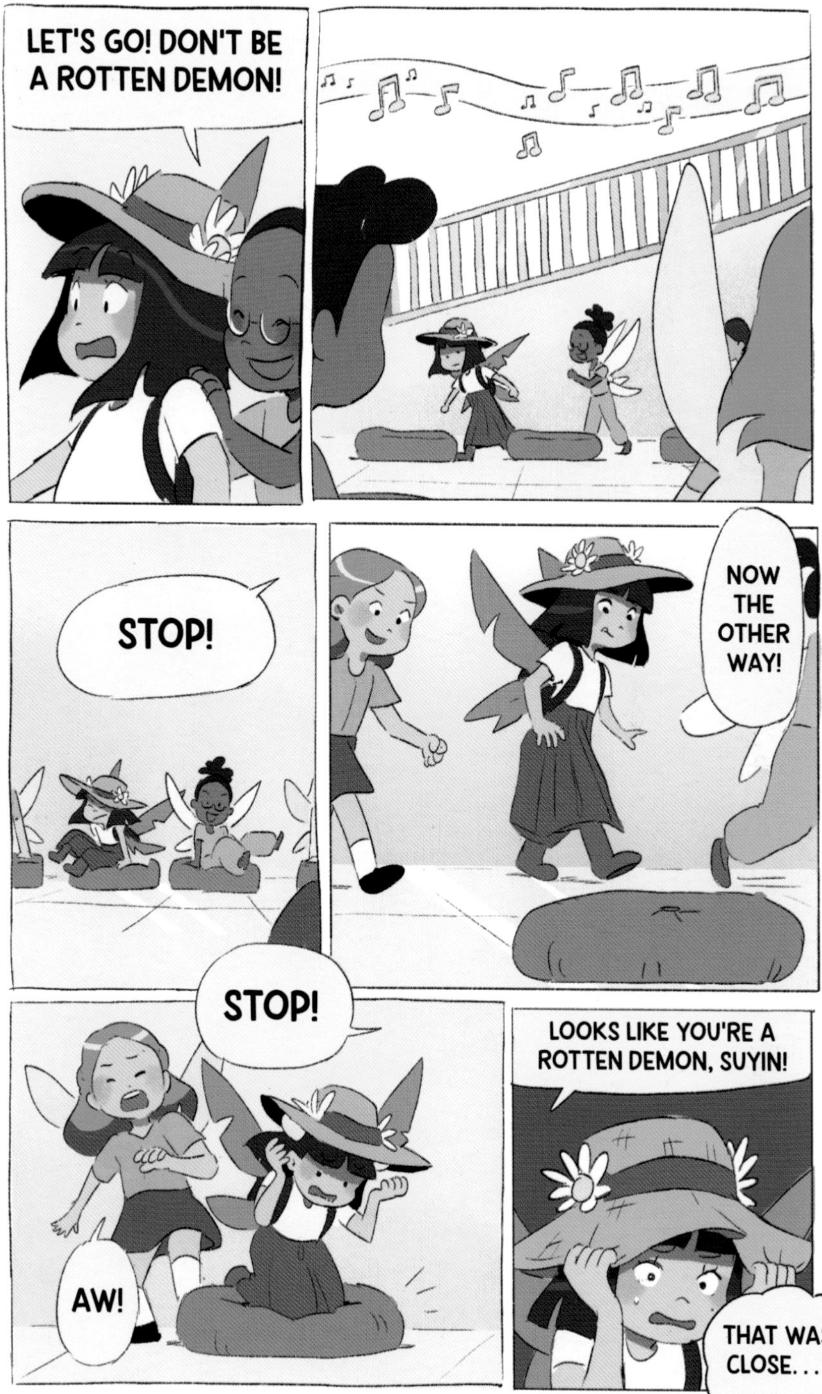
LET'S GO! DON'T BE A ROTTEN DEMON!
STOP!
NOW THE OTHER WAY!
STOP!
AW!
LOOKS LIKE YOU'RE A ROTTEN DEMON, SUYIN!
THAT WAS CLOSE. . . .

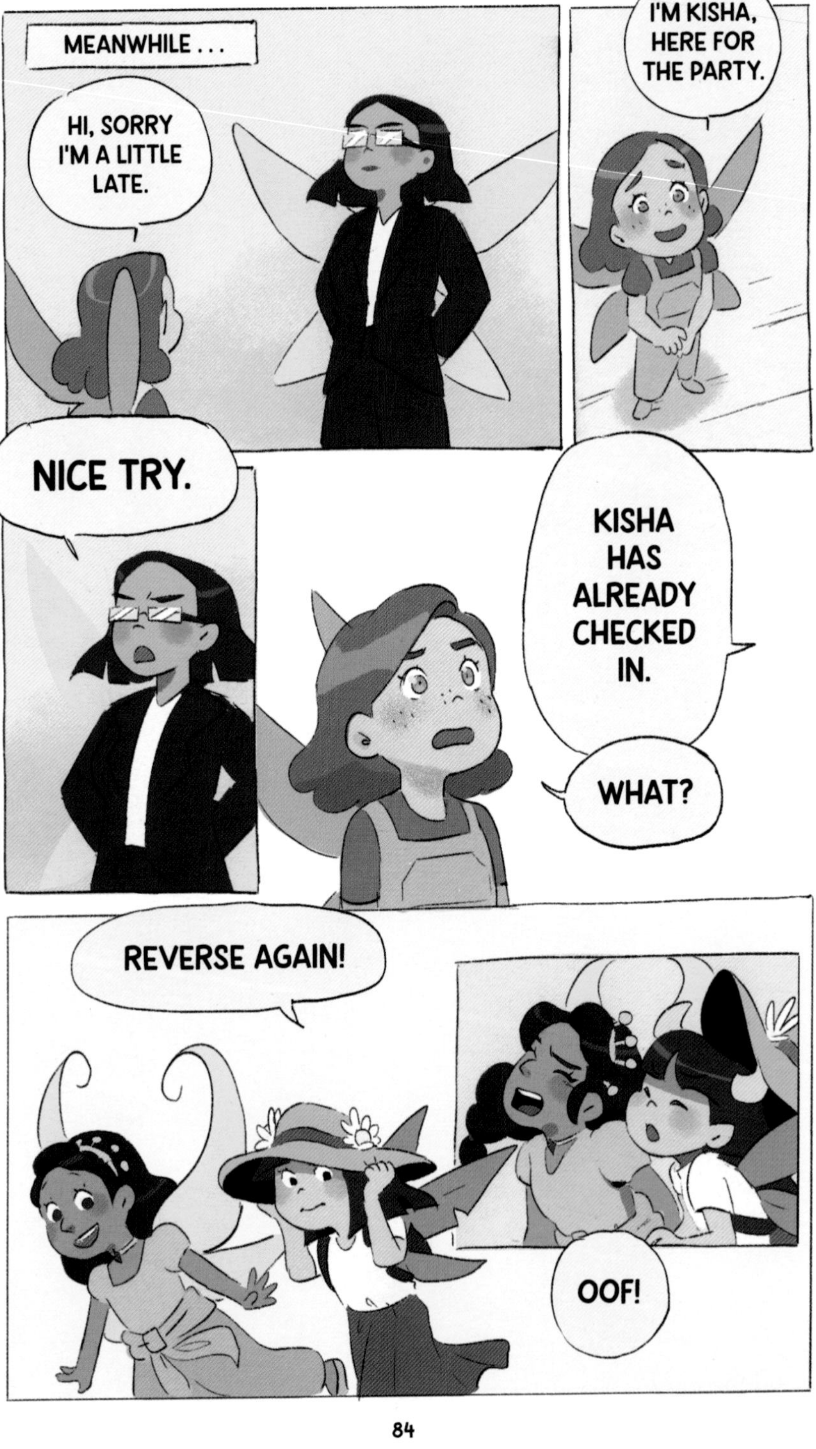
MEANWHILE . . .
HI, SORRY I'M A LITTLE LATE.
I'M KISHA, HERE FOR THE PARTY.
NICE TRY.
KISHA HAS ALREADY CHECKED IN.
WHAT?
REVERSE AGAIN!
OOF!

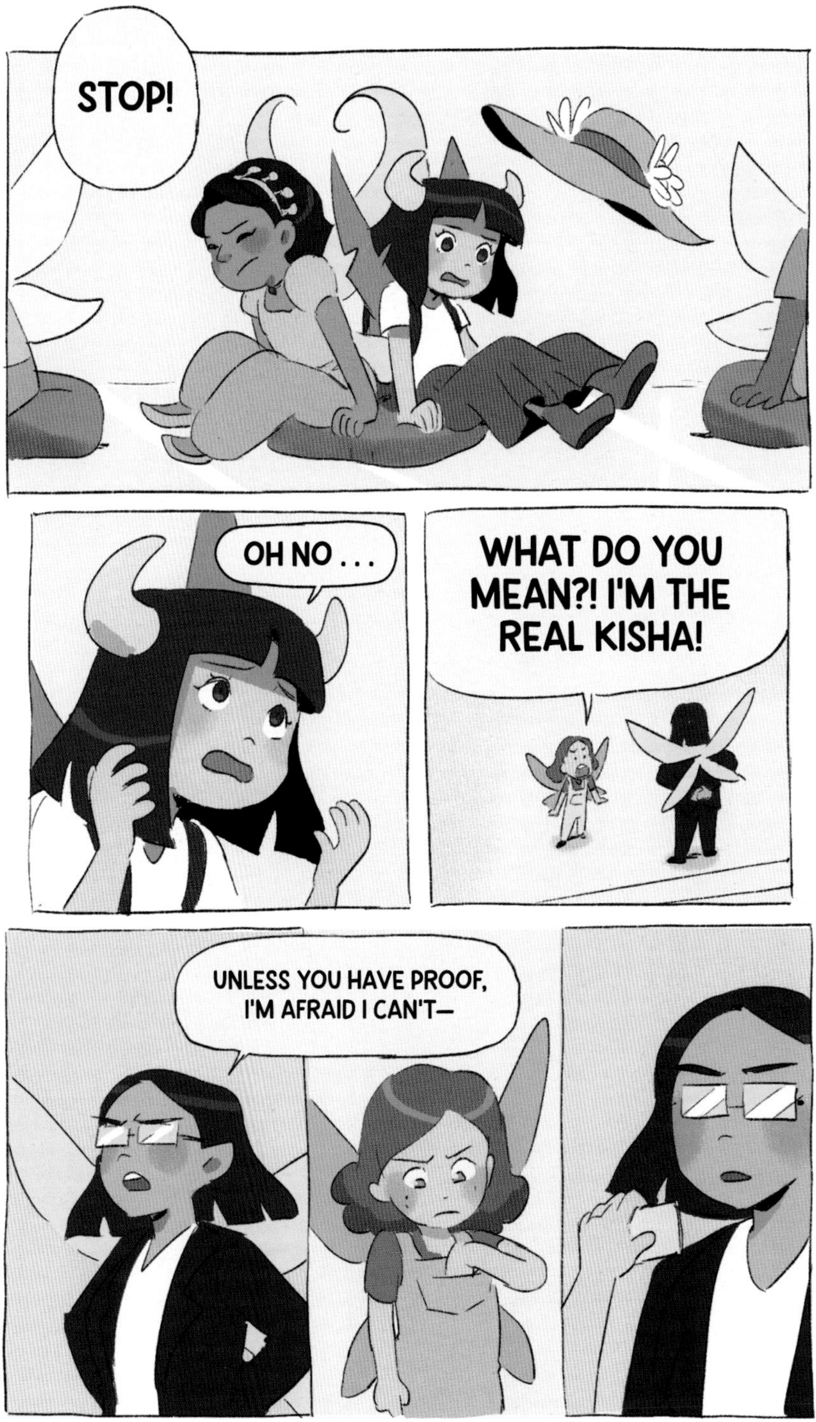
STOP!
OH NO . . .
WHAT DO YOU MEAN?! I'M THE REAL KISHA!
UNLESS YOU HAVE PROOF, I'M AFRAID I CAN'T—

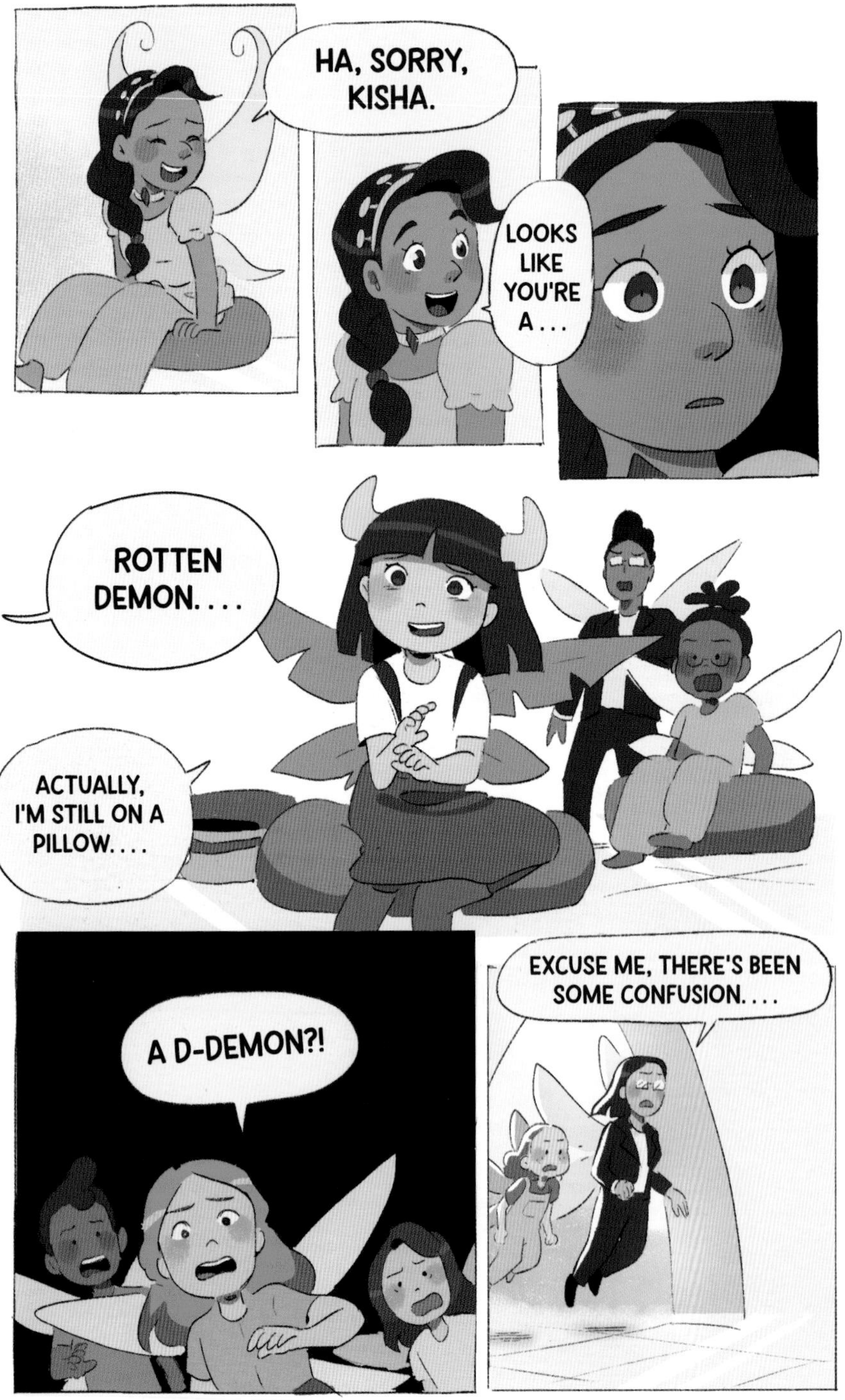
HA, SORRY, KISHA.
LOOKS LIKE YOU'RE A . . .
ROTTEN DEMON. . . .
ACTUALLY, I'M STILL ON A PILLOW. . . .
A D-DEMON?!
EXCUSE ME, THERE'S BEEN SOME CONFUSION. . . .

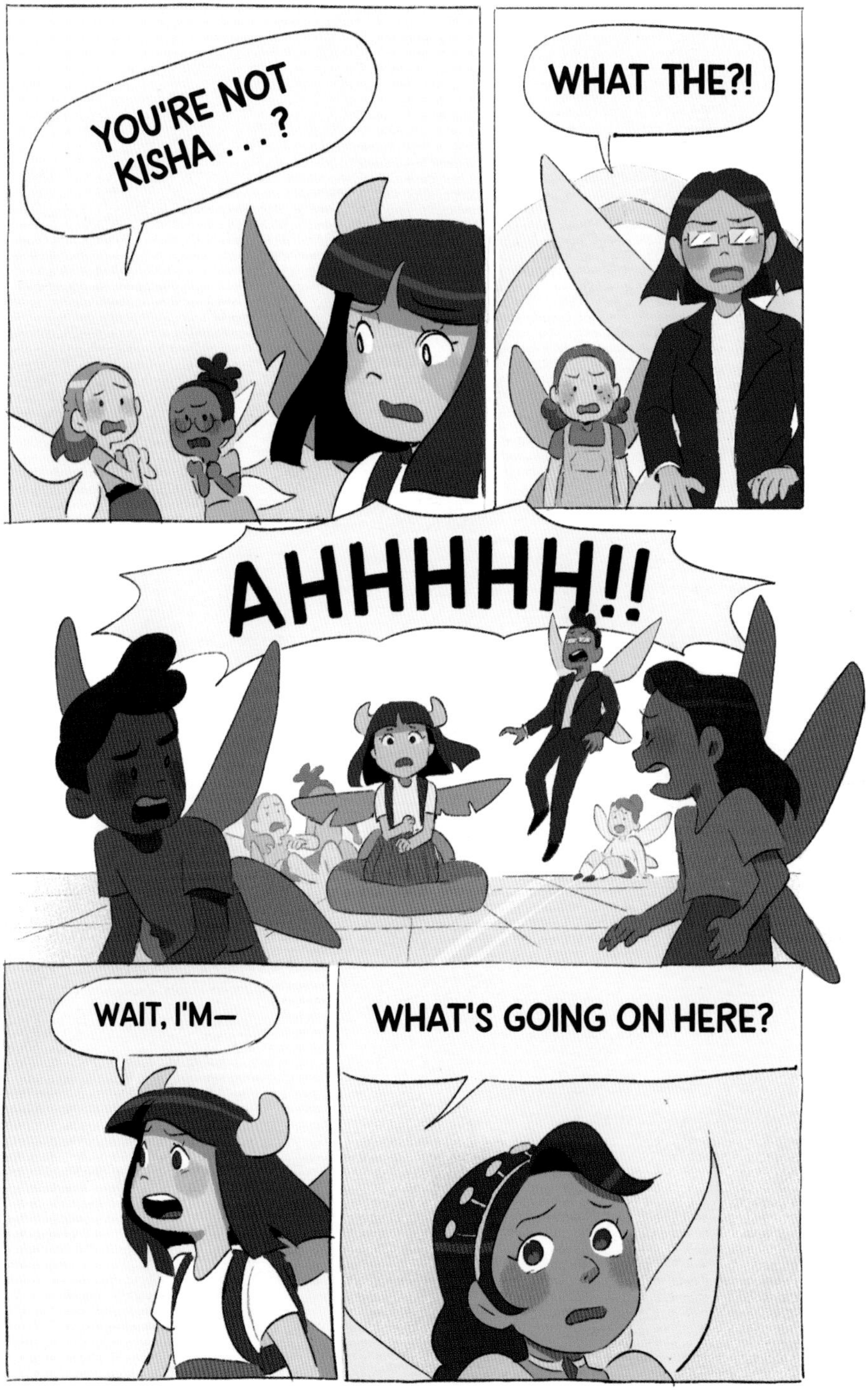
YOU'RE NOT KISHA . . . ?
WHAT THE?!
AHHHHH!!
WAIT, I'M—
WHAT'S GOING ON HERE?

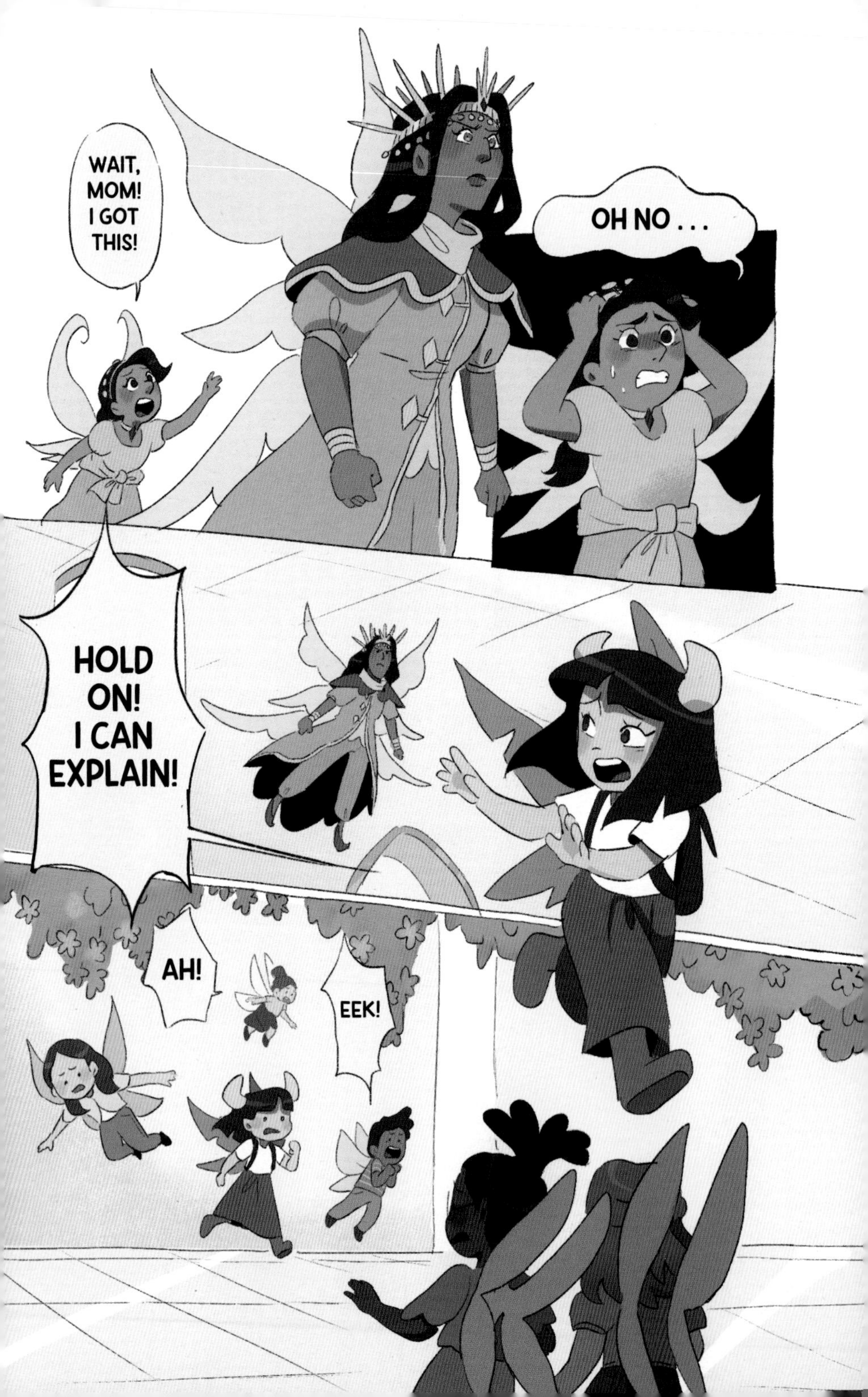
WAIT, MOM! I GOT THIS!
OH NO . . .
HOLD ON! I CAN EXPLAIN!
AH!
EEK!

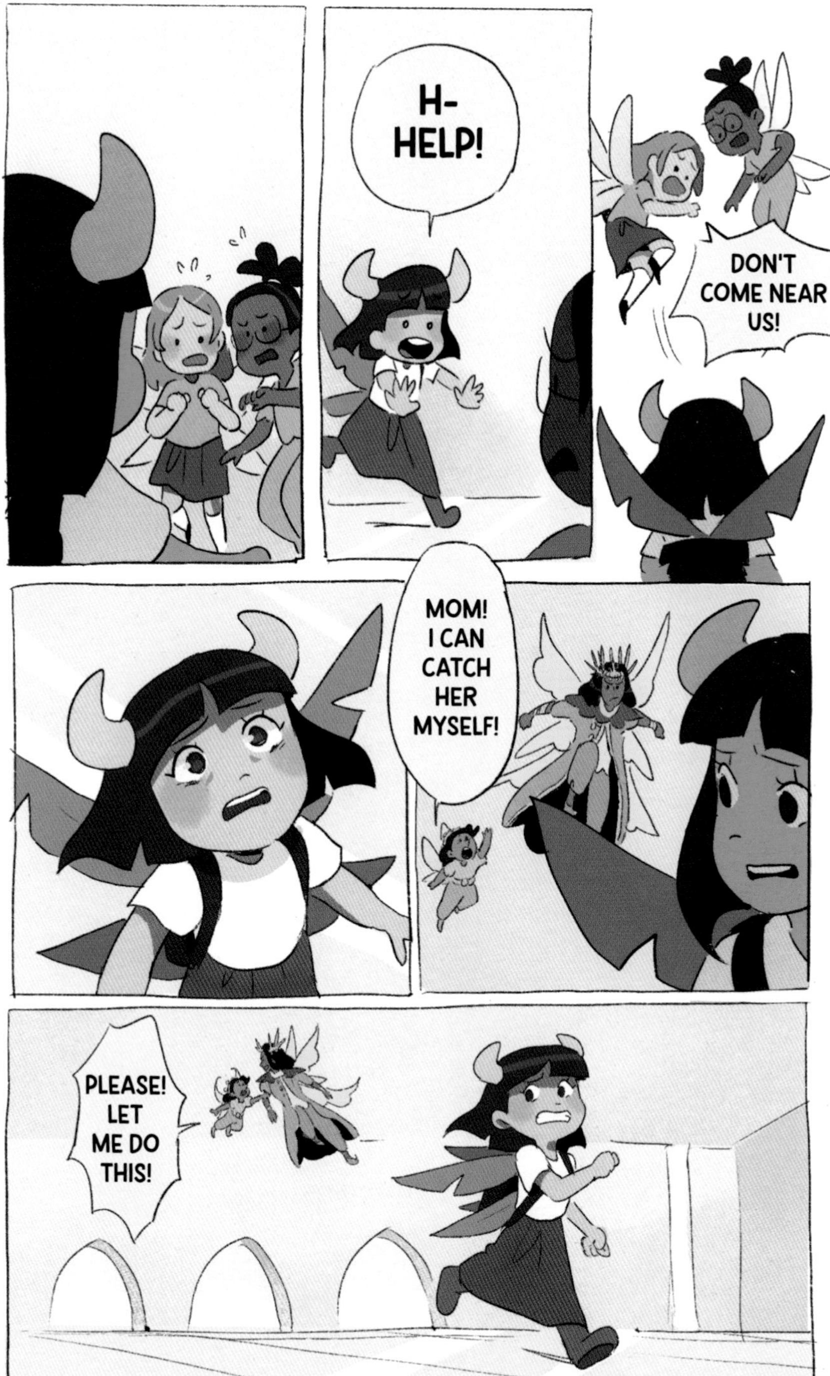
H-
HELP!
DON'T COME NEAR US!
MOM! I CAN CATCH HER MYSELF!
PLEASE! LET ME DO THIS!

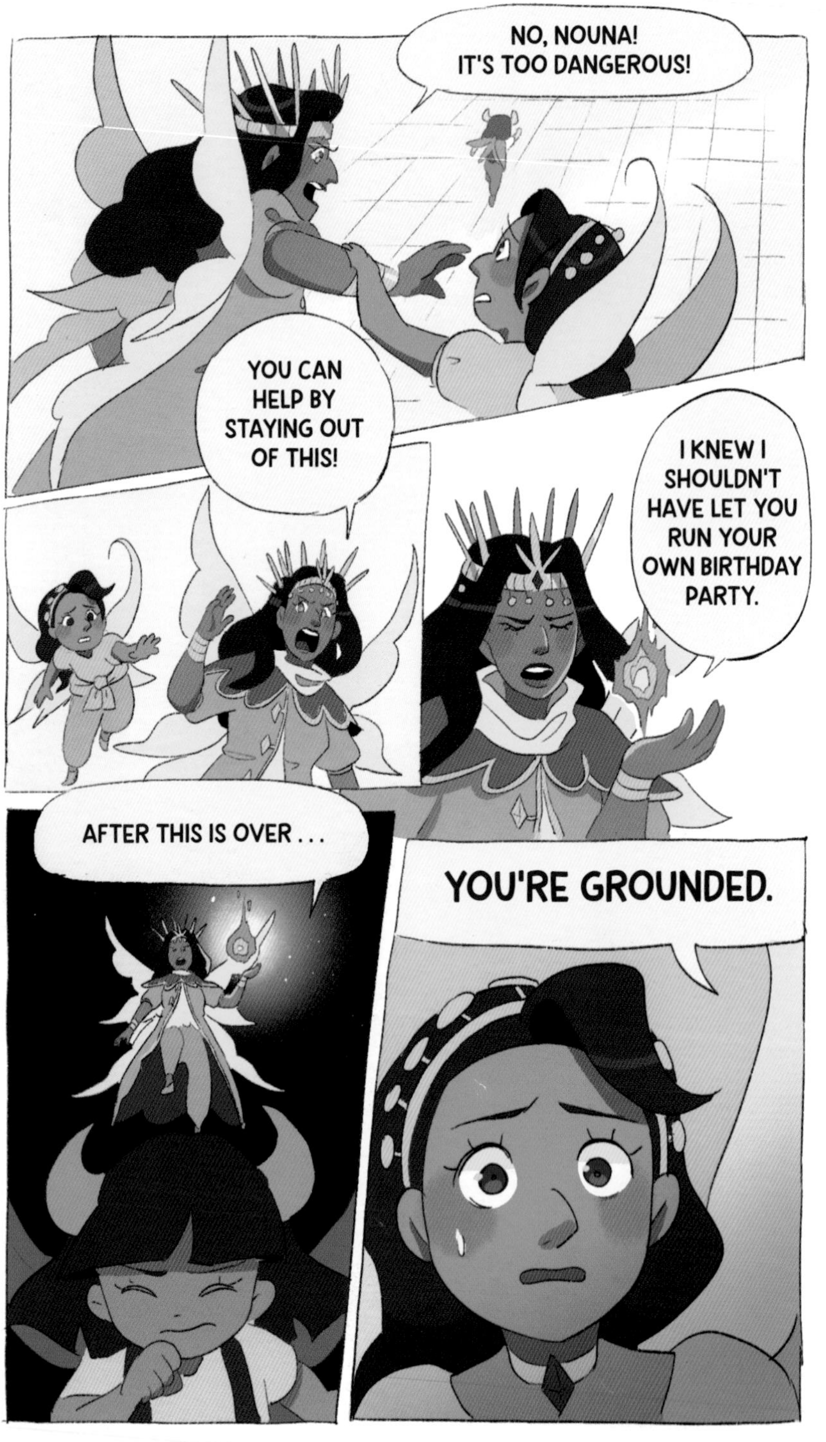
NO, NOUNA!
IT'S TOO DANGEROUS!
YOU CAN HELP BY STAYING OUT OF THIS!
I KNEW I SHOULDN'T HAVE LET YOU RUN YOUR OWN BIRTHDAY PARTY.
AFTER THIS IS OVER . . .
YOU'RE GROUNDED.

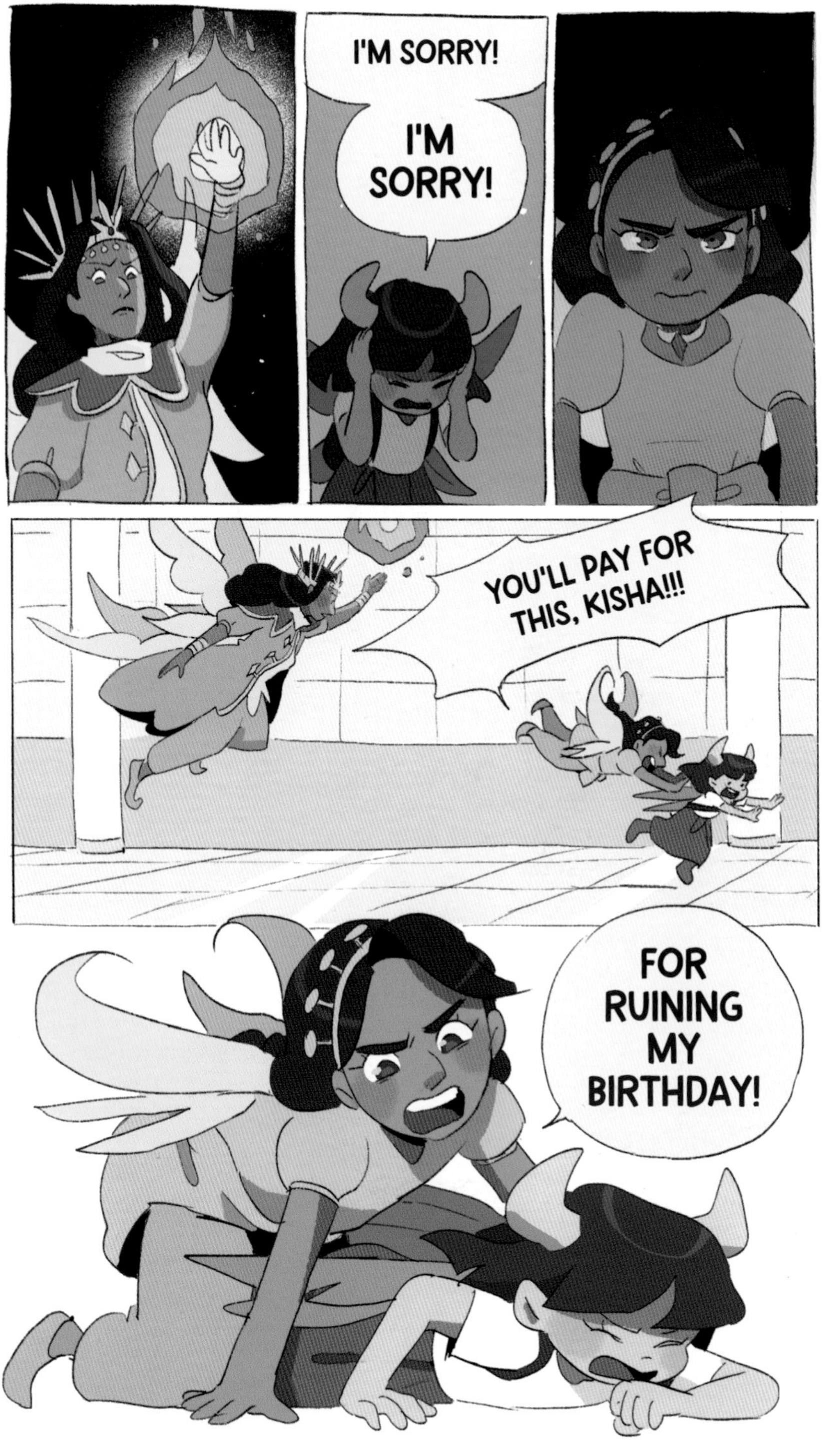
I'M SORRY!
I'M SORRY!
YOU'LL PAY FOR THIS, KISHA!!!
FOR RUINING MY BIRTHDAY!

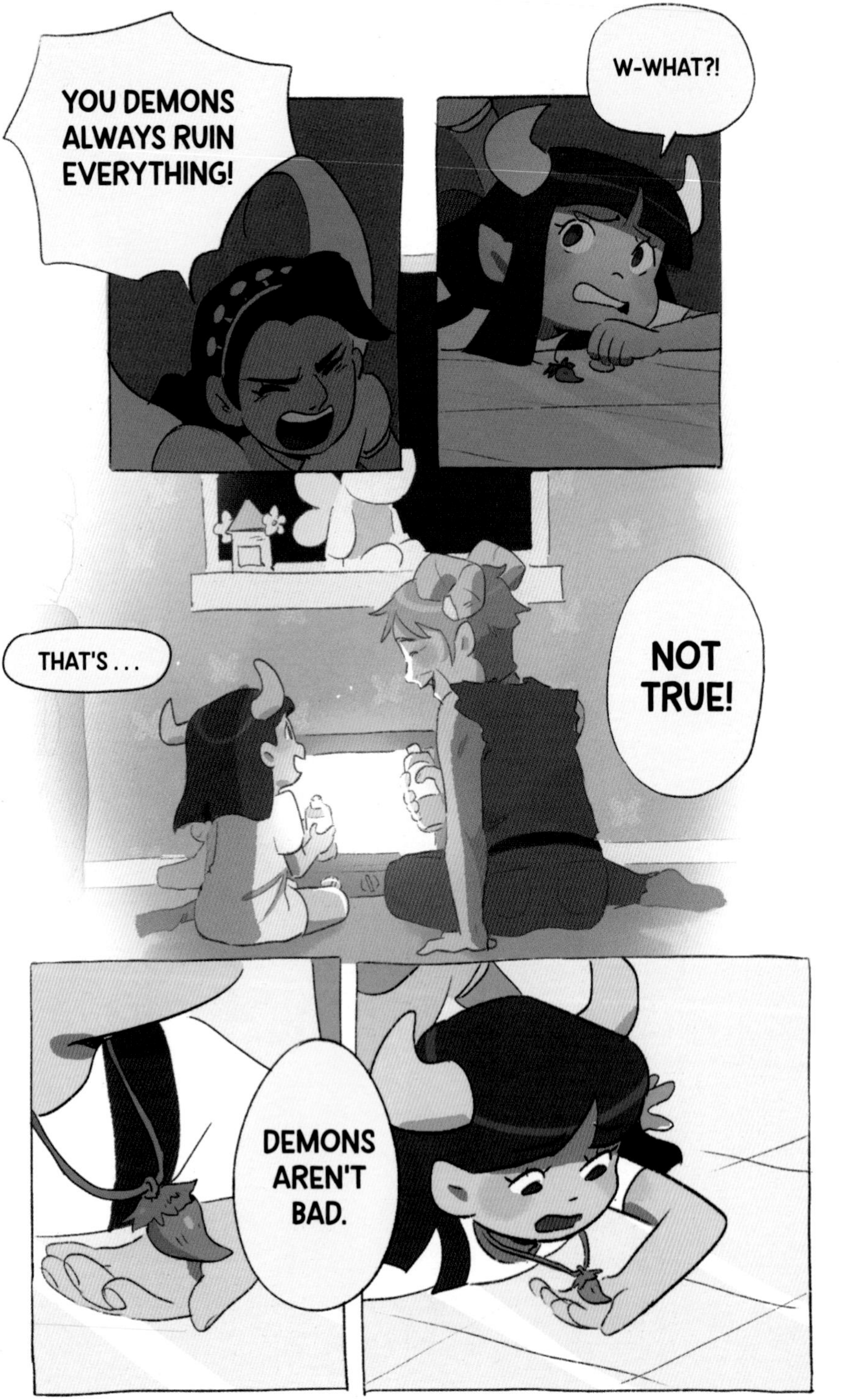
YOU DEMONS ALWAYS RUIN EVERYTHING!
W-WHAT?!
THAT'S . . .
NOT TRUE!
DEMONS AREN'T BAD.

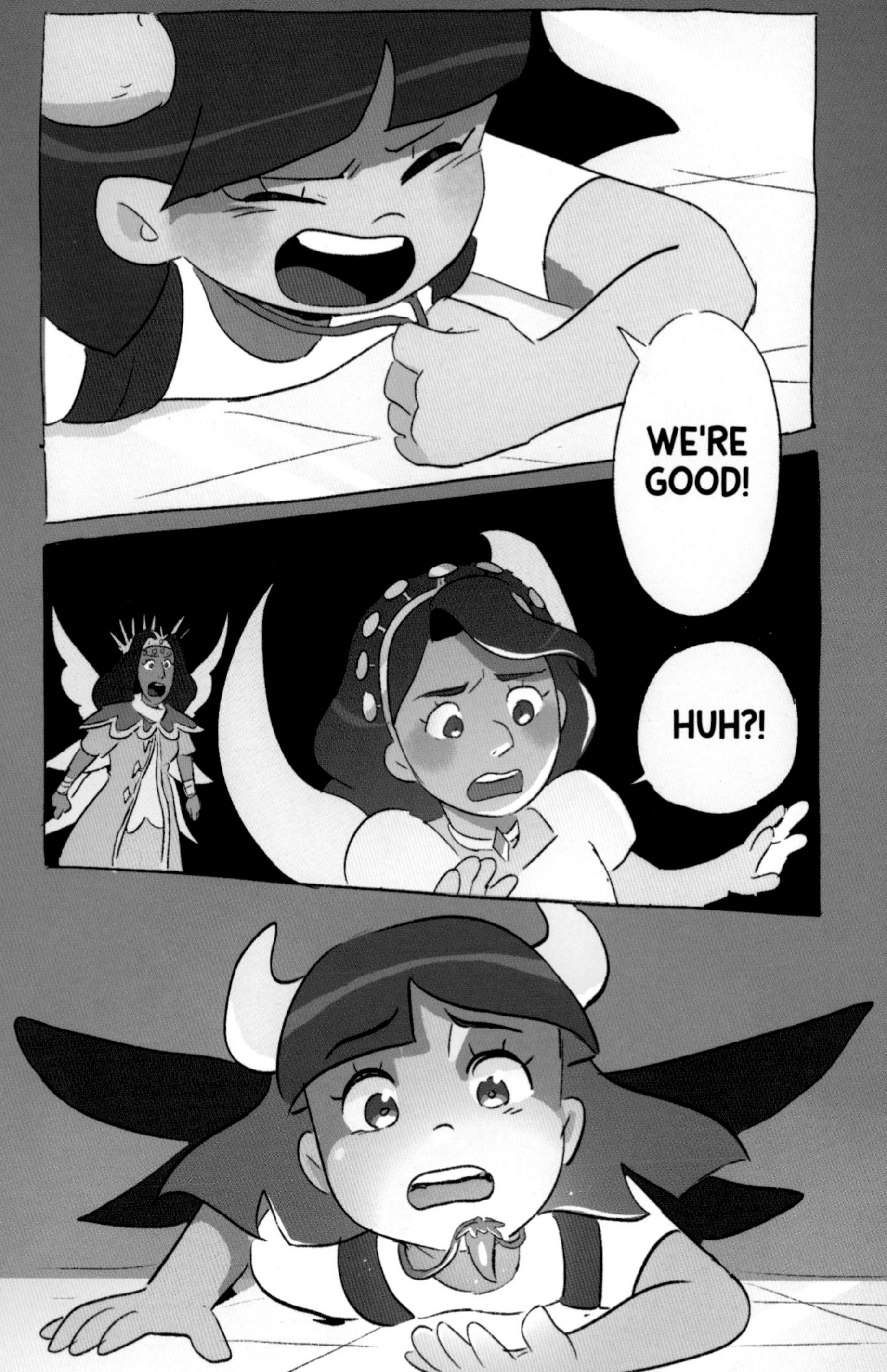
WE'RE GOOD!
HUH?!

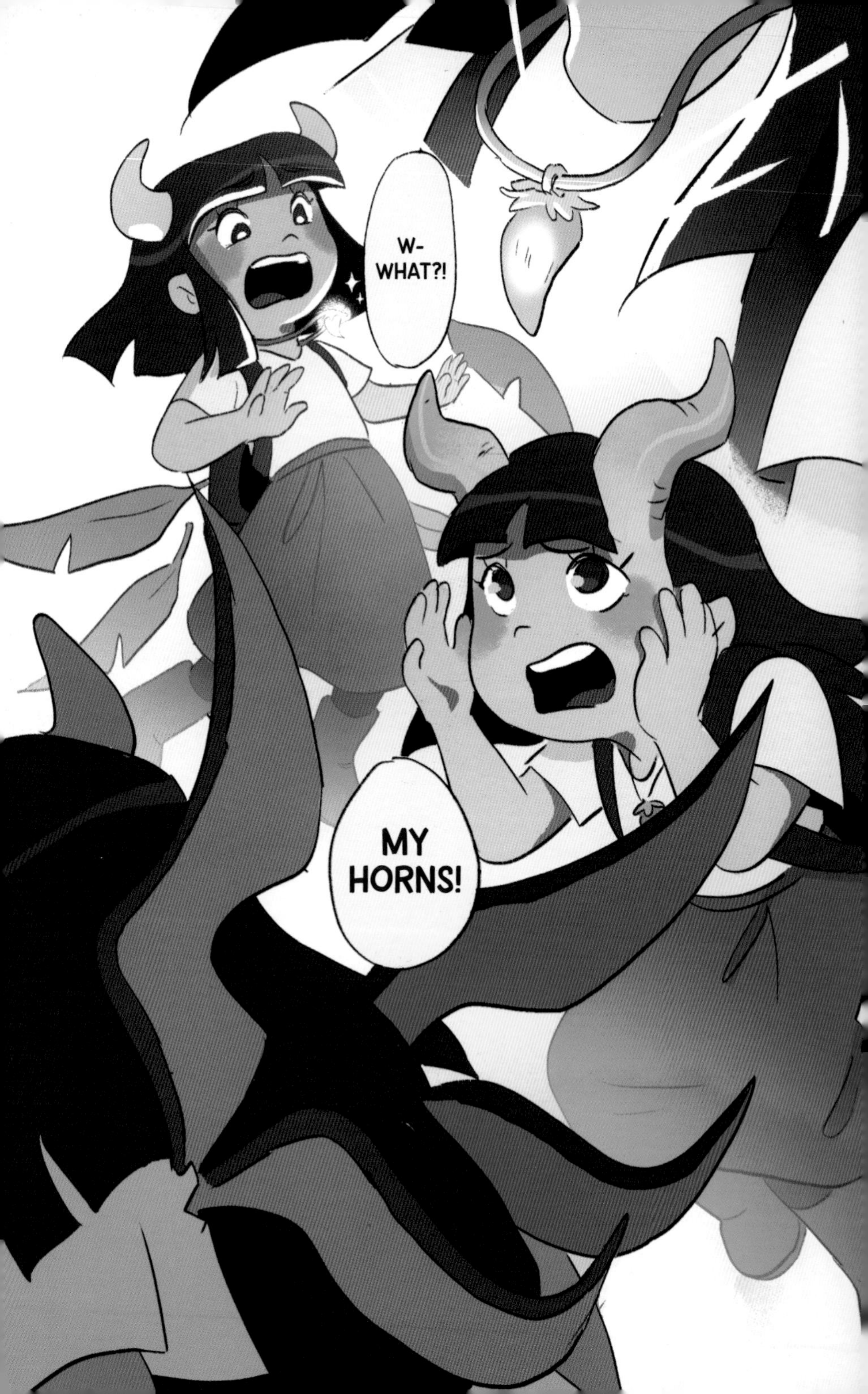
W-
WHAT?!
MY
HORNS!

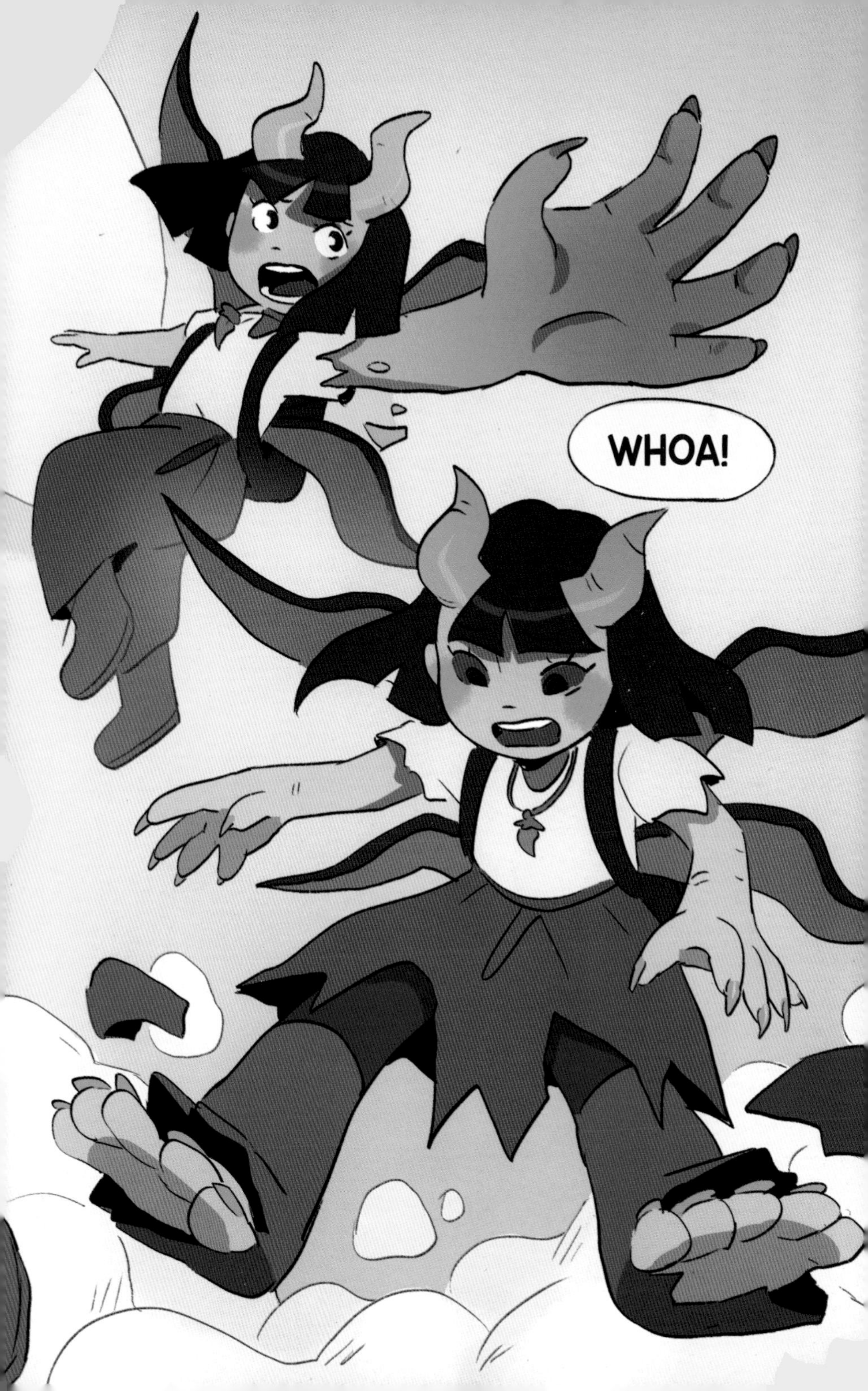
WHOA!

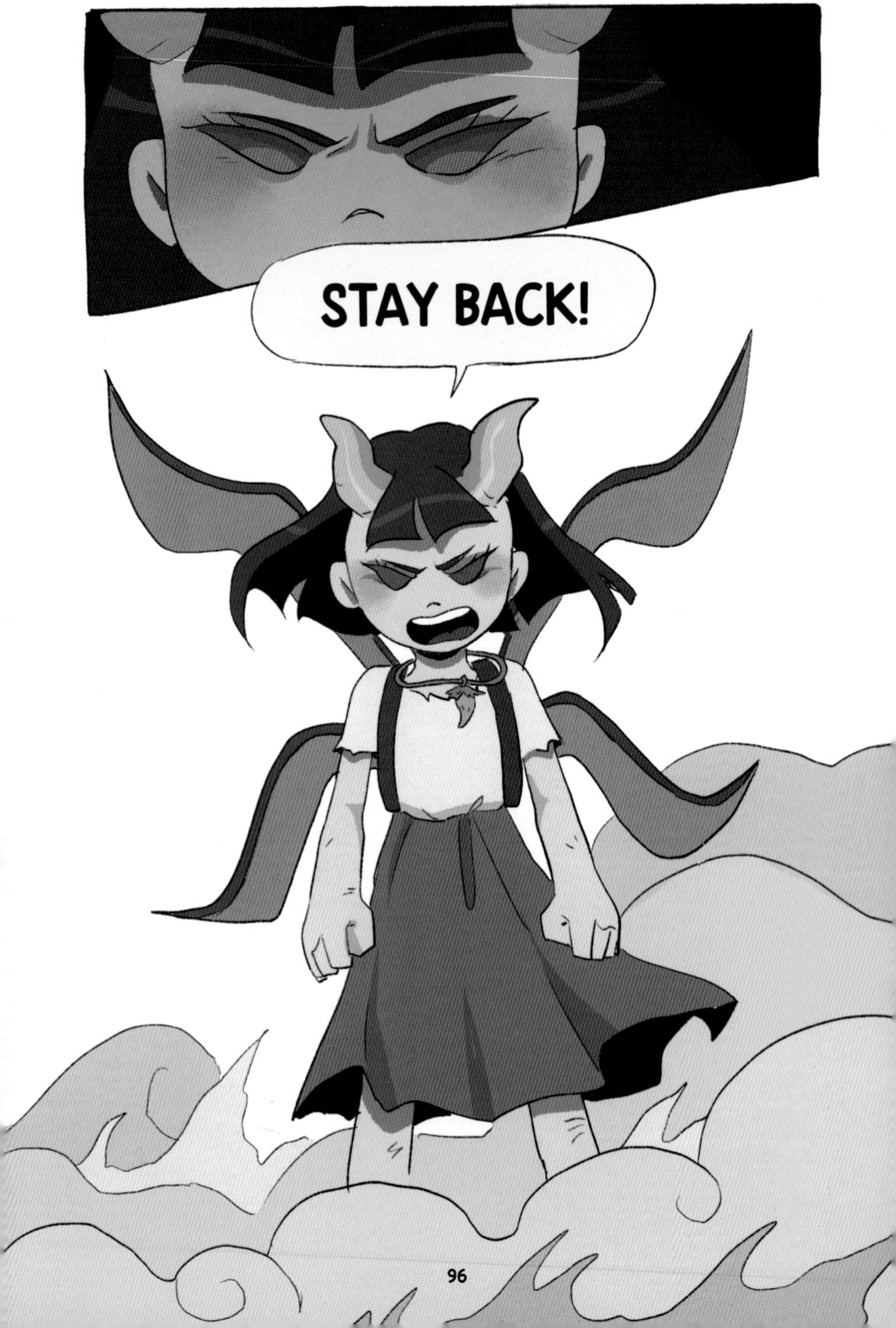
STAY BACK!

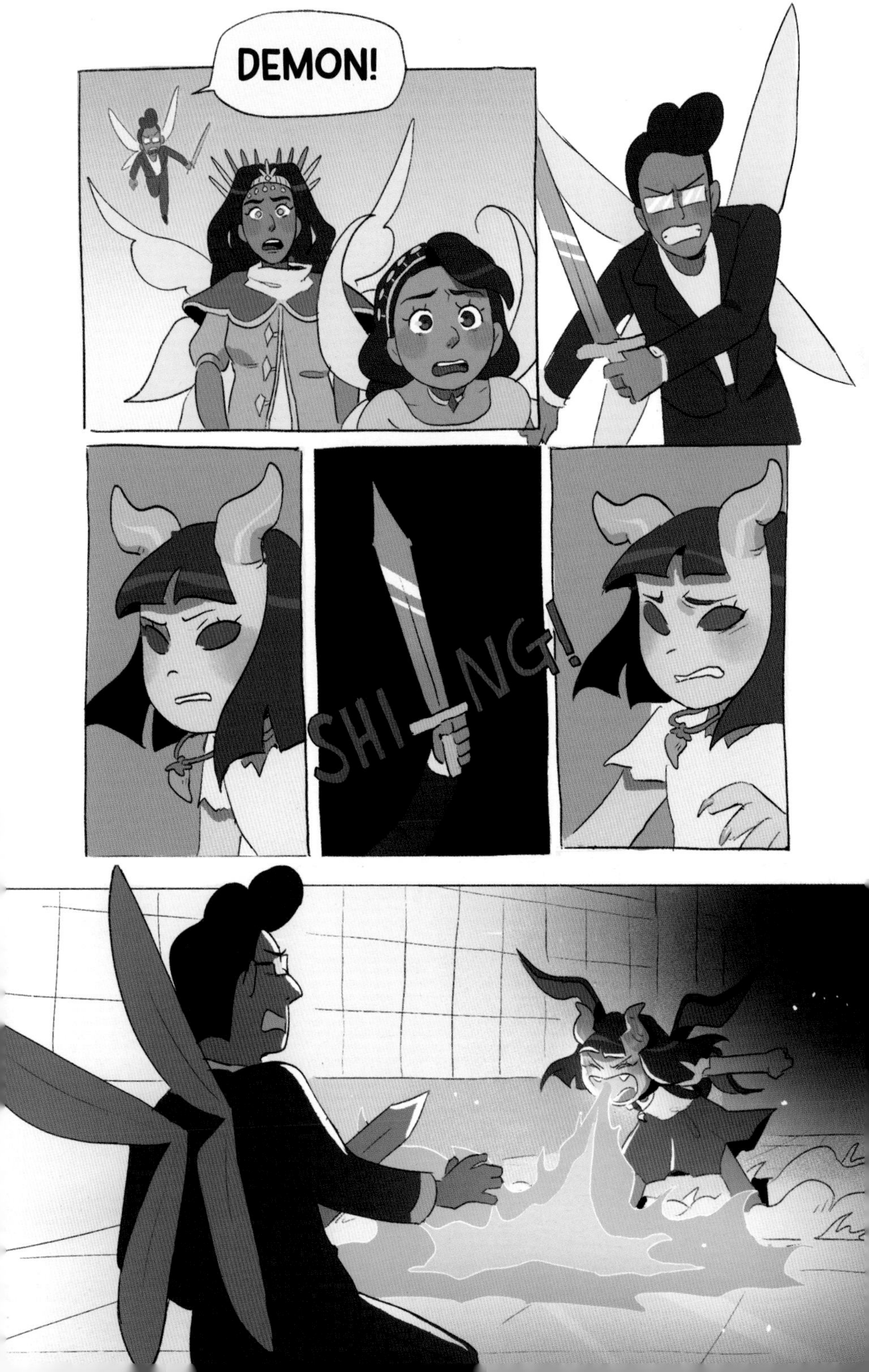
DEMON!
SHING!

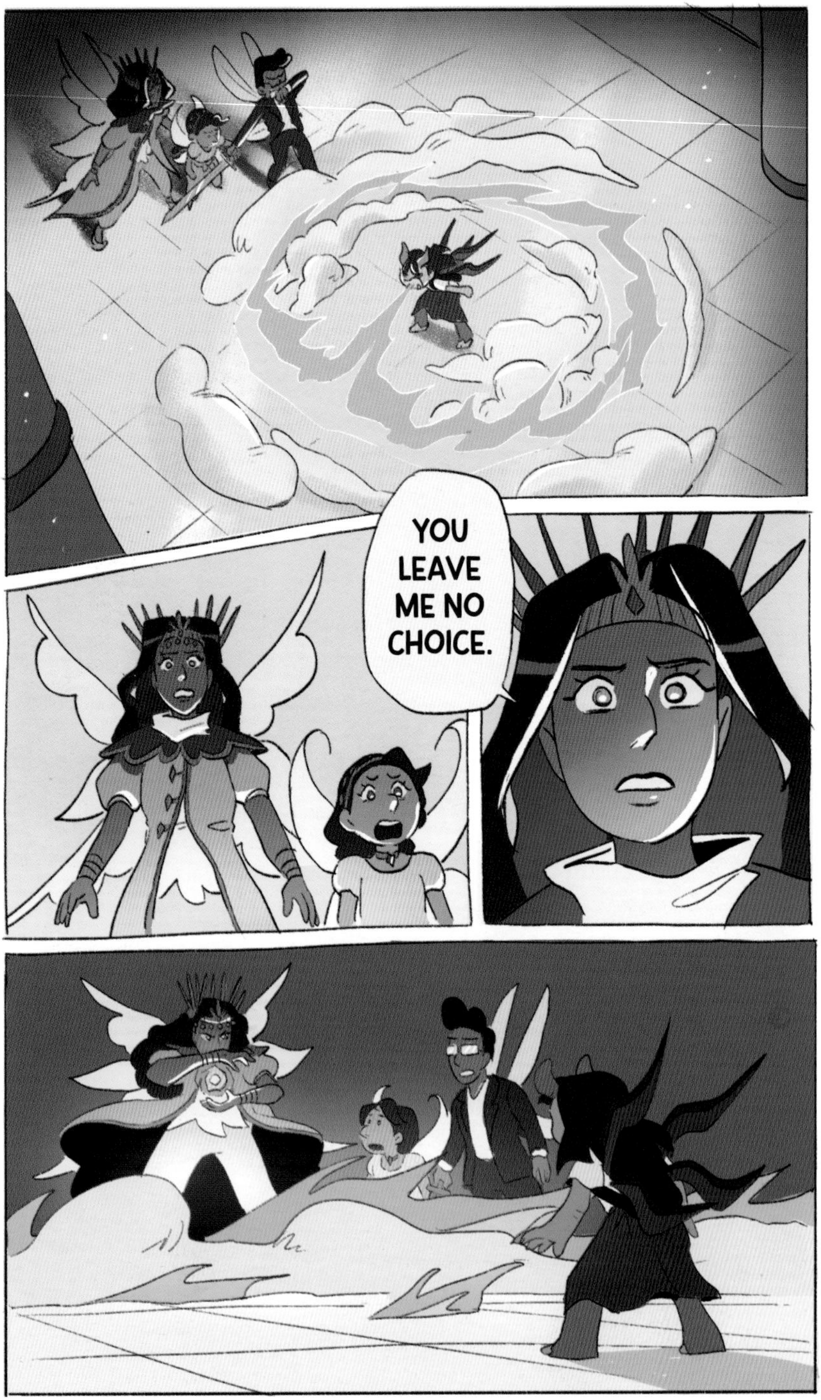
YOU LEAVE ME NO CHOICE.

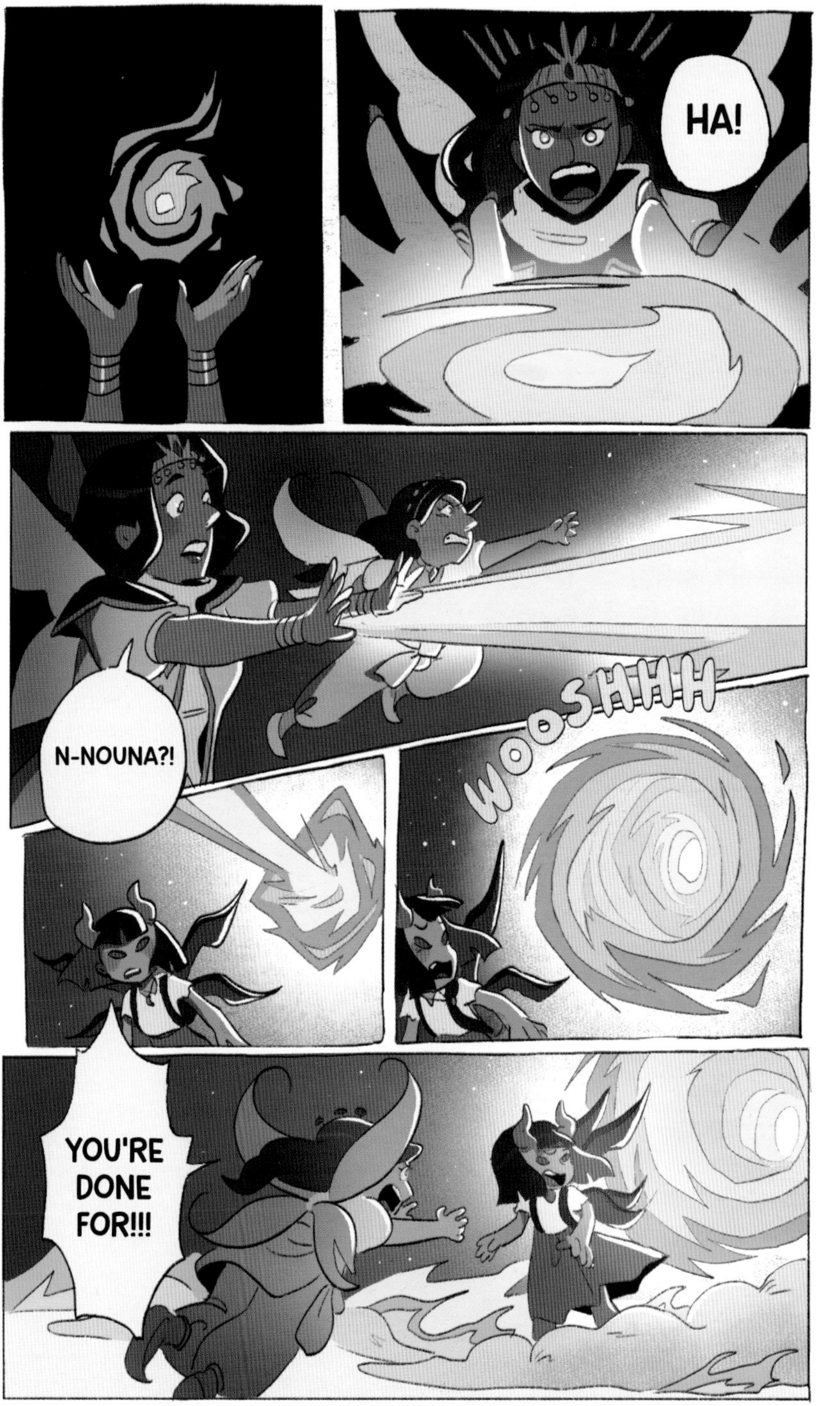
HA!
N-NOUNA?!
WOOSHHH
YOU'RE DONE FOR!!!

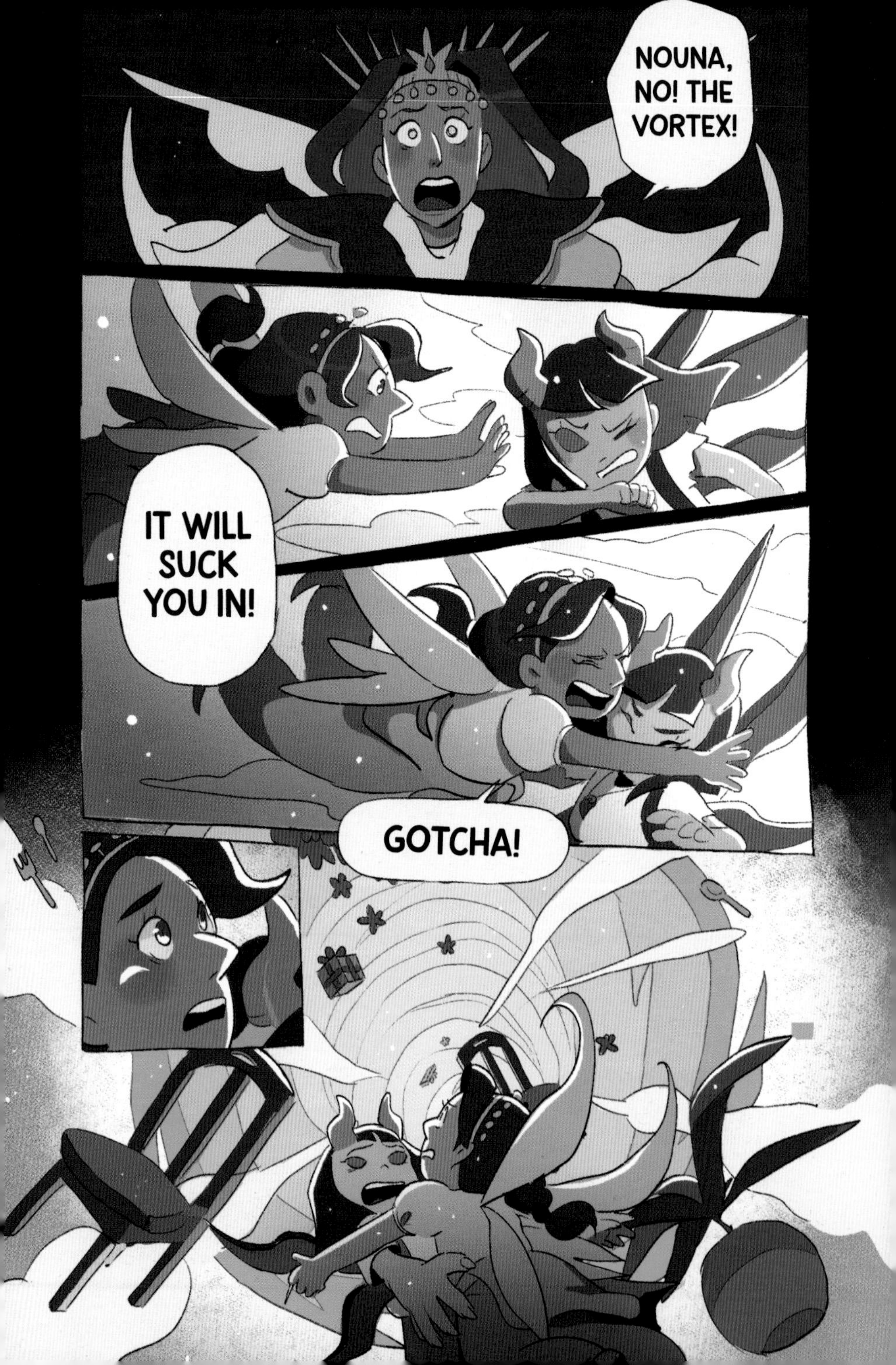
NOUNA, NO! THE VORTEX!
IT WILL SUCK YOU IN!
GOTCHA!

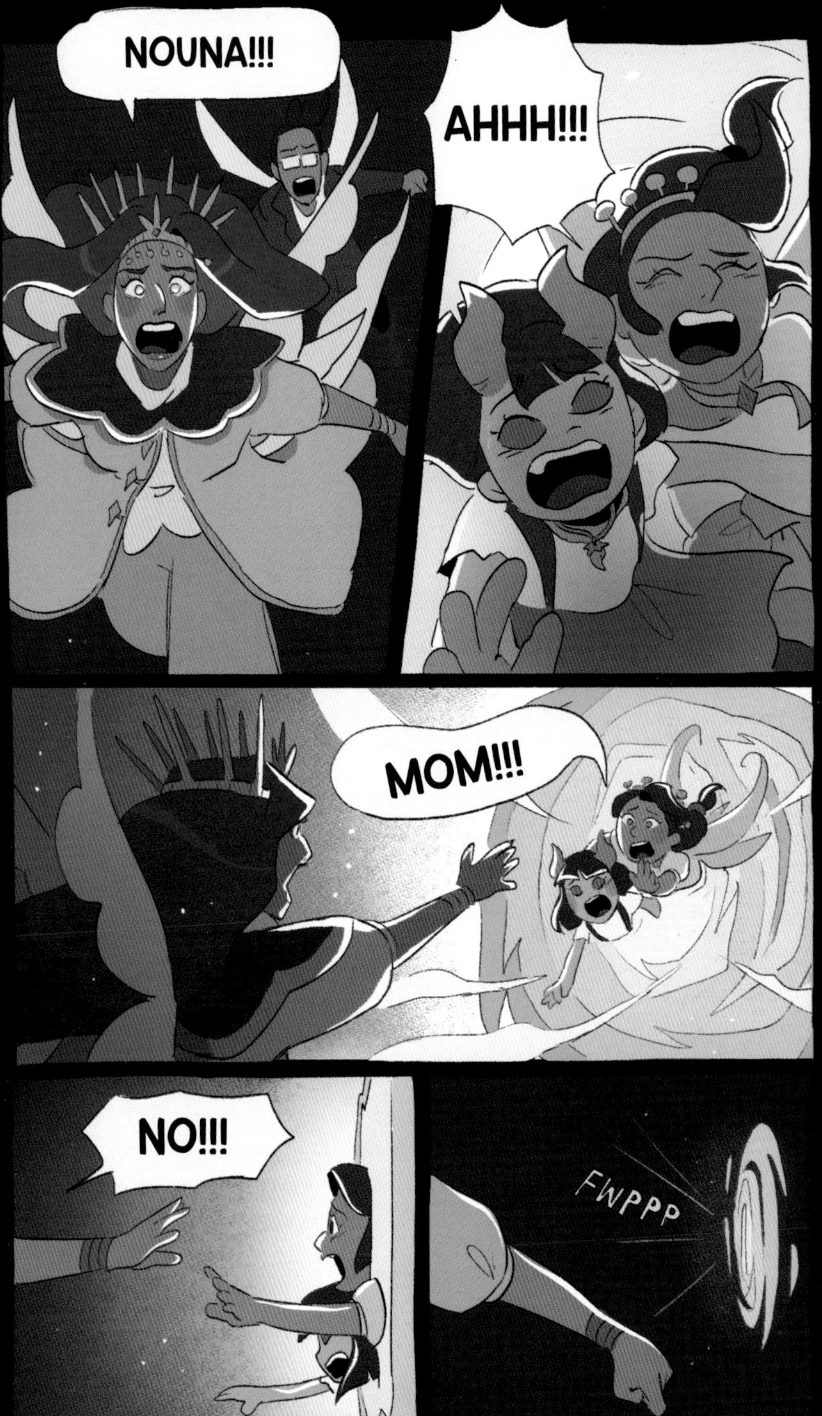
NOUNA!!!
AHHH!!!
MOM!!!
NO!!!
FWPPP

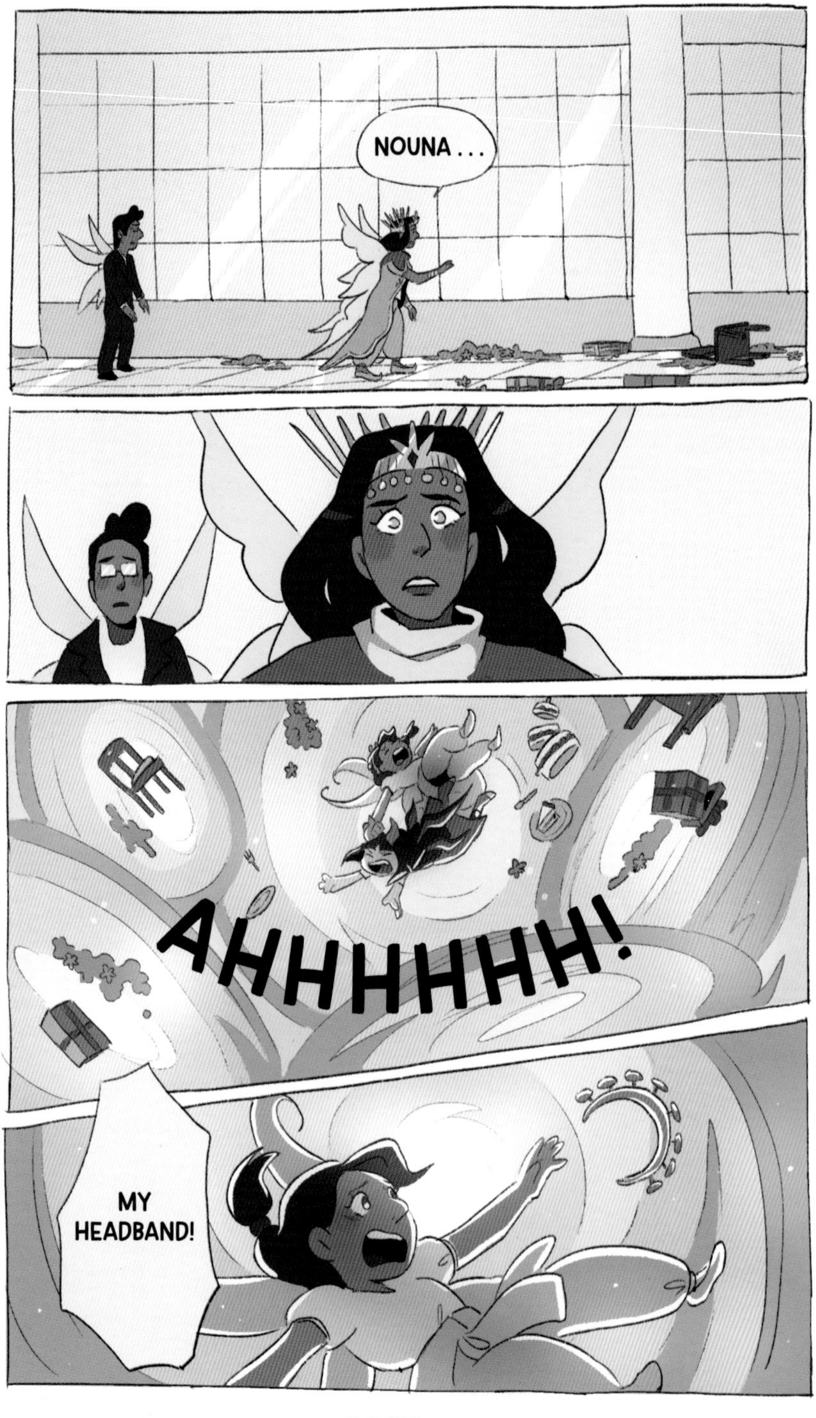
NOUNA . . .
AHHHHHH!
MY HEADBAND!

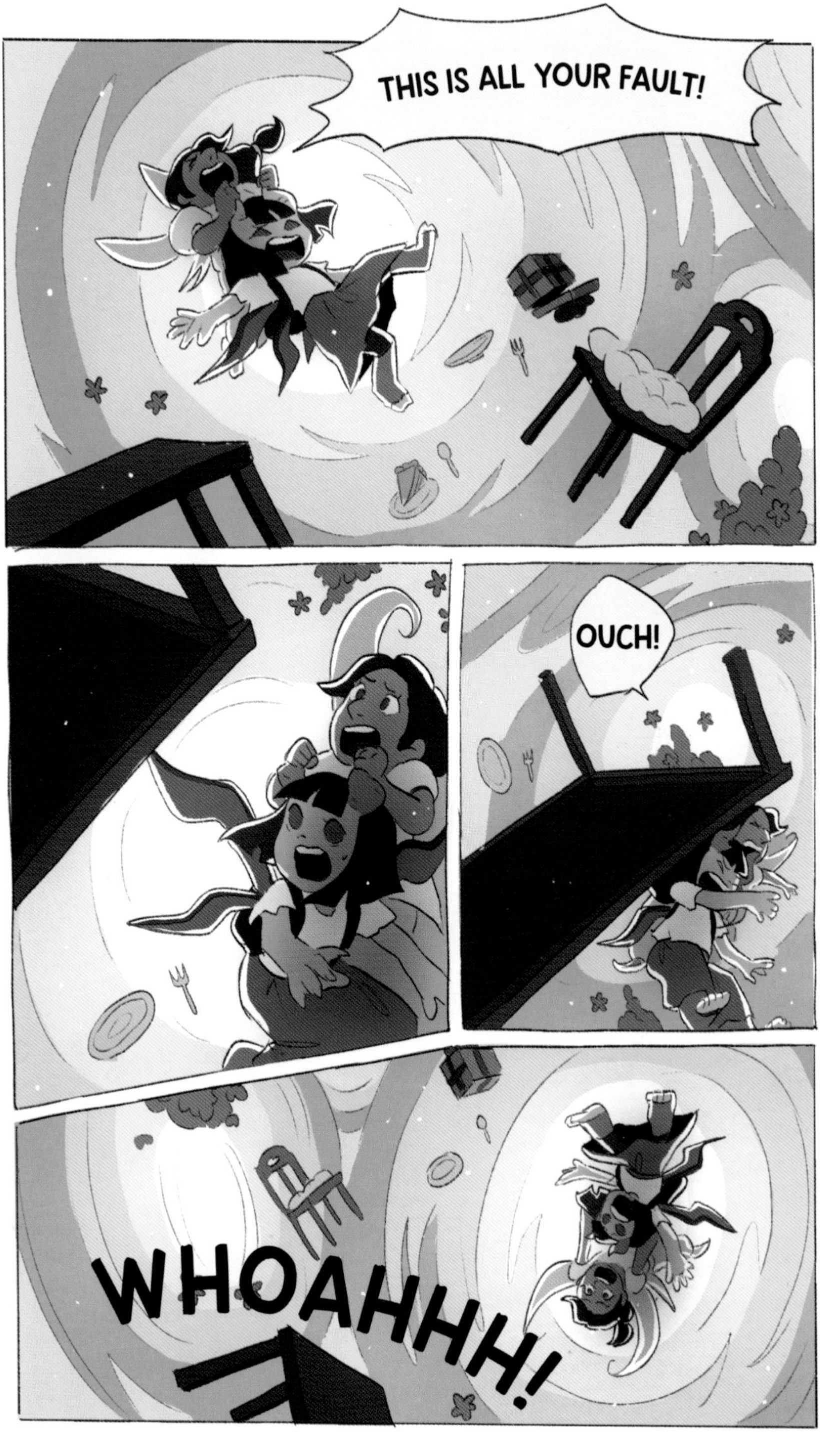
THIS IS ALL YOUR FAULT!
OUCH!
WHOAHHH!

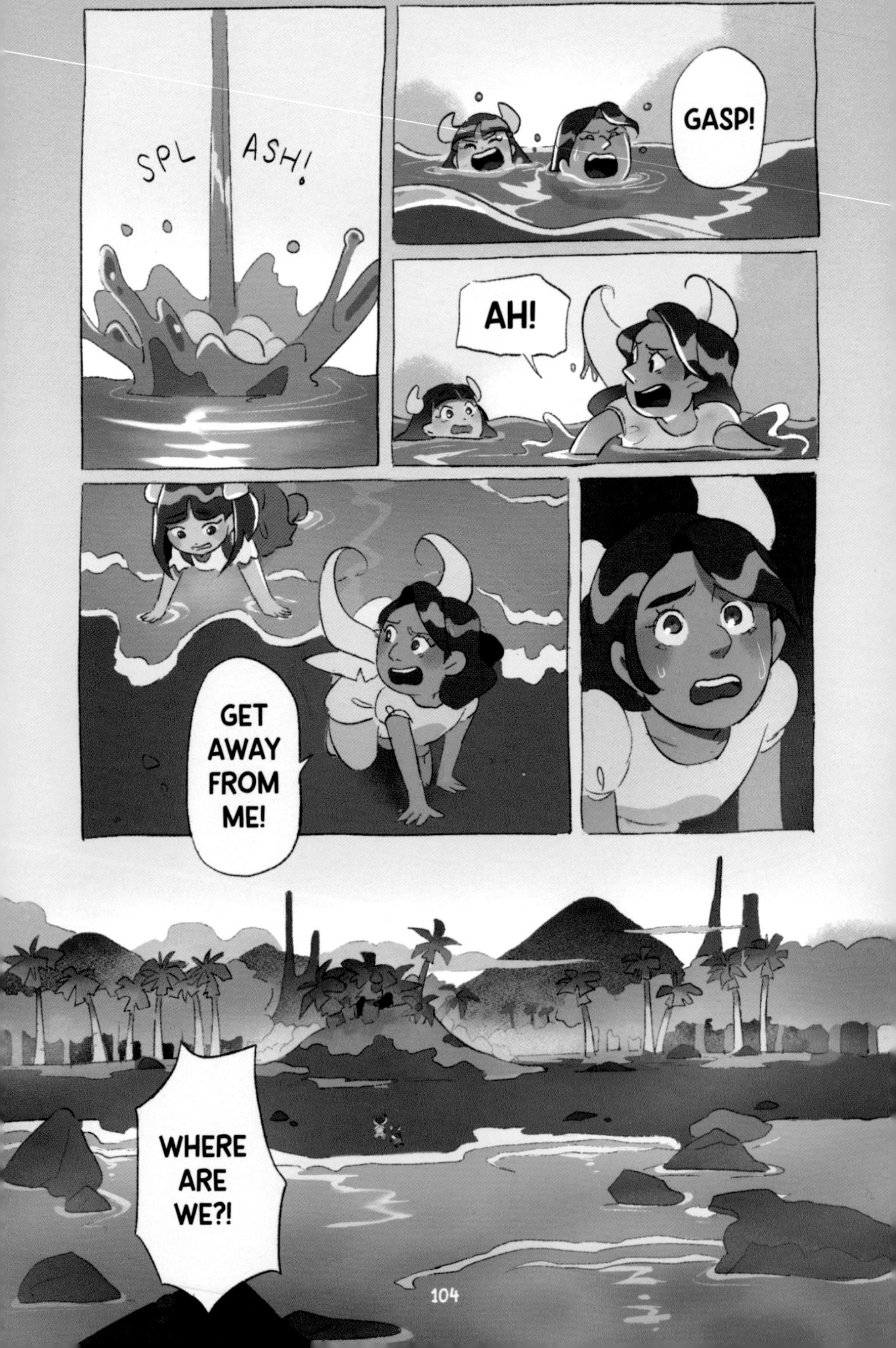
SPL ASH!
GASP!
AH!
GET AWAY FROM ME!
WHERE ARE WE?!

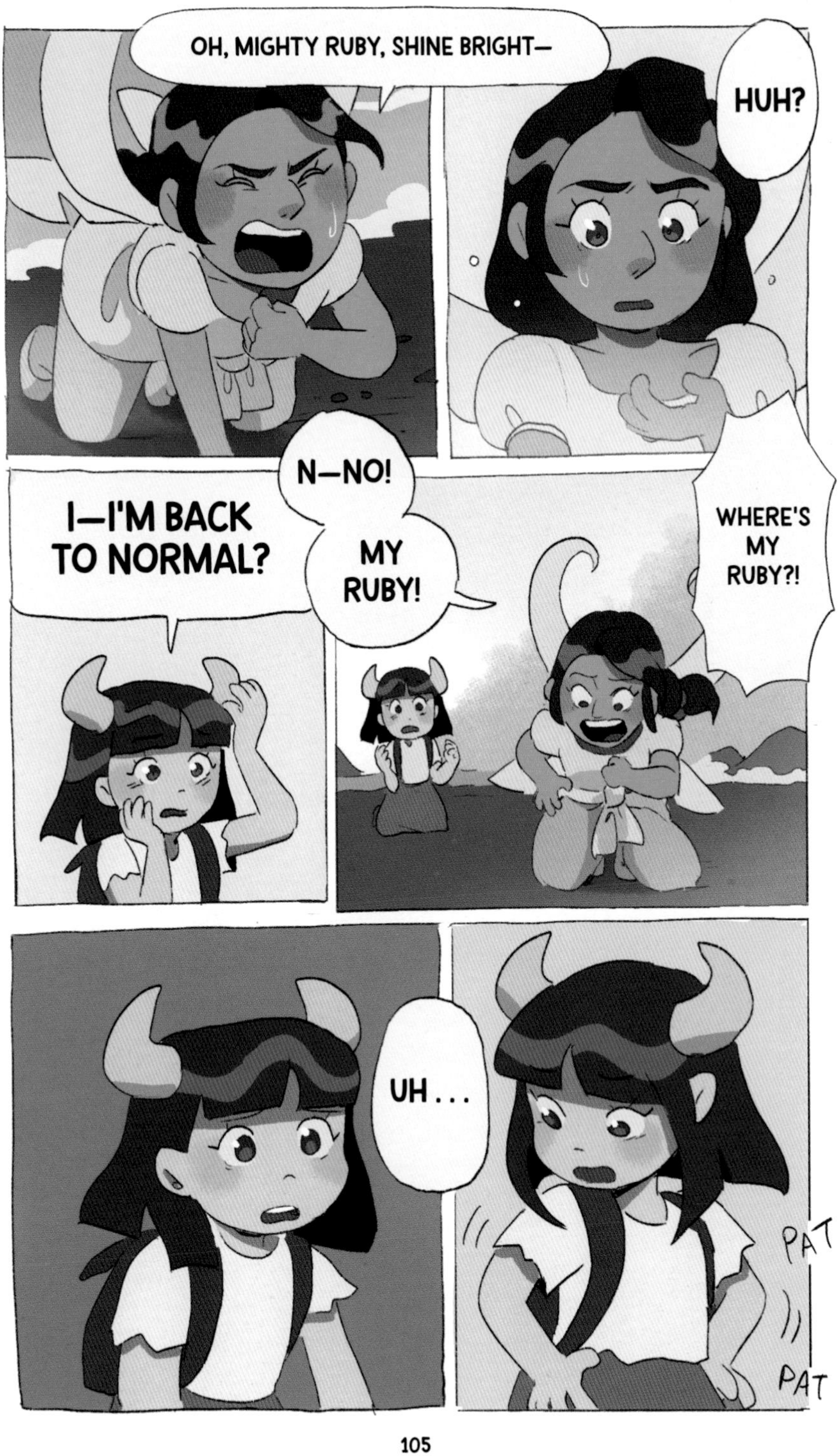
OH, MIGHTY RUBY, SHINE BRIGHT—
HUH?
I—I'M BACK TO NORMAL?
N—NO!
MY RUBY!
WHERE'S MY RUBY?!
UH . . .
PAT
PAT

I'M SO DEAD.
UHH . . .
IT COULDN'T HAVE GONE TOO FAR!
IT COULD BE SOMEWHERE ON THIS BEACH!

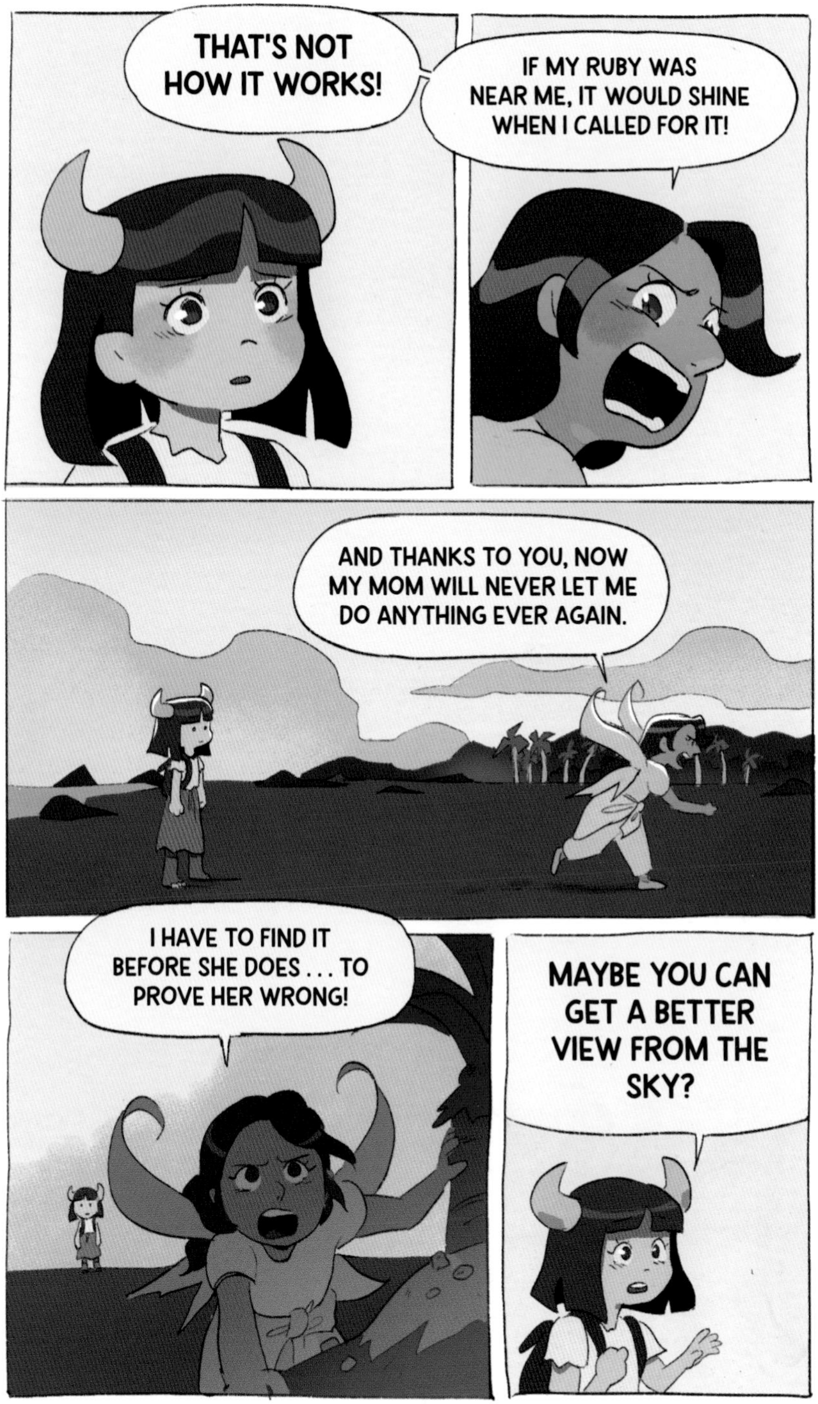
THAT'S NOT HOW IT WORKS!
IF MY RUBY WAS NEAR ME, IT WOULD SHINE WHEN I CALLED FOR IT!
AND THANKS TO YOU, NOW MY MOM WILL NEVER LET ME DO ANYTHING EVER AGAIN.
I HAVE TO FIND IT BEFORE SHE DOES . . . TO PROVE HER WRONG!
MAYBE YOU CAN GET A BETTER VIEW FROM THE SKY?

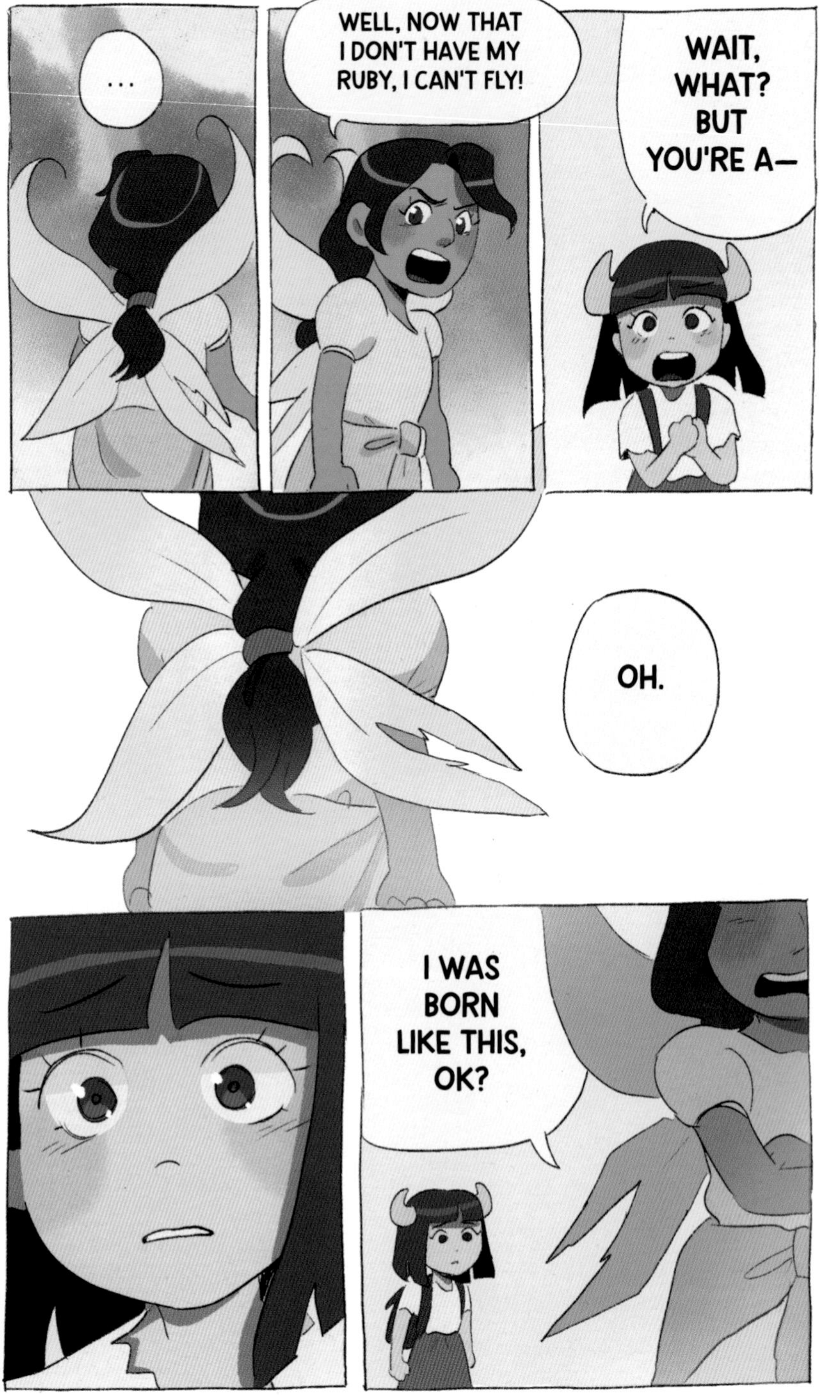
...
WELL, NOW THAT I DON'T HAVE MY RUBY, I CAN'T FLY!
WAIT, WHAT? BUT YOU'RE A—
OH.
I WAS BORN LIKE THIS, OK?

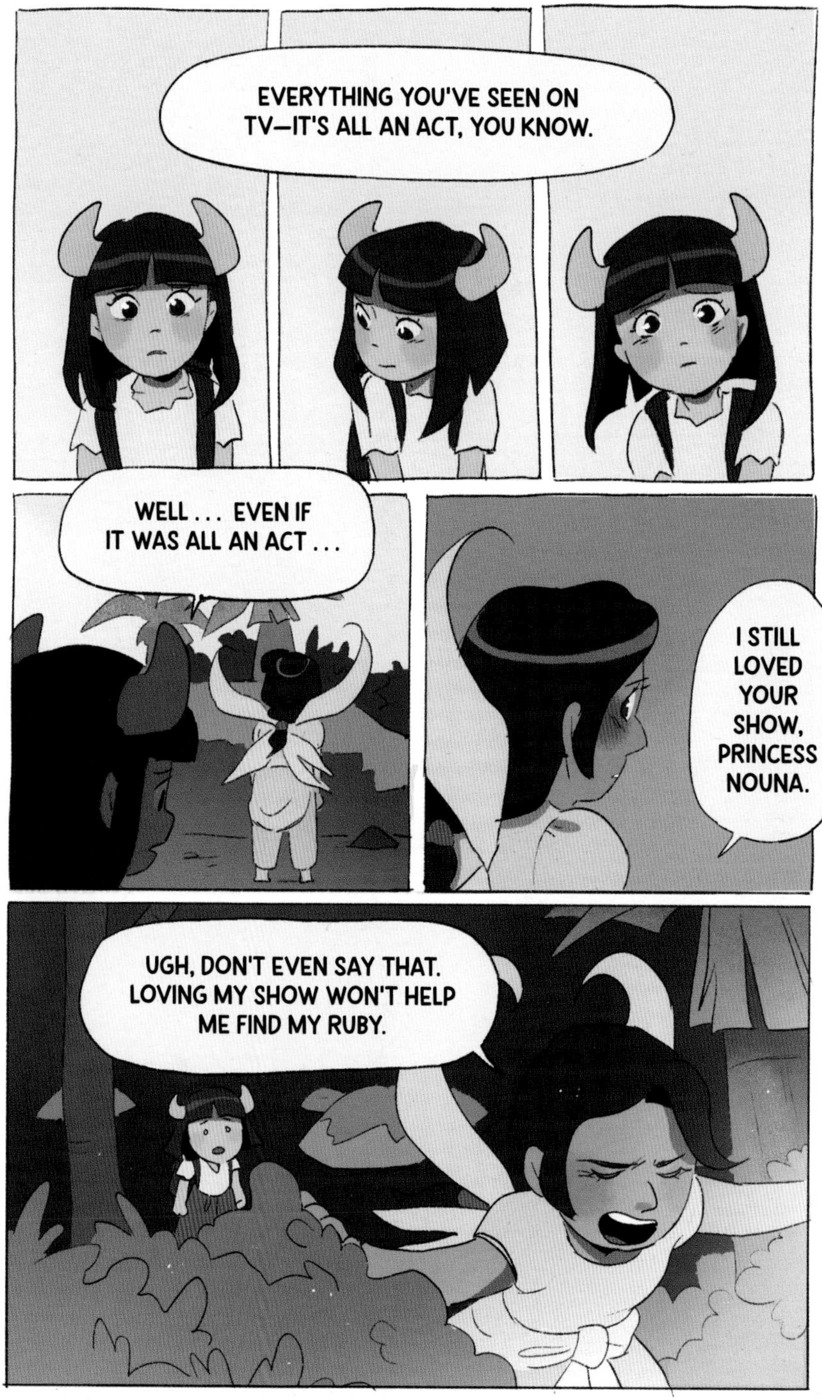
EVERYTHING YOU'VE SEEN ON TV—IT'S ALL AN ACT, YOU KNOW.
WELL . . . EVEN IF IT WAS ALL AN ACT . . .
I STILL LOVED YOUR SHOW, PRINCESS NOUNA.
UGH, DON'T EVEN SAY THAT. LOVING MY SHOW WON'T HELP ME FIND MY RUBY.

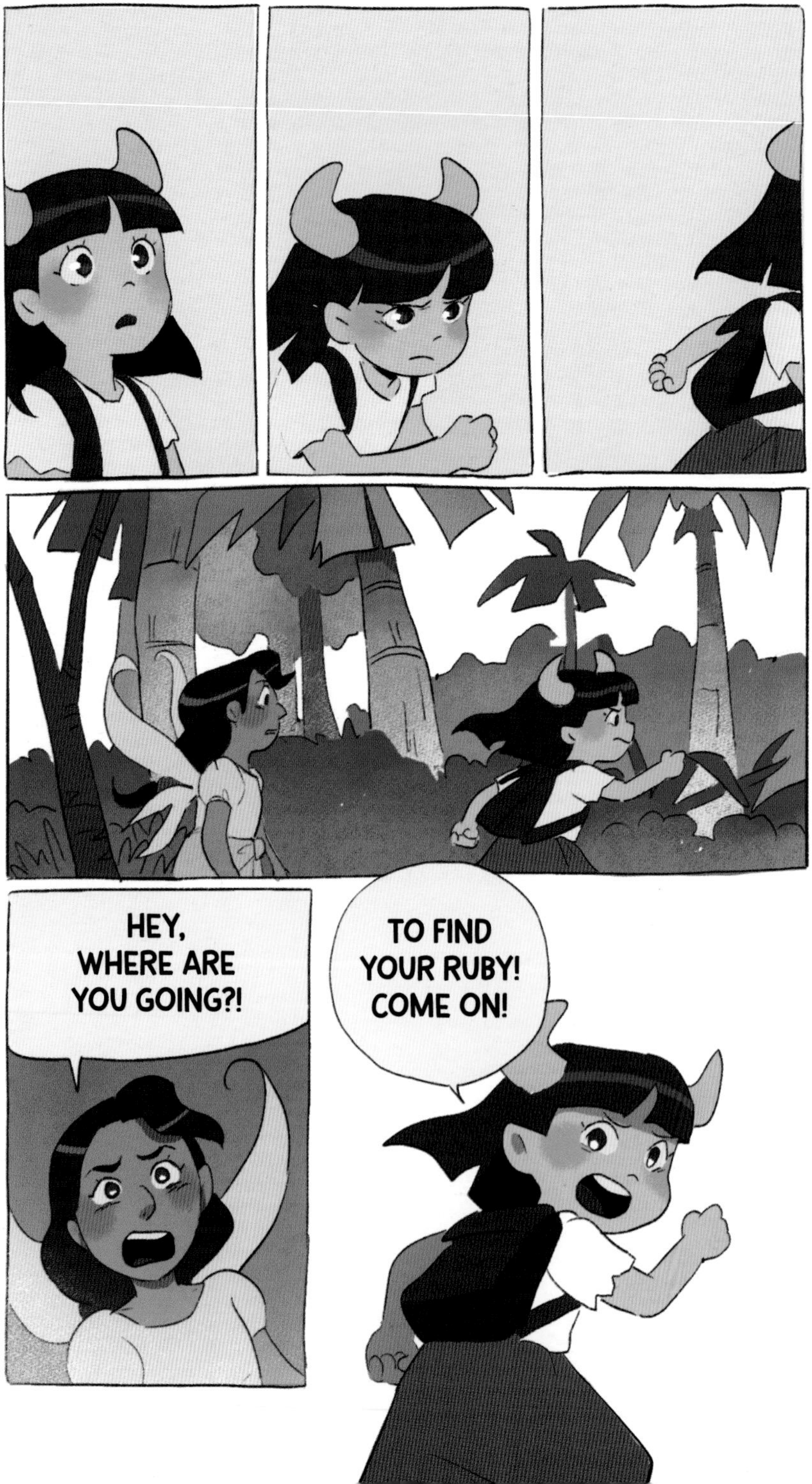
HEY, WHERE ARE YOU GOING?!
TO FIND YOUR RUBY! COME ON!

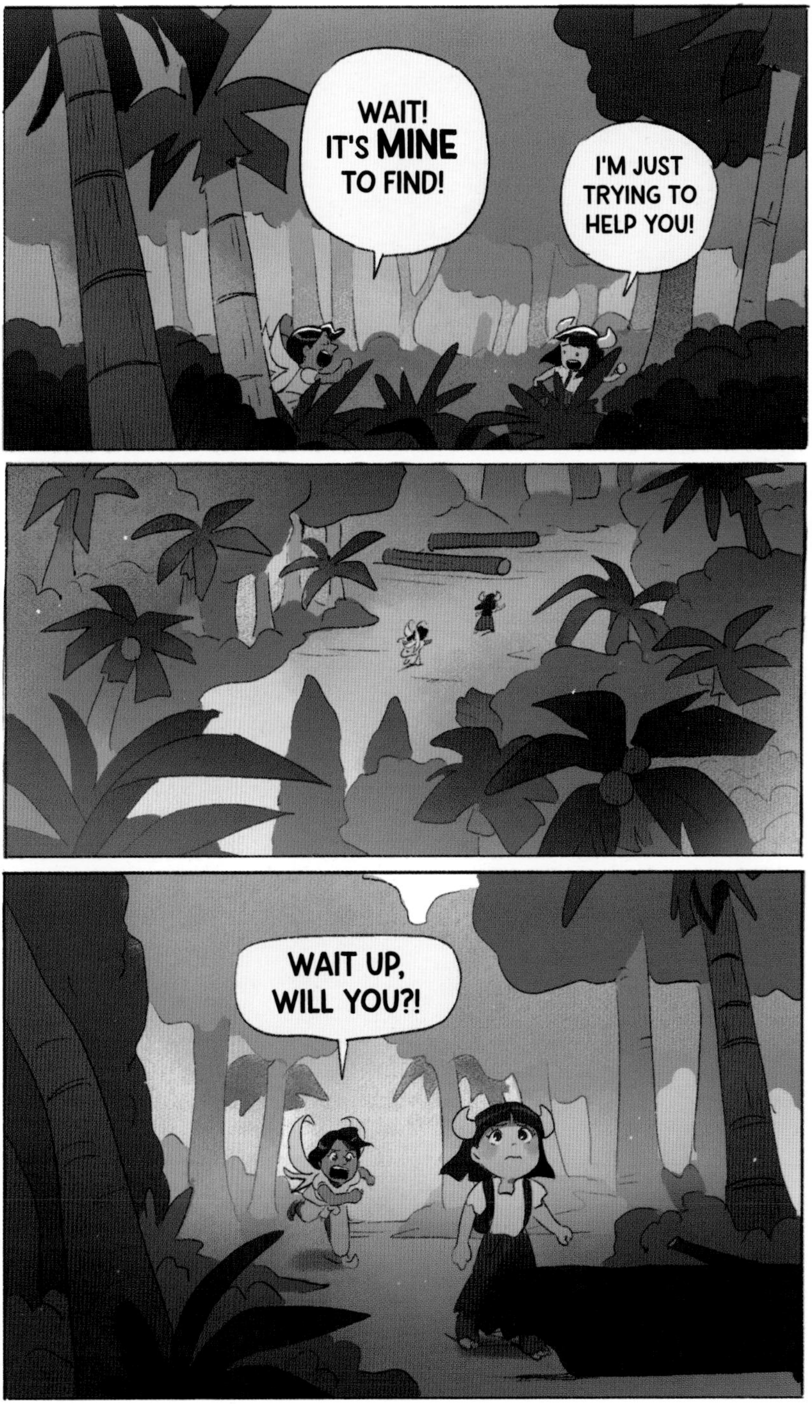
WAIT!
IT'S **MINE**
TO FIND!
I'M JUST TRYING TO HELP YOU!
WAIT UP, WILL YOU?!

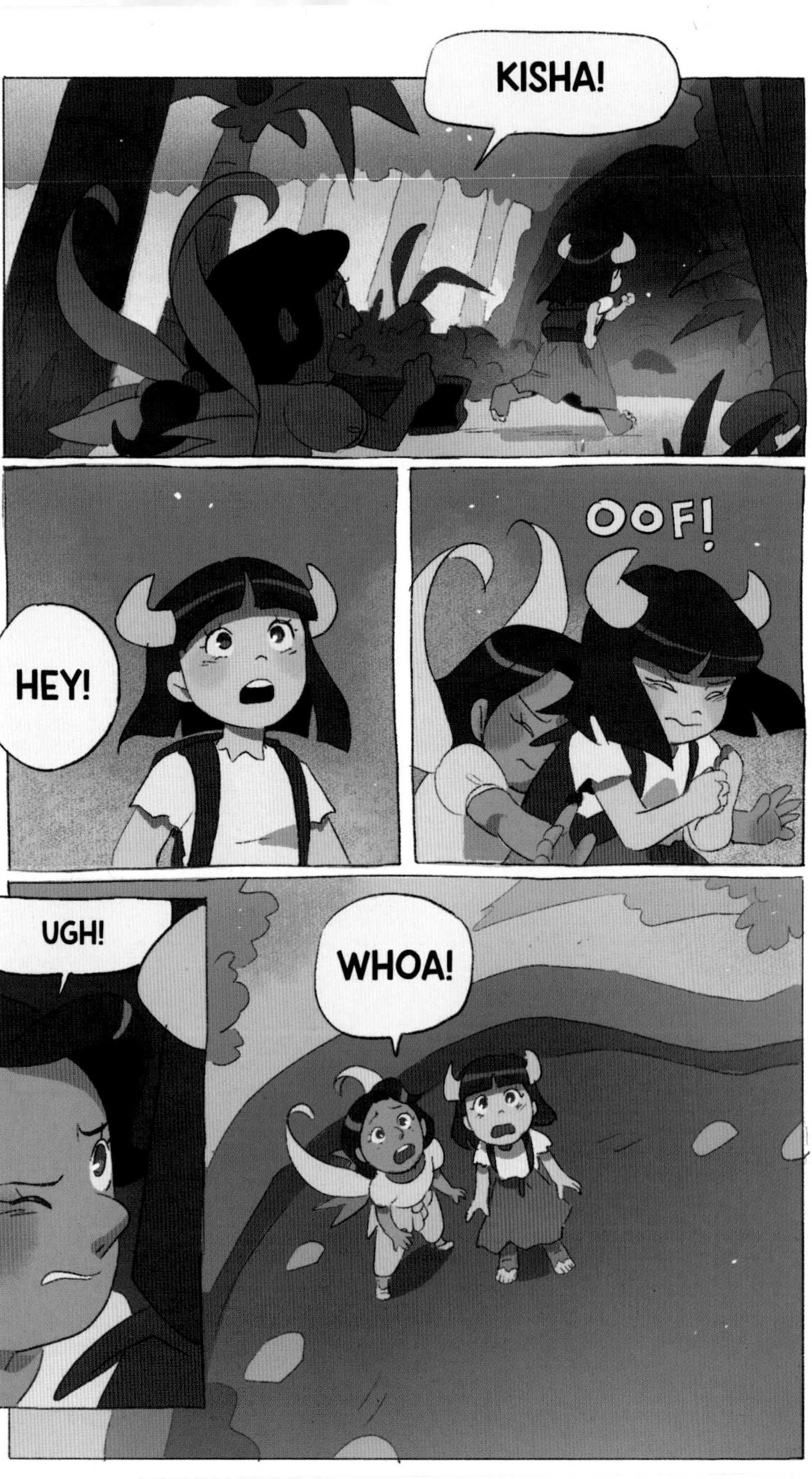
KISHA!
HEY!
OOF!
UGH!
WHOA!

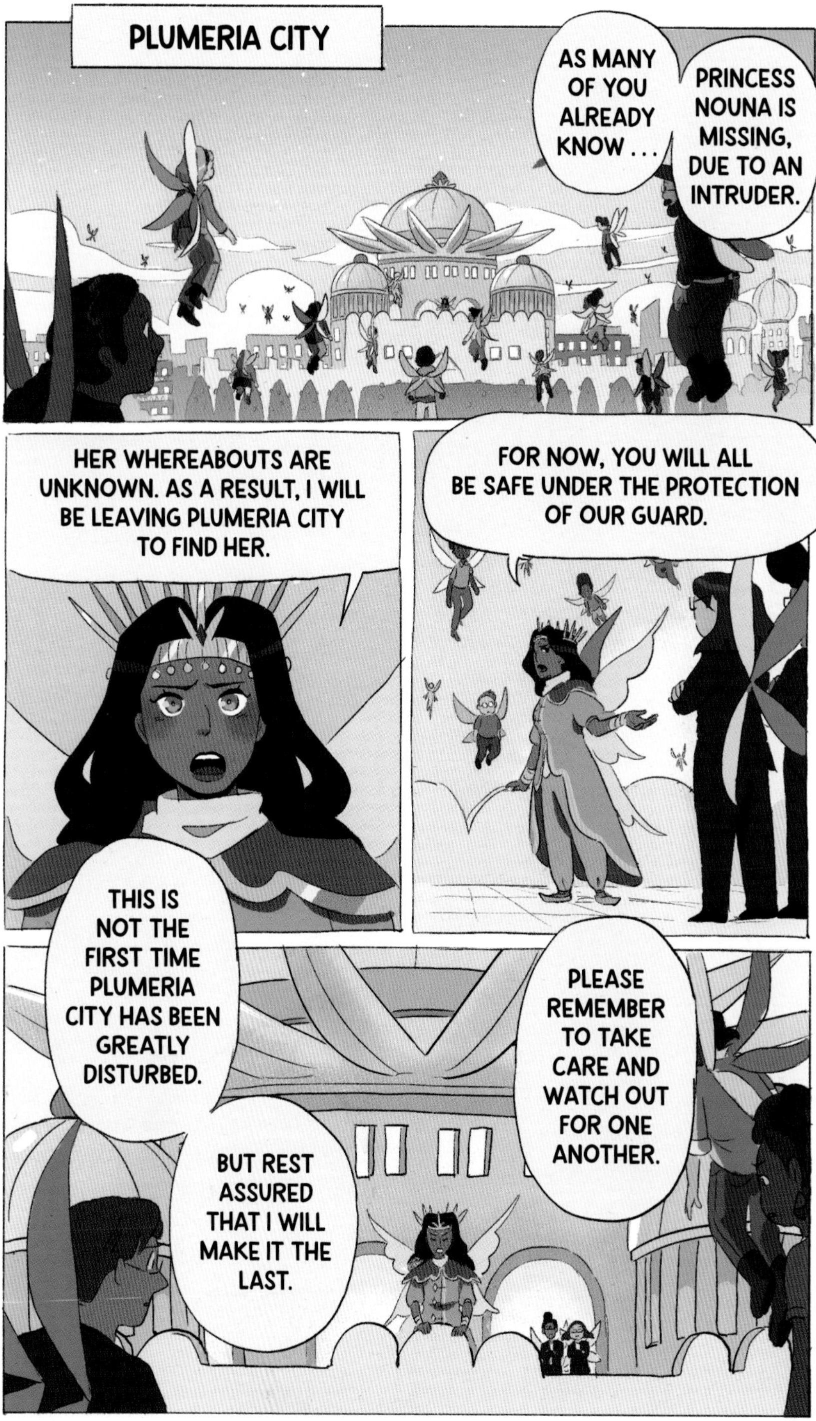
PLUMERIA CITY
AS MANY OF YOU ALREADY KNOW . . .
PRINCESS NOUNA IS MISSING, DUE TO AN INTRUDER.
HER WHEREABOUTS ARE UNKNOWN. AS A RESULT, I WILL BE LEAVING PLUMERIA CITY TO FIND HER.
FOR NOW, YOU WILL ALL BE SAFE UNDER THE PROTECTION OF OUR GUARD.
THIS IS NOT THE FIRST TIME PLUMERIA CITY HAS BEEN GREATLY DISTURBED.
BUT REST ASSURED THAT I WILL MAKE IT THE LAST.
PLEASE REMEMBER TO TAKE CARE AND WATCH OUT FOR ONE ANOTHER.

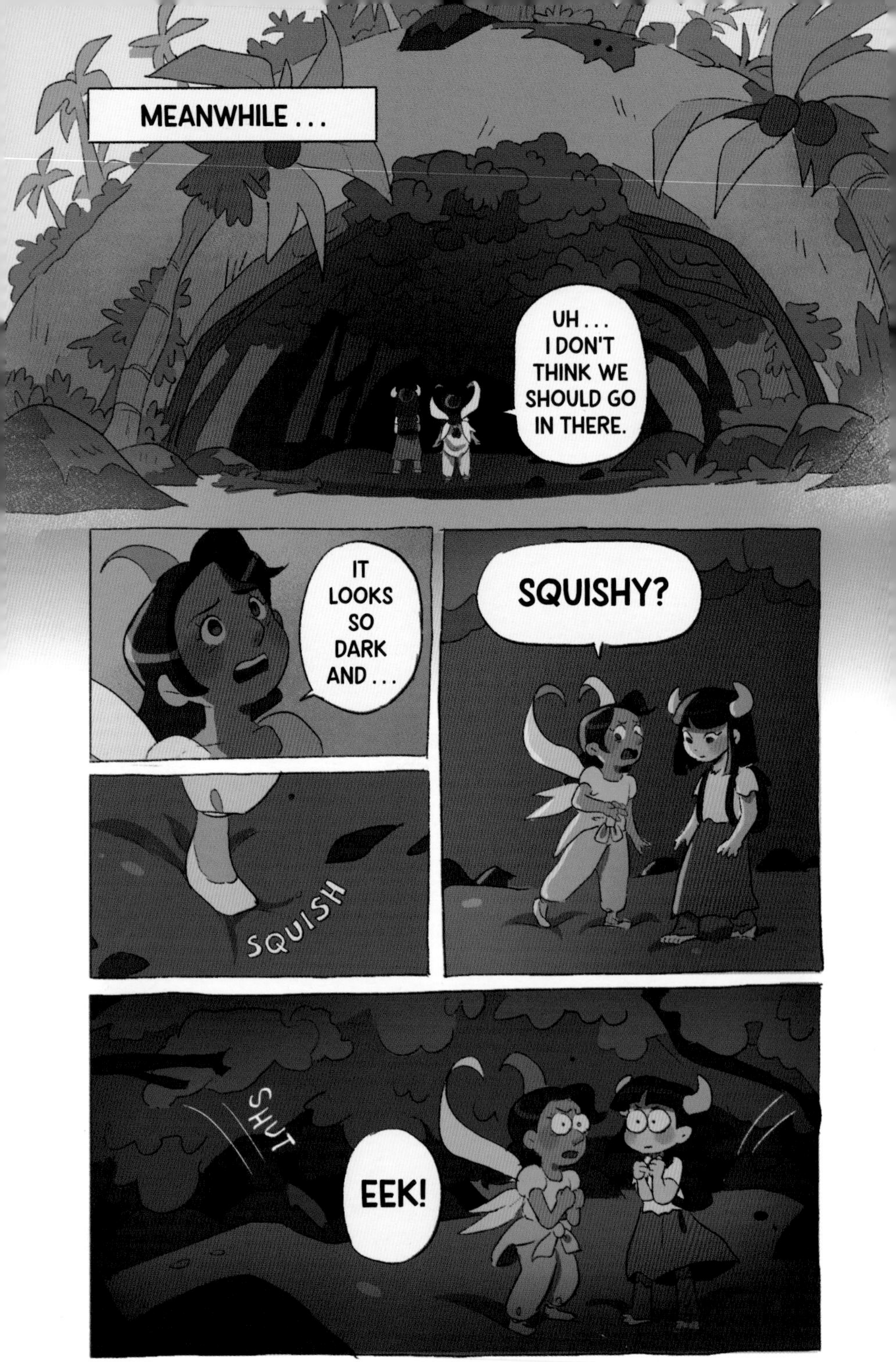
MEANWHILE . . .
UH . . . I DON'T THINK WE SHOULD GO IN THERE.
IT LOOKS SO DARK AND . . .
SQUISH
SQUISHY?
SHUT
EEK!

OK, I HAVE ANOTHER PLAN!
ON THE COUNT OF THREE, JUMP!
ONE . . .
TWO . . .
THREE!

119

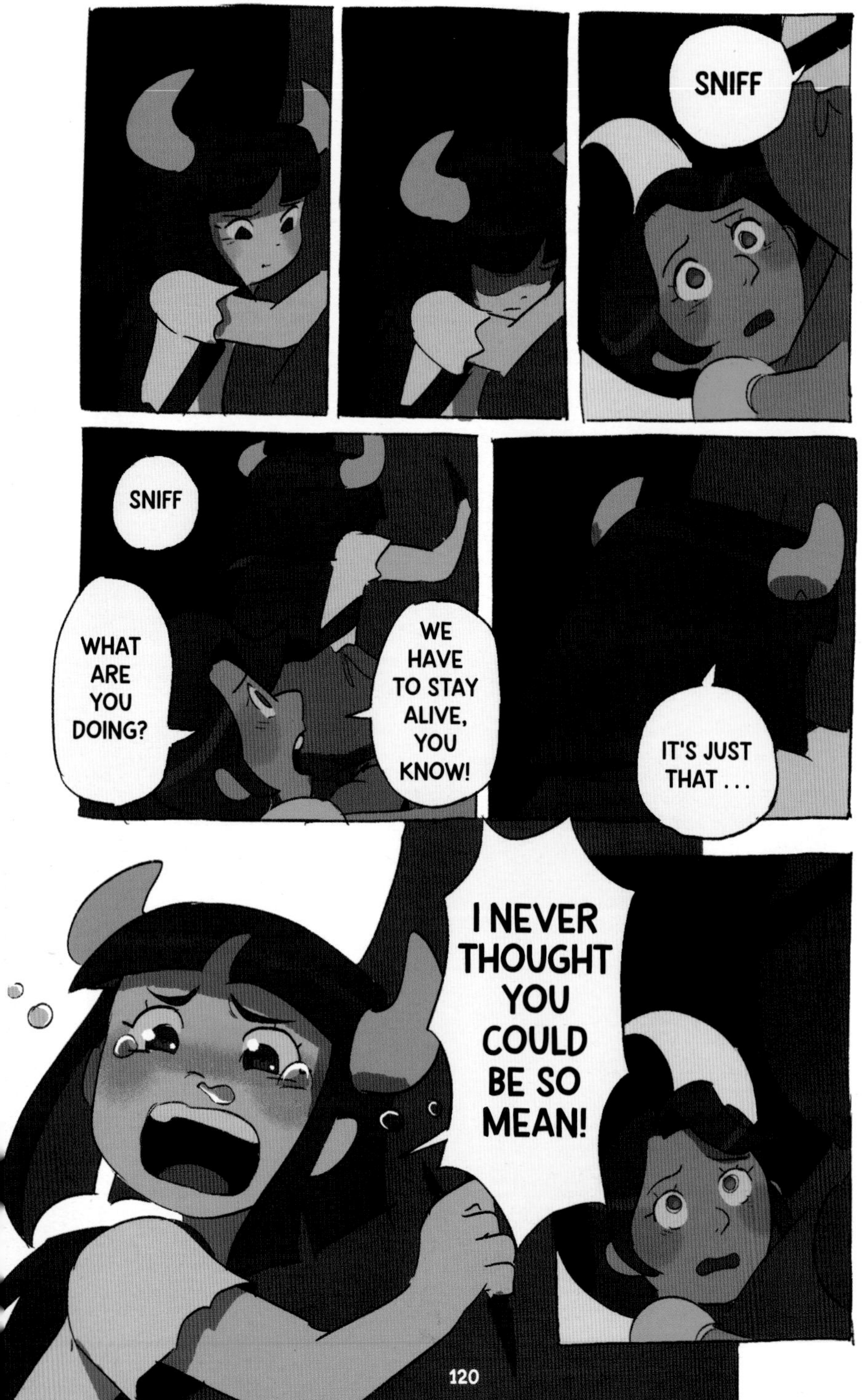
SNIFF
SNIFF
WHAT ARE YOU DOING?
WE HAVE TO STAY ALIVE, YOU KNOW!
IT'S JUST THAT . . .
I NEVER THOUGHT YOU COULD BE SO MEAN!

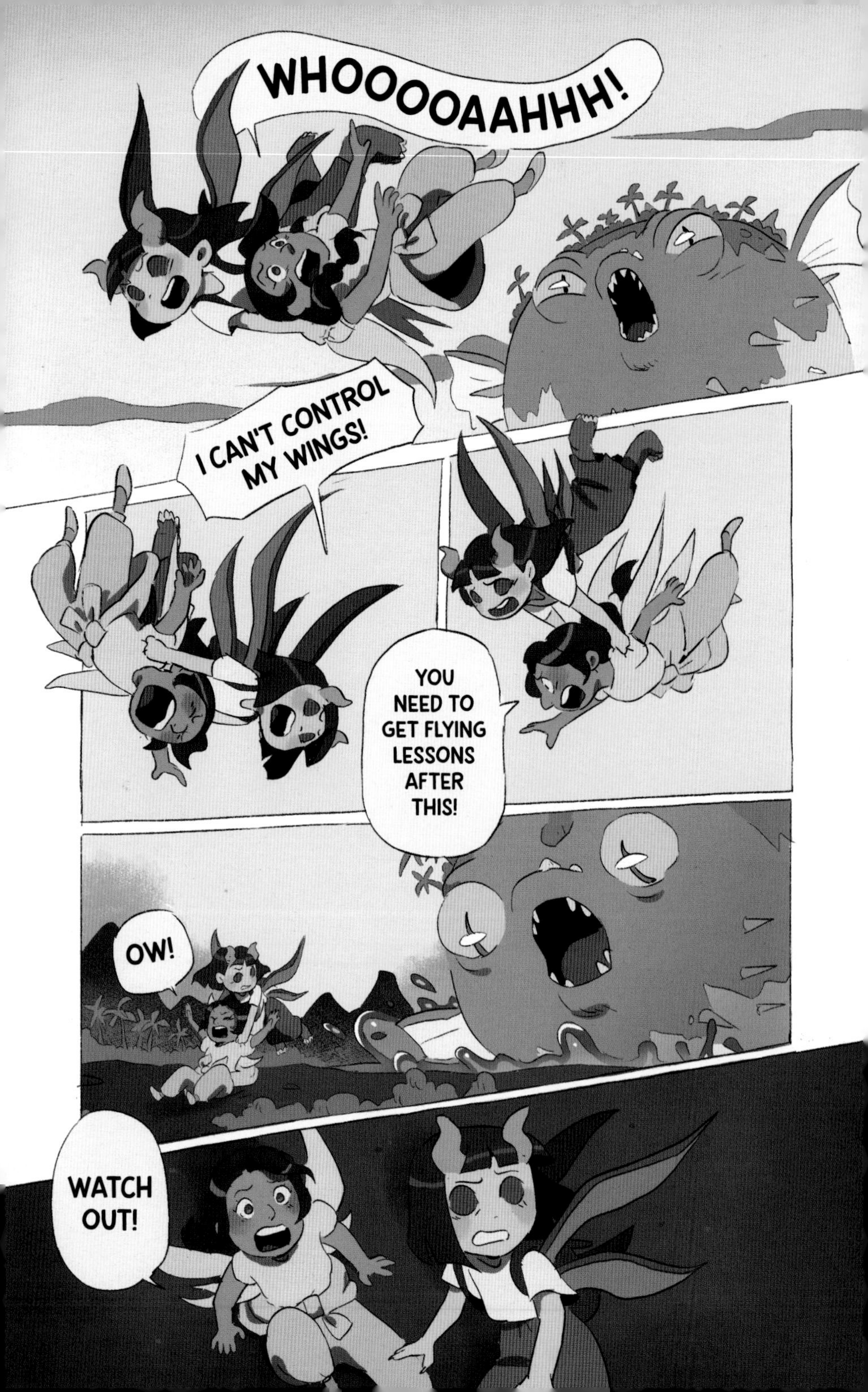
WHOOOOAAHHH!
I CAN'T CONTROL MY WINGS!
YOU NEED TO GET FLYING LESSONS AFTER THIS!
OW!
WATCH OUT!

UHHH . . .

POINT IT AT THAT!

ZZZ zz zz

HEY, YOU OK?

HNG . . .

128

PLUMERIA CITY

BE RIGHT BACK.
GONNA TRASH THIS.

HEY,
I HAVE
BAD
NEWS.

MEANWHILE

SO . . .

ONCE YOU GET THE HANG OF FLYING, YOU GOTTA TEACH ME.

WHAT? NO WAY. YOU SHOULD BE TEACHING **ME** WHEN WE GET YOUR RUBY BACK.

WELL, I'D LIKE TO LEARN TO FLY WITHOUT IT SOMEDAY.

. . .

NOUNA?

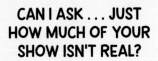
CAN I ASK . . . JUST HOW MUCH OF YOUR SHOW ISN'T REAL?

AND I DON'T MEAN THAT IN A BAD WAY!

I STILL LOVE IT, NO MATTER WHAT. . . .

A LOT OF IT.

MOST FAIRY PARENTS TEACH THEIR KIDS HOW TO FLY WHEN THEY'RE BABIES.

BUT WITH MY BROKEN WING, IT MADE IT HARDER FOR MY MOM TO TEACH ME. ESPECIALLY SINCE SHE'S SO BUSY PROTECTING THE FAIRY WORLD.

THE RUBY CONTAINS SOME OF MY MOM'S POWER. THAT'S HOW IT HELPS ME FLY.

BUT WITHOUT IT, I CAN'T.

HONESTLY, I'M SCARED OF OTHER FAIRIES FINDING OUT THE TRUTH.

BUT IF I COULD JUST LEARN TO FLY BY MYSELF, I WOULDN'T HAVE TO WORRY ABOUT THAT.

WELL, I'M PRETTY SURE THAT THE FAIRIES WOULD STILL LOVE YOU EVEN IF YOU CAN'T FLY.

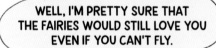

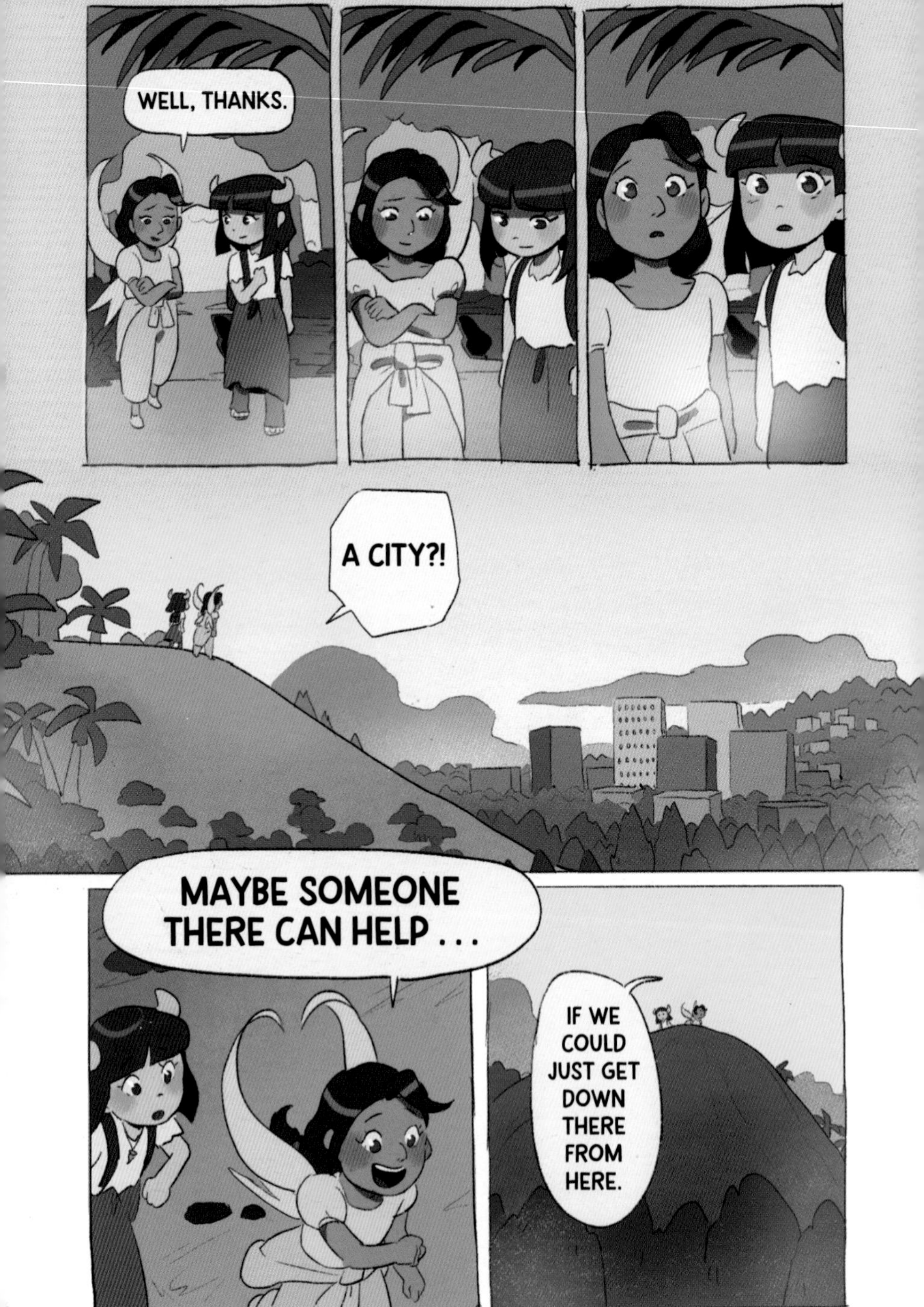
WELL, THANKS.
A CITY?!
MAYBE SOMEONE THERE CAN HELP . . .
IF WE COULD JUST GET DOWN THERE FROM HERE.

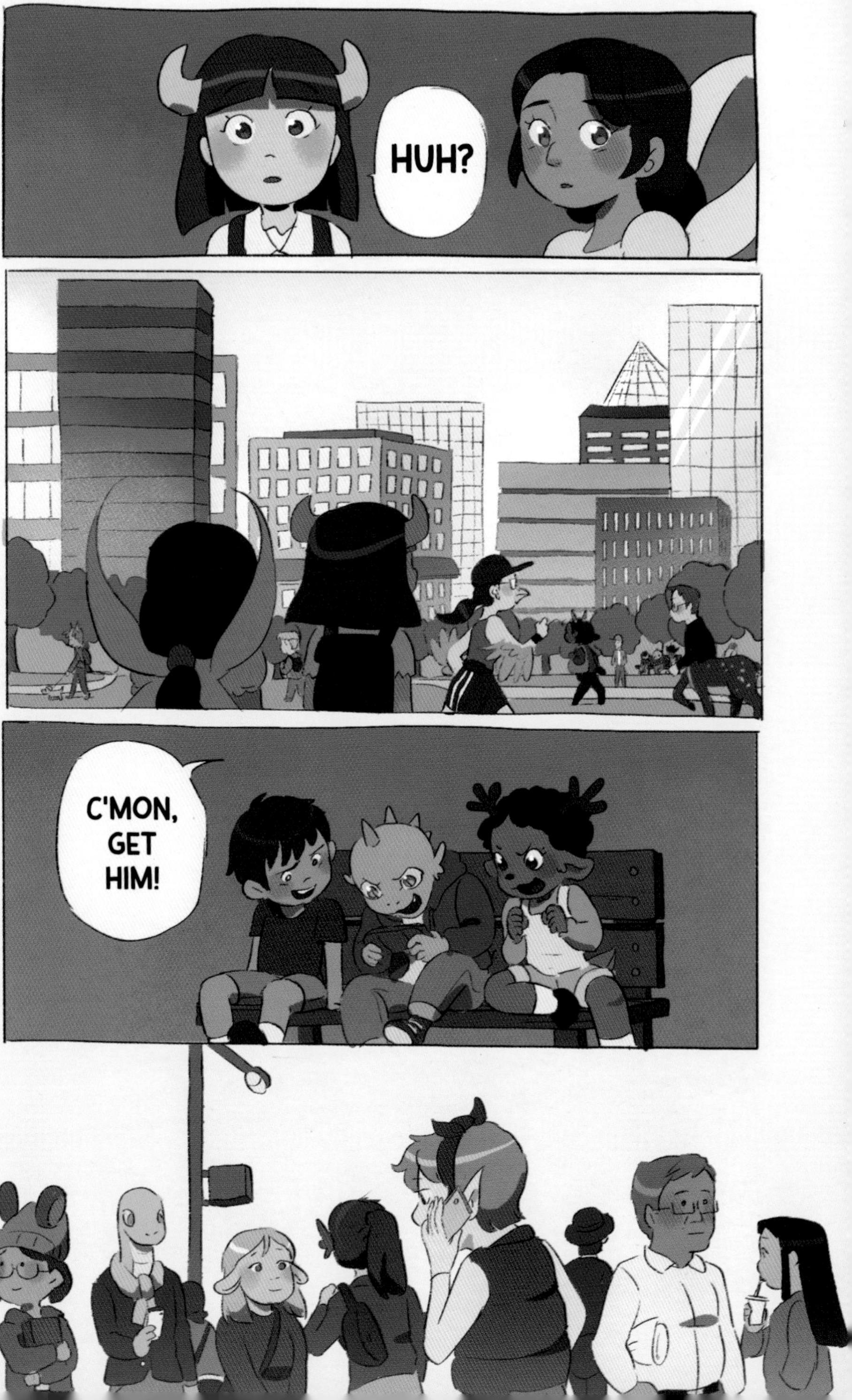
HUH?
C'MON, GET HIM!

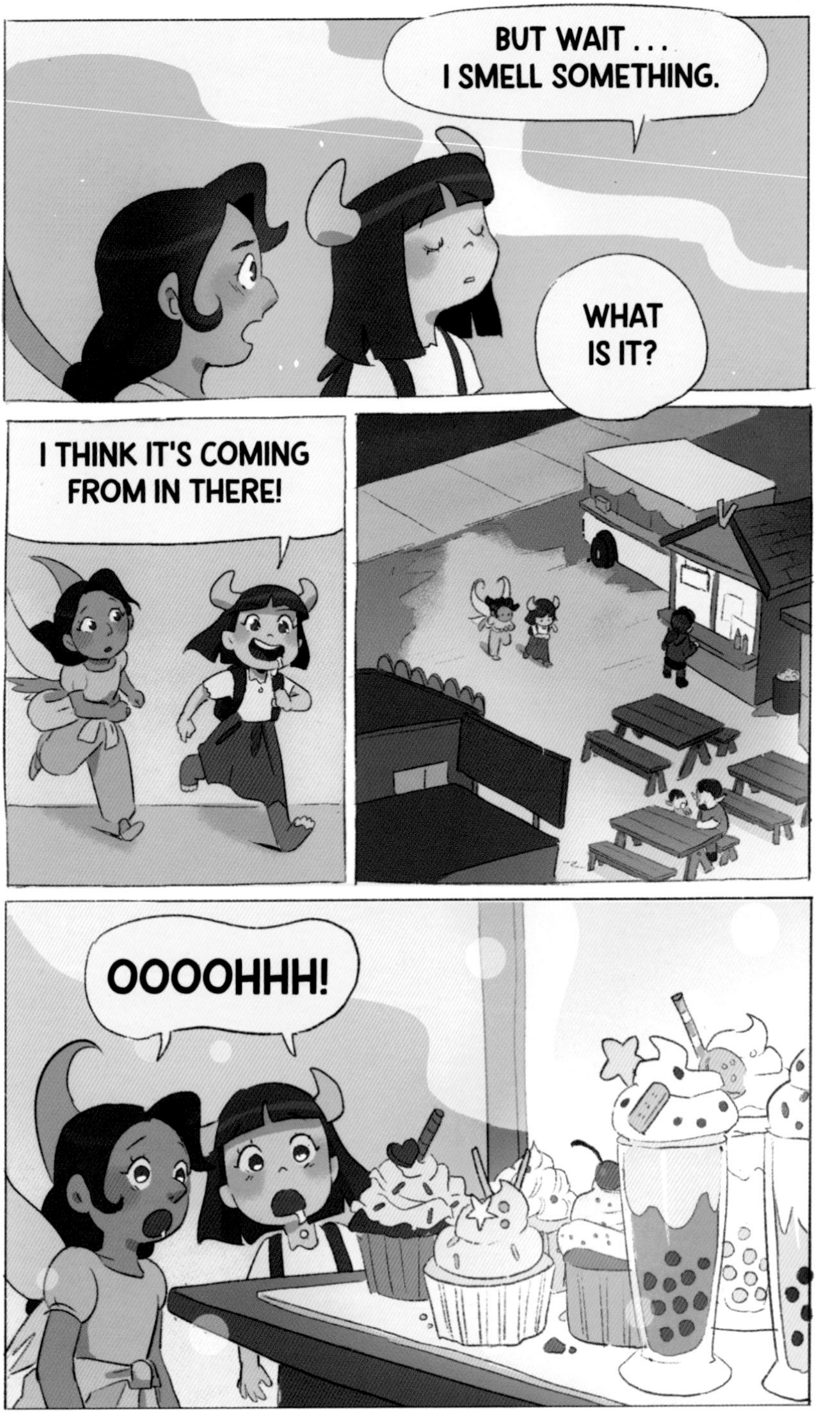
BUT WAIT . . .
I SMELL SOMETHING.
WHAT IS IT?
I THINK IT'S COMING FROM IN THERE!
OOOOHHH!

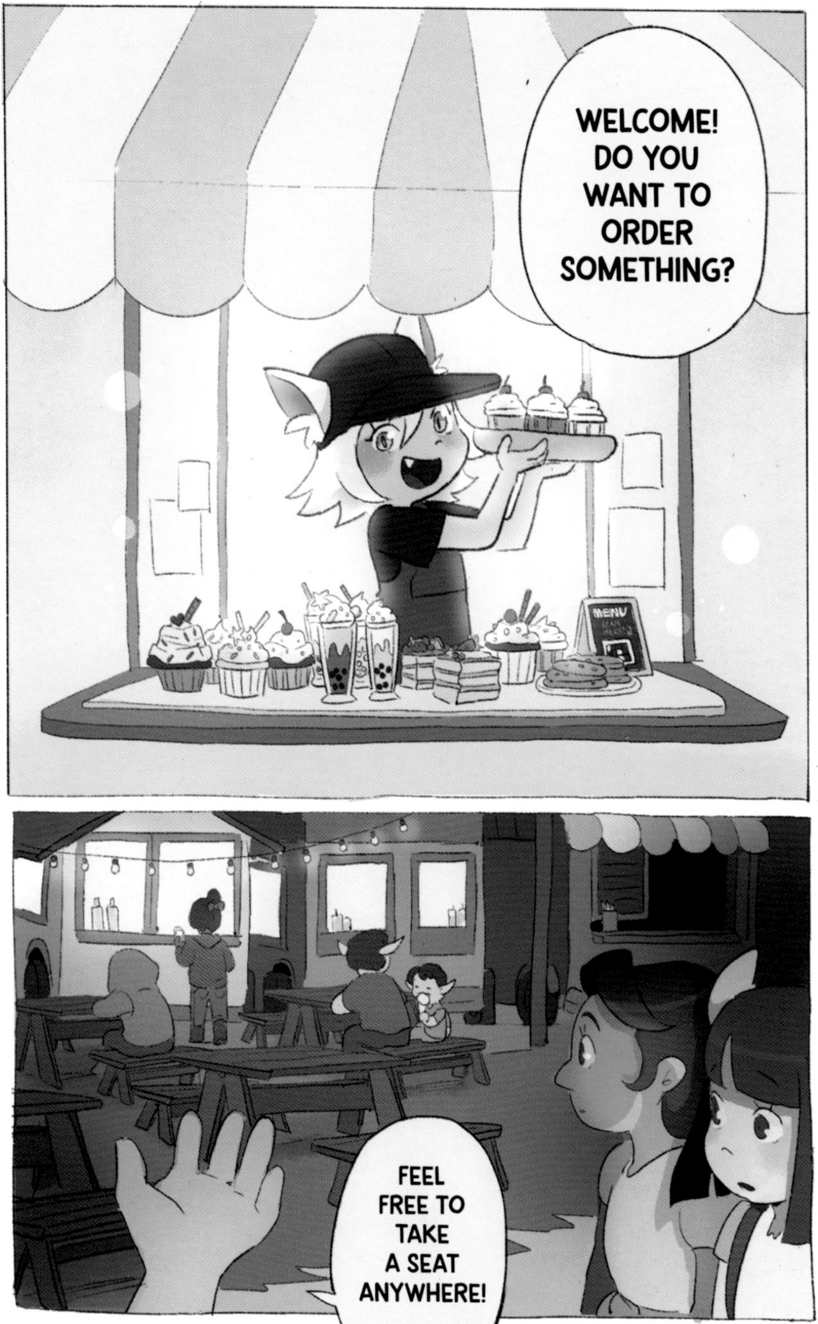
WELCOME! DO YOU WANT TO ORDER SOMETHING?
MENU
FEEL FREE TO TAKE A SEAT ANYWHERE!

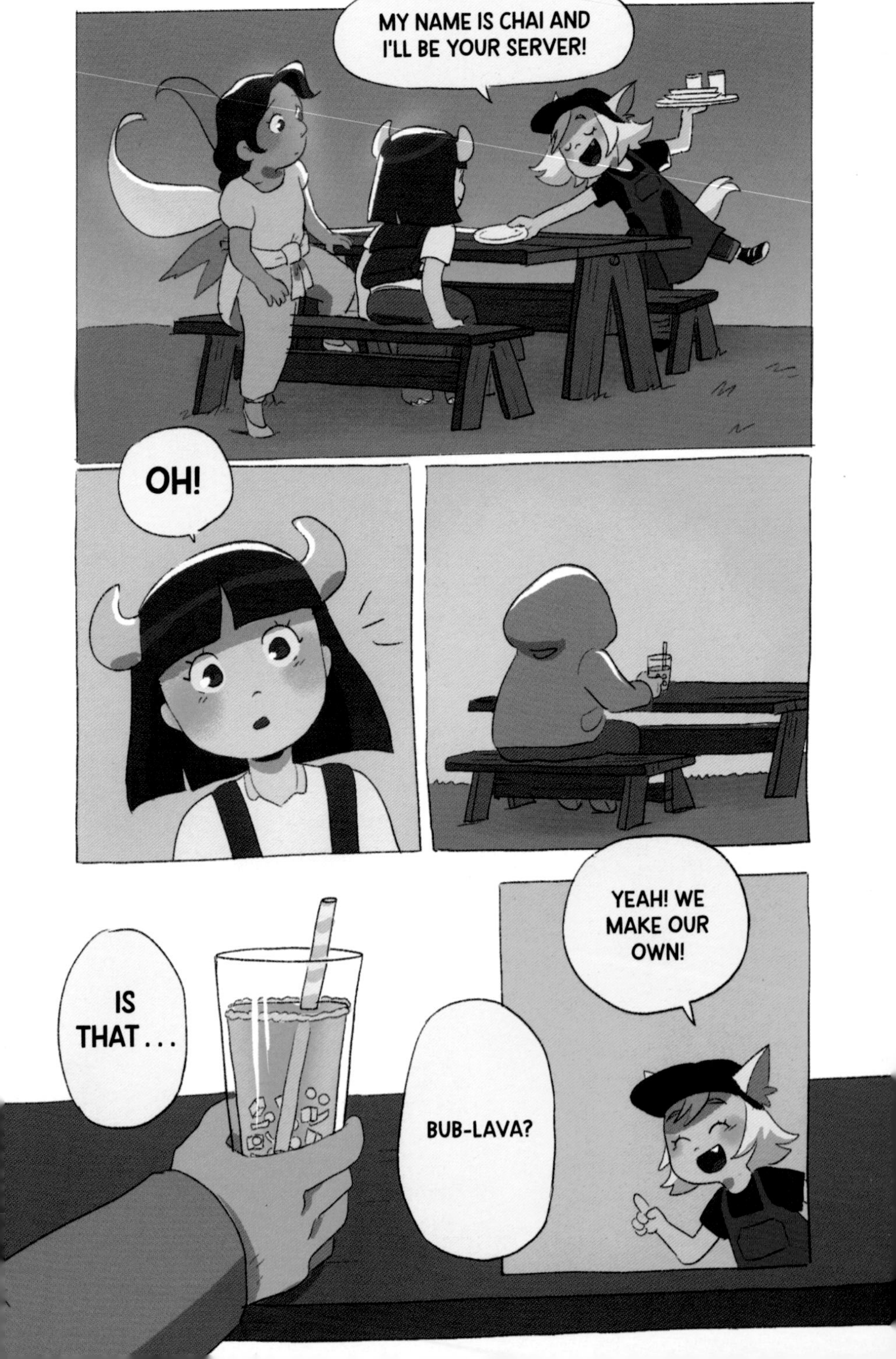
MY NAME IS CHAI AND I'LL BE YOUR SERVER!
OH!
IS THAT . . .
BUB-LAVA?
YEAH! WE MAKE OUR OWN!

WHAT ARE YOU
DOING HERE?!

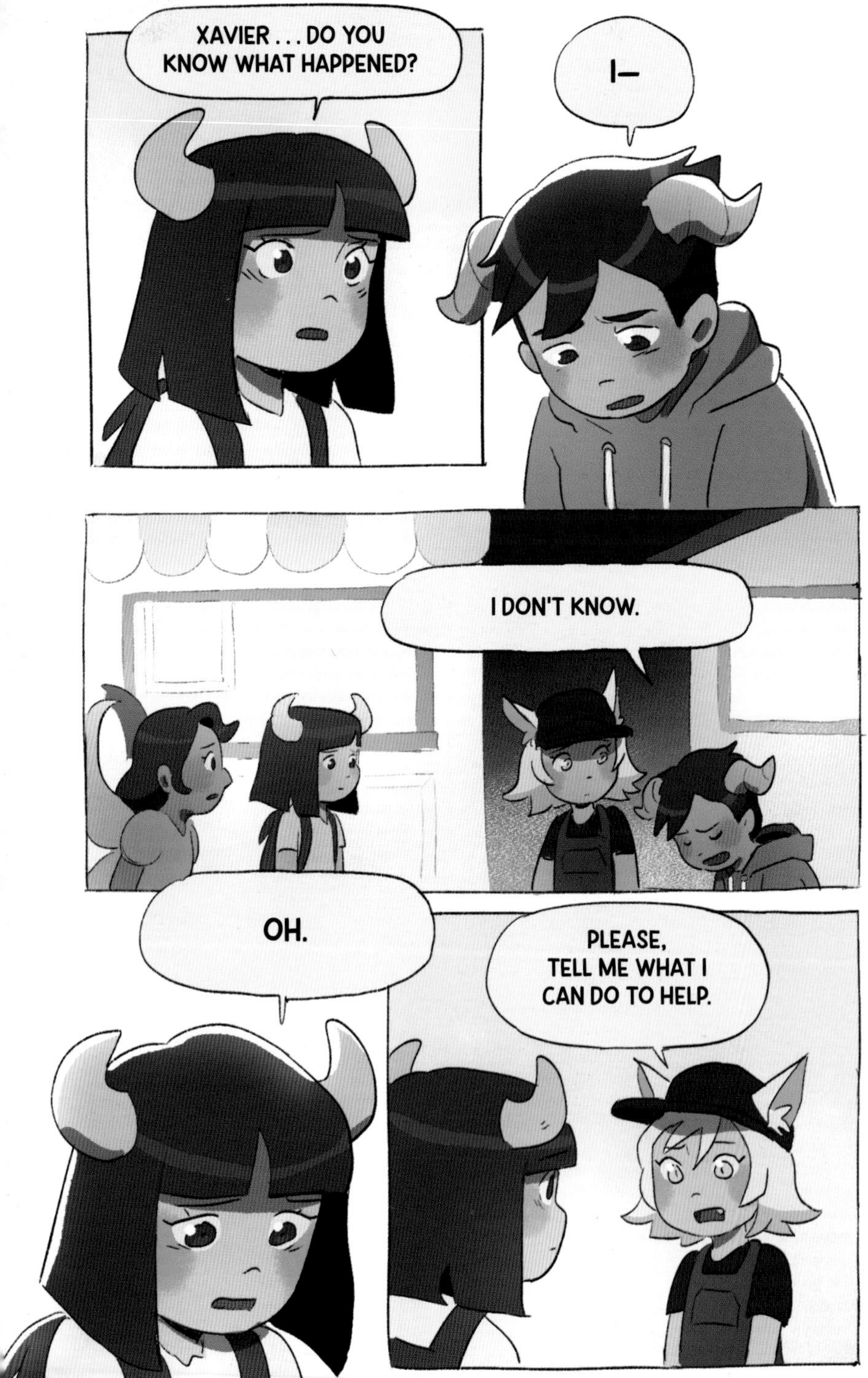
XAVIER . . . DO YOU KNOW WHAT HAPPENED?
I—
I DON'T KNOW.
OH.
PLEASE, TELL ME WHAT I CAN DO TO HELP.

WELL, YOU SEE, THE REASON I RUN THE CAFÉ IS BECAUSE MY FAMILY RELIES ON IT.

WE WERE ALSO FORCED OUT OF OUR HOME.

I'M SO SORRY. HOW DID THAT HAPPEN?

OH NO.

WE'VE NEVER KNOWN FOR SURE. BUT WHAT IF IT WAS THE SAME CAUSE AS MOUNT MAGMA?

WE NEED TO FIND MY RUBY.

I HAVE NO IDEA WHERE IT IS NOW, BUT . . .

IT HAS MAGICAL POWERS THAT MIGHT BE ABLE TO HELP. MEESH THINKS IT COULD SAVE MOUNT MAGMA.

WELL, I'VE NEVER SEEN ONE BEFORE . . .

A . . . FAIRY RUBY?

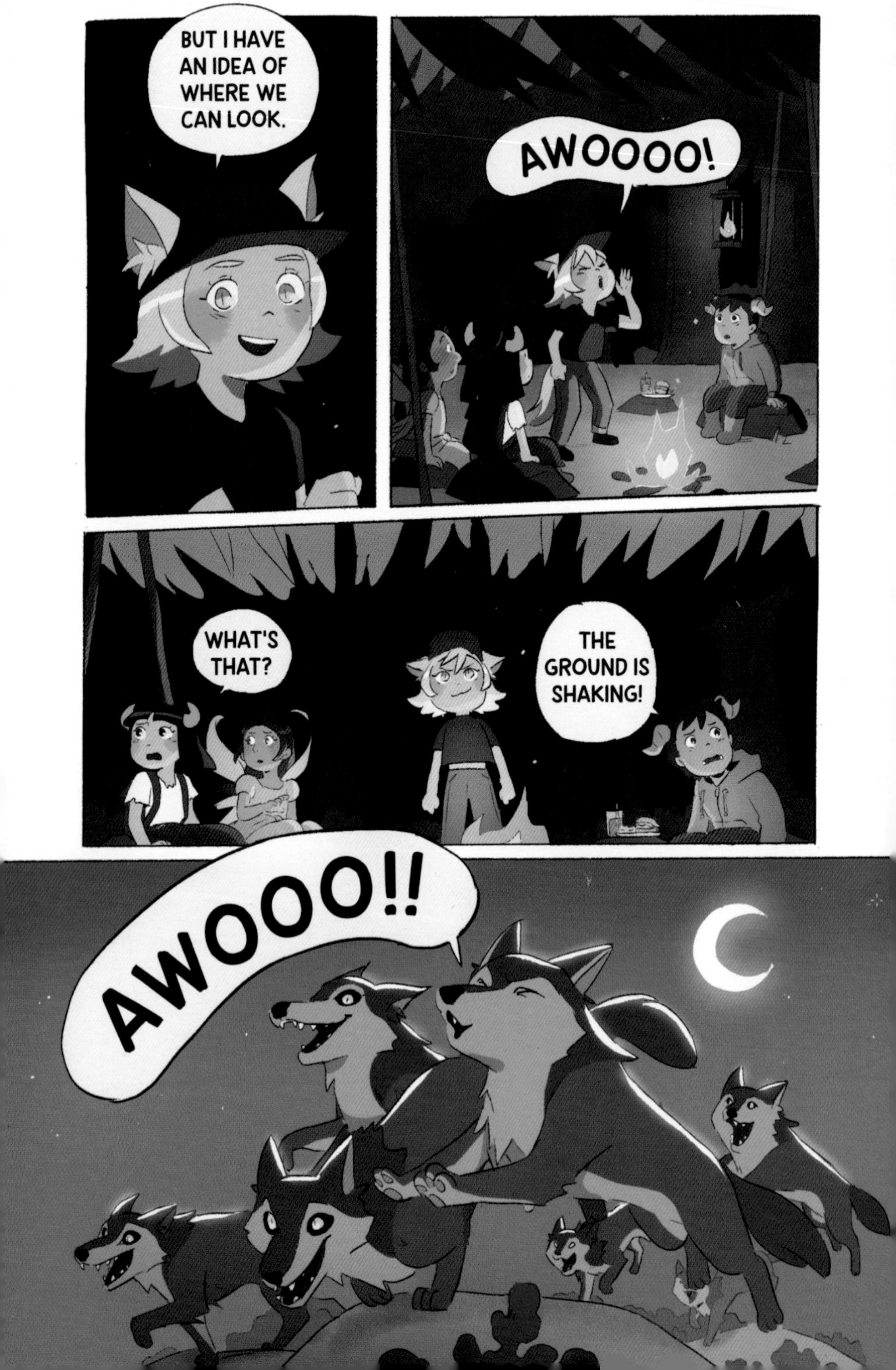
BUT I HAVE AN IDEA OF WHERE WE CAN LOOK.
AWOOOO!
WHAT'S THAT?
THE GROUND IS SHAKING!
AWOOO!!

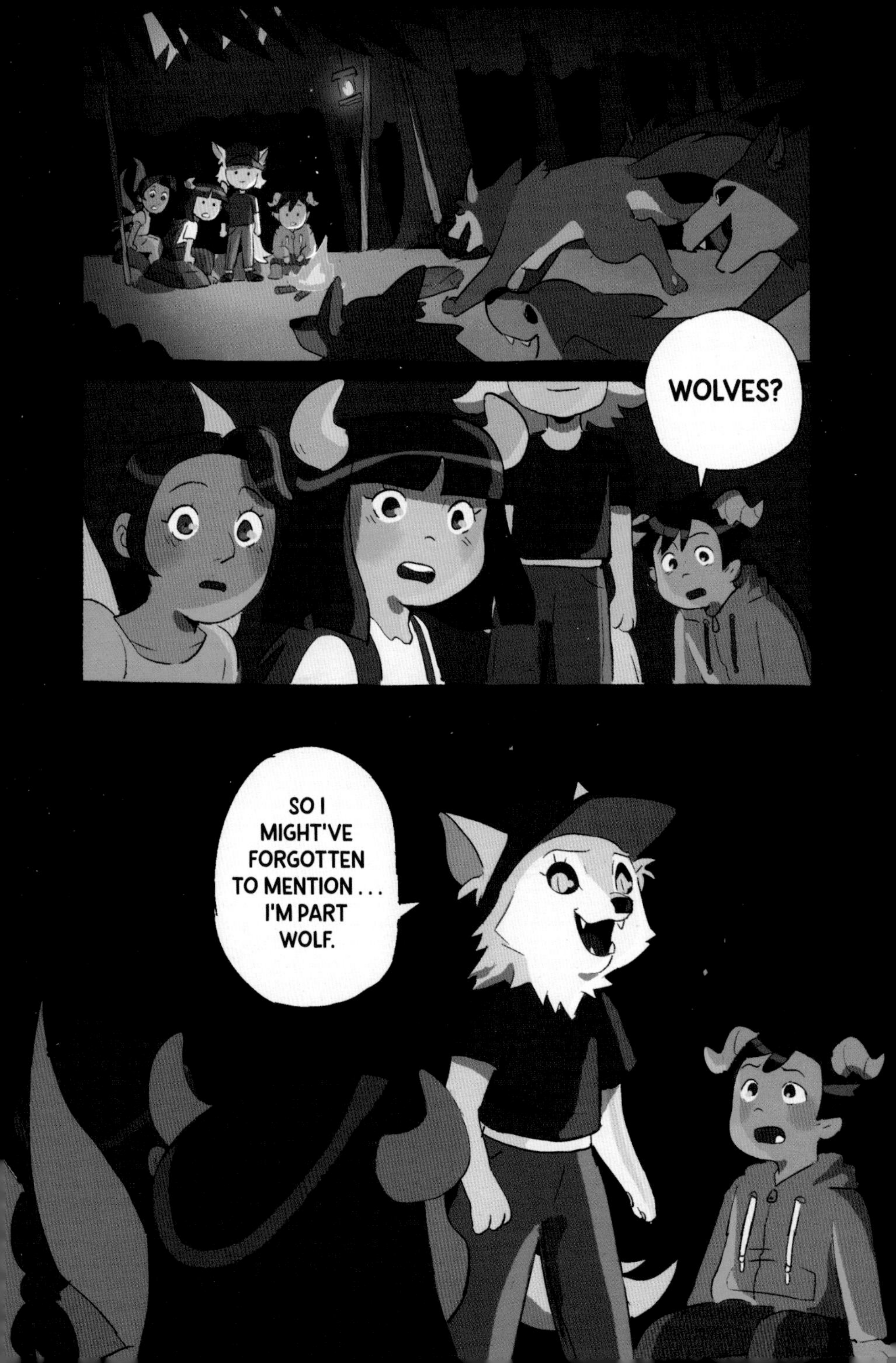
WOLVES?
SO I MIGHT'VE FORGOTTEN TO MENTION . . . I'M PART WOLF.

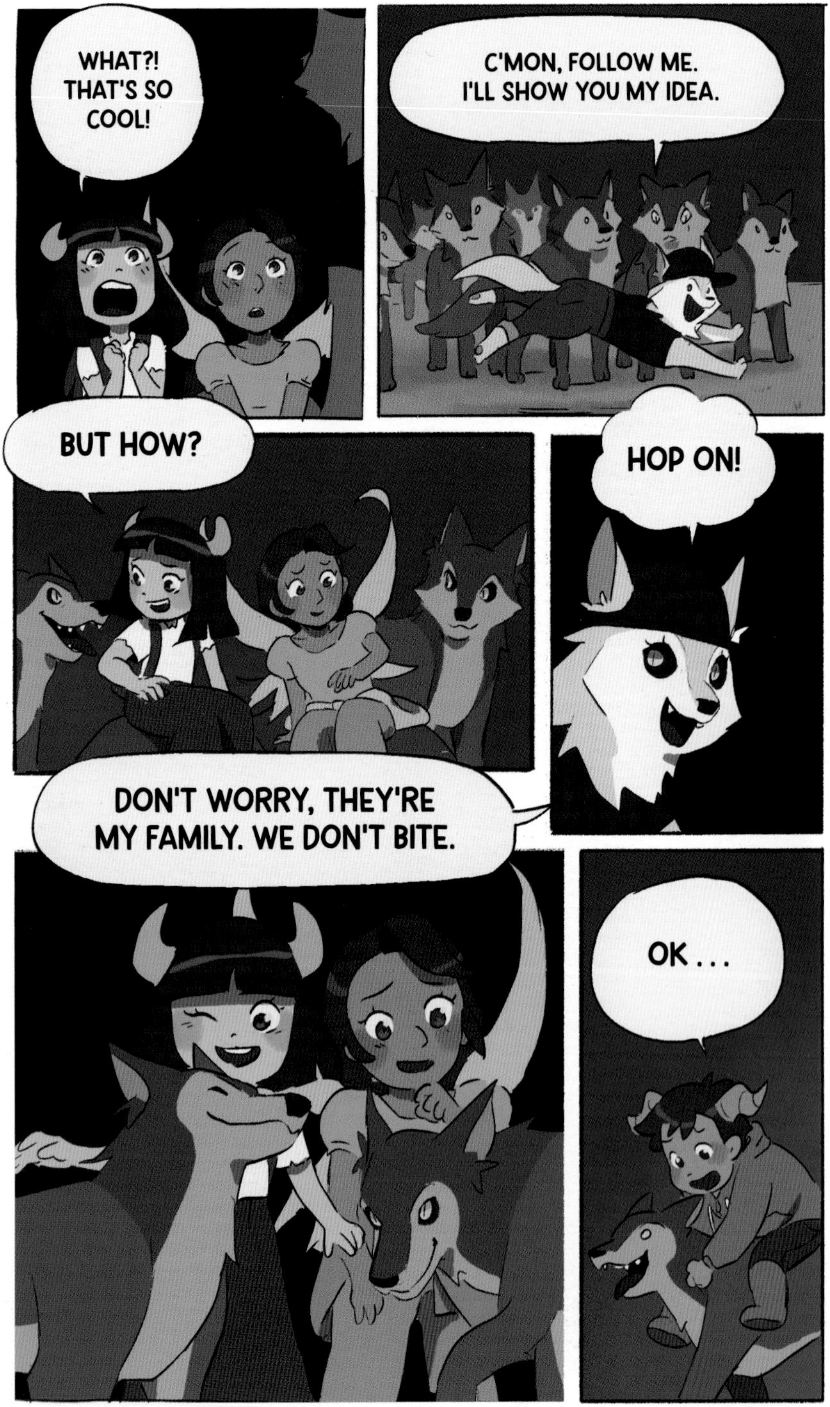
WHAT?! THAT'S SO COOL!
C'MON, FOLLOW ME. I'LL SHOW YOU MY IDEA.
BUT HOW?
HOP ON!
DON'T WORRY, THEY'RE MY FAMILY. WE DON'T BITE.
OK . . .

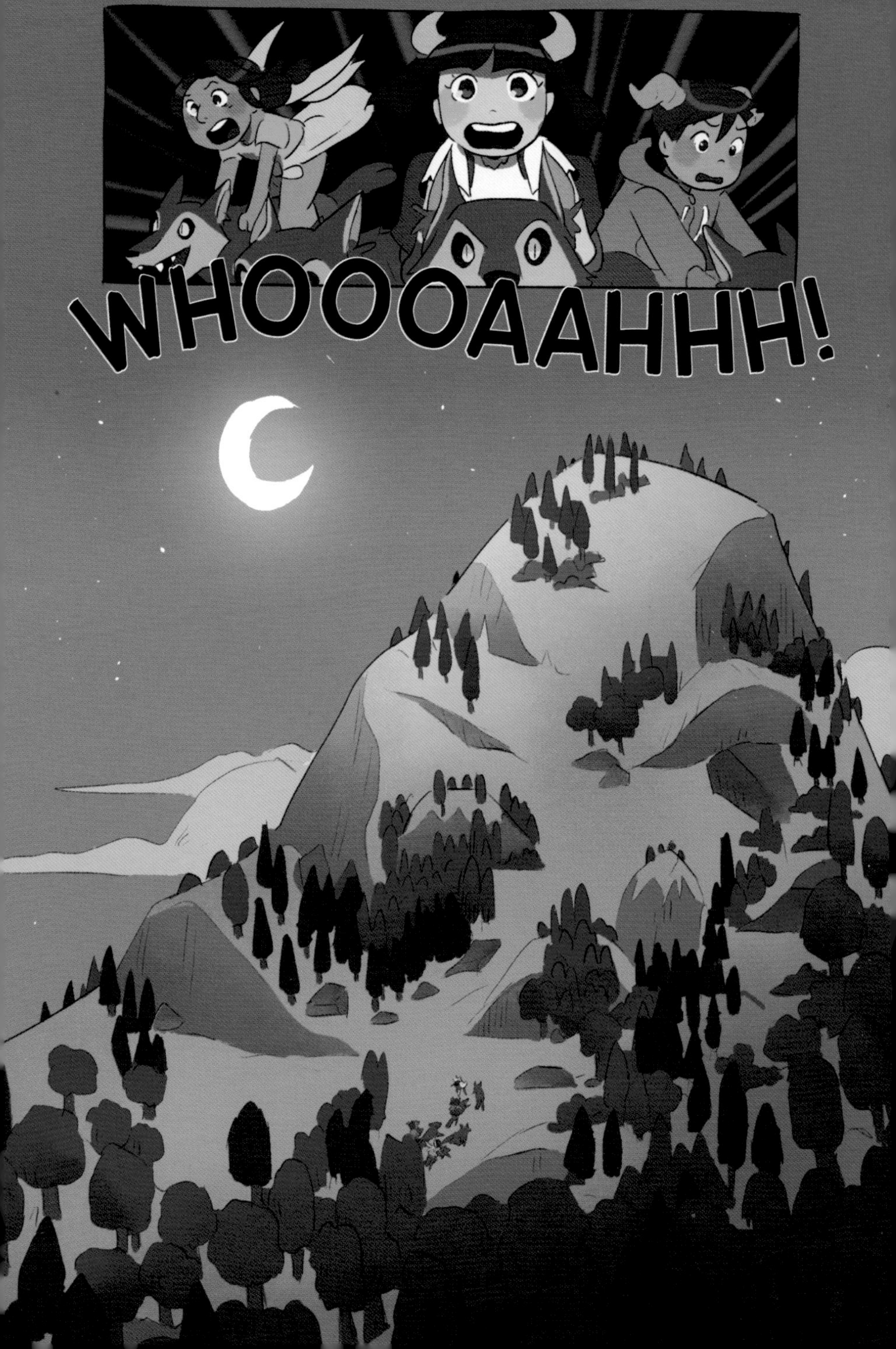
WHOOOAAHHH!

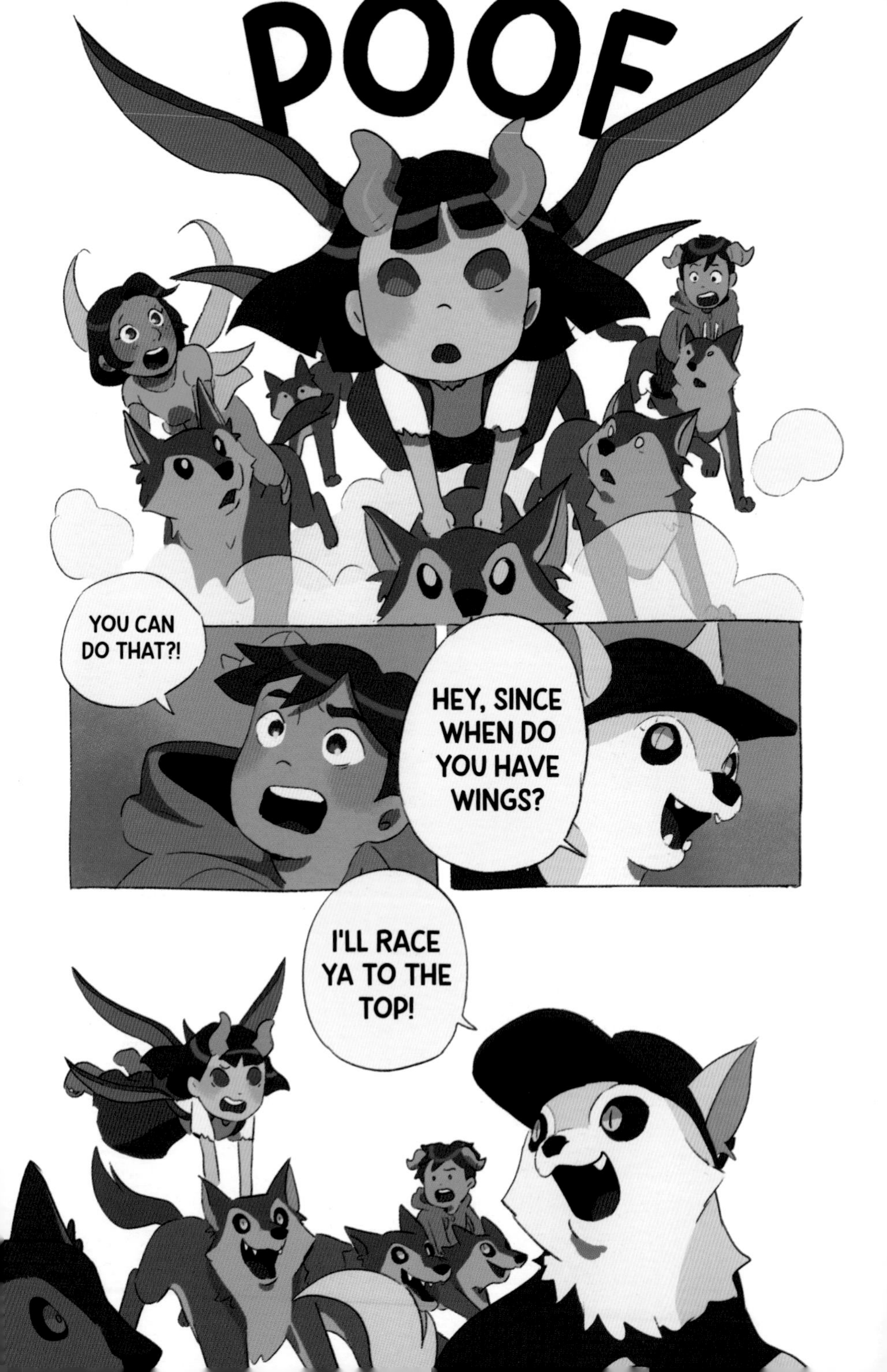
POOF
YOU CAN DO THAT?!
HEY, SINCE WHEN DO YOU HAVE WINGS?
I'LL RACE YA TO THE TOP!

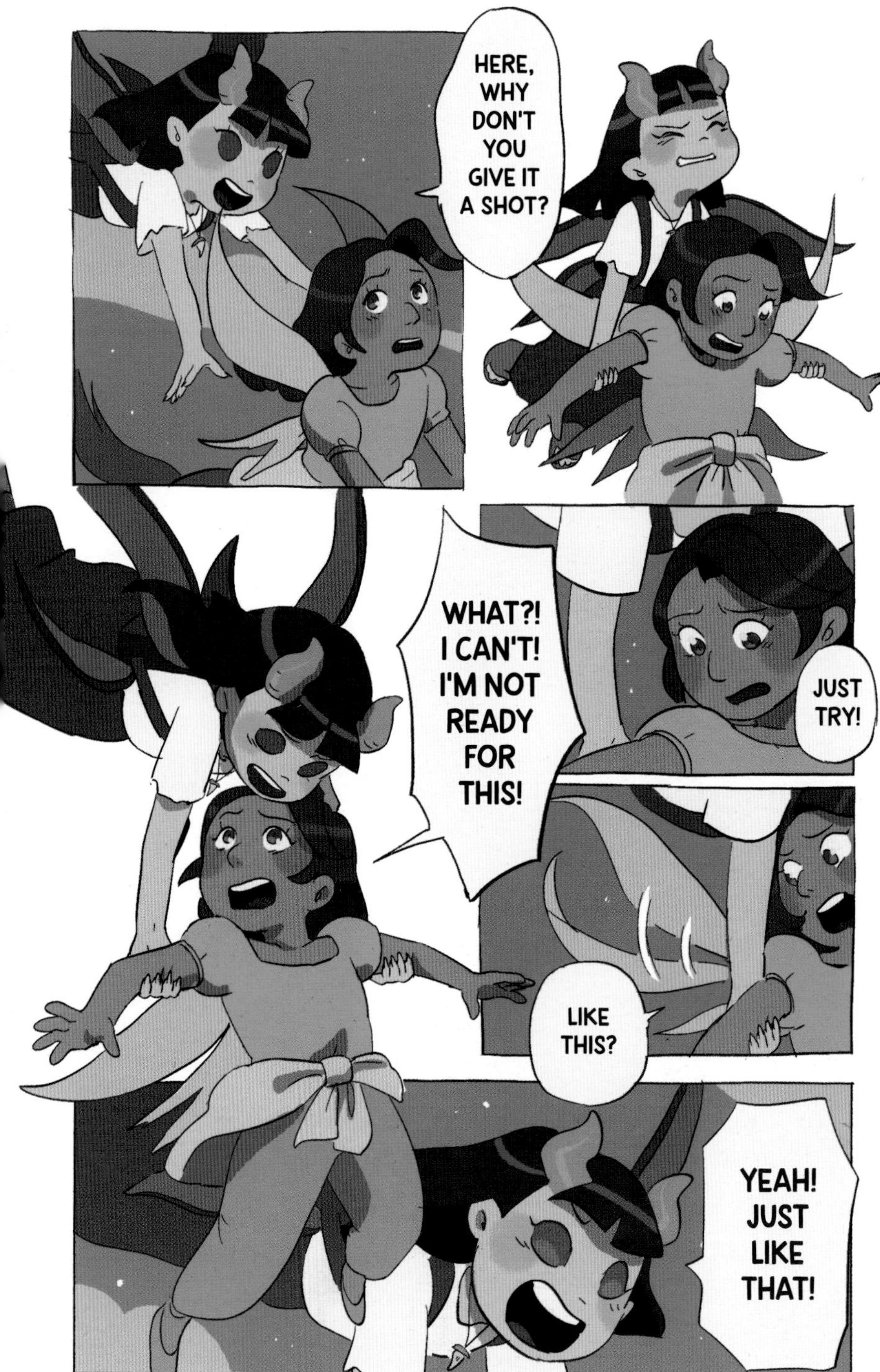
HERE, WHY DON'T YOU GIVE IT A SHOT?
WHAT?! I CAN'T! I'M NOT READY FOR THIS!
JUST TRY!
LIKE THIS?
YEAH! JUST LIKE THAT!

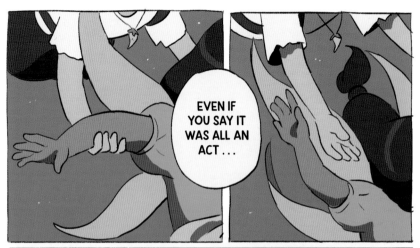

EVEN IF YOU SAY IT WAS ALL AN ACT . . .

TO ME . . .

YOU WERE ALWAYS REAL!

OH MY LAVA . . .

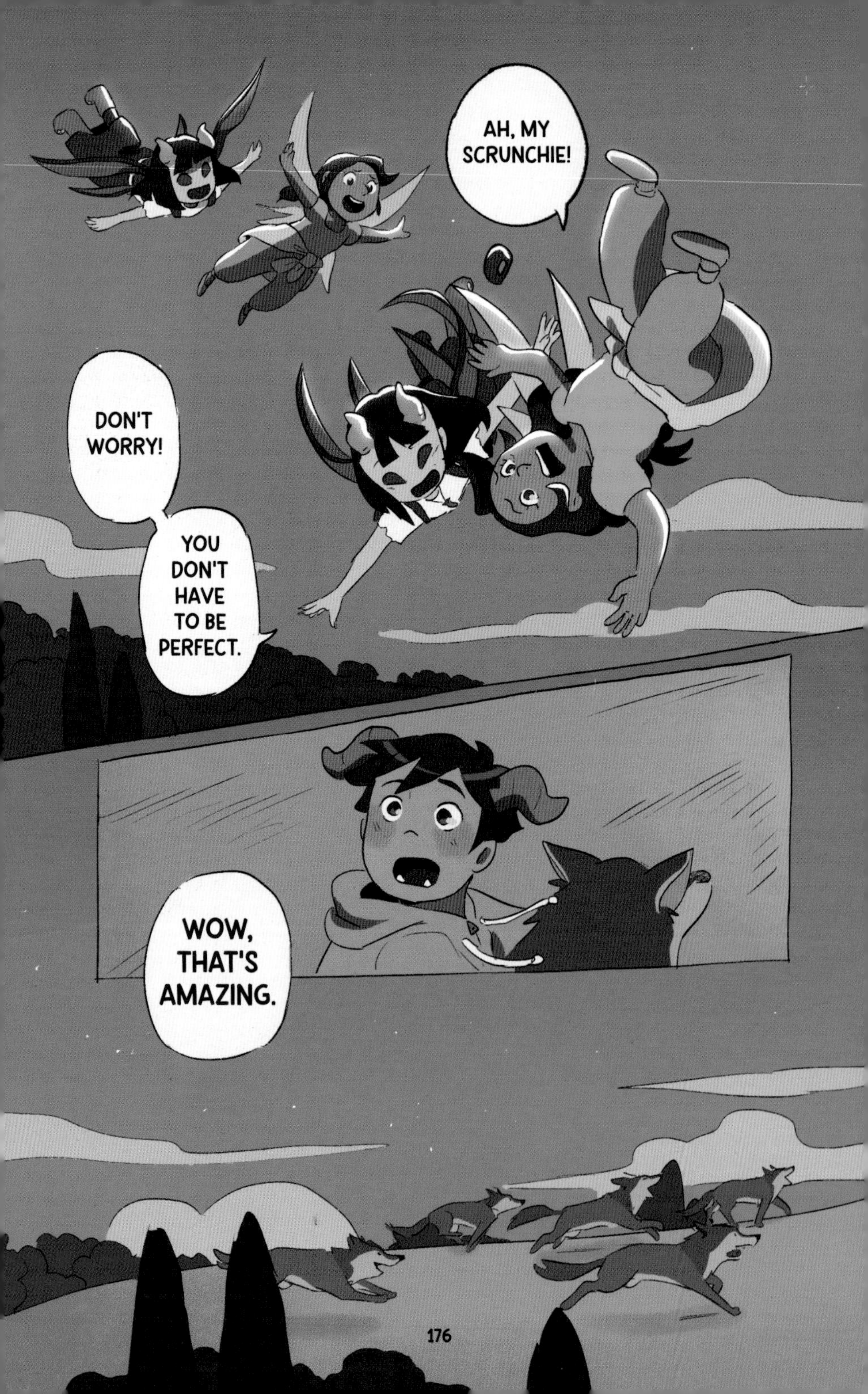
AH, MY SCRUNCHIE!
DON'T WORRY!
YOU DON'T HAVE TO BE PERFECT.
WOW, THAT'S AMAZING.

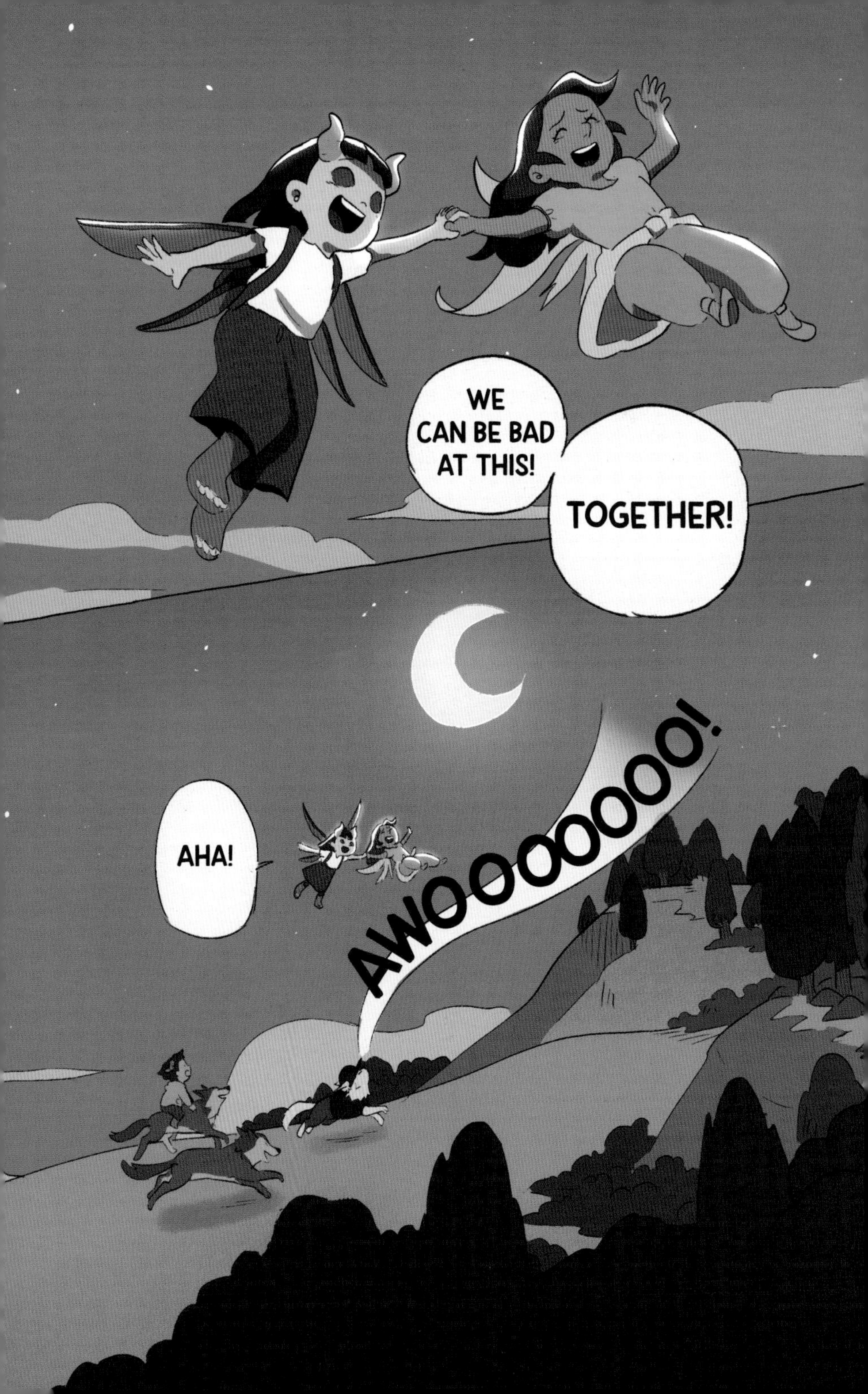
WE CAN BE BAD AT THIS!
TOGETHER!
AHA!
AWOOOOOOOO!

178

SOMETIMES YOU CAN SEE PLUMERIA CITY UP THERE.

AND, UH . . . MOUNT MAGMA. . . .

SORRY, IT'S FOGGIER THAN USUAL TODAY.

179

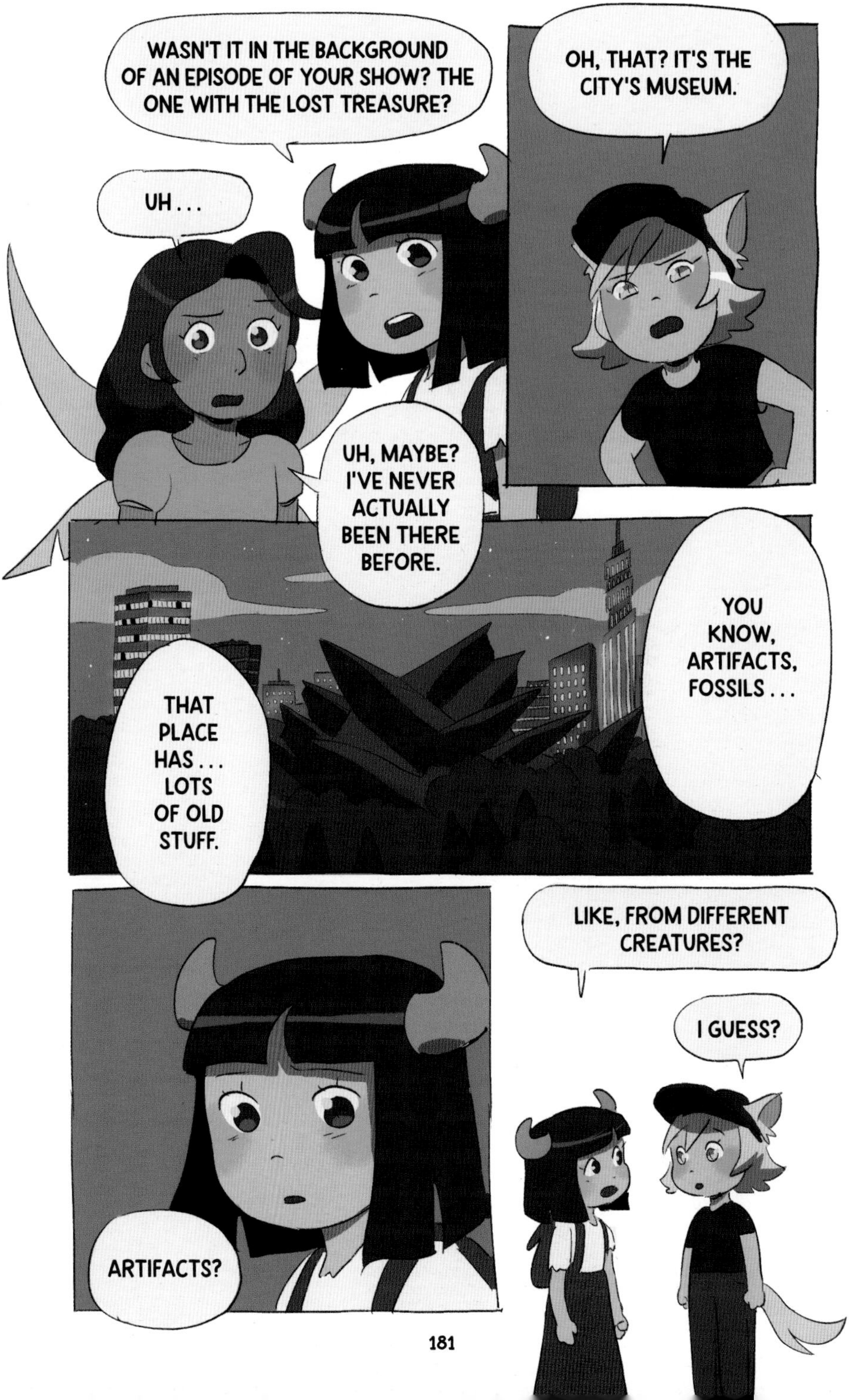
WASN'T IT IN THE BACKGROUND OF AN EPISODE OF YOUR SHOW? THE ONE WITH THE LOST TREASURE?
UH . . .
OH, THAT? IT'S THE CITY'S MUSEUM.
UH, MAYBE? I'VE NEVER ACTUALLY BEEN THERE BEFORE.
YOU KNOW, ARTIFACTS, FOSSILS . . .
THAT PLACE HAS . . . LOTS OF OLD STUFF.
ARTIFACTS?
LIKE, FROM DIFFERENT CREATURES?
I GUESS?

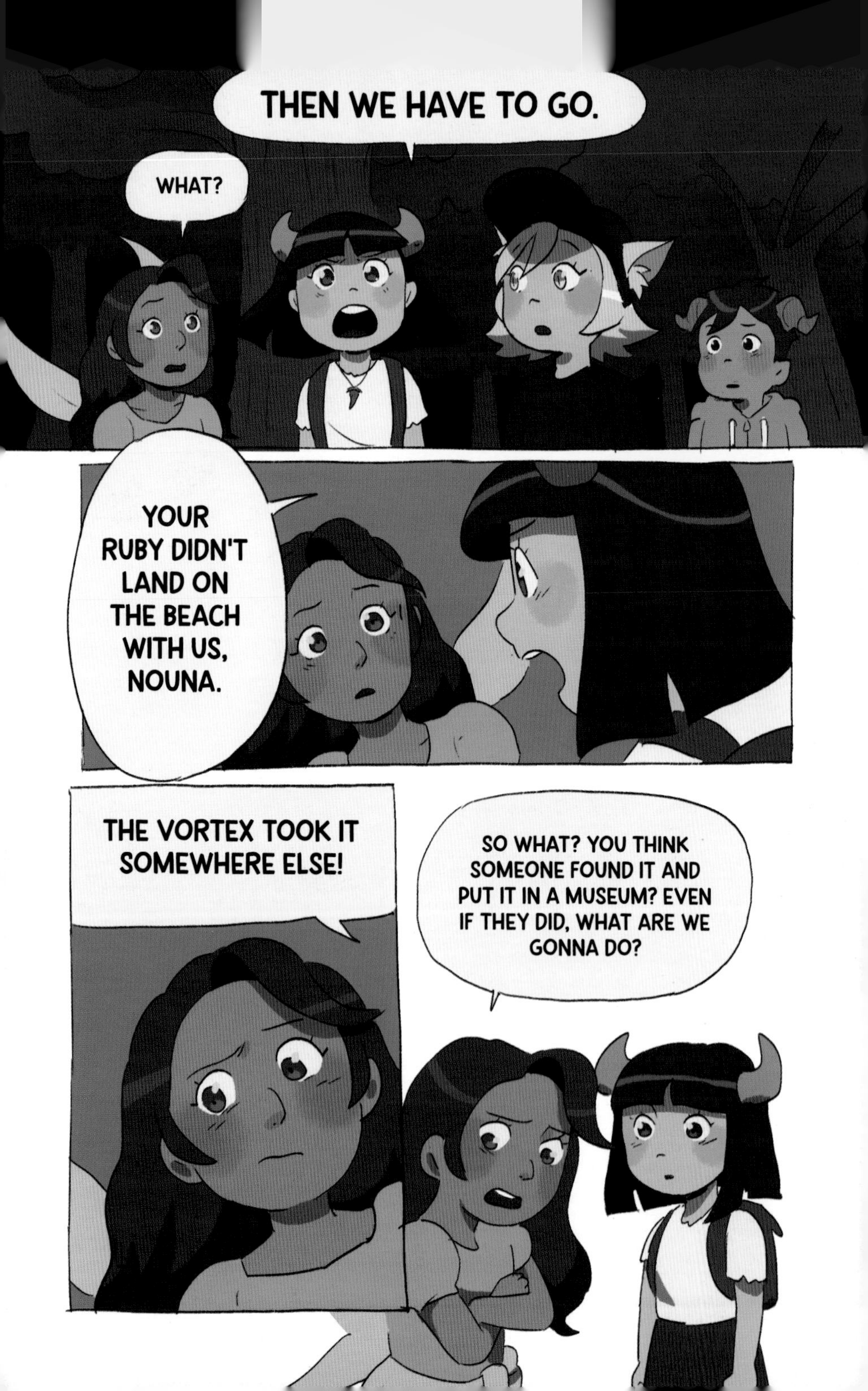
THEN WE HAVE TO GO.
WHAT?
YOUR RUBY DIDN'T LAND ON THE BEACH WITH US, NOUNA.
THE VORTEX TOOK IT SOMEWHERE ELSE!
SO WHAT? YOU THINK SOMEONE FOUND IT AND PUT IT IN A MUSEUM? EVEN IF THEY DID, WHAT ARE WE GONNA DO?

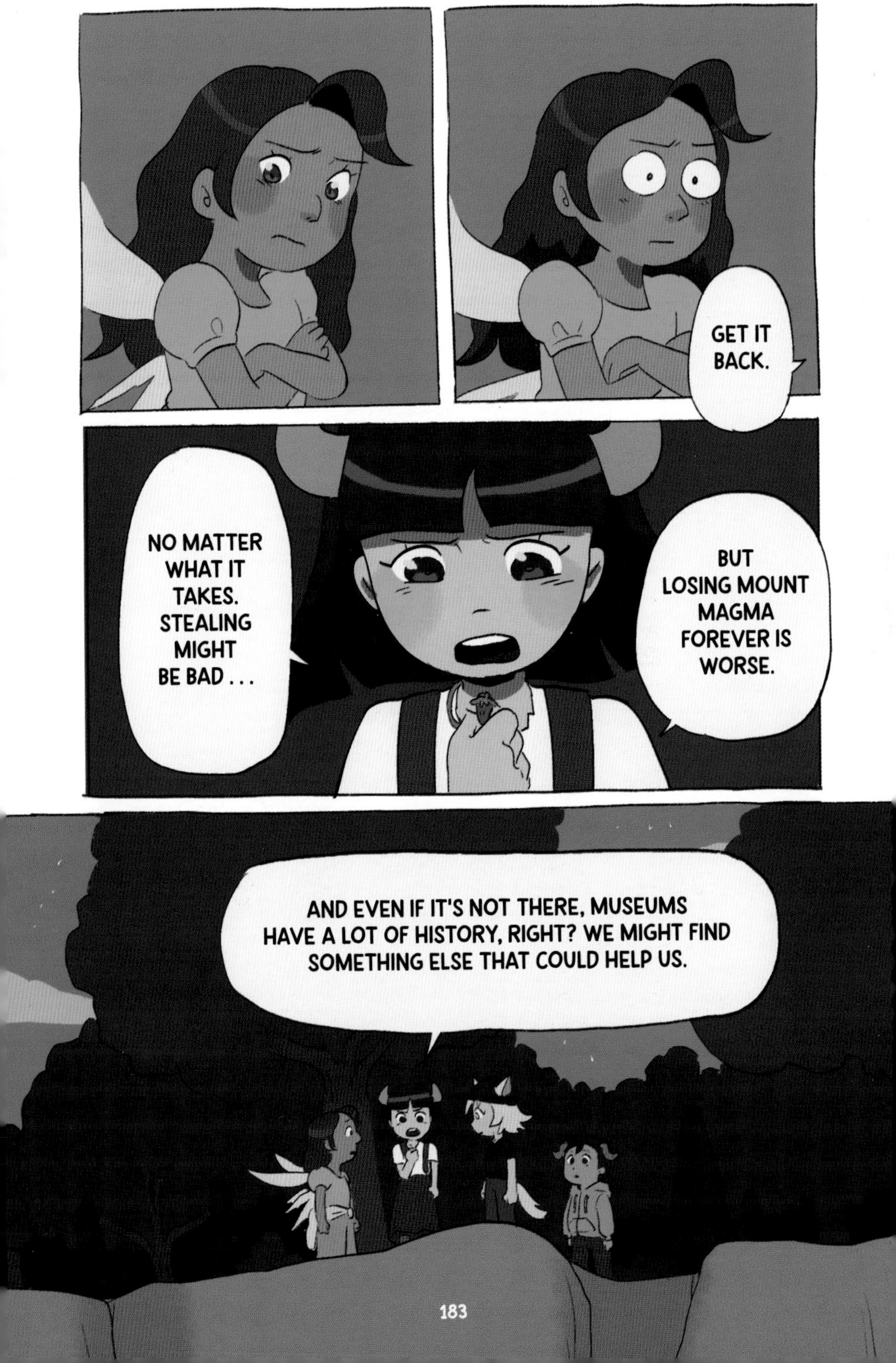
GET IT BACK.
NO MATTER WHAT IT TAKES. STEALING MIGHT BE BAD . . .
BUT LOSING MOUNT MAGMA FOREVER IS WORSE.
AND EVEN IF IT'S NOT THERE, MUSEUMS HAVE A LOT OF HISTORY, RIGHT? WE MIGHT FIND SOMETHING ELSE THAT COULD HELP US.

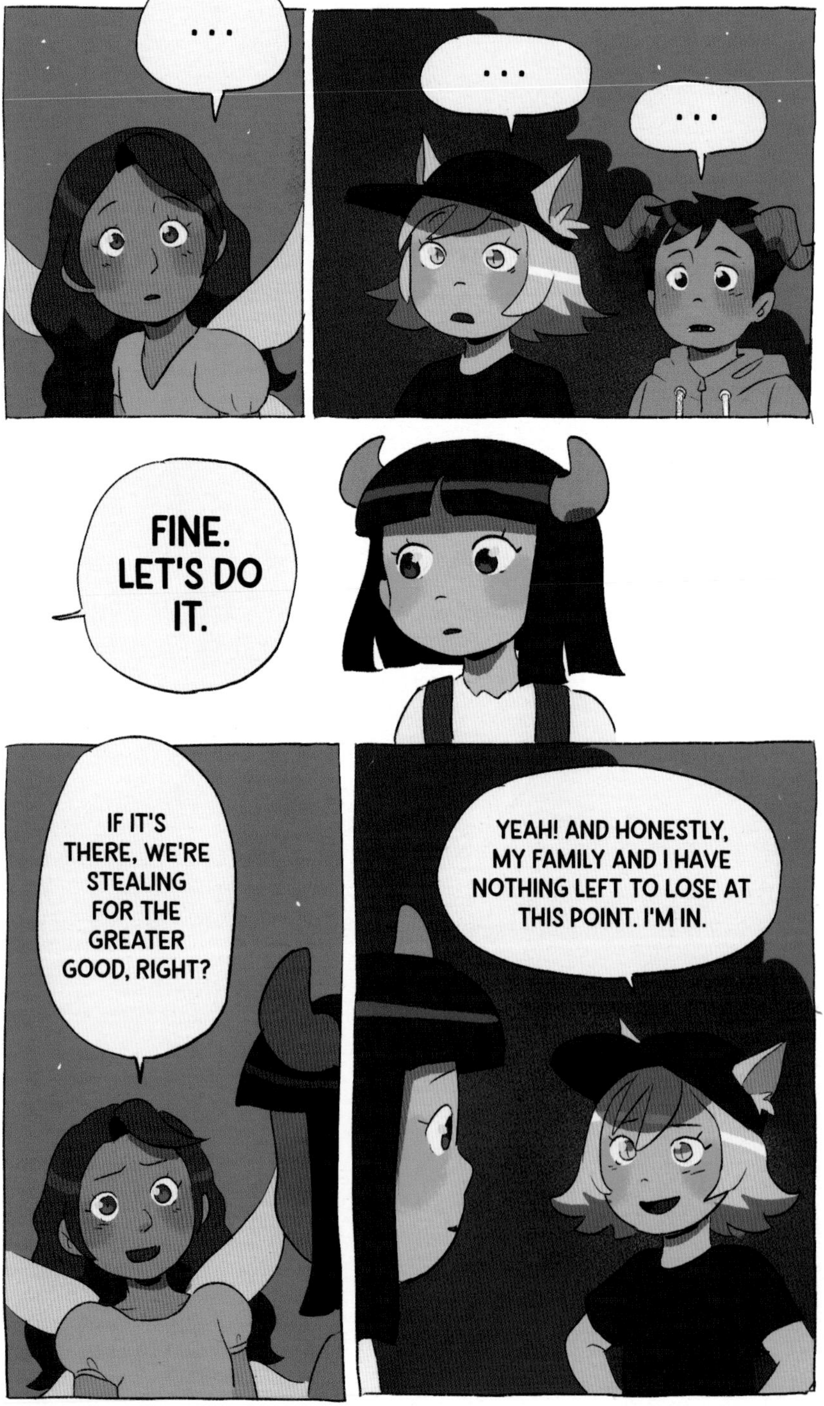
...
...
...
FINE. LET'S DO IT.
IF IT'S THERE, WE'RE STEALING FOR THE GREATER GOOD, RIGHT?
YEAH! AND HONESTLY, MY FAMILY AND I HAVE NOTHING LEFT TO LOSE AT THIS POINT. I'M IN.

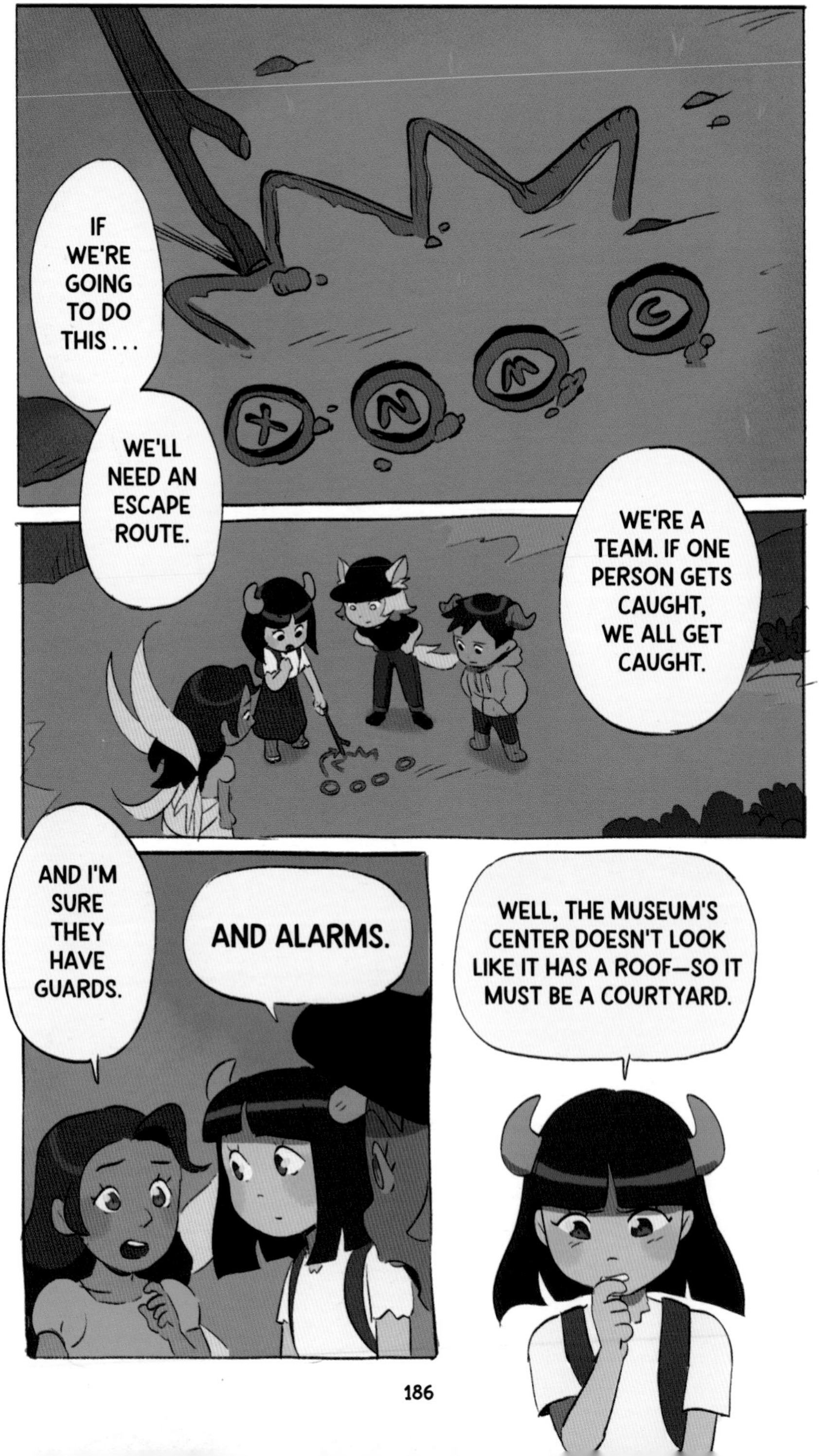
IF WE'RE GOING TO DO THIS . . .
WE'LL NEED AN ESCAPE ROUTE.
WE'RE A TEAM. IF ONE PERSON GETS CAUGHT, WE ALL GET CAUGHT.
AND I'M SURE THEY HAVE GUARDS.
AND ALARMS.
WELL, THE MUSEUM'S CENTER DOESN'T LOOK LIKE IT HAS A ROOF—SO IT MUST BE A COURTYARD.

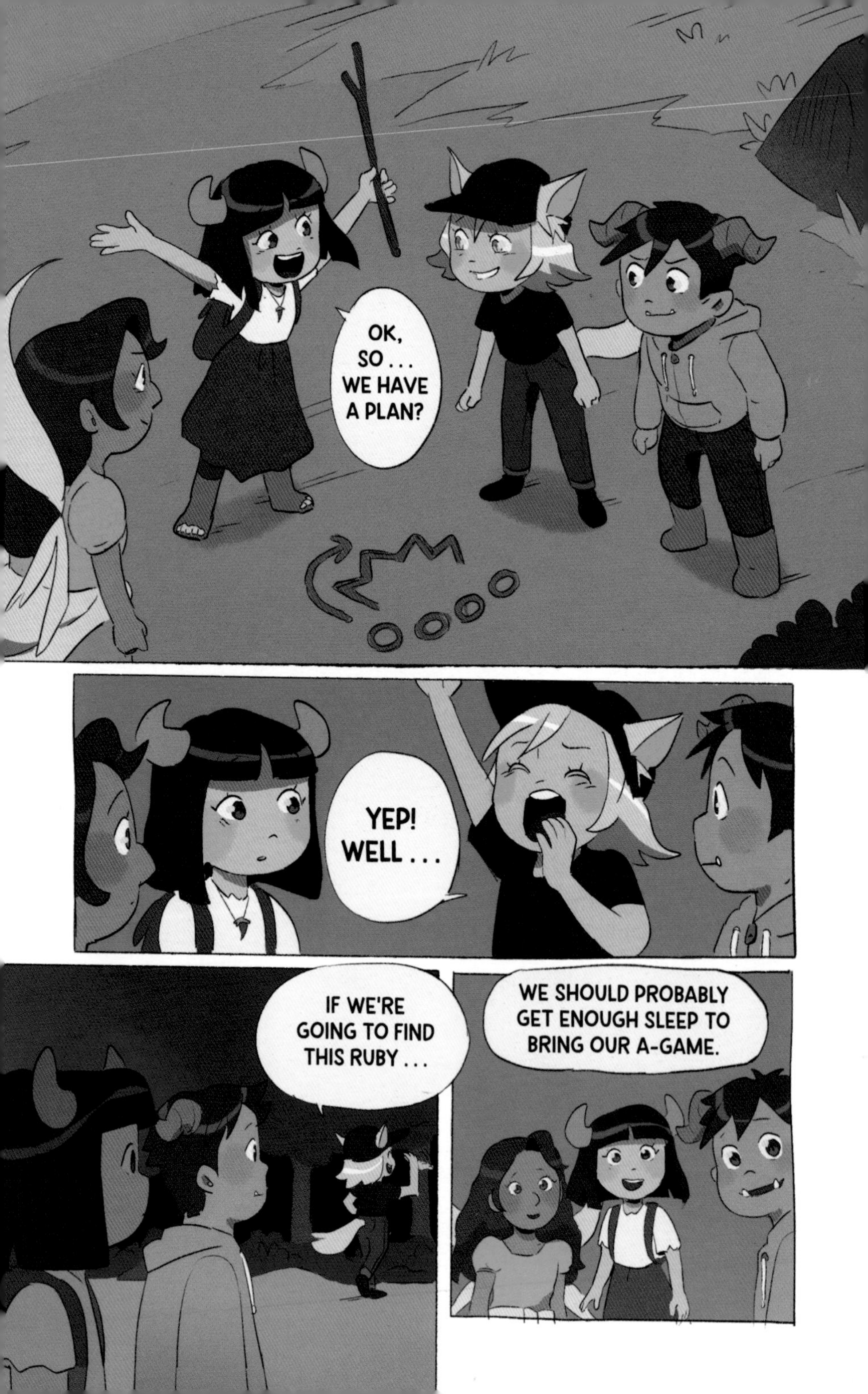
OK, SO . . . WE HAVE A PLAN?
YEP! WELL . . .
IF WE'RE GOING TO FIND THIS RUBY . . .
WE SHOULD PROBABLY GET ENOUGH SLEEP TO BRING OUR A-GAME.

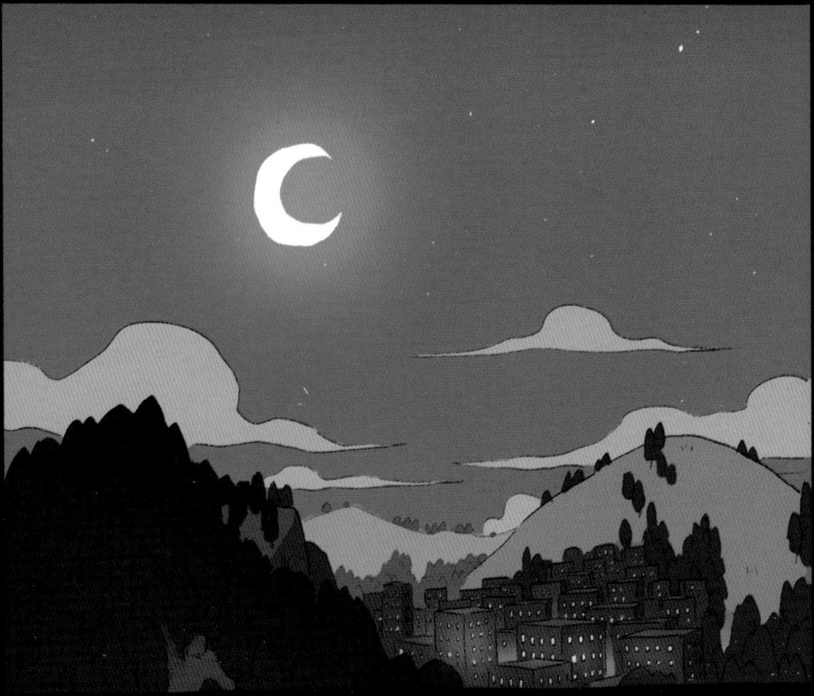

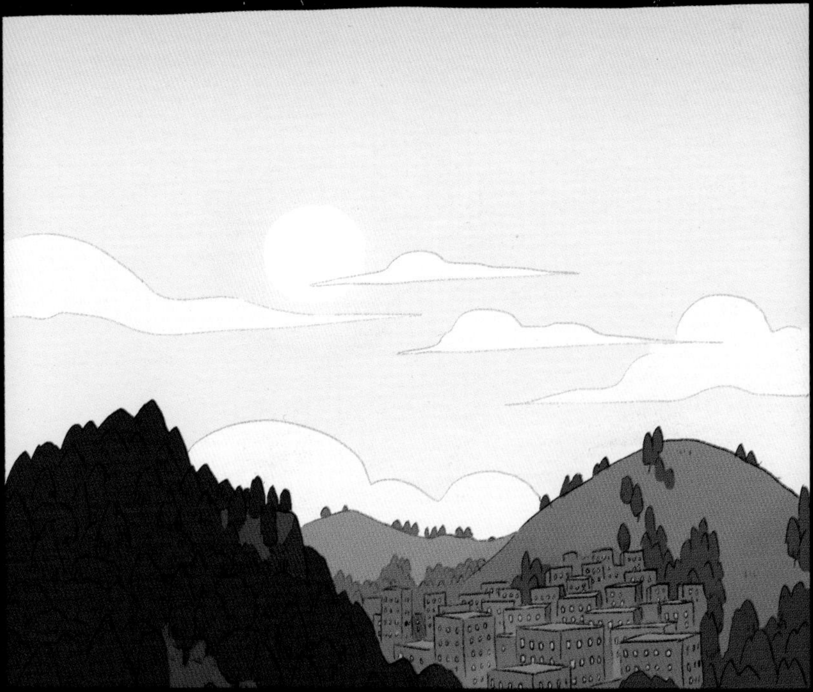

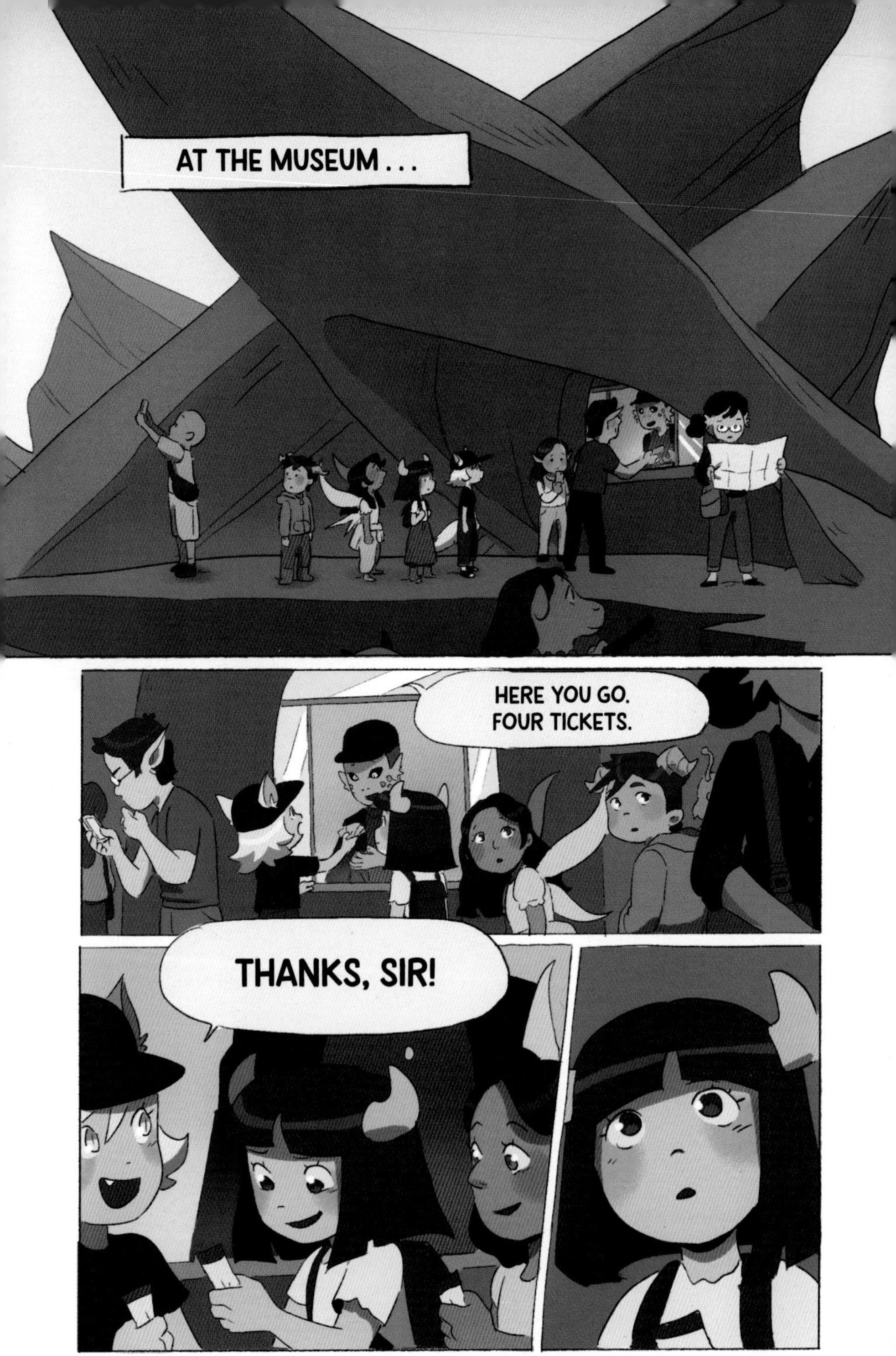
AT THE MUSEUM . . .
HERE YOU GO. FOUR TICKETS.
THANKS, SIR!

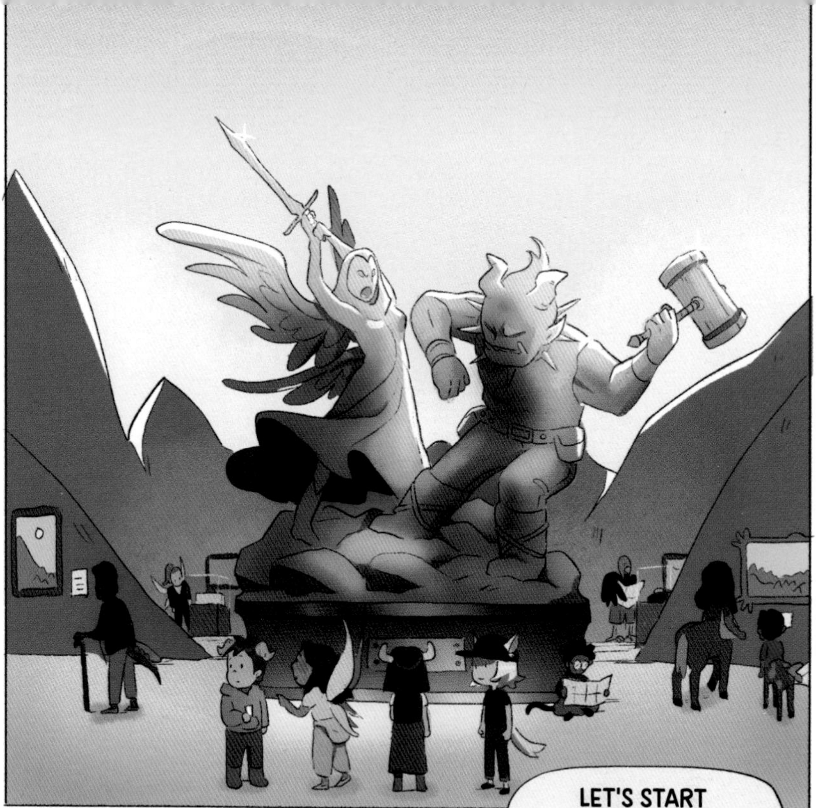

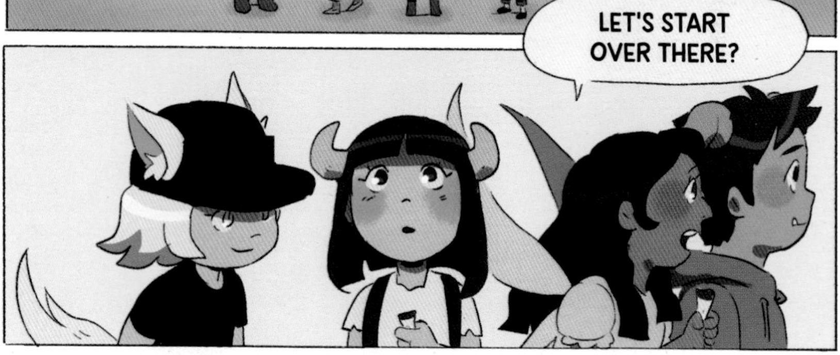
LET'S START OVER THERE?

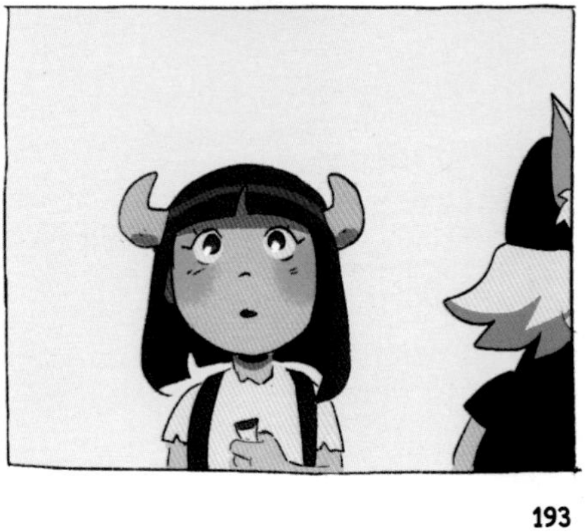

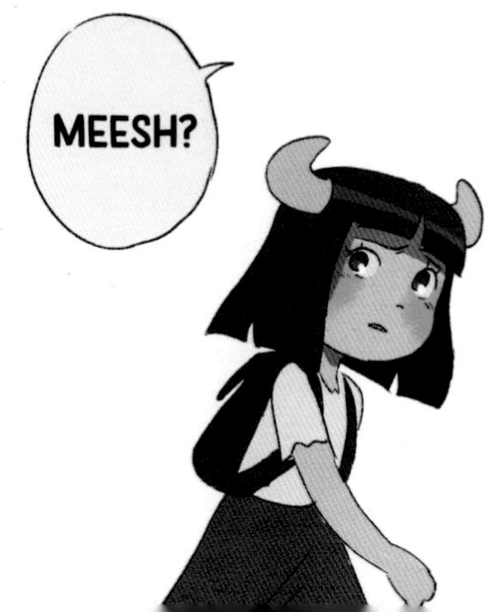
MEESH?

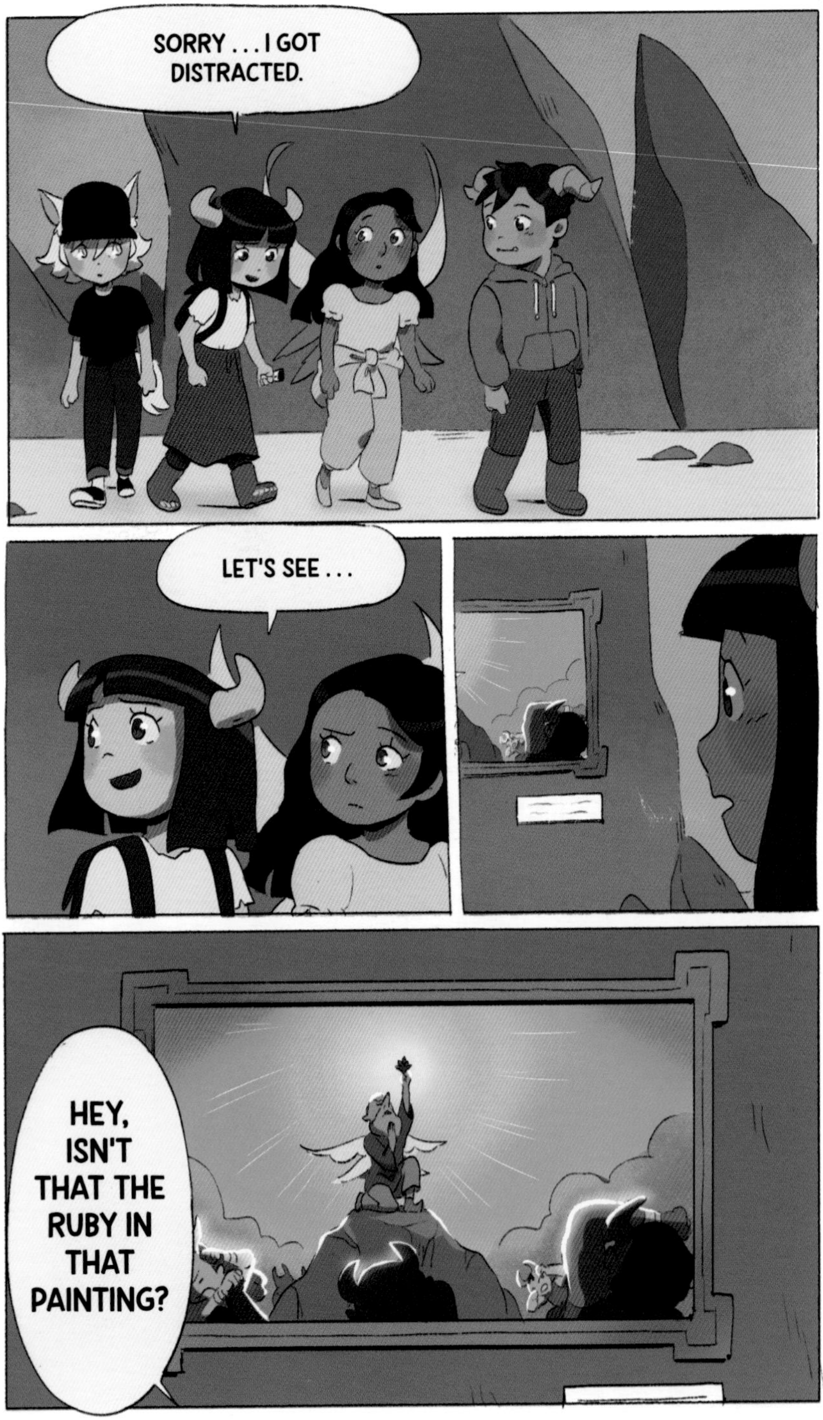
SORRY . . . I GOT DISTRACTED.
LET'S SEE . . .
HEY, ISN'T THAT THE RUBY IN THAT PAINTING?

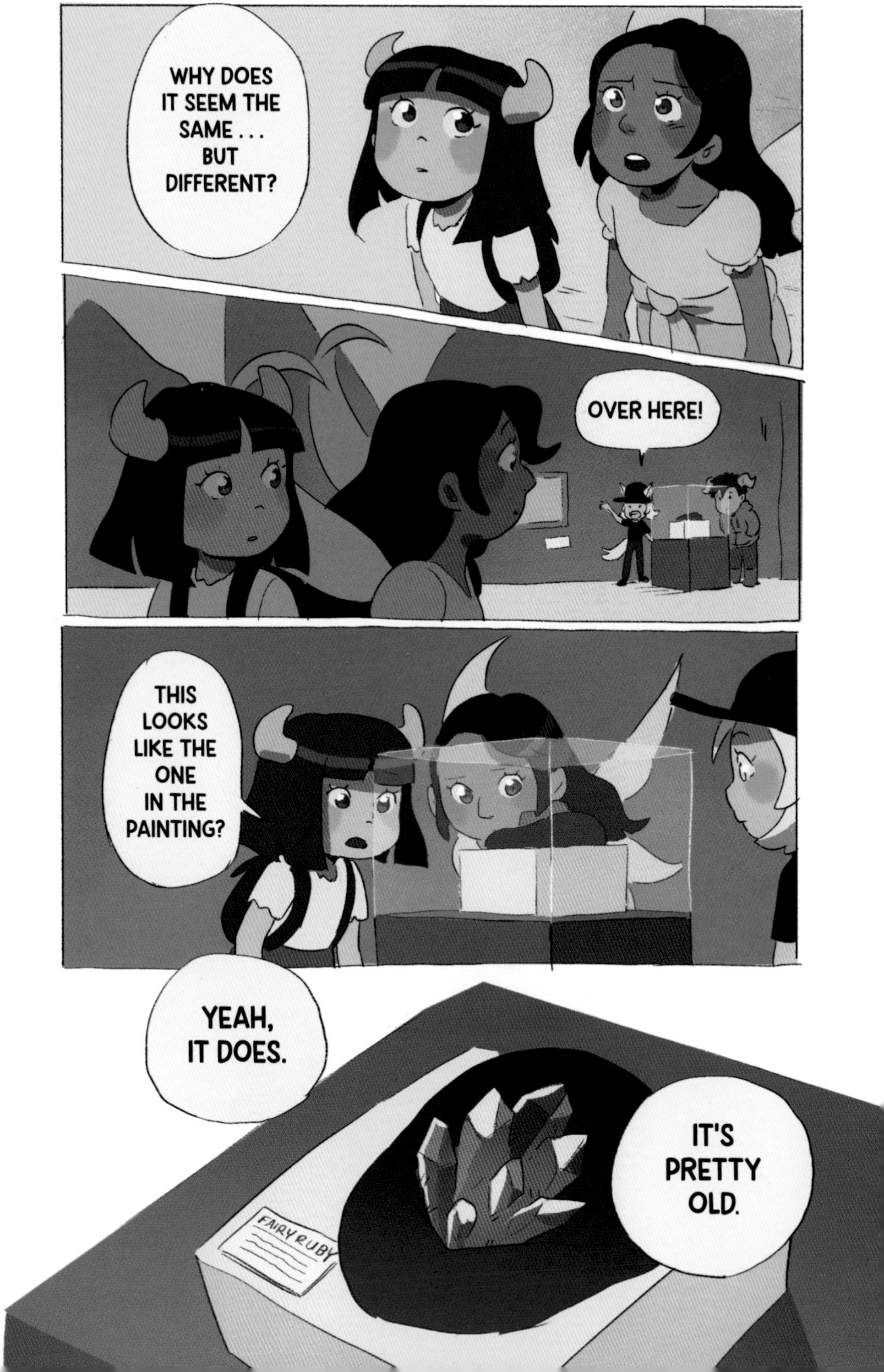
WHY DOES IT SEEM THE SAME . . . BUT DIFFERENT?
OVER HERE!
THIS LOOKS LIKE THE ONE IN THE PAINTING?
YEAH, IT DOES.
IT'S PRETTY OLD.
FAIRY RUBY

NO
WAY . . .

GUARDS.
OF COURSE.

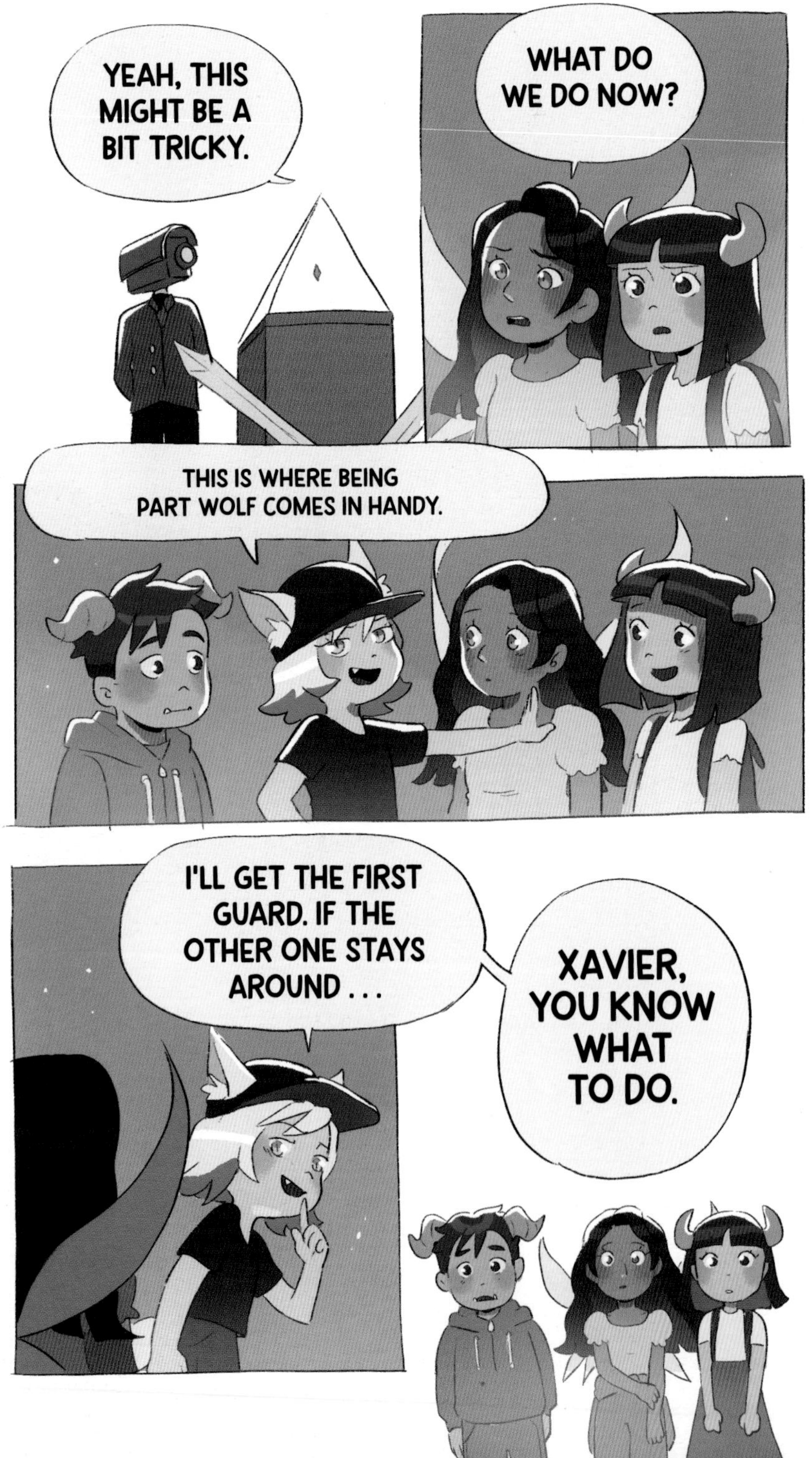
YEAH, THIS MIGHT BE A BIT TRICKY.
WHAT DO WE DO NOW?
THIS IS WHERE BEING PART WOLF COMES IN HANDY.
I'LL GET THE FIRST GUARD. IF THE OTHER ONE STAYS AROUND . . .
XAVIER, YOU KNOW WHAT TO DO.

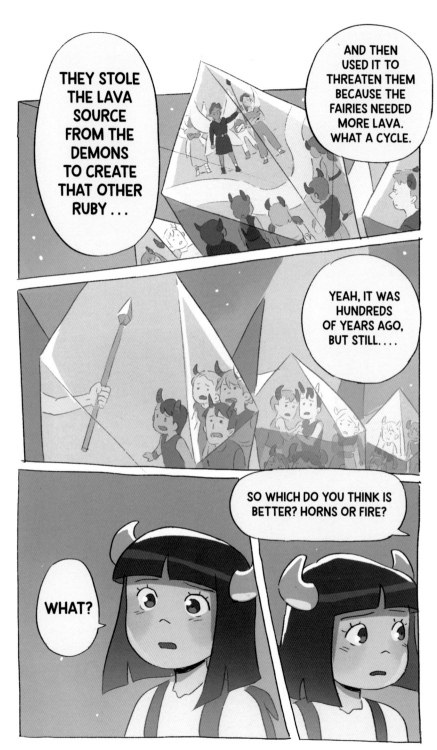

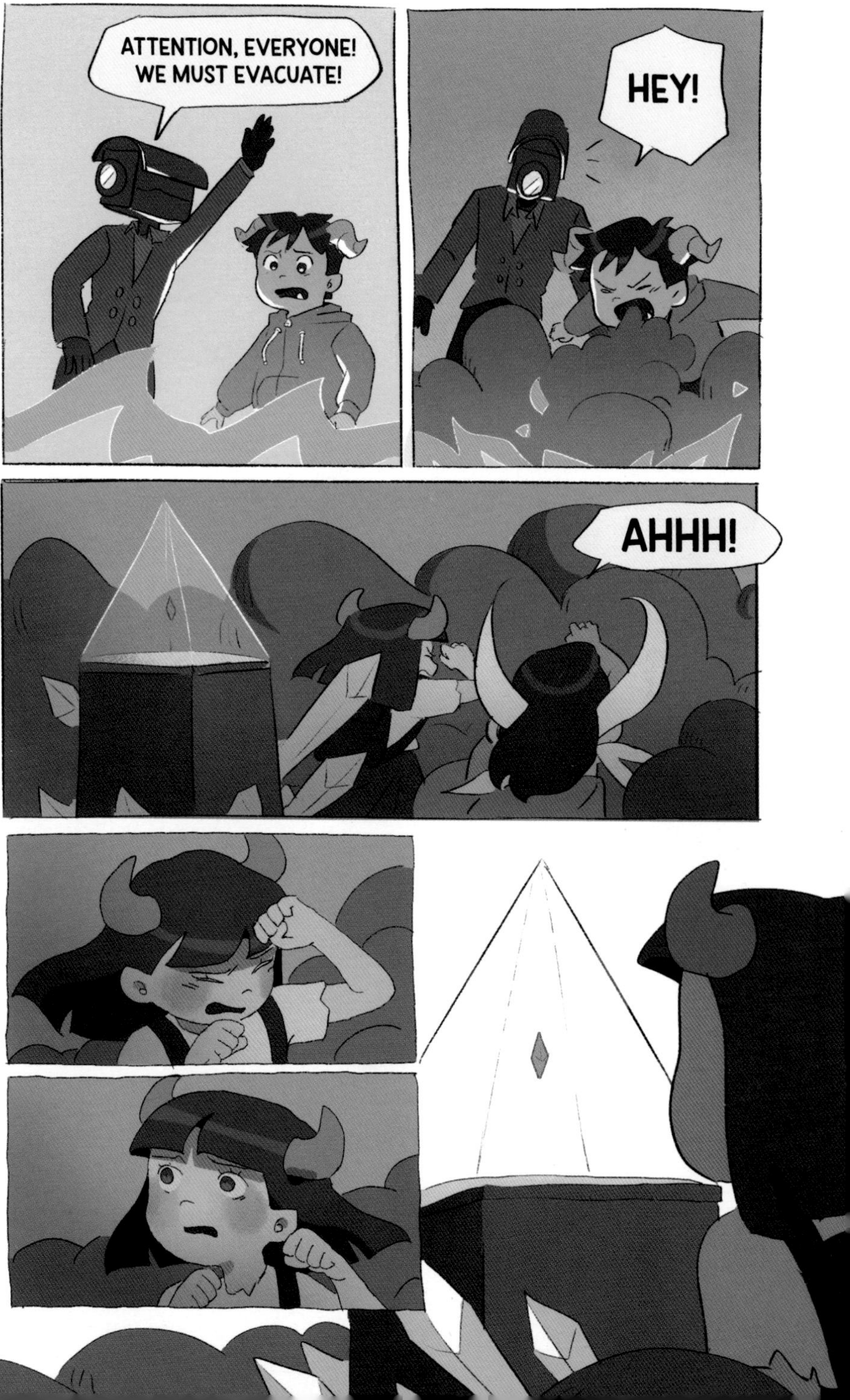
ATTENTION, EVERYONE! WE MUST EVACUATE!
HEY!
AHHH!

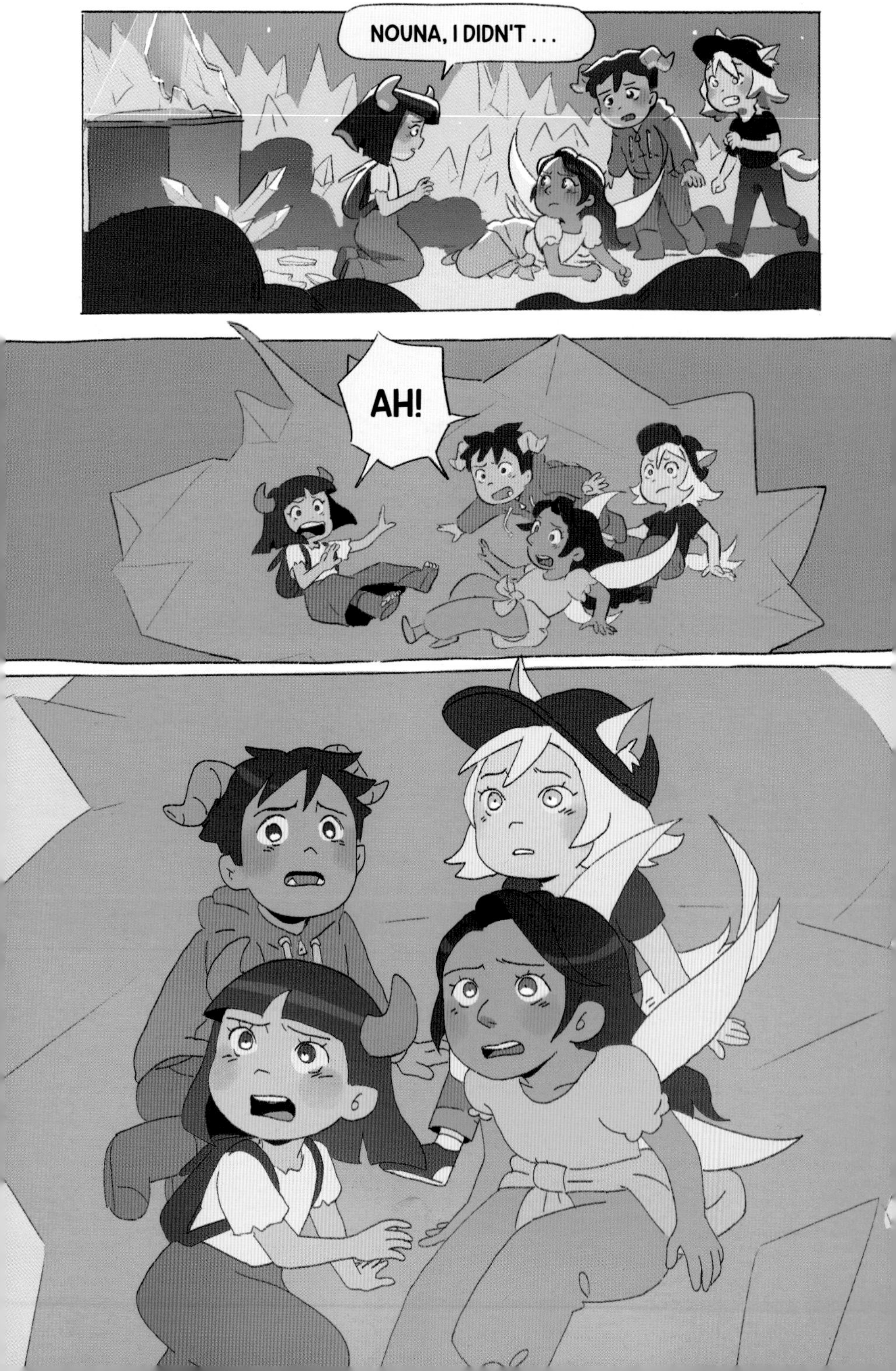
NOUNA, I DIDN'T . . .
AH!

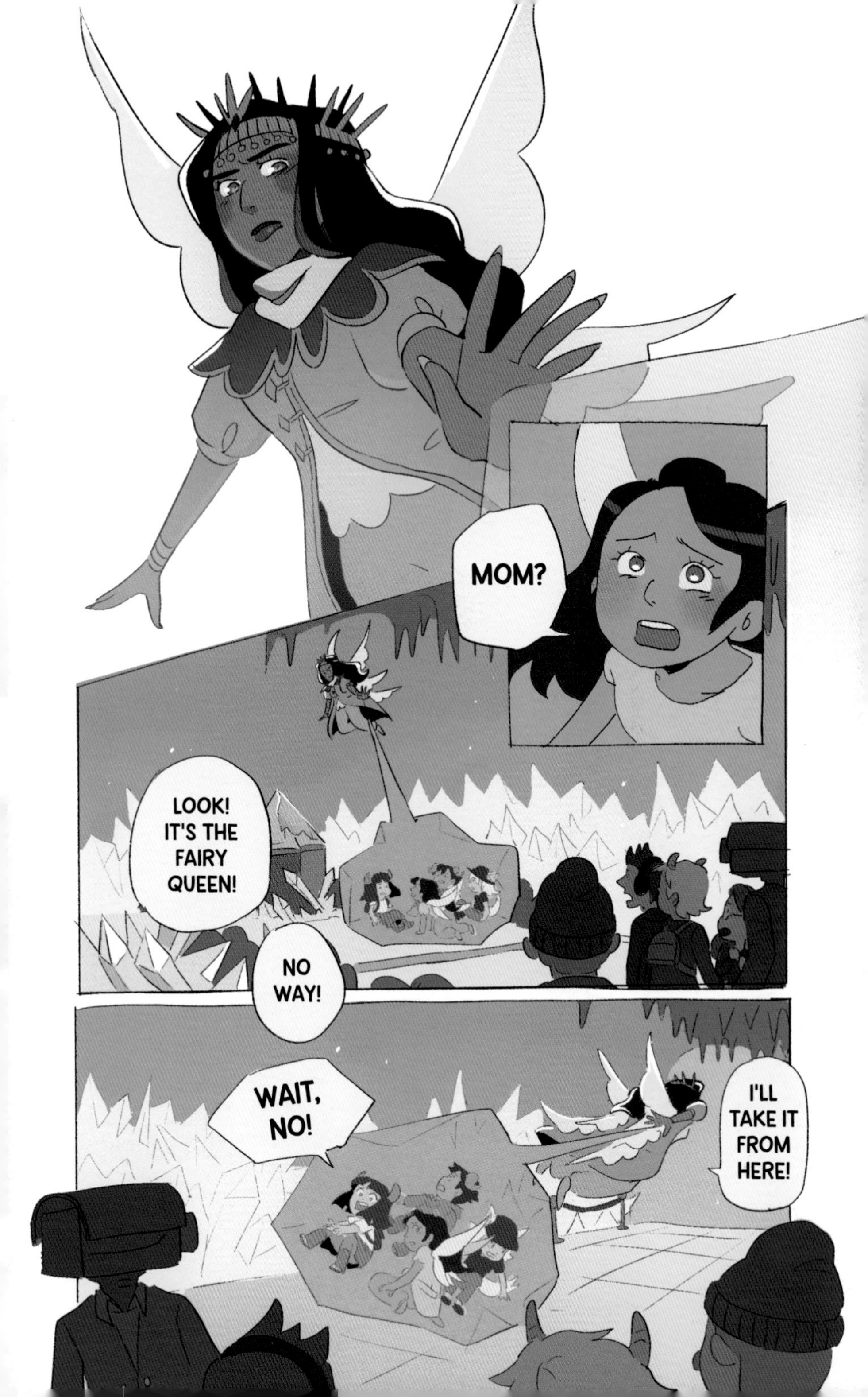
MOM?
LOOK! IT'S THE FAIRY QUEEN!
NO WAY!
WAIT, NO!
I'LL TAKE IT FROM HERE!

220

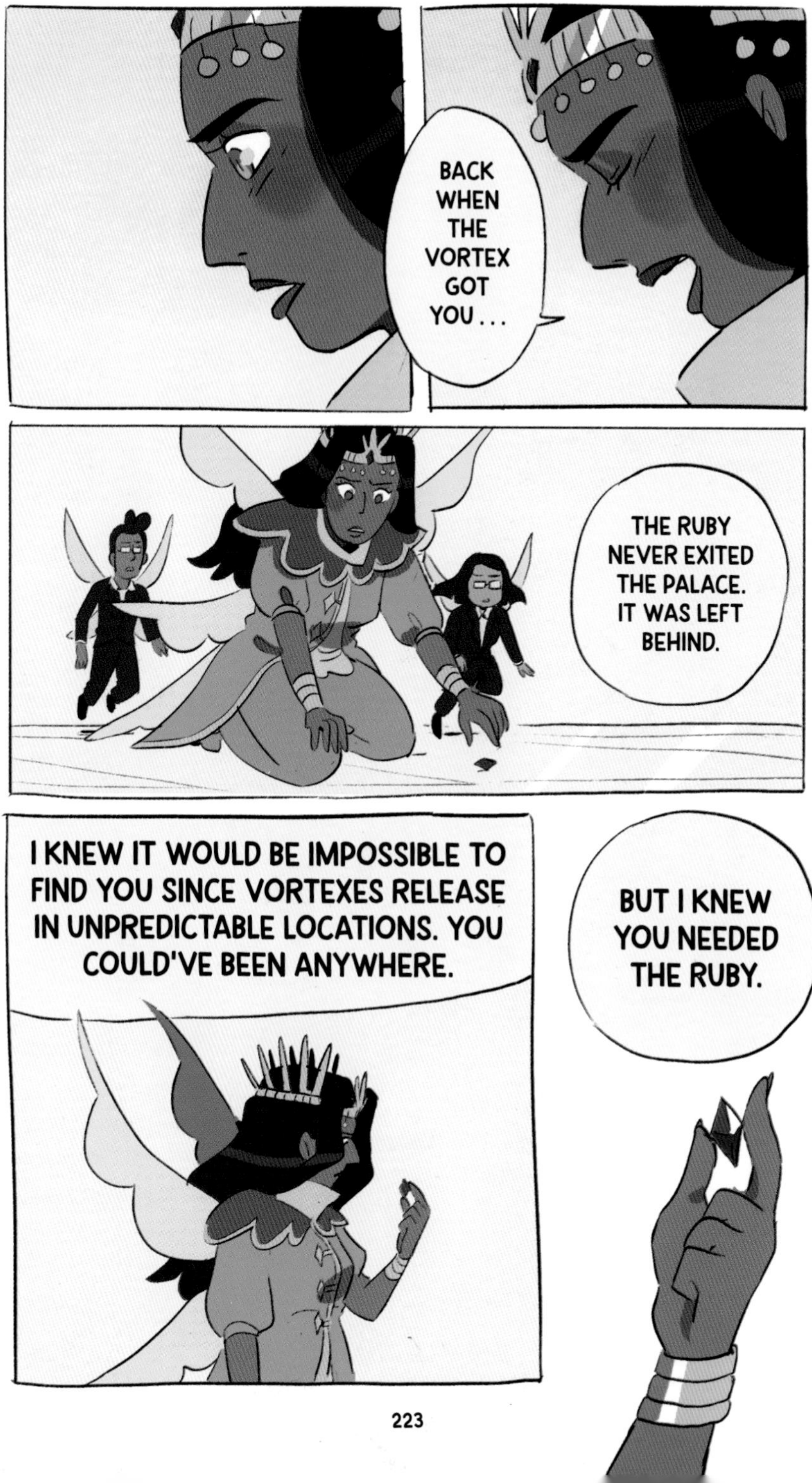
BACK WHEN THE VORTEX GOT YOU . . .
THE RUBY NEVER EXITED THE PALACE. IT WAS LEFT BEHIND.
I KNEW IT WOULD BE IMPOSSIBLE TO FIND YOU SINCE VORTEXES RELEASE IN UNPREDICTABLE LOCATIONS. YOU COULD'VE BEEN ANYWHERE.
BUT I KNEW YOU NEEDED THE RUBY.

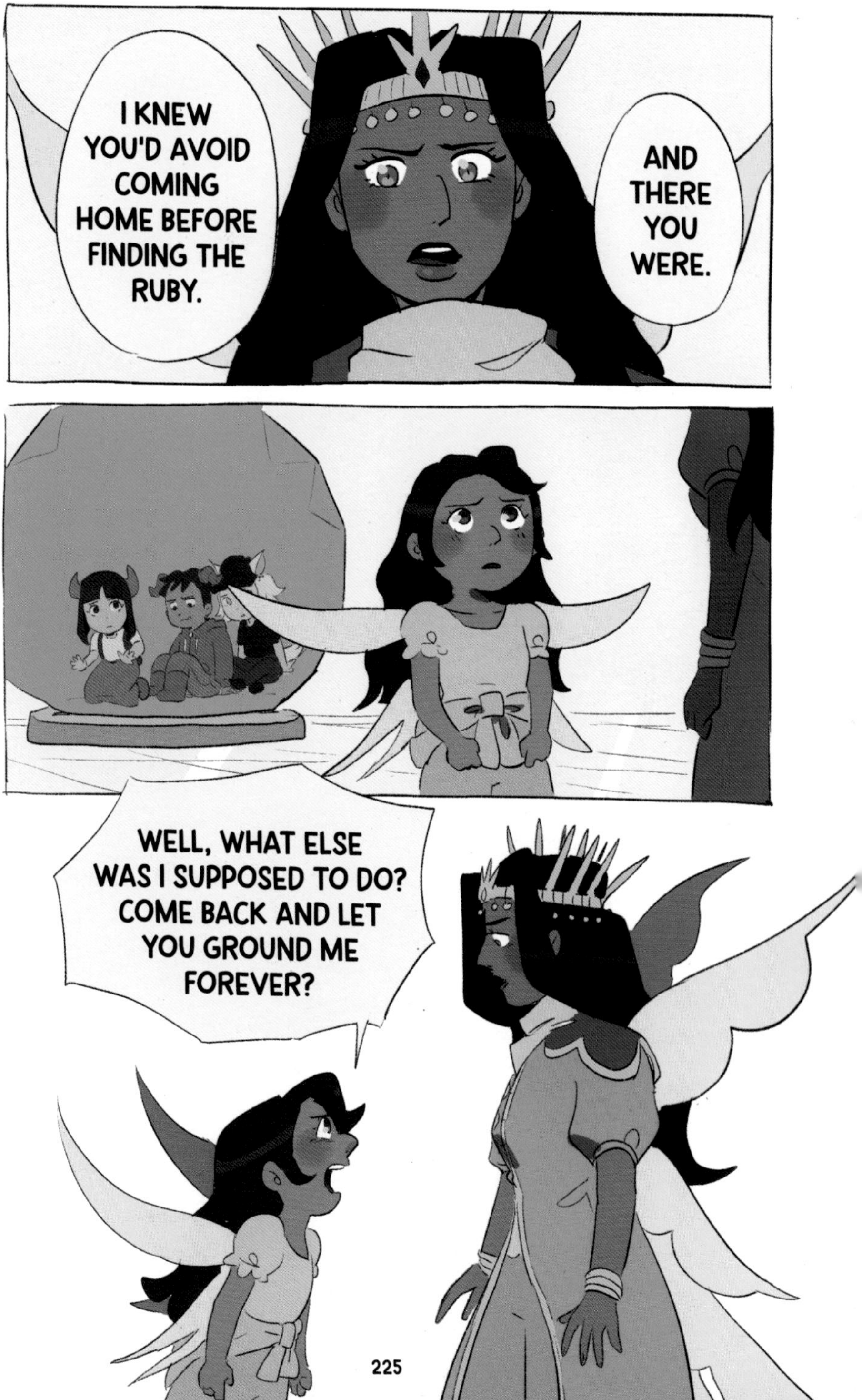
I KNEW YOU'D AVOID COMING HOME BEFORE FINDING THE RUBY.
AND THERE YOU WERE.
WELL, WHAT ELSE WAS I SUPPOSED TO DO? COME BACK AND LET YOU GROUND ME FOREVER?

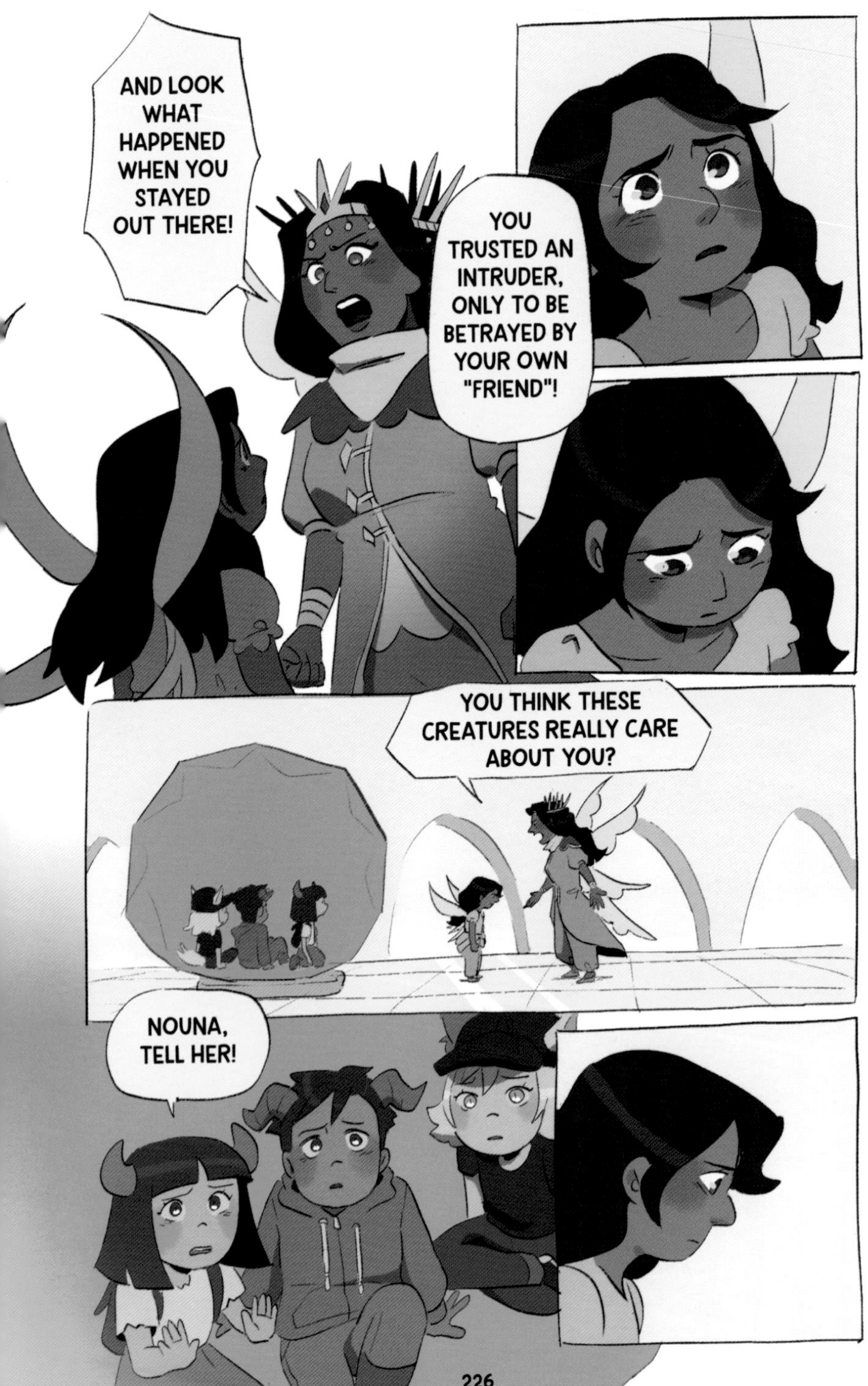
AND LOOK WHAT HAPPENED WHEN YOU STAYED OUT THERE!
YOU TRUSTED AN INTRUDER, ONLY TO BE BETRAYED BY YOUR OWN "FRIEND"!
YOU THINK THESE CREATURES REALLY CARE ABOUT YOU?
NOUNA, TELL HER!

SIGH.

ENOUGH. WHERE ARE YOUR PARENTS? THEY NEED TO BE HELD ACCOUNTABLE FOR THIS. FOR YOU TRYING TO STEAL A FAIRY ARTIFACT!

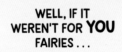

WELL, IF IT WEREN'T FOR **YOU** FAIRIES . . .

MY GRANDMA WOULD BE HERE. BUT SHE ISN'T. BECAUSE **YOU** POISONED MOUNT MAGMA!

WHAT IN THE WORLD ARE YOU TALKING ABOUT?

THE GREEN GLOW? IN THE LAVA? TURNING EVERYONE INTO STONE?

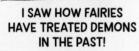

I SAW HOW FAIRIES HAVE TREATED DEMONS IN THE PAST!

HOW DARE YOU ACCUSE—

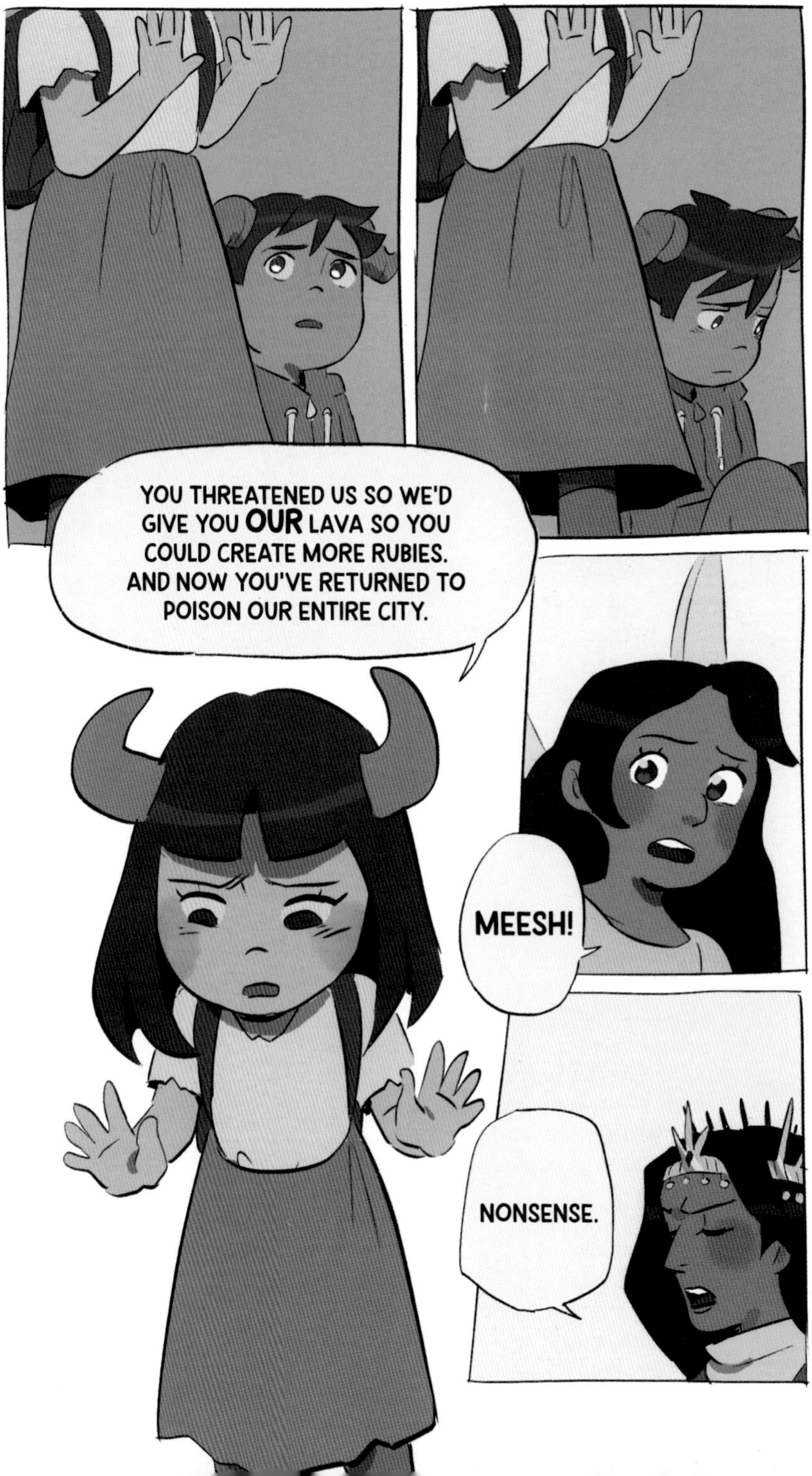
YOU THREATENED US SO WE'D GIVE YOU **OUR** LAVA SO YOU COULD CREATE MORE RUBIES. AND NOW YOU'VE RETURNED TO POISON OUR ENTIRE CITY.
MEESH!
NONSENSE.

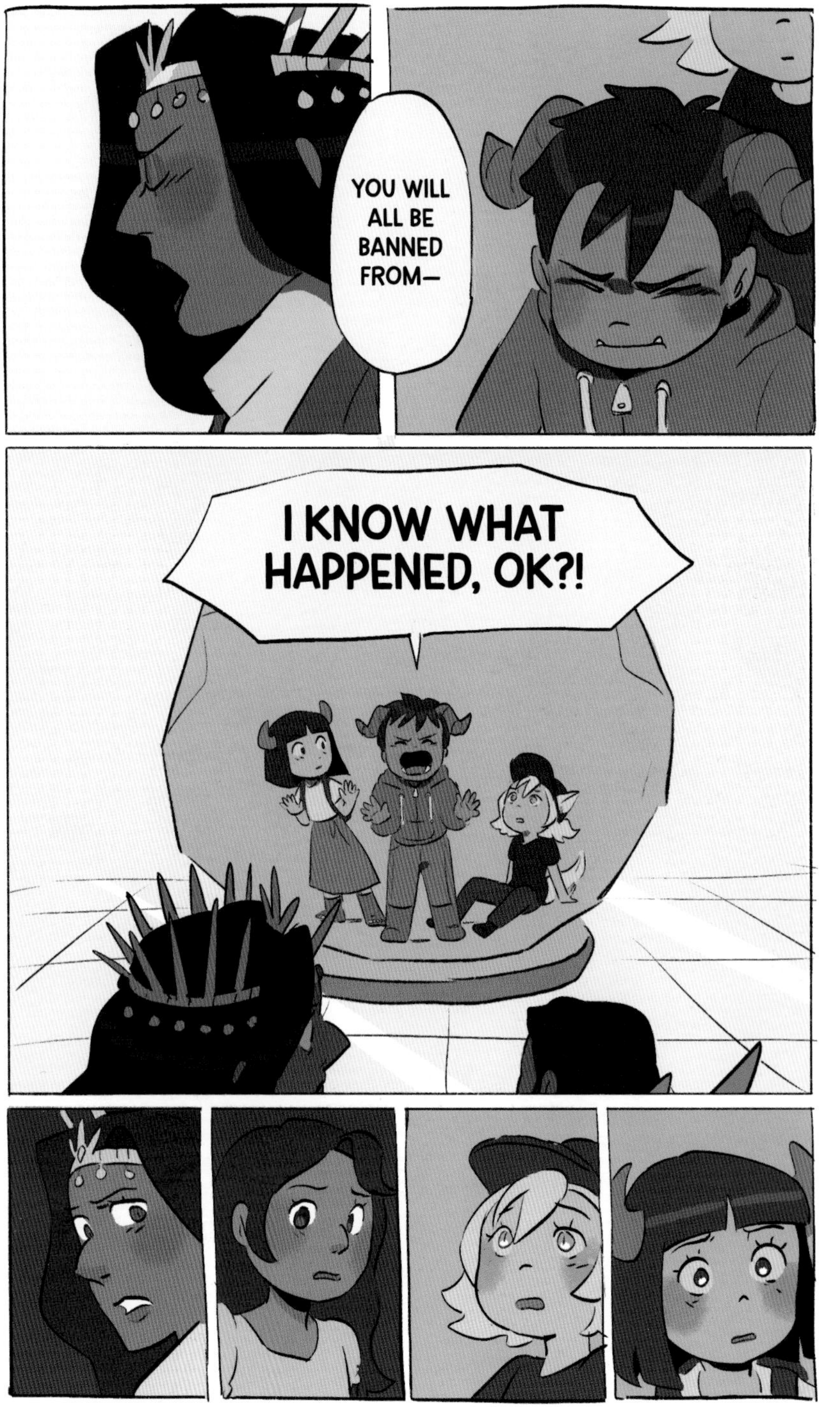
YOU WILL ALL BE BANNED FROM—
I KNOW WHAT HAPPENED, OK?!

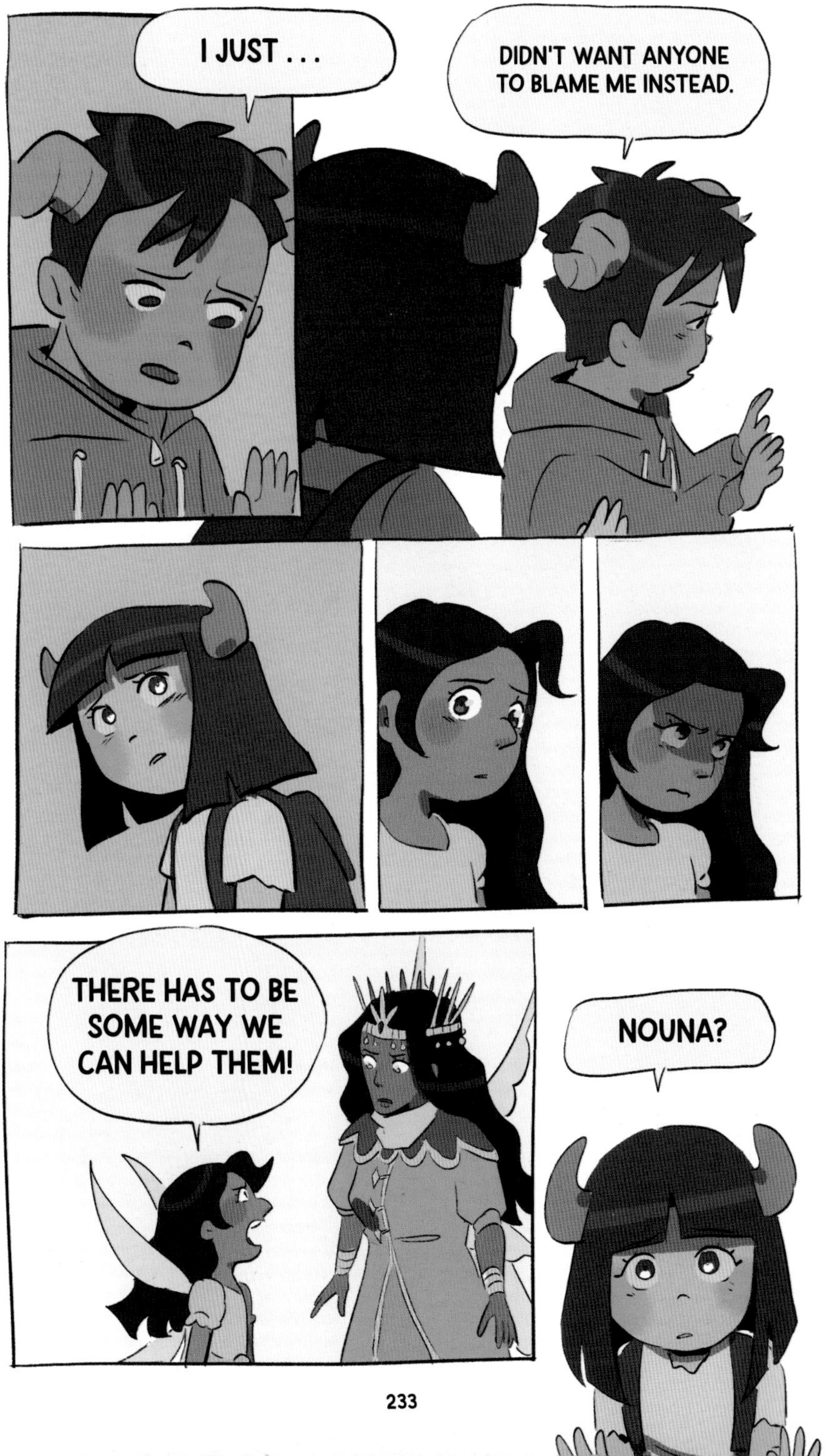
I JUST . . .
DIDN'T WANT ANYONE TO BLAME ME INSTEAD.
THERE HAS TO BE SOME WAY WE CAN HELP THEM!
NOUNA?

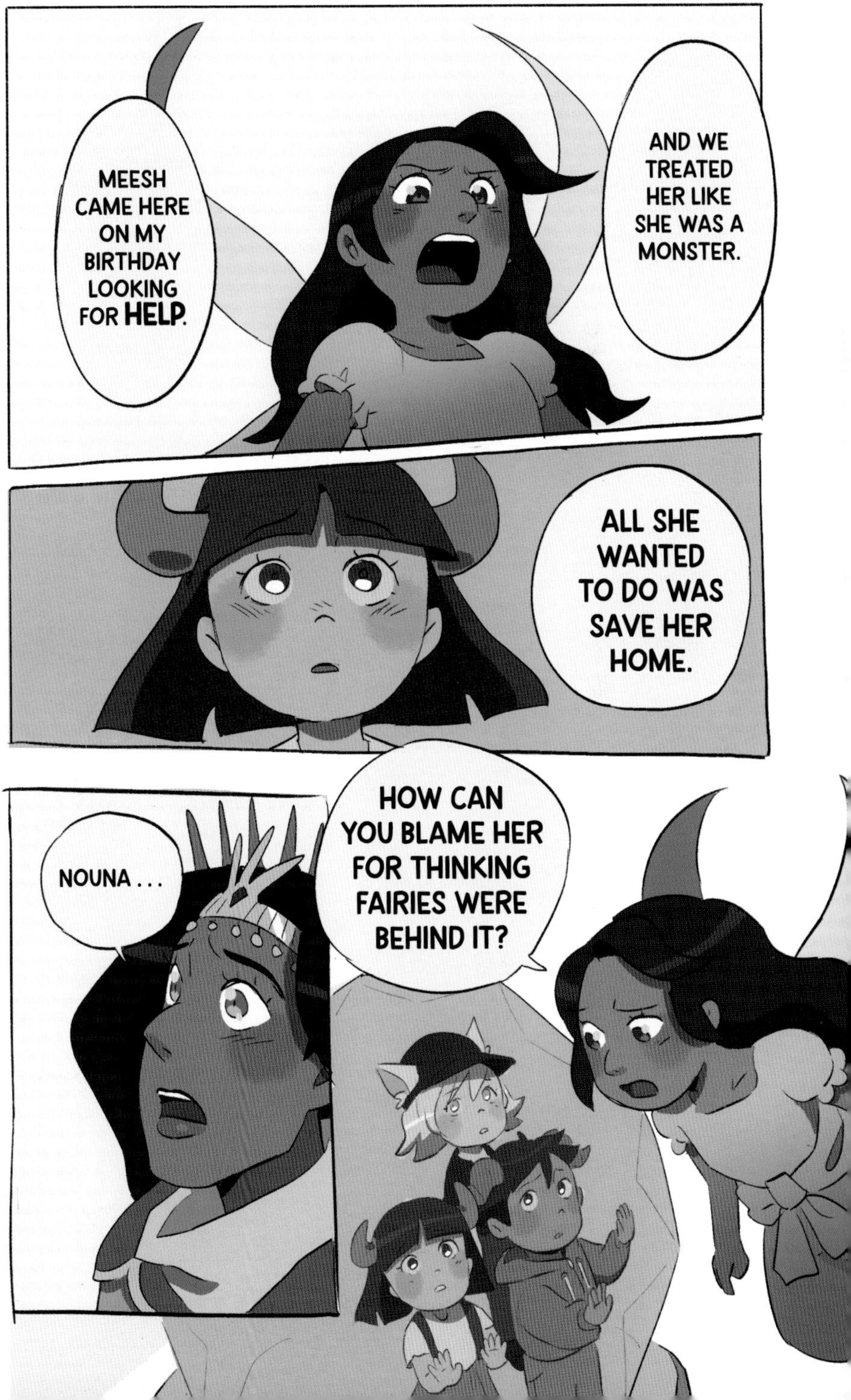
MEESH CAME HERE ON MY BIRTHDAY LOOKING FOR **HELP**.
AND WE TREATED HER LIKE SHE WAS A MONSTER.
ALL SHE WANTED TO DO WAS SAVE HER HOME.
NOUNA . . .
HOW CAN YOU BLAME HER FOR THINKING FAIRIES WERE BEHIND IT?

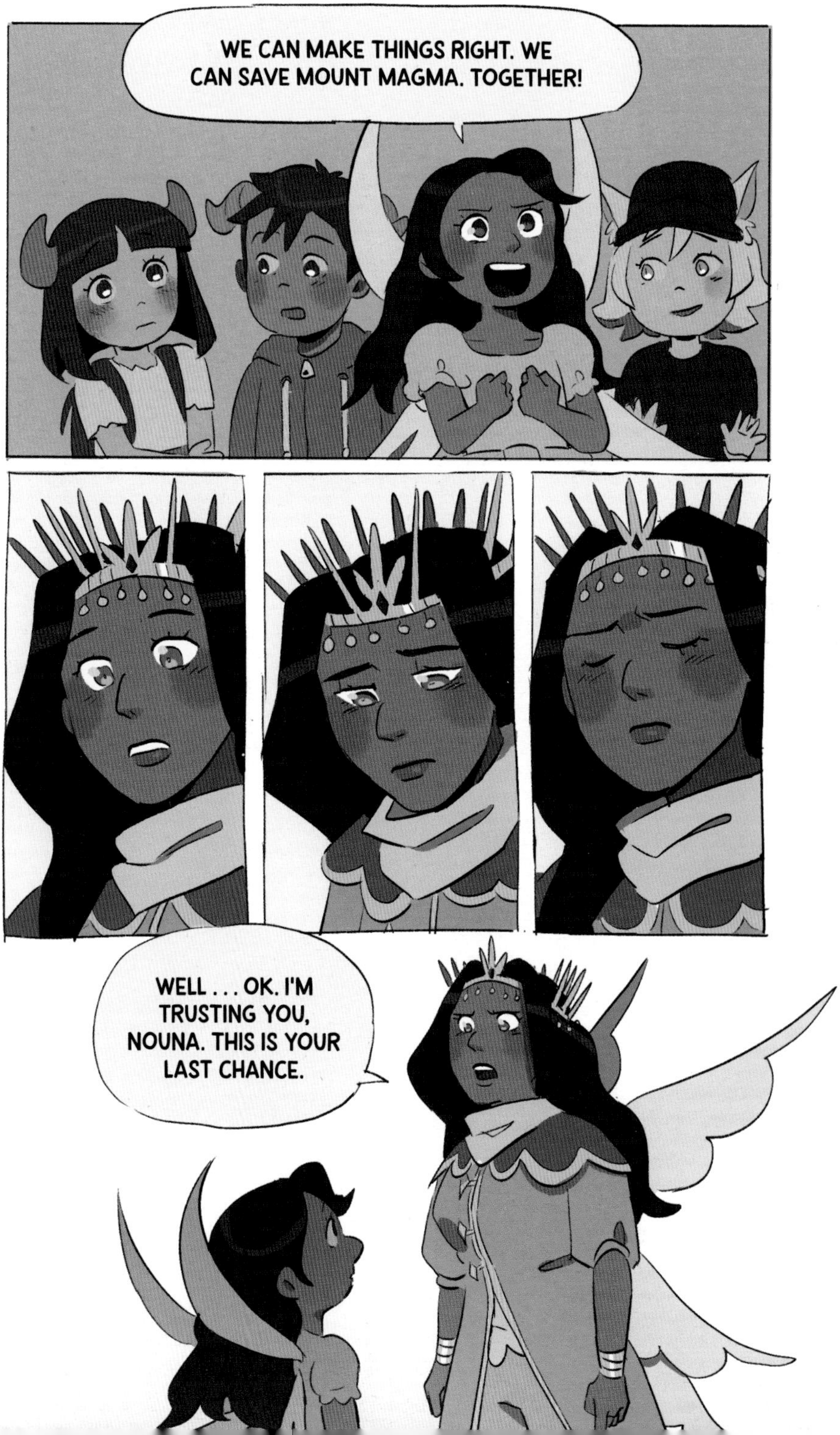
WE CAN MAKE THINGS RIGHT. WE CAN SAVE MOUNT MAGMA. TOGETHER!
WELL . . . OK. I'M TRUSTING YOU, NOUNA. THIS IS YOUR LAST CHANCE.

WE'LL HAVE TO RETURN TO THE SOURCE. IT'S THE ONLY WAY TO FIGURE OUT IF WE **CAN** HELP.

WE'LL LEAVE NOW.

SO . . . YOU'RE SAYING YOU'LL TRY?

nod

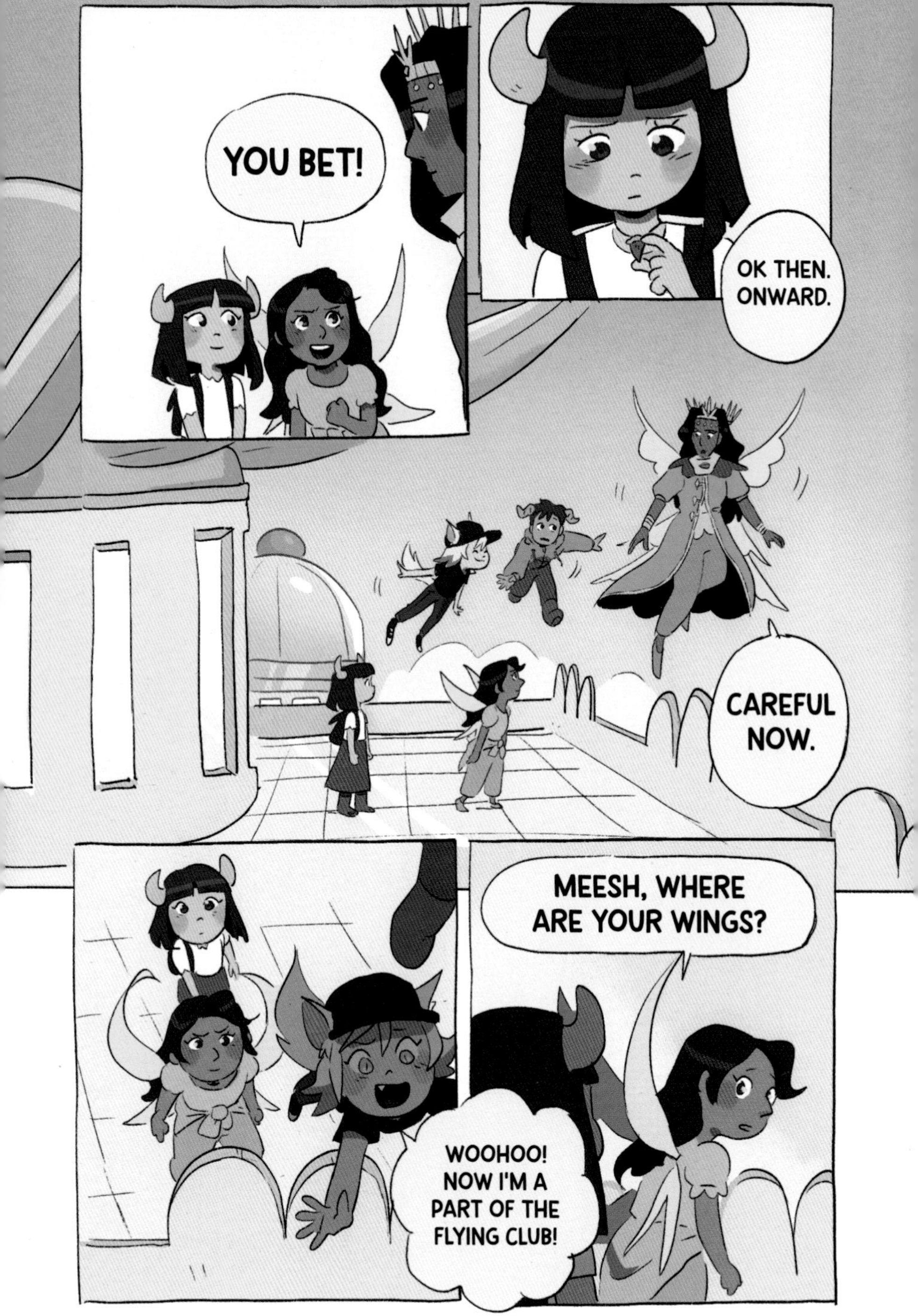
YOU BET!
OK THEN. ONWARD.
CAREFUL NOW.
WOOHOO! NOW I'M A PART OF THE FLYING CLUB!
MEESH, WHERE ARE YOUR WINGS?

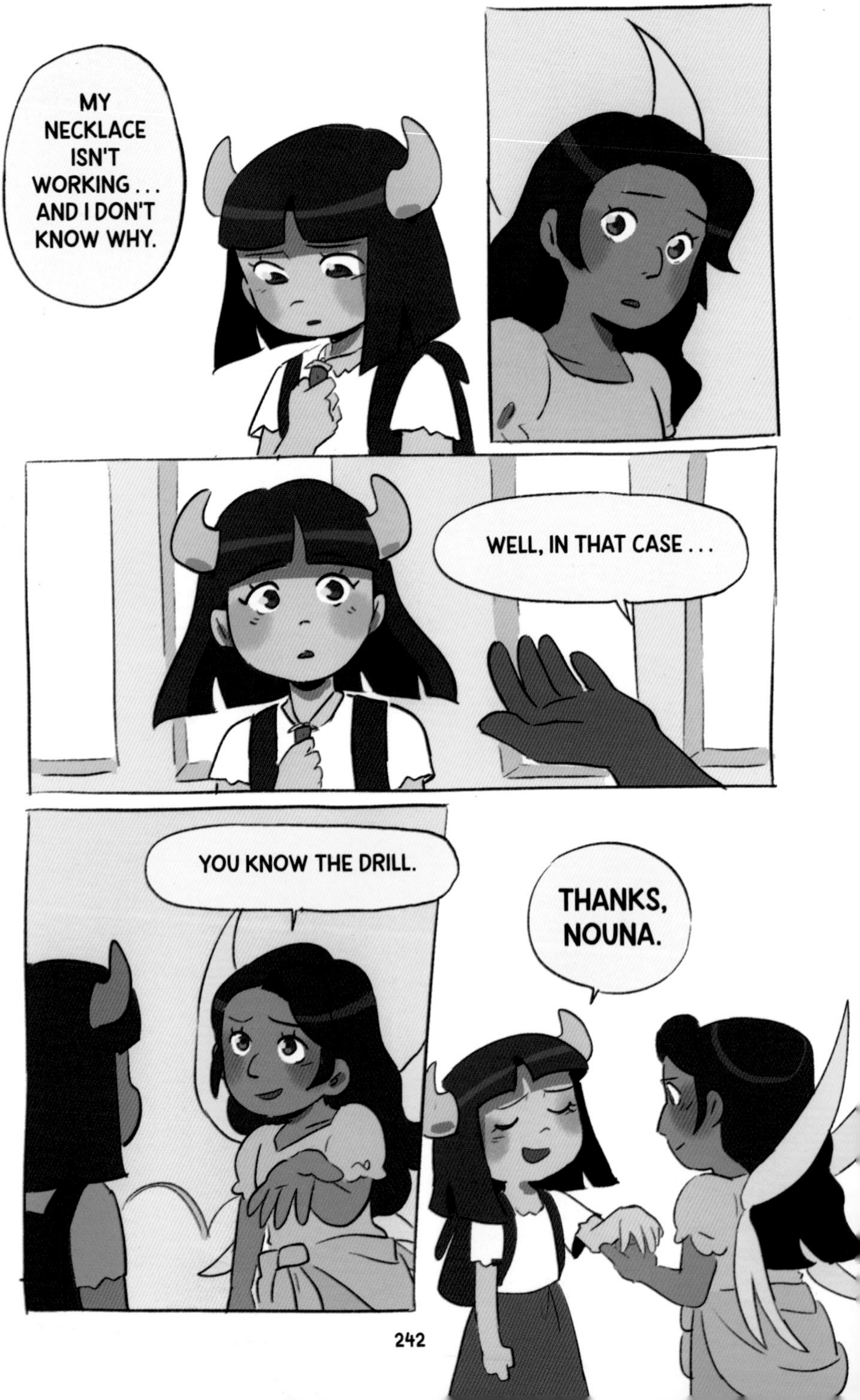
MY NECKLACE ISN'T WORKING . . . AND I DON'T KNOW WHY.
WELL, IN THAT CASE . . .
YOU KNOW THE DRILL.
THANKS, NOUNA.

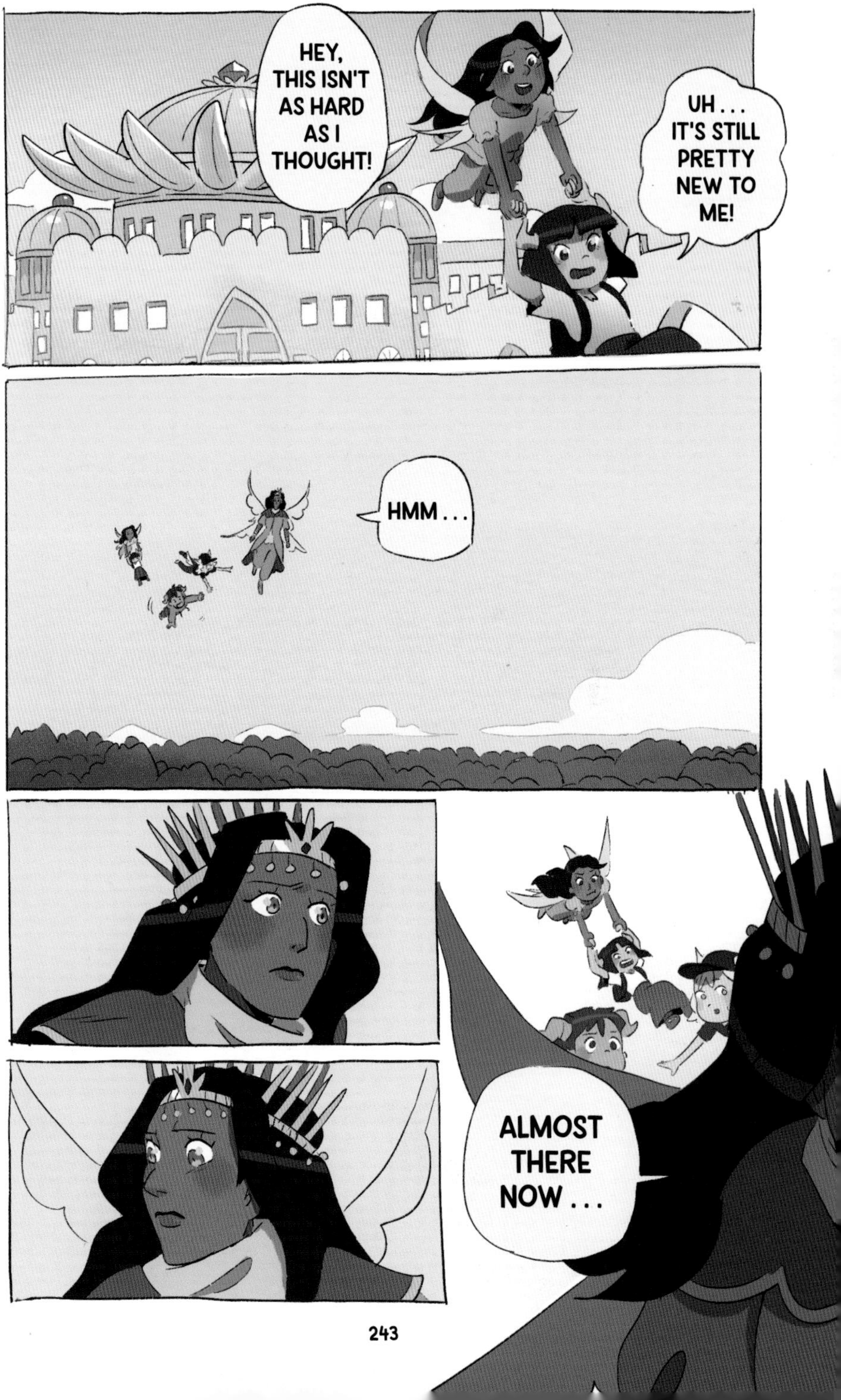
HEY, THIS ISN'T AS HARD AS I THOUGHT!
UH . . . IT'S STILL PRETTY NEW TO ME!
HMM . . .
ALMOST THERE NOW . . .

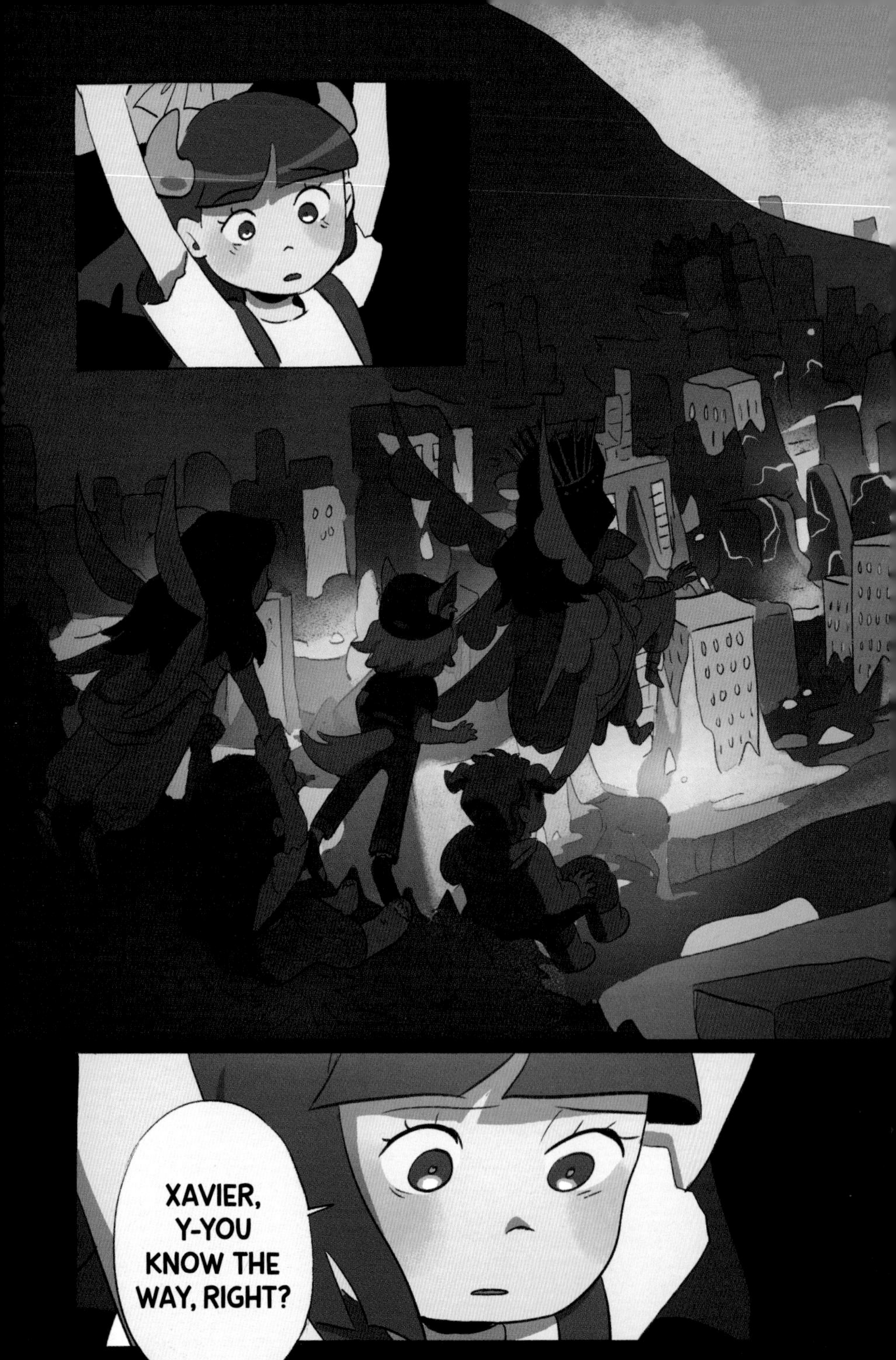
XAVIER, Y-YOU KNOW THE WAY, RIGHT?

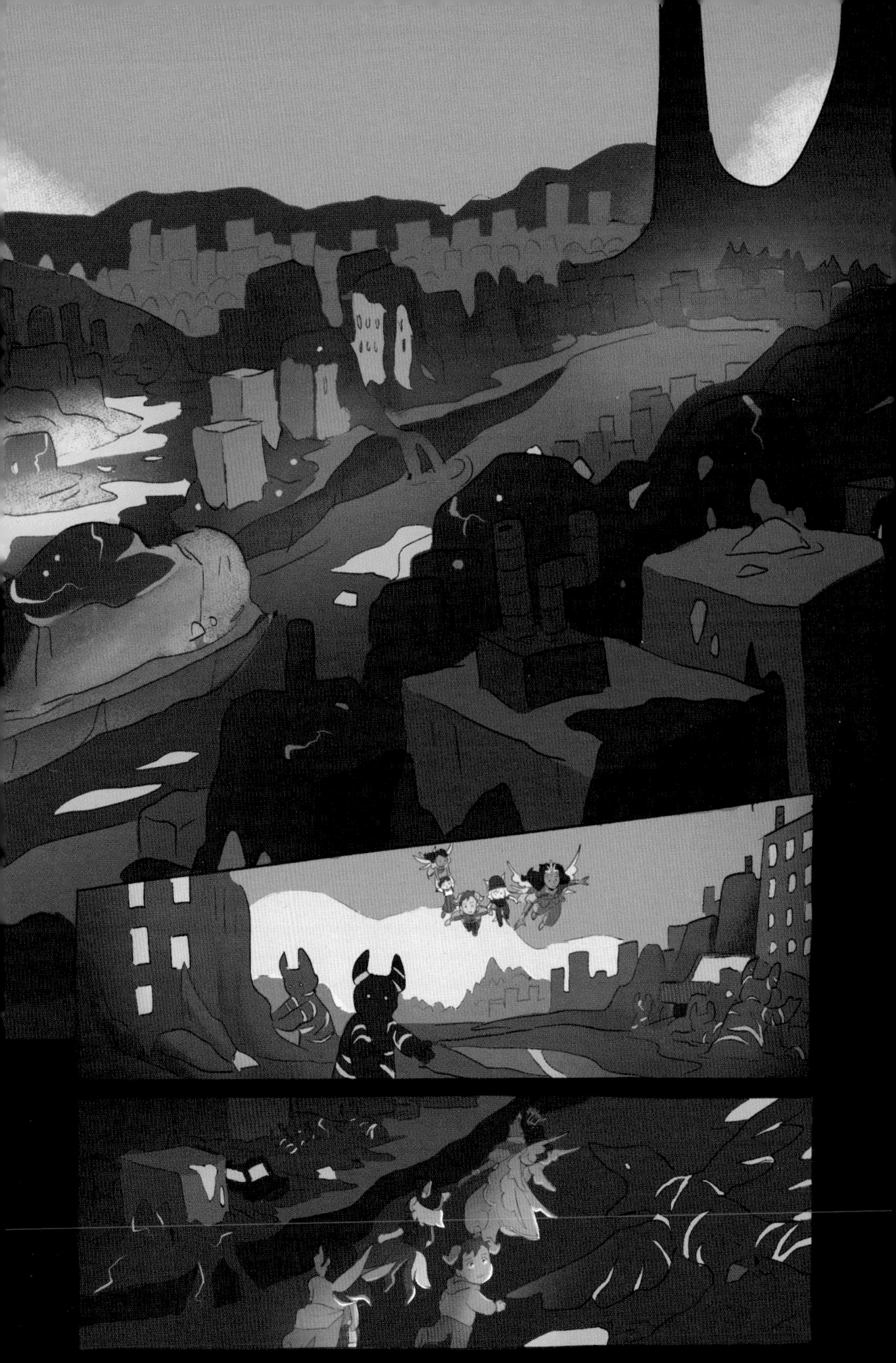

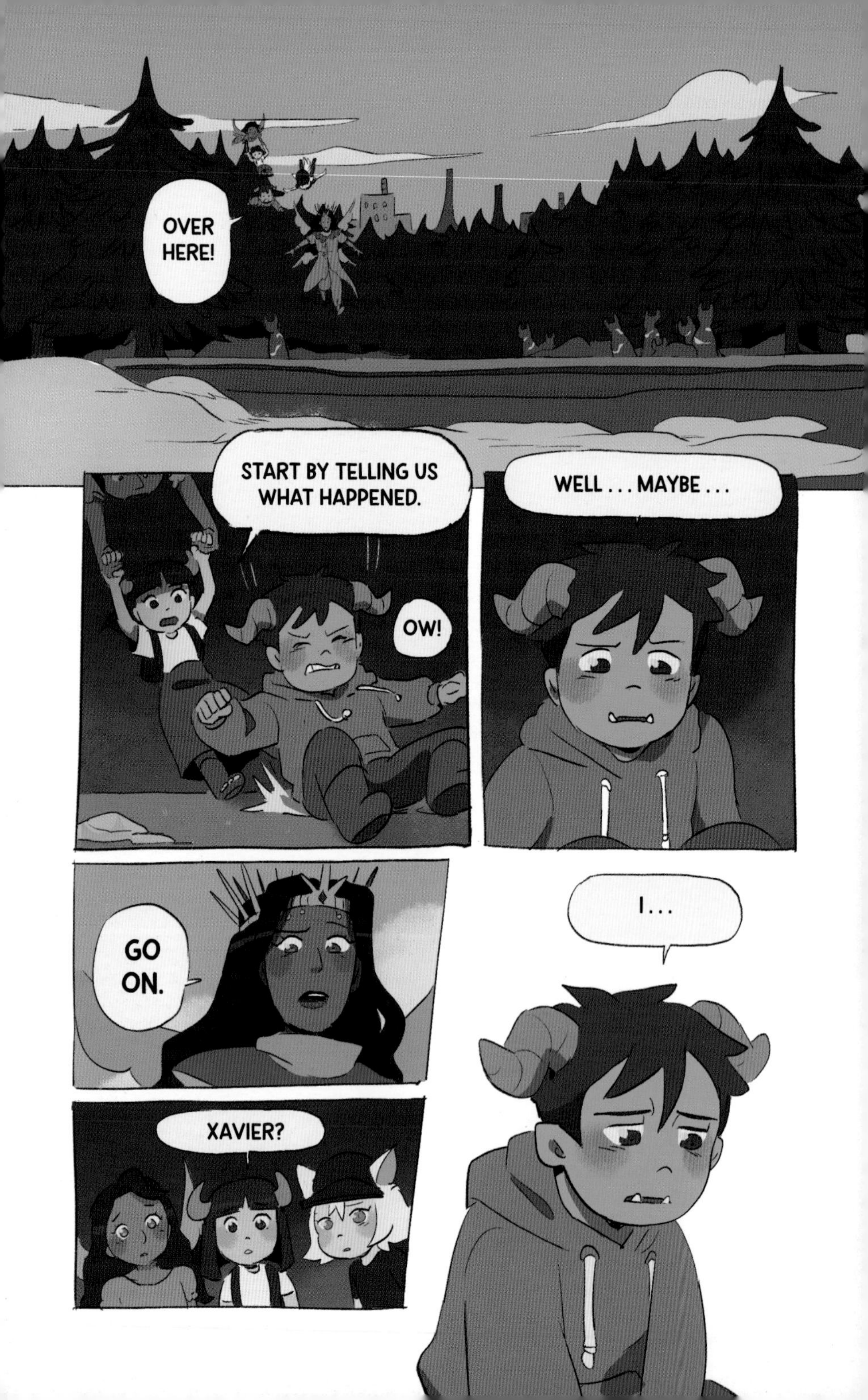
OVER HERE!
START BY TELLING US WHAT HAPPENED.
OW!
WELL . . . MAYBE . . .
GO ON.
I . . .
XAVIER?

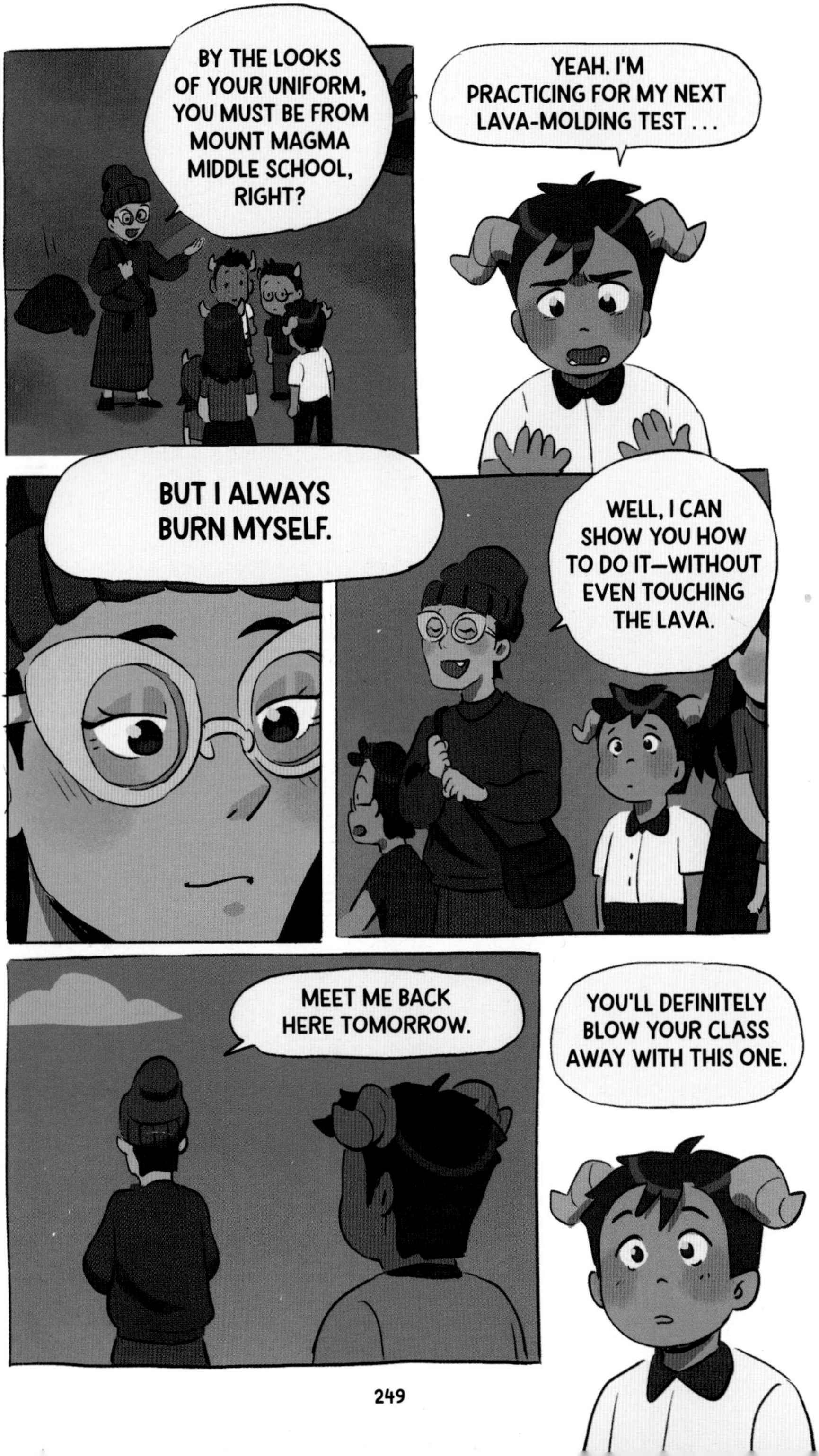
BY THE LOOKS OF YOUR UNIFORM, YOU MUST BE FROM MOUNT MAGMA MIDDLE SCHOOL, RIGHT?
YEAH. I'M PRACTICING FOR MY NEXT LAVA-MOLDING TEST . . .
BUT I ALWAYS BURN MYSELF.
WELL, I CAN SHOW YOU HOW TO DO IT—WITHOUT EVEN TOUCHING THE LAVA.
MEET ME BACK HERE TOMORROW.
YOU'LL DEFINITELY BLOW YOUR CLASS AWAY WITH THIS ONE.

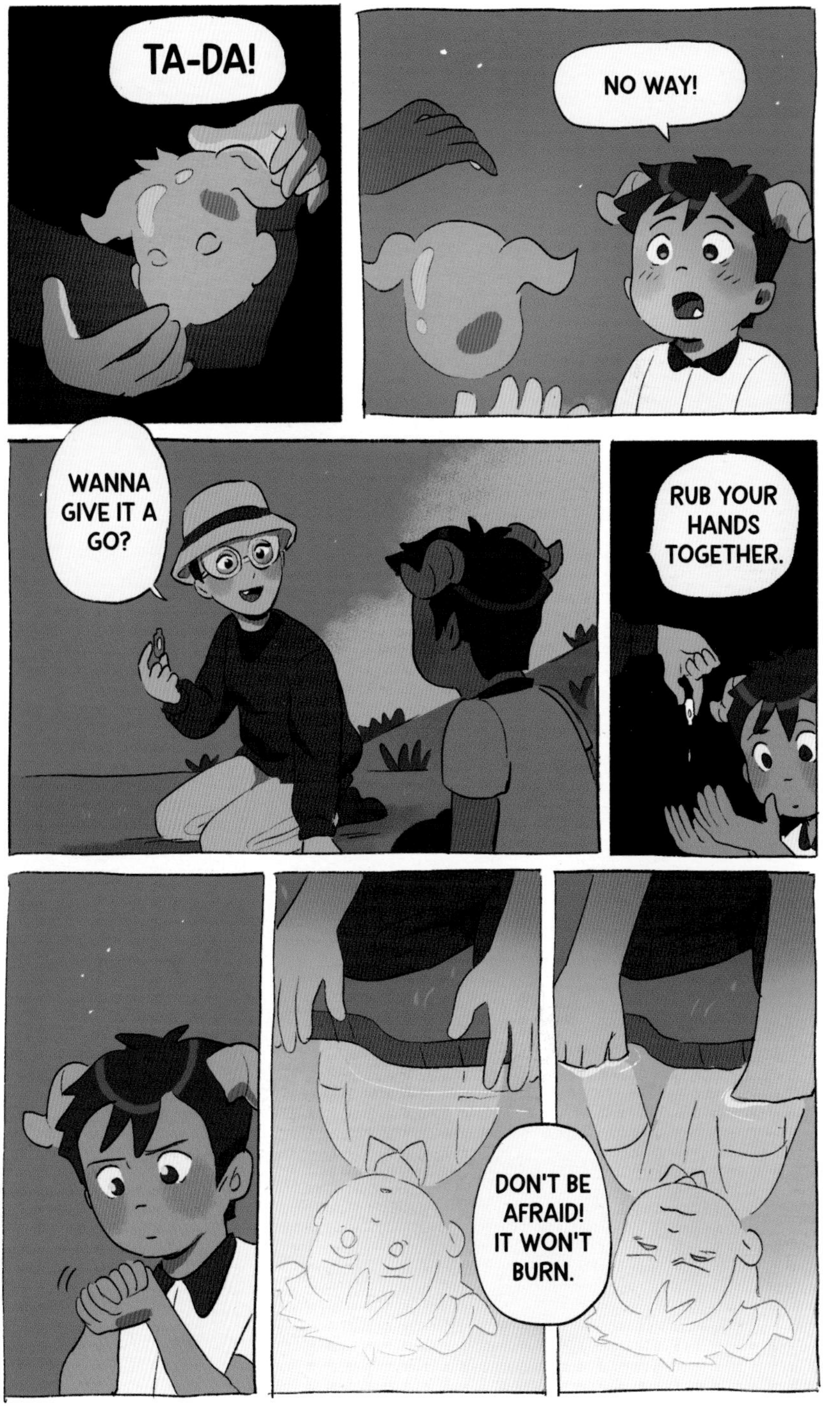
TA-DA!
NO WAY!
WANNA GIVE IT A GO?
RUB YOUR HANDS TOGETHER.
DON'T BE AFRAID! IT WON'T BURN.

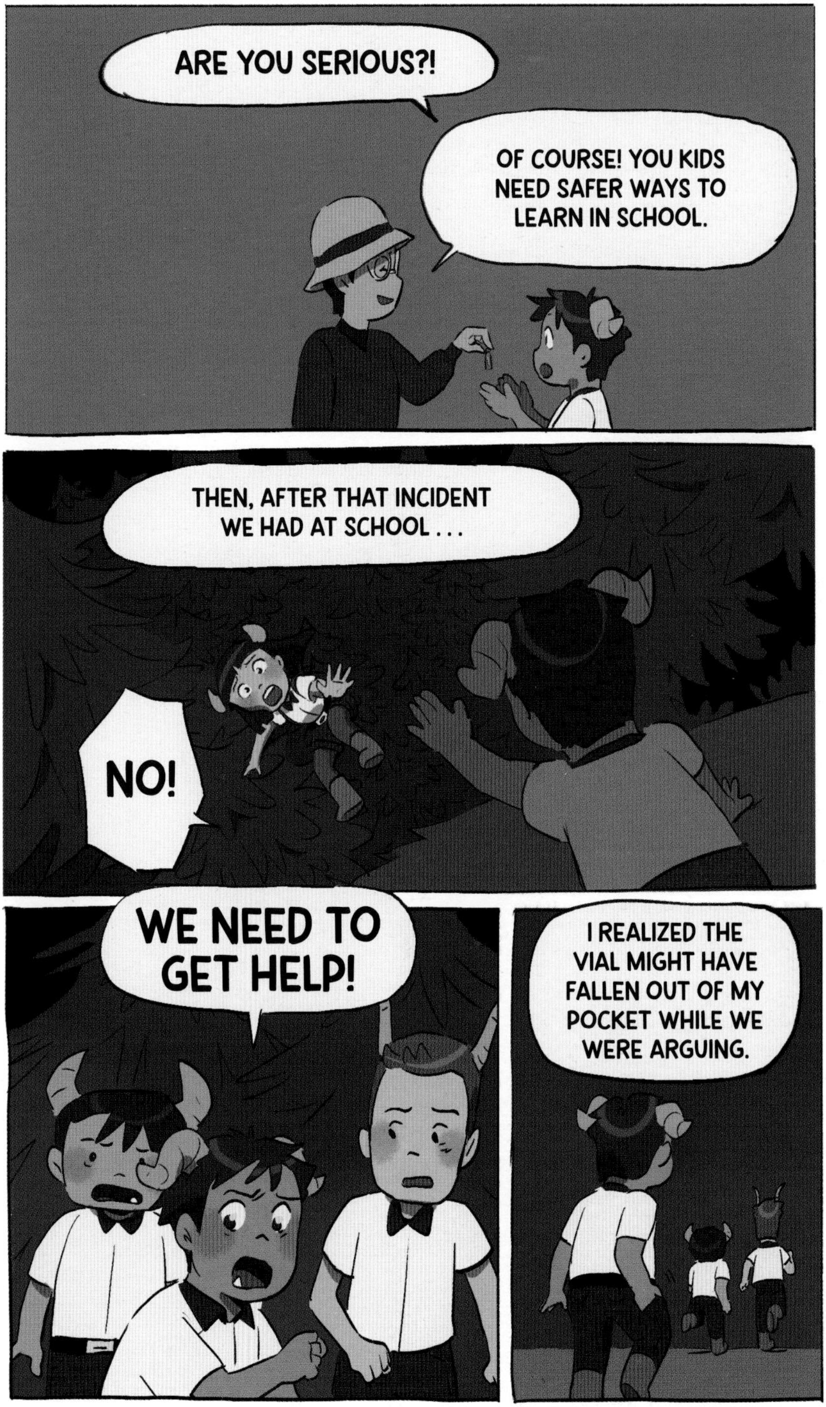
ARE YOU SERIOUS?!
OF COURSE! YOU KIDS NEED SAFER WAYS TO LEARN IN SCHOOL.
THEN, AFTER THAT INCIDENT WE HAD AT SCHOOL . . .
NO!
WE NEED TO GET HELP!
I REALIZED THE VIAL MIGHT HAVE FALLEN OUT OF MY POCKET WHILE WE WERE ARGUING.

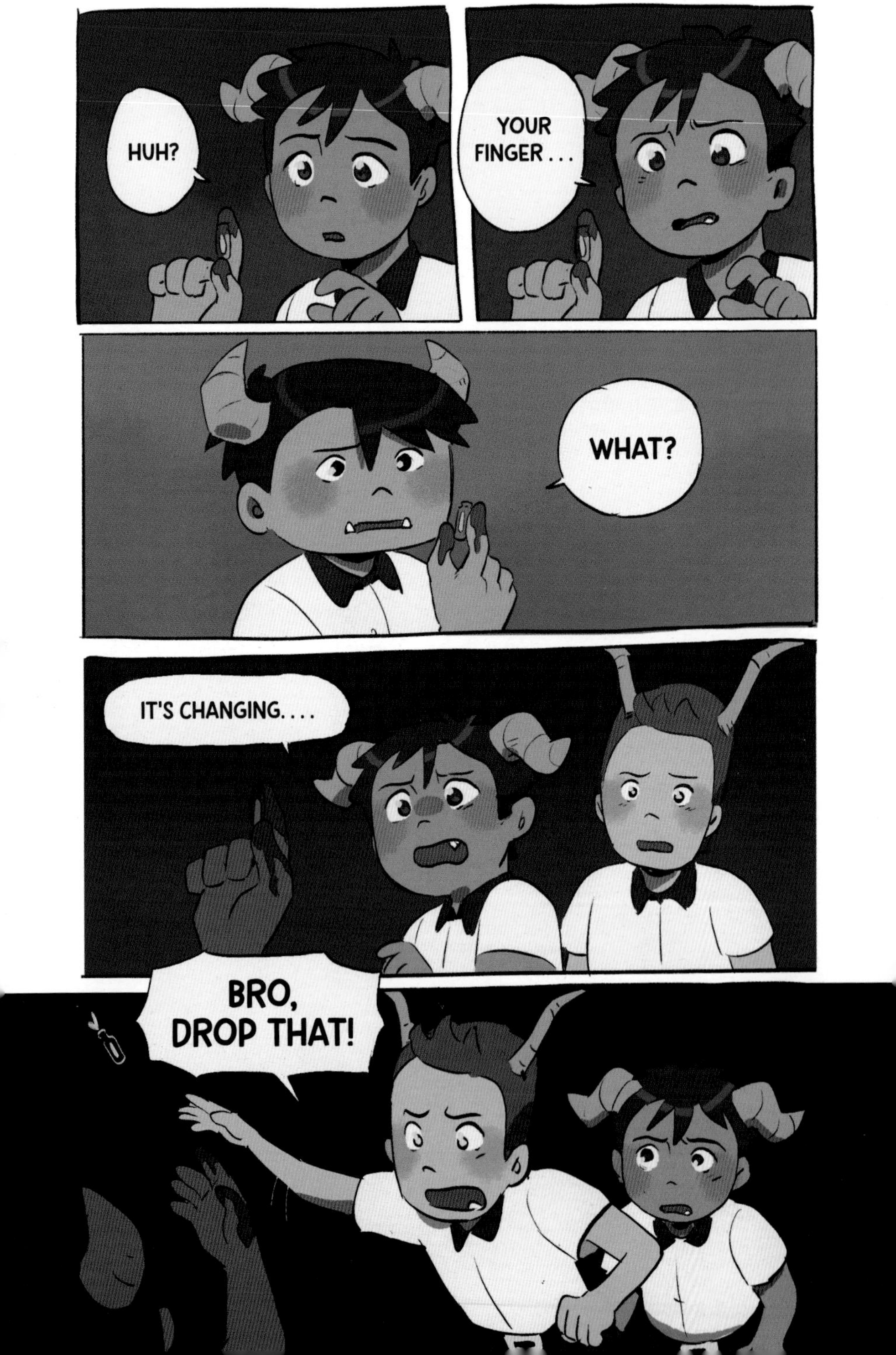
HUH?
YOUR FINGER . . .
WHAT?
IT'S CHANGING. . . .
BRO, DROP THAT!

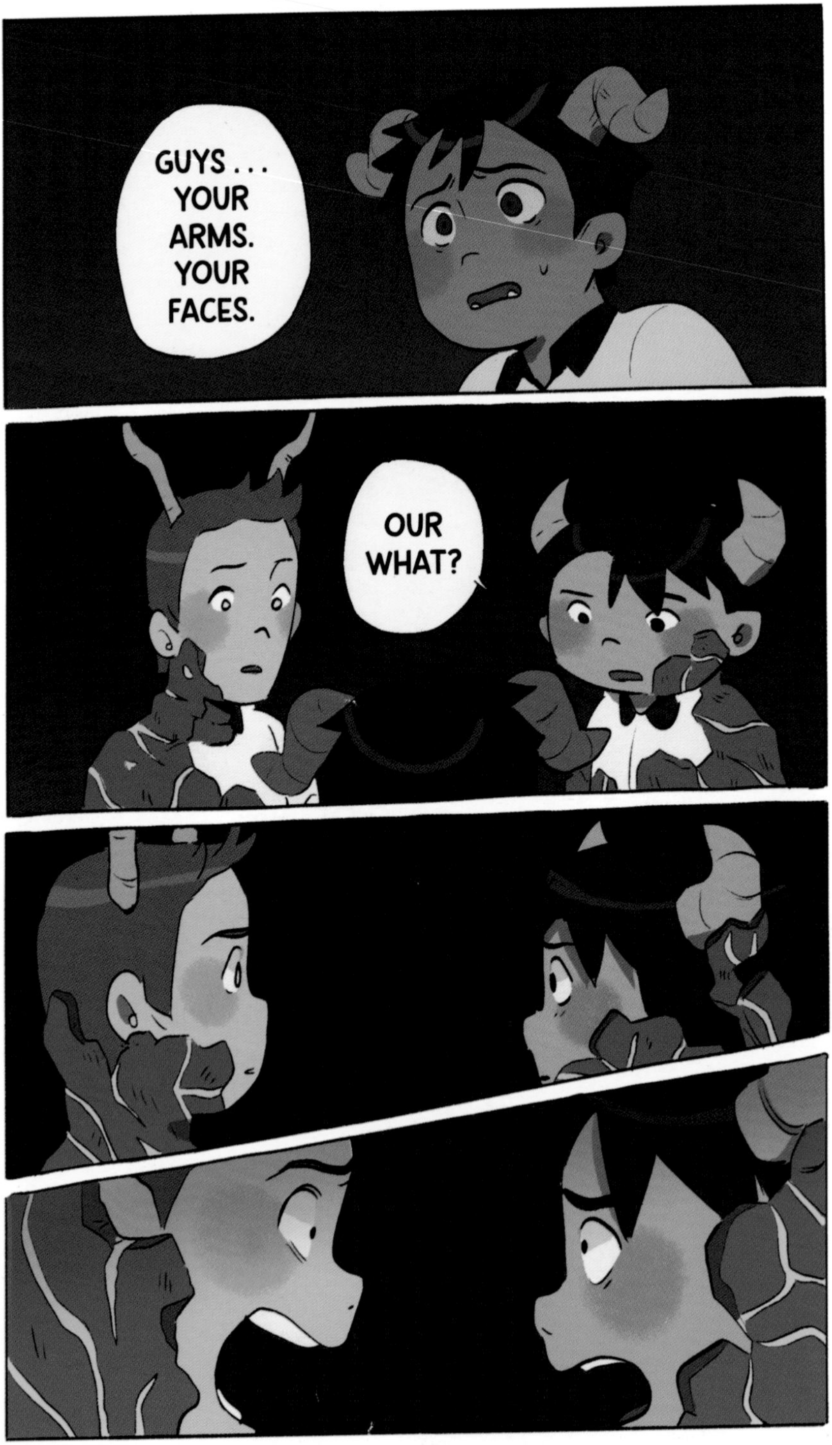
GUYS . . .
YOUR ARMS.
YOUR FACES.
OUR WHAT?

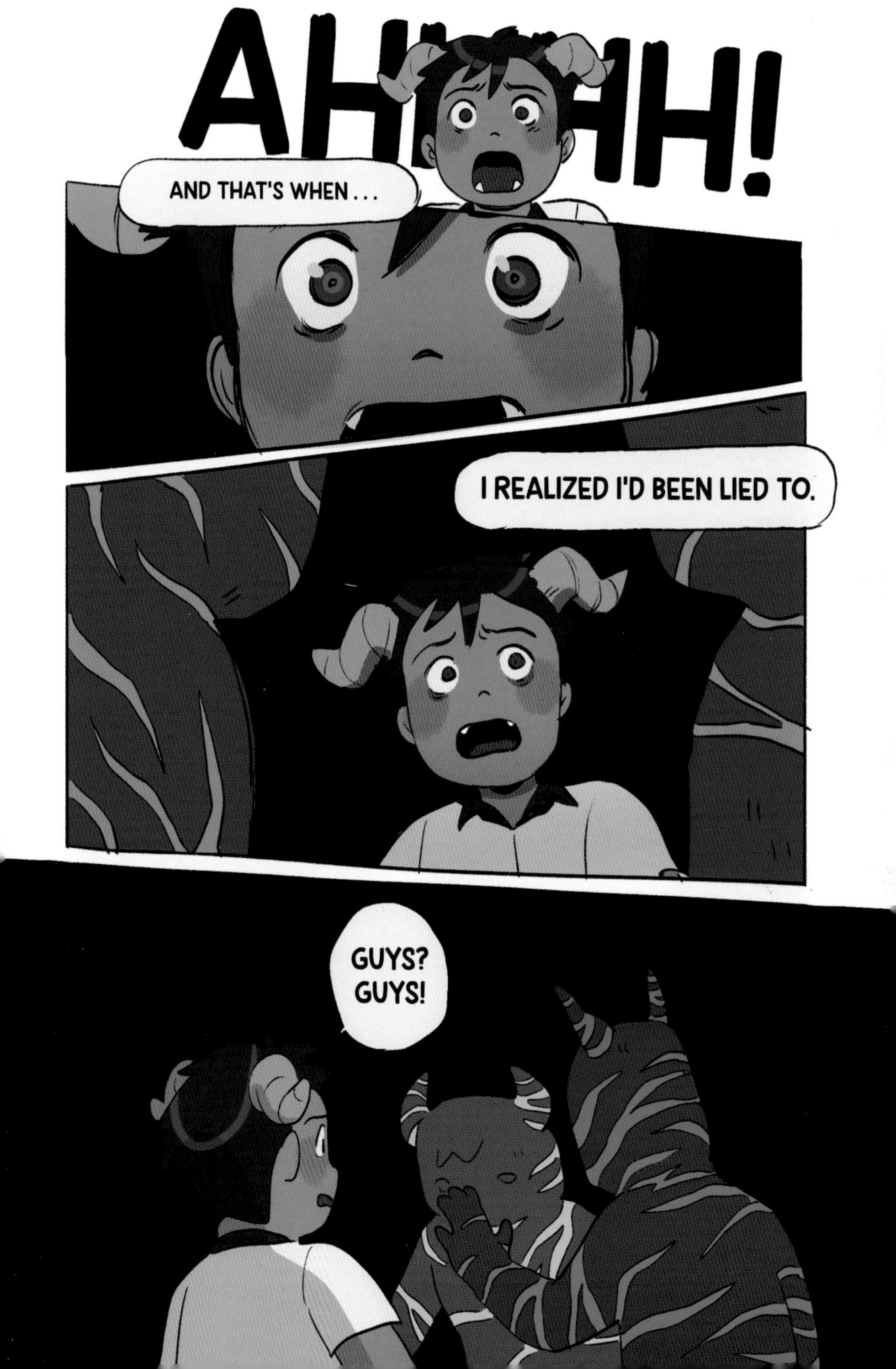
AHHHHH!
AND THAT'S WHEN . . .
I REALIZED I'D BEEN LIED TO.
GUYS?
GUYS!

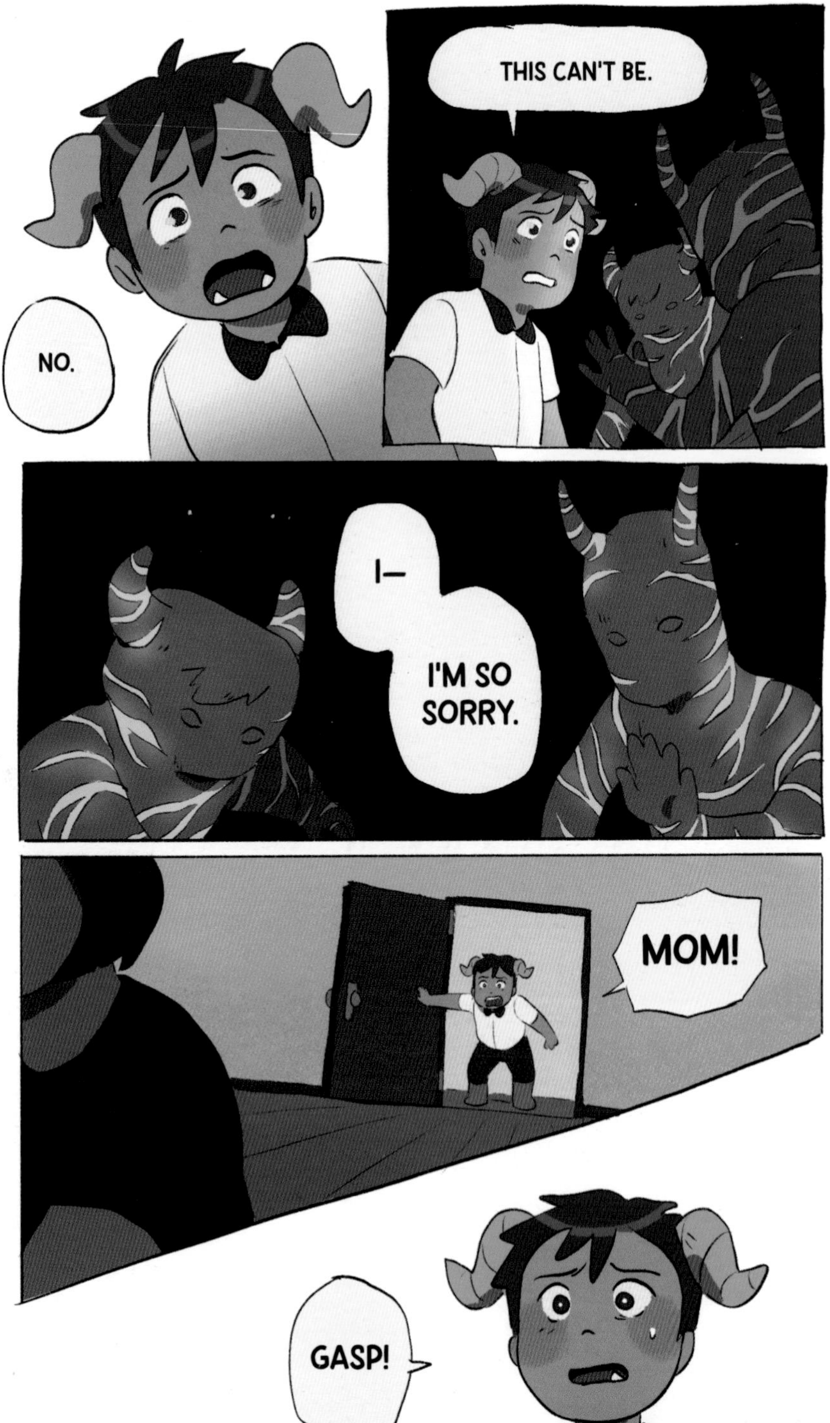
NO.
THIS CAN'T BE.
I—
I'M SO SORRY.
MOM!
GASP!

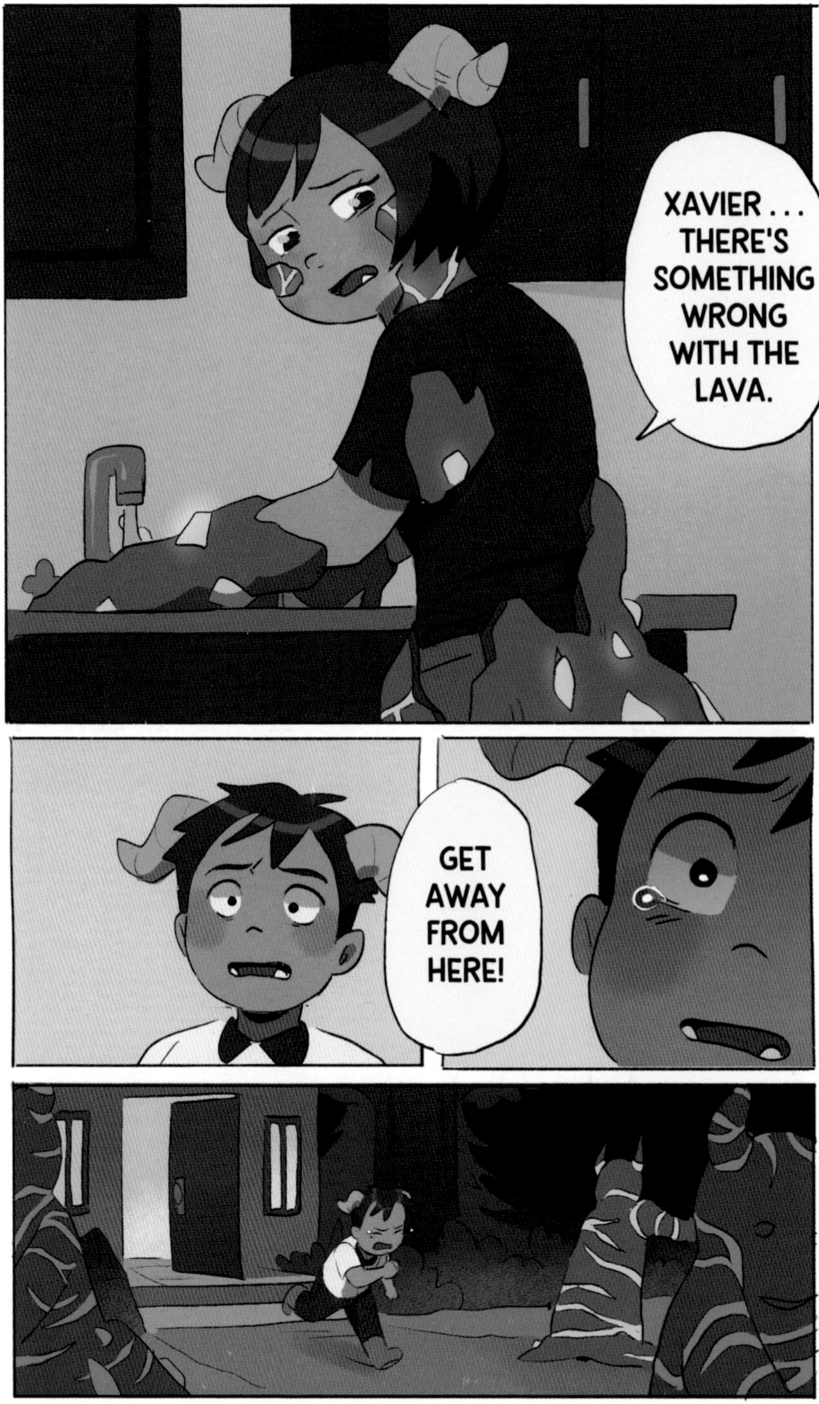
XAVIER . . . THERE'S SOMETHING WRONG WITH THE LAVA.
GET AWAY FROM HERE!

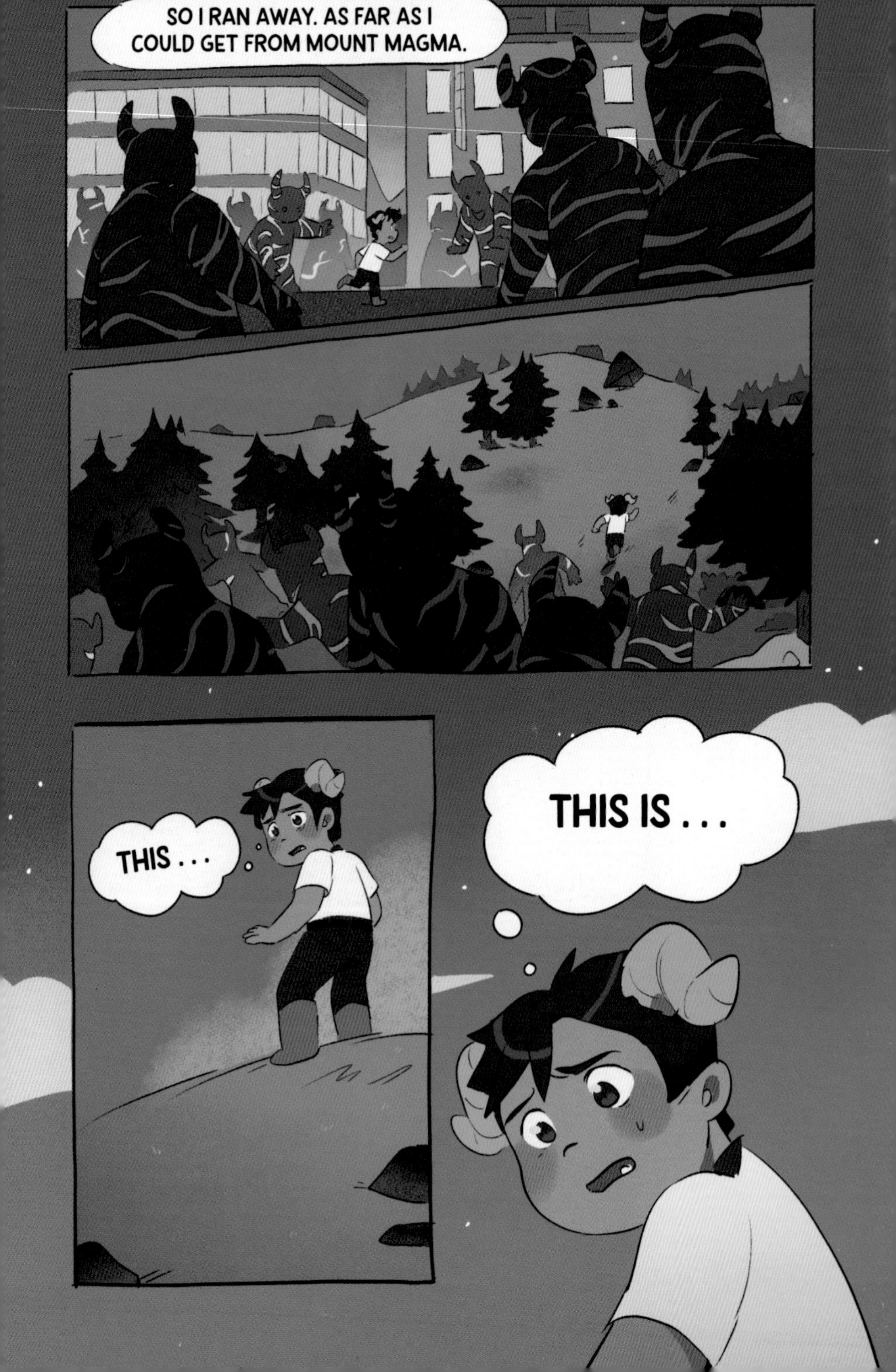
SO I RAN AWAY. AS FAR AS I COULD GET FROM MOUNT MAGMA.
THIS . . .
THIS IS . . .

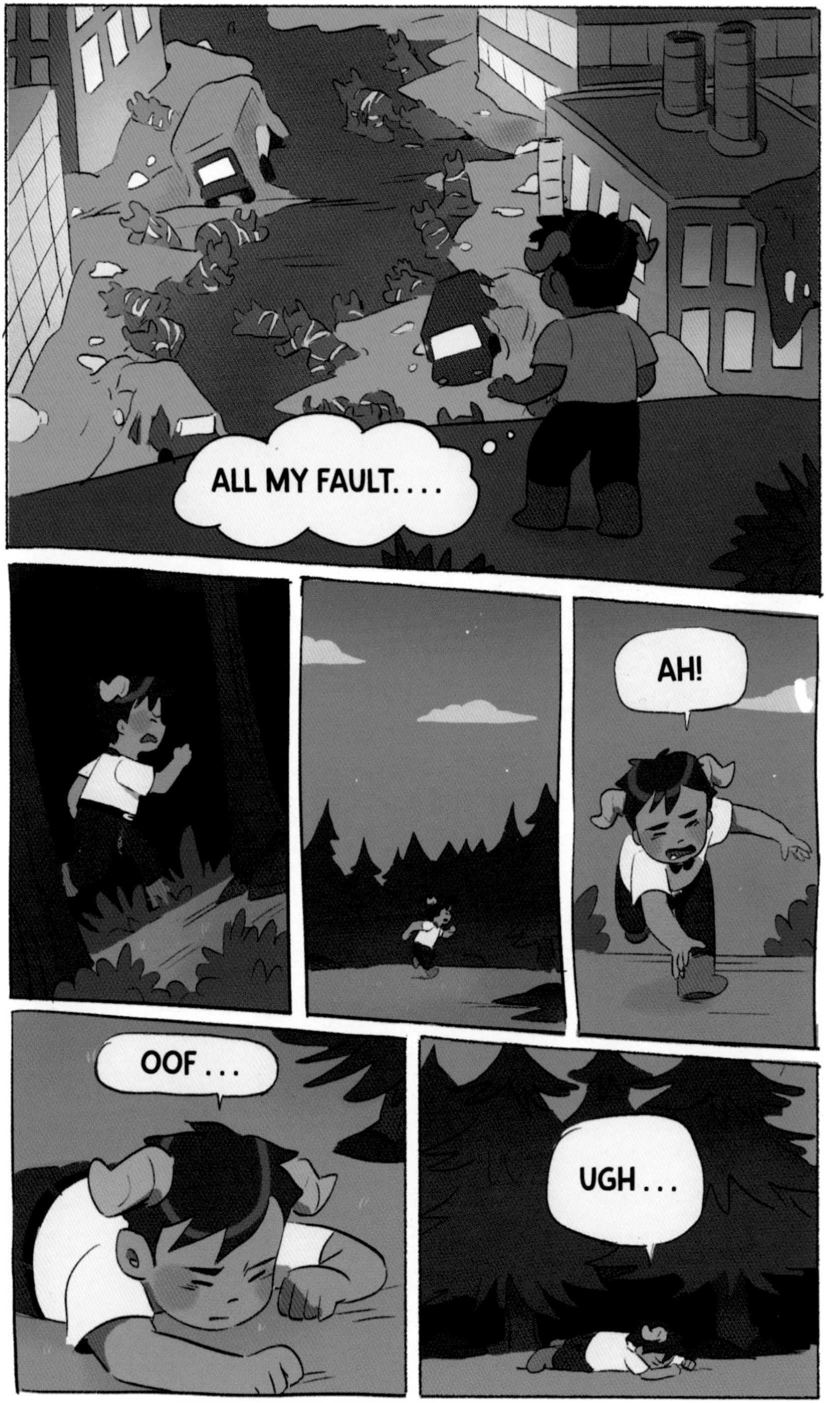
ALL MY FAULT. . . .
AH!
OOF . . .
UGH . . .

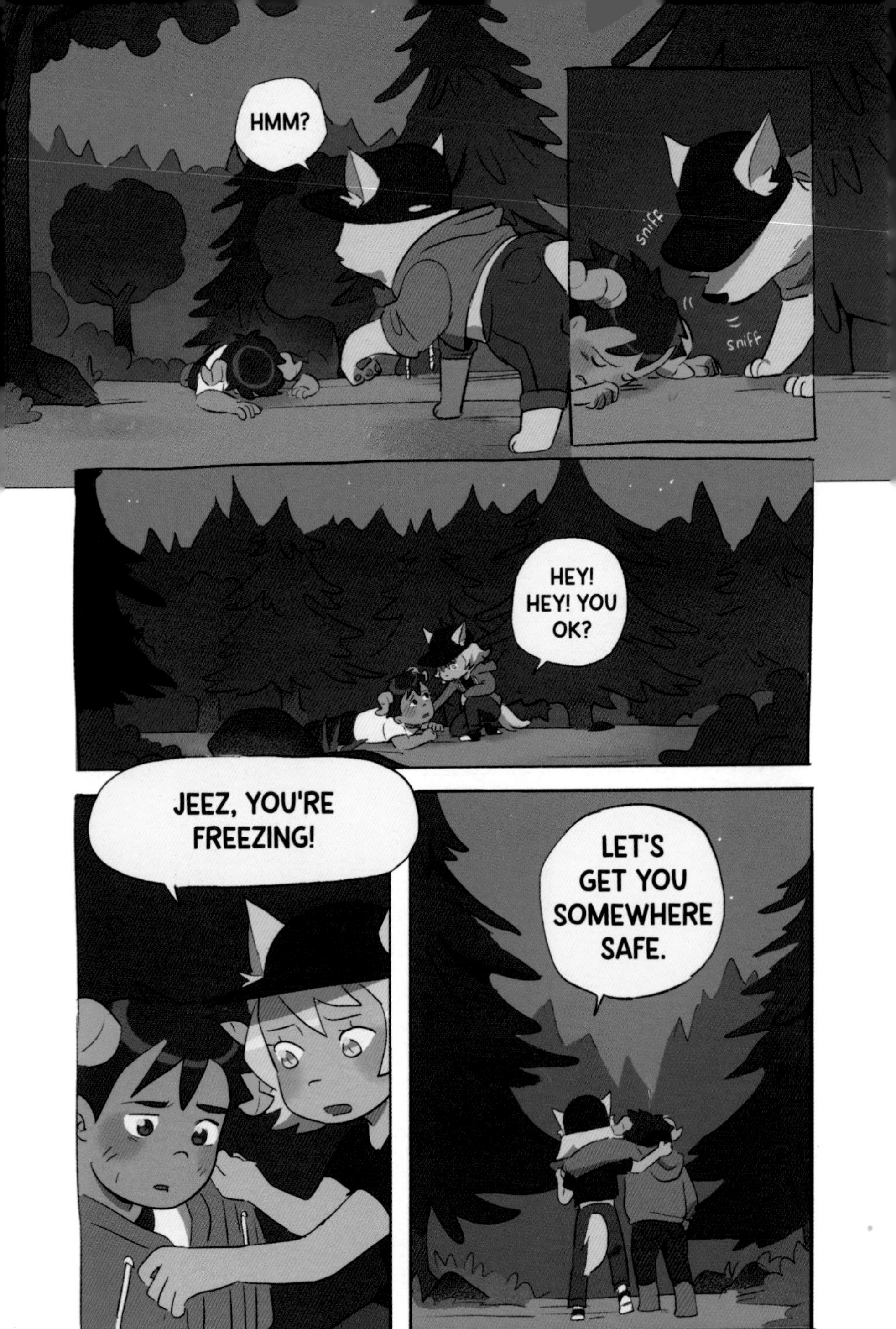
HMM?
sniff
sniff
HEY! HEY! YOU OK?
JEEZ, YOU'RE FREEZING!
LET'S GET YOU SOMEWHERE SAFE.

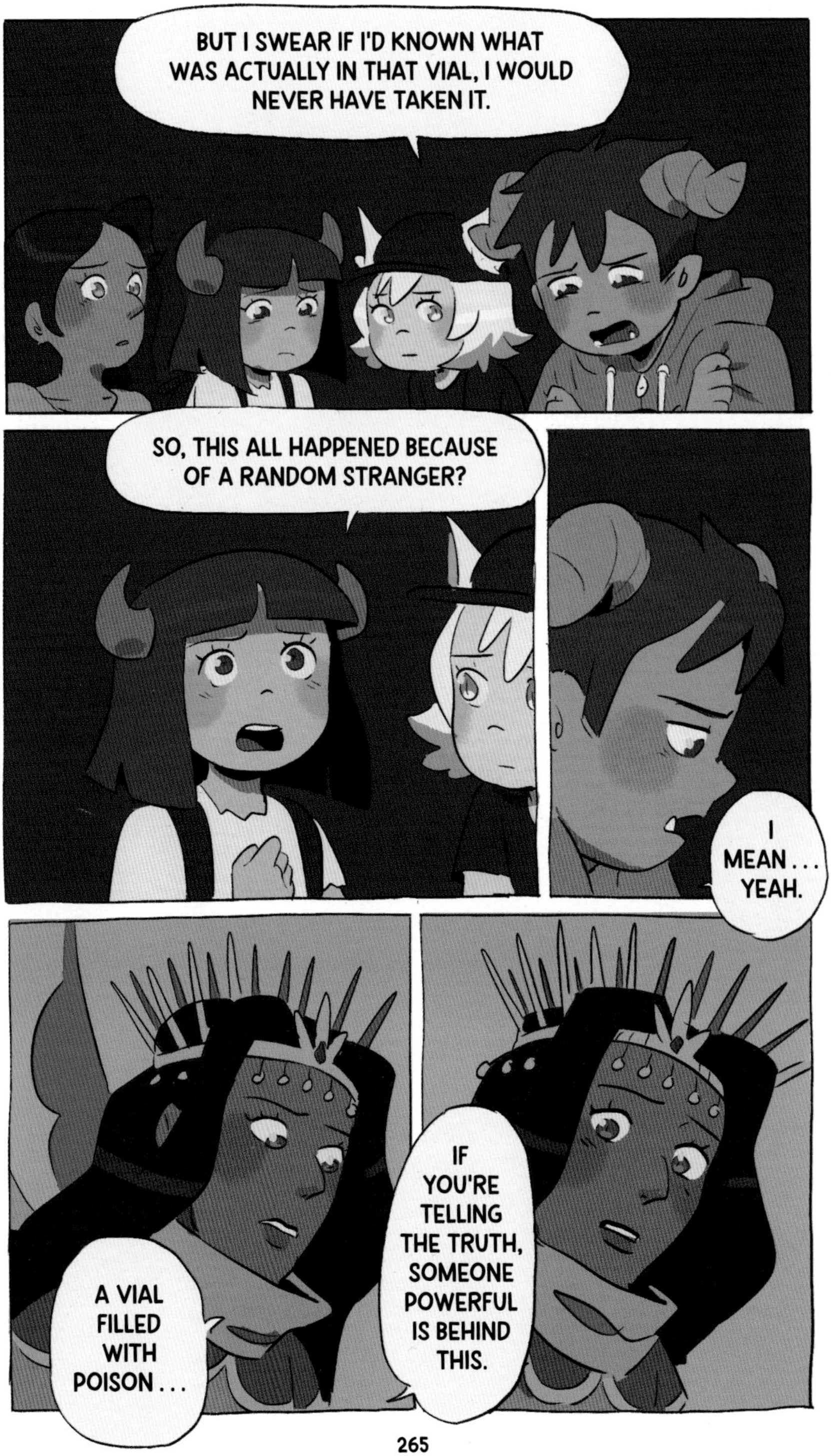

BUT I SWEAR IF I'D KNOWN WHAT WAS ACTUALLY IN THAT VIAL, I WOULD NEVER HAVE TAKEN IT.
SO, THIS ALL HAPPENED BECAUSE OF A RANDOM STRANGER?
I MEAN . . . YEAH.
A VIAL FILLED WITH POISON . . .
IF YOU'RE TELLING THE TRUTH, SOMEONE POWERFUL IS BEHIND THIS.

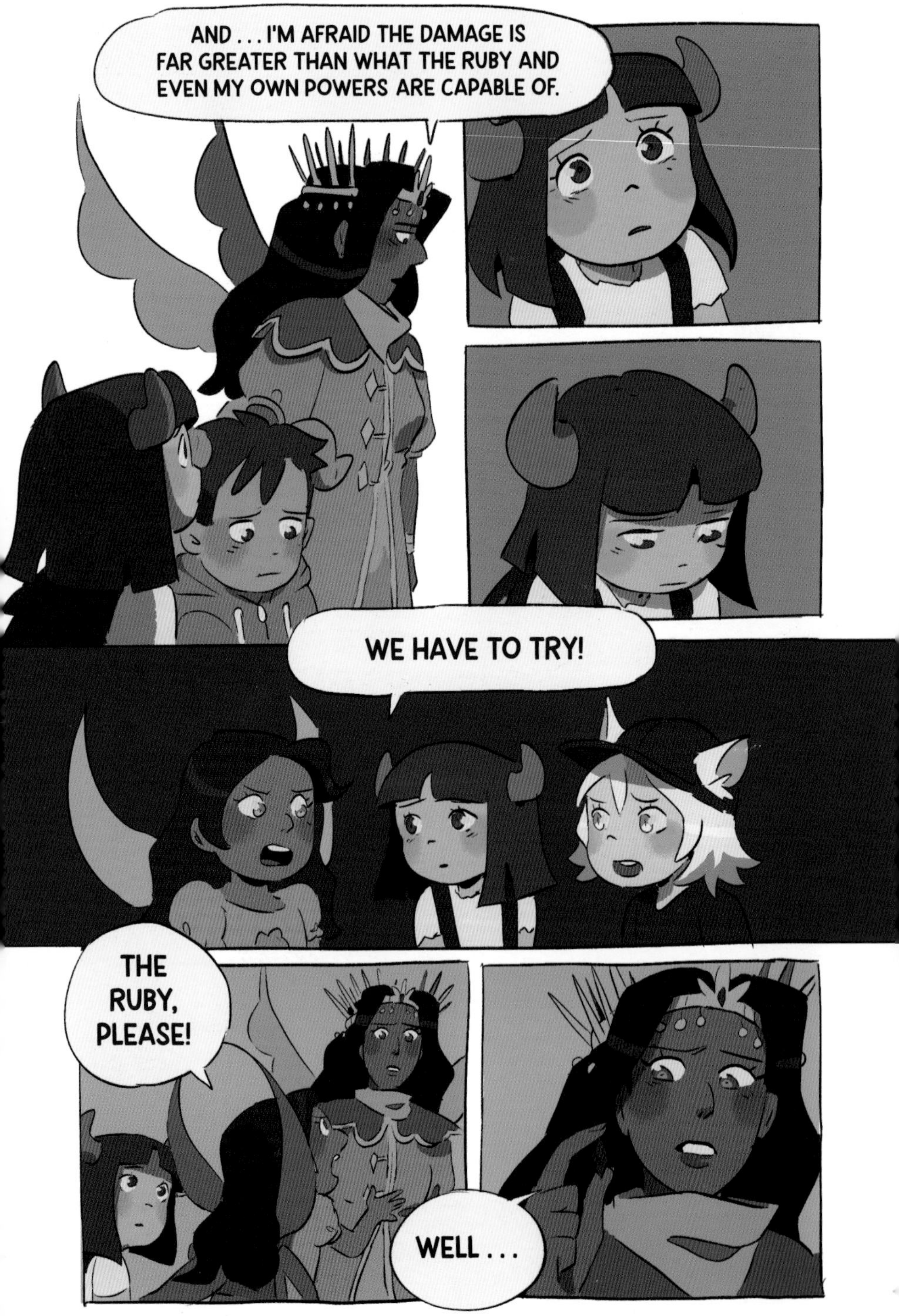

AND . . . I'M AFRAID THE DAMAGE IS FAR GREATER THAN WHAT THE RUBY AND EVEN MY OWN POWERS ARE CAPABLE OF.
WE HAVE TO TRY!
THE RUBY, PLEASE!
WELL . . .

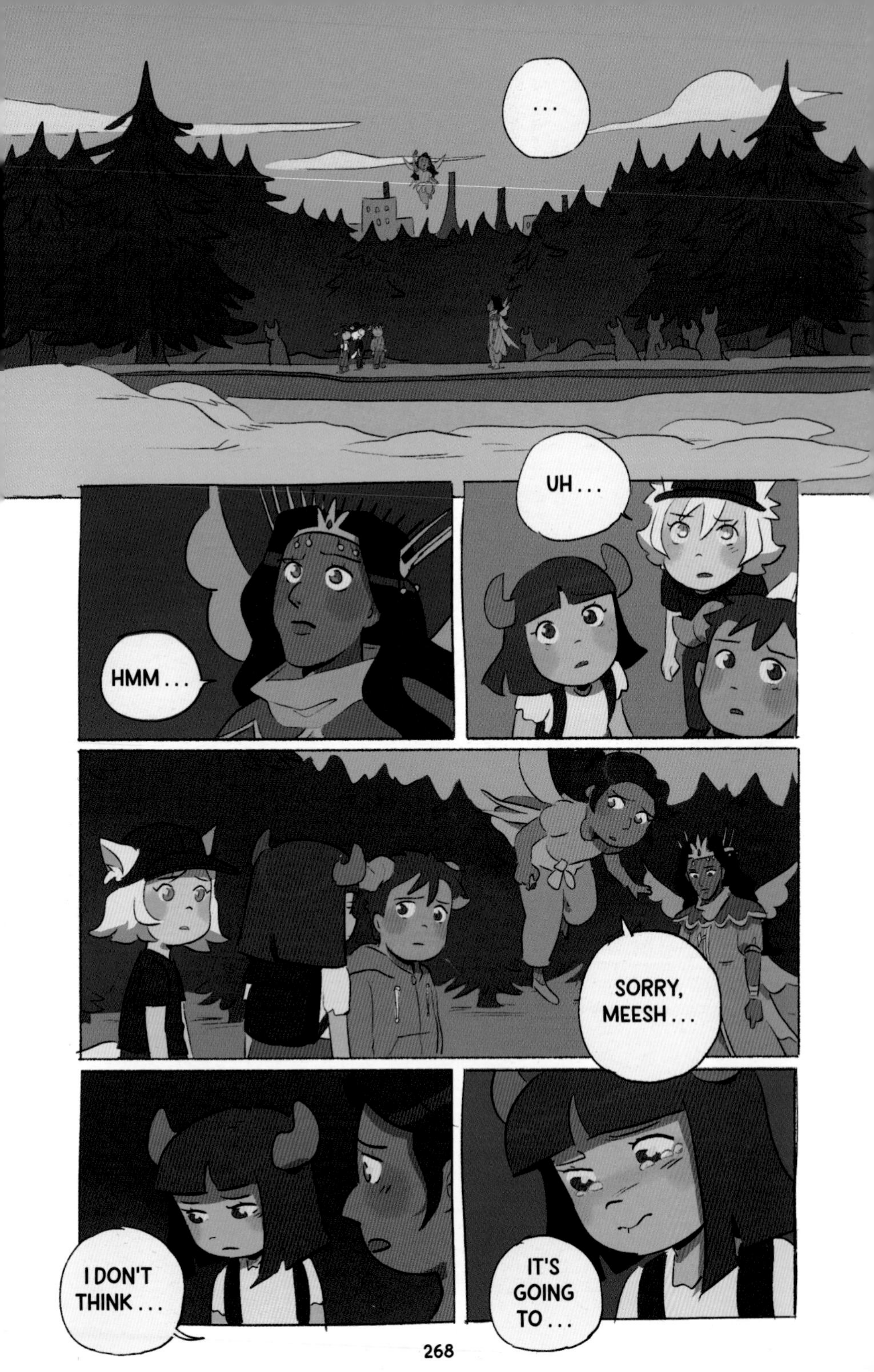
...
HMM...
UH...
SORRY, MEESH...
I DON'T THINK...
IT'S GOING TO...

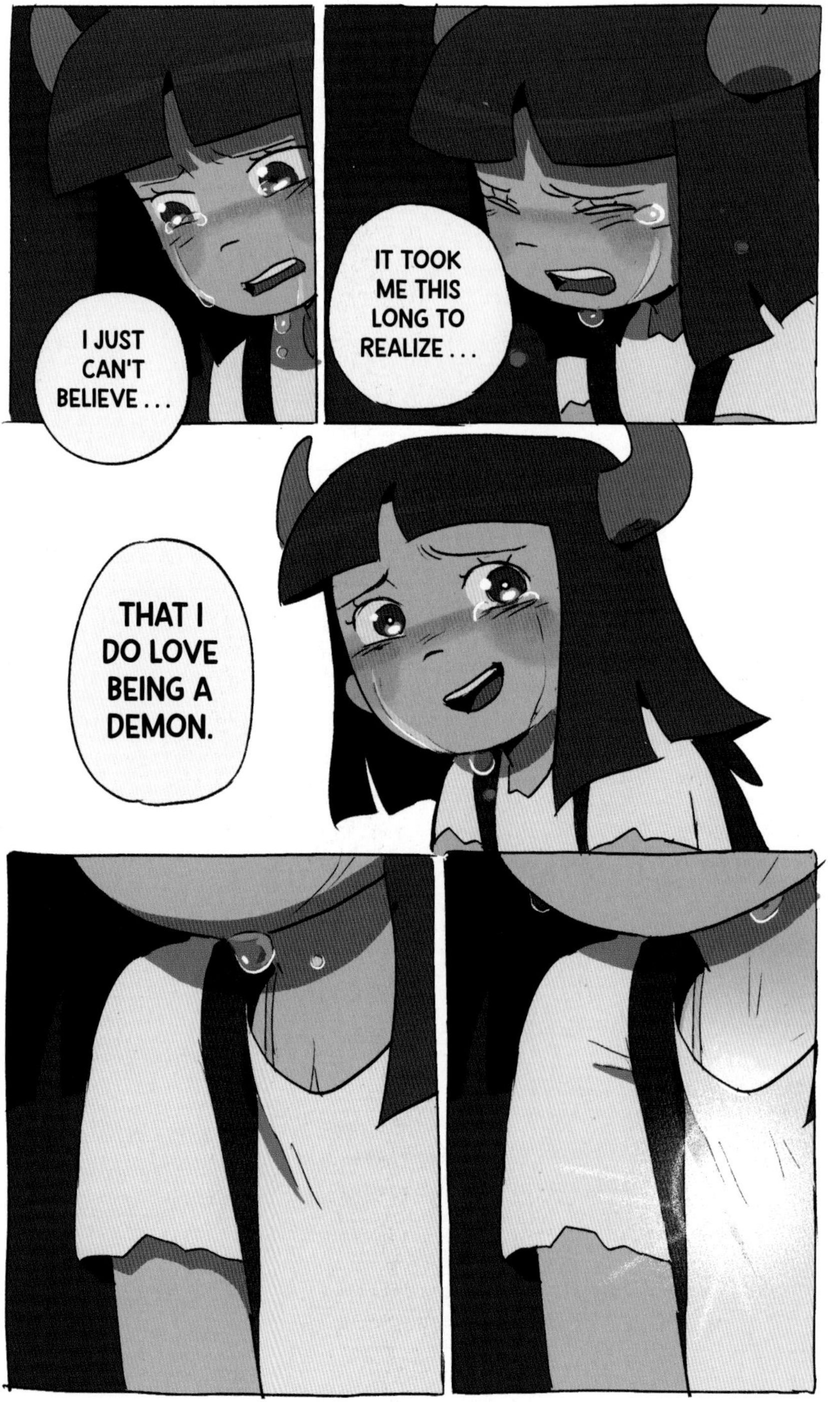
I JUST CAN'T BELIEVE . . .
IT TOOK ME THIS LONG TO REALIZE . . .
THAT I DO LOVE BEING A DEMON.

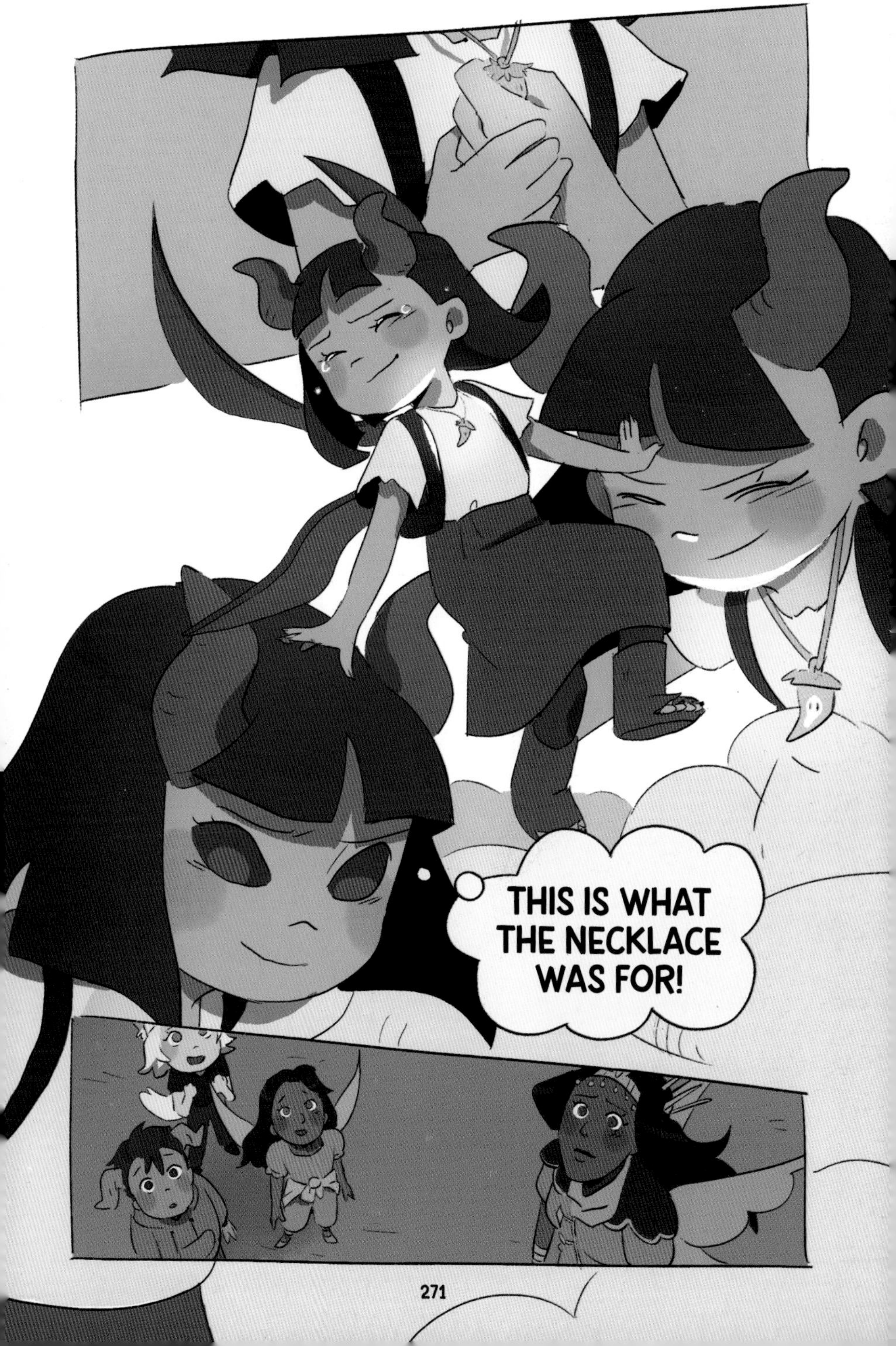
THIS IS WHAT THE NECKLACE WAS FOR!

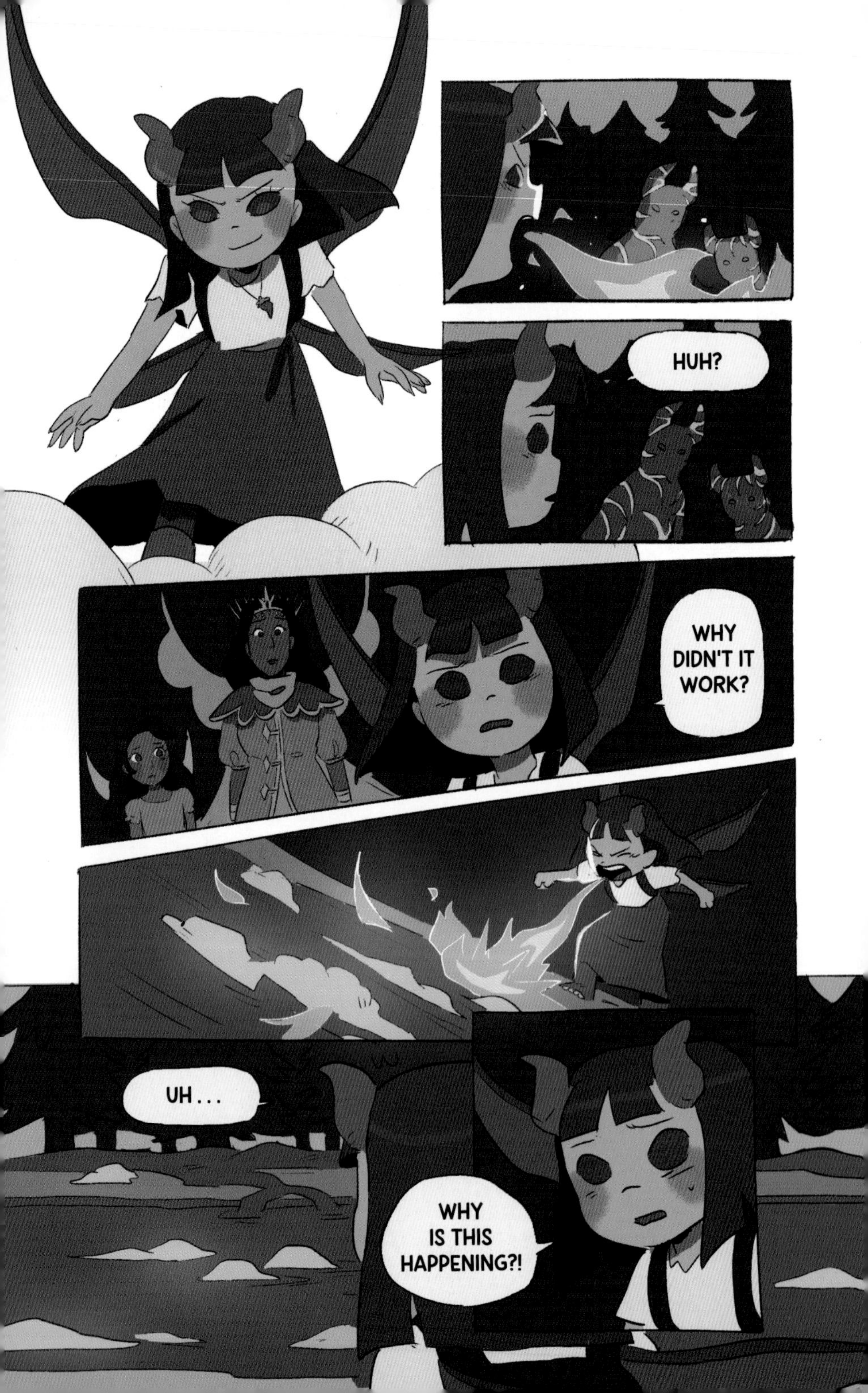
HUH?
WHY DIDN'T IT WORK?
UH . . .
WHY IS THIS HAPPENING?!

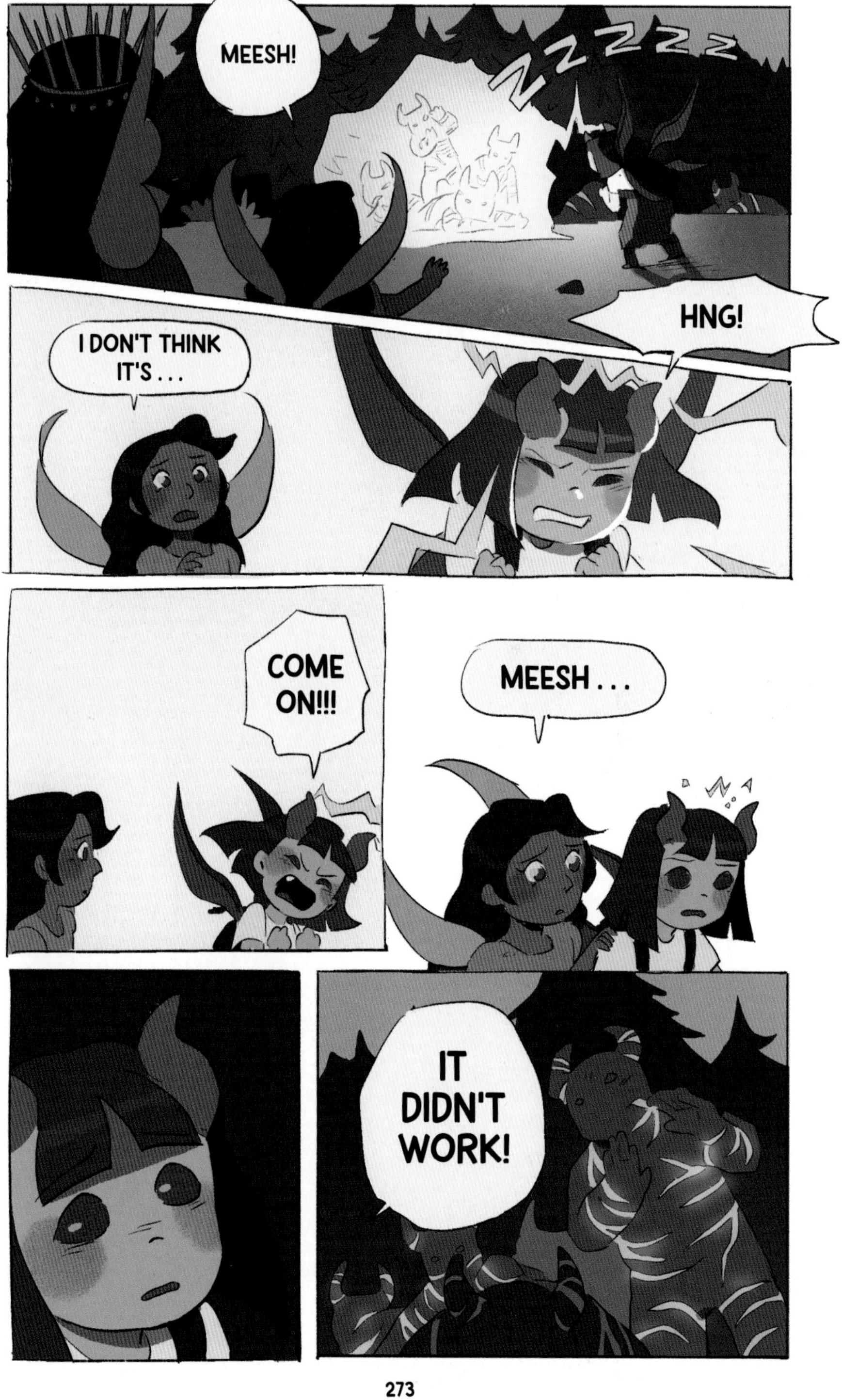
MEESH!
ZZZZZZ
I DON'T THINK IT'S . . .
HNG!
COME ON!!!
MEESH . . .
IT DIDN'T WORK!

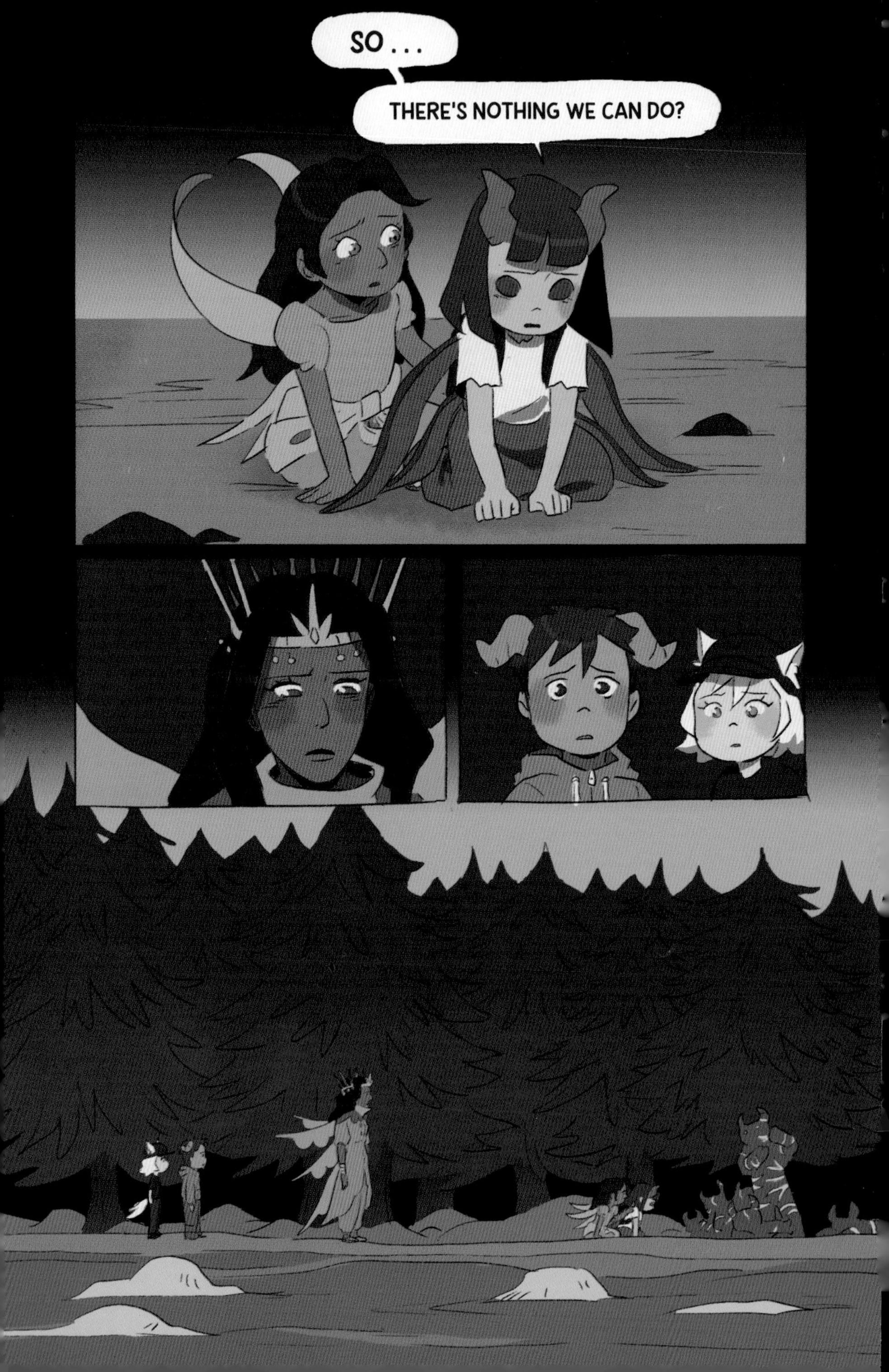
SO . . .
THERE'S NOTHING WE CAN DO?

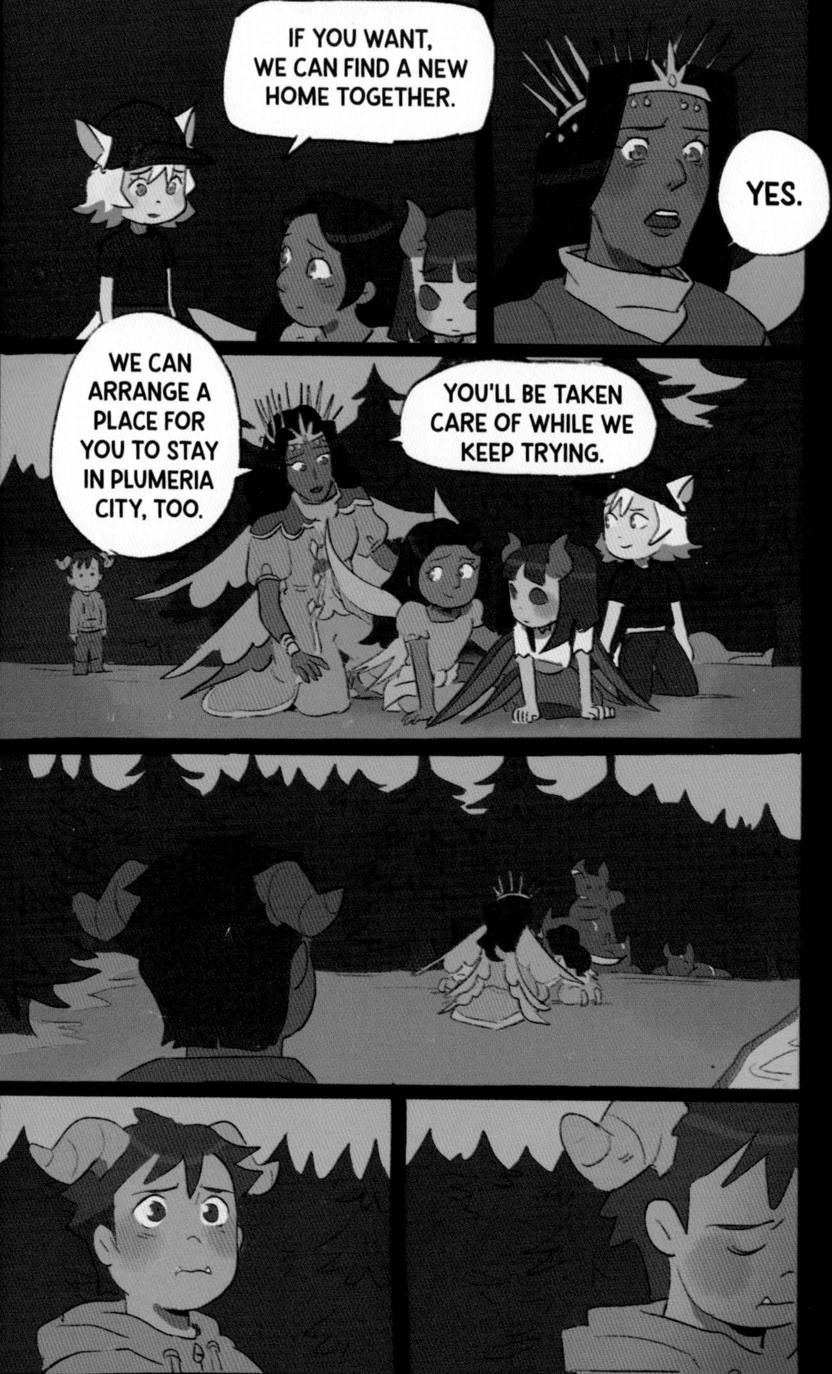
IF YOU WANT, WE CAN FIND A NEW HOME TOGETHER.
YES.
WE CAN ARRANGE A PLACE FOR YOU TO STAY IN PLUMERIA CITY, TOO.
YOU'LL BE TAKEN CARE OF WHILE WE KEEP TRYING.

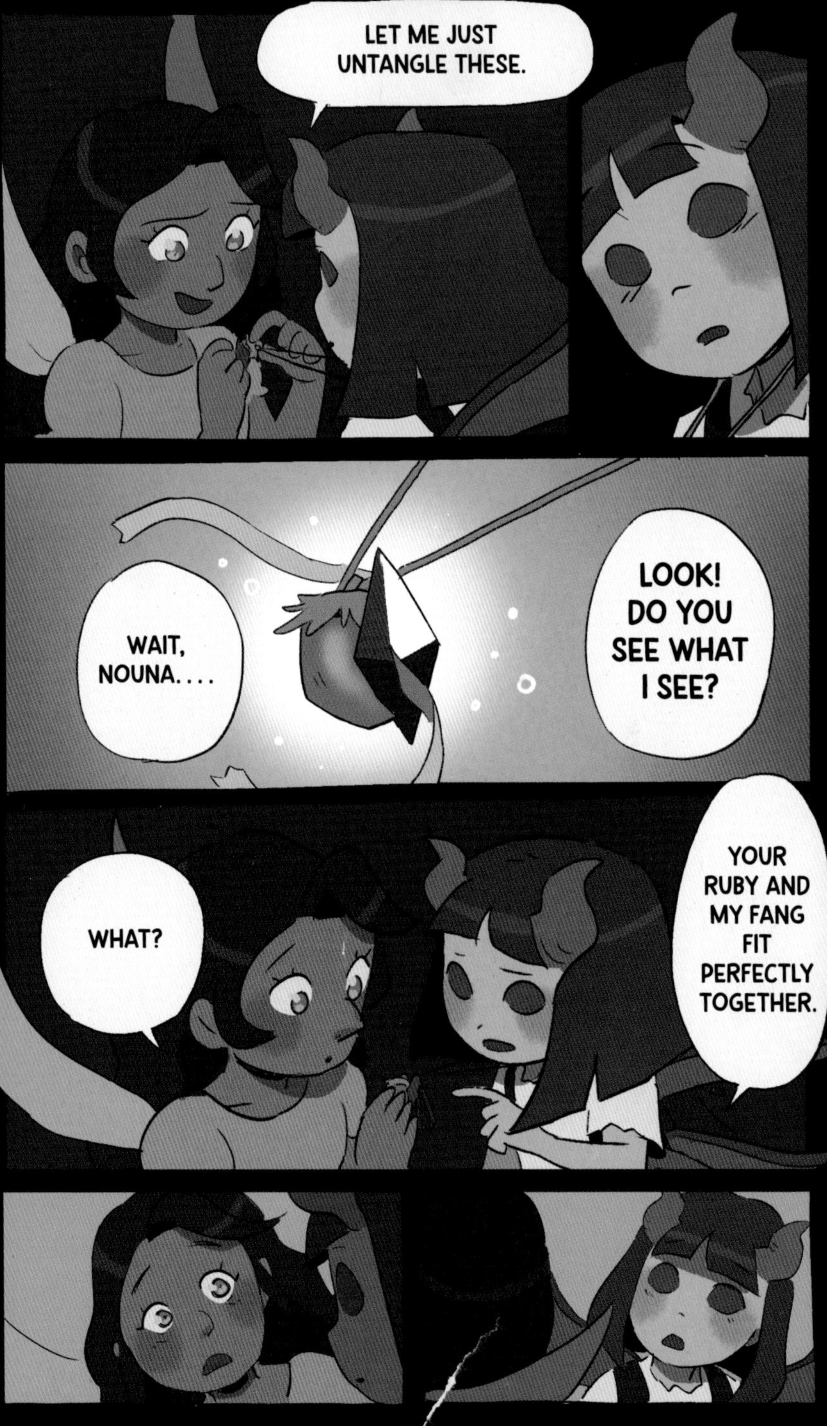
LET ME JUST UNTANGLE THESE.
WAIT, NOUNA. . . .
LOOK! DO YOU SEE WHAT I SEE?
WHAT?
YOUR RUBY AND MY FANG FIT PERFECTLY TOGETHER.

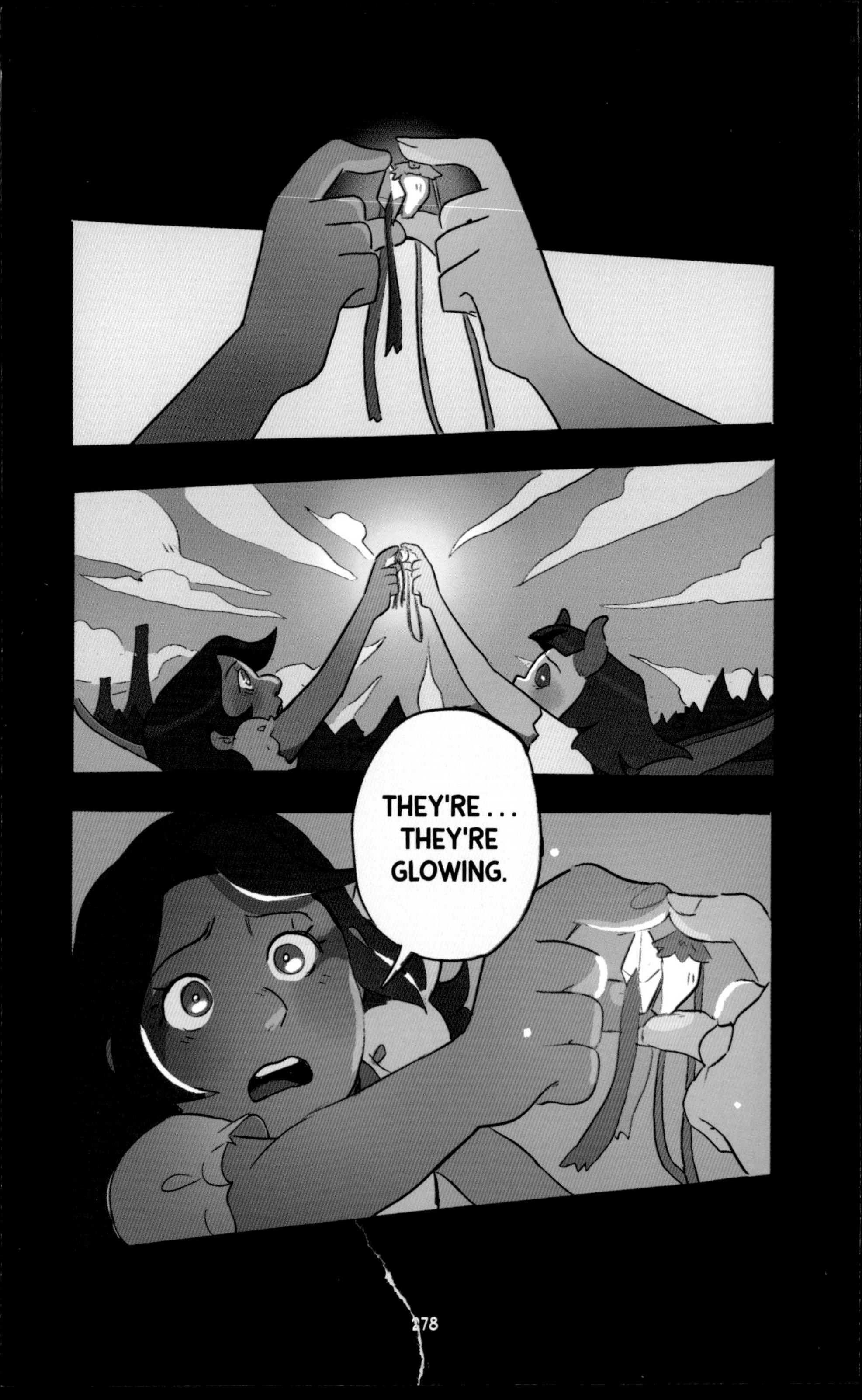
THEY'RE . . .
THEY'RE
GLOWING.

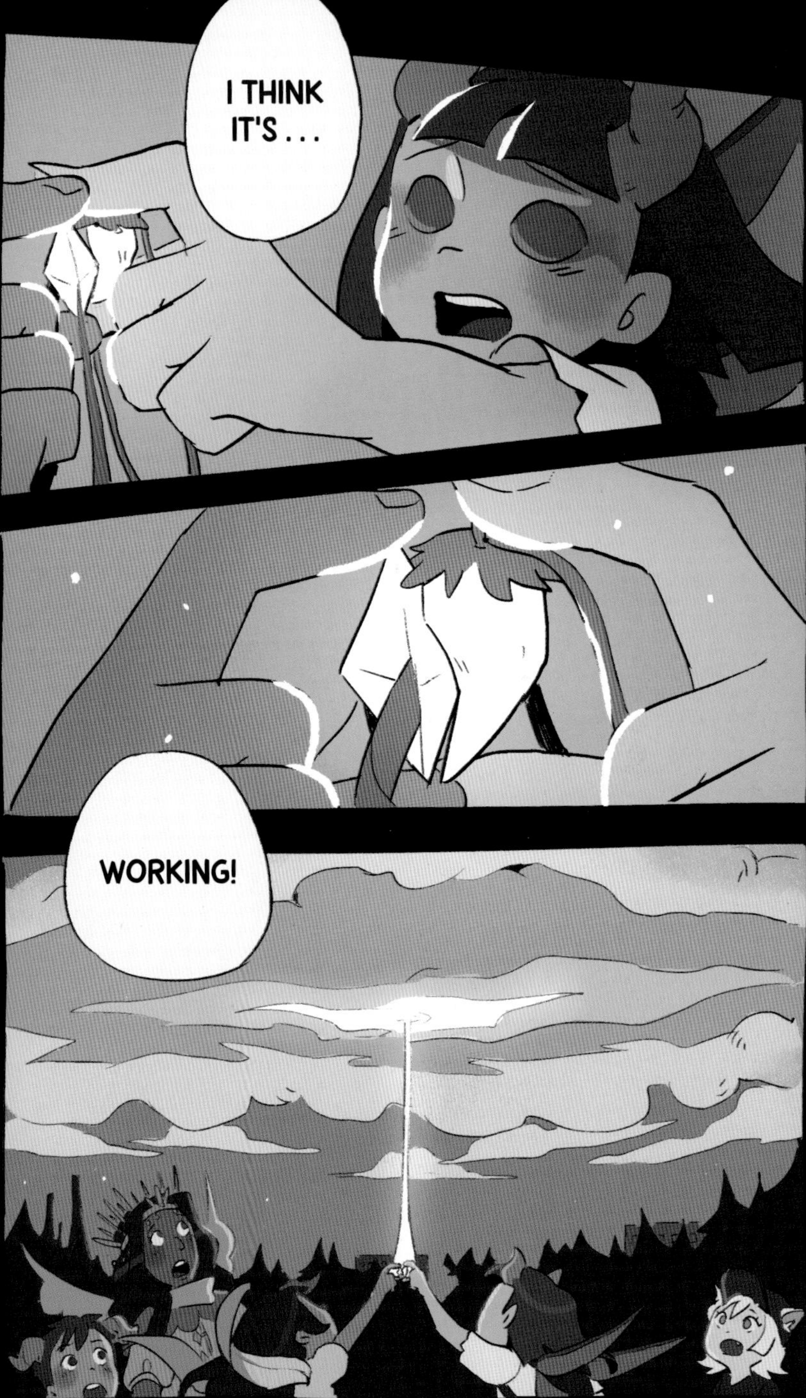
I THINK IT'S . . .
WORKING!

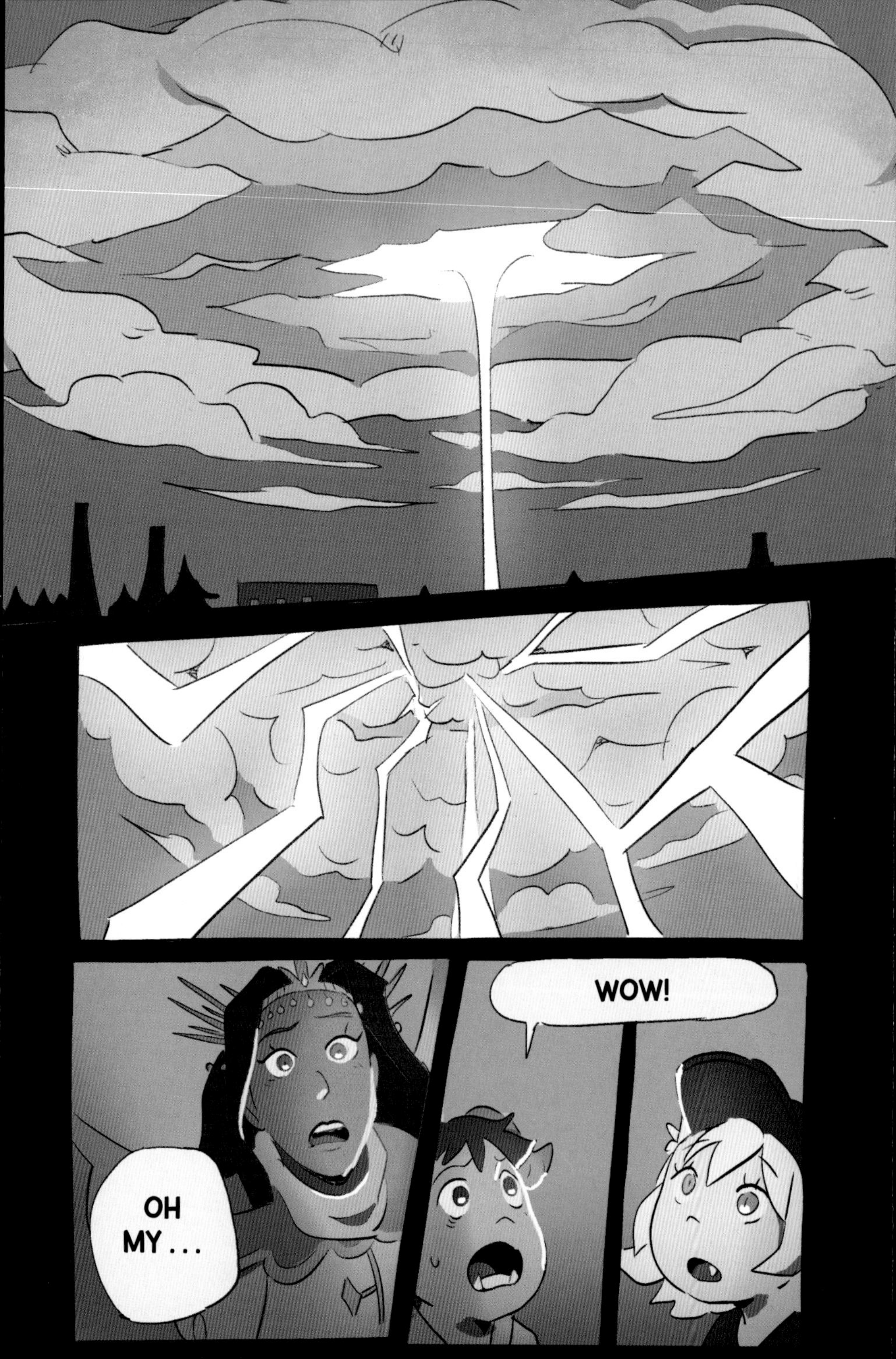
OH MY . . .
WOW!

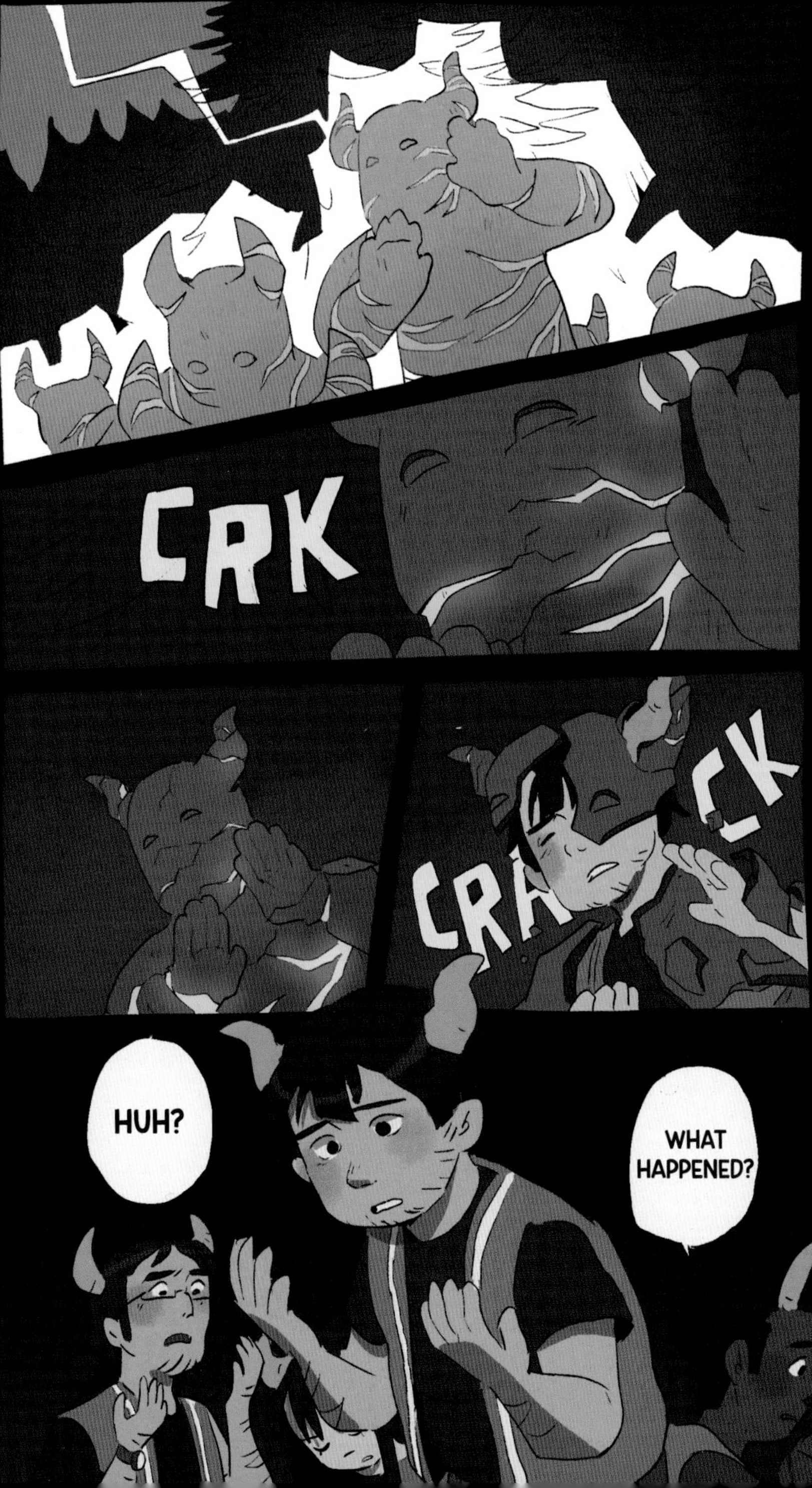
CRK
CRA
CK
HUH?
WHAT HAPPENED?

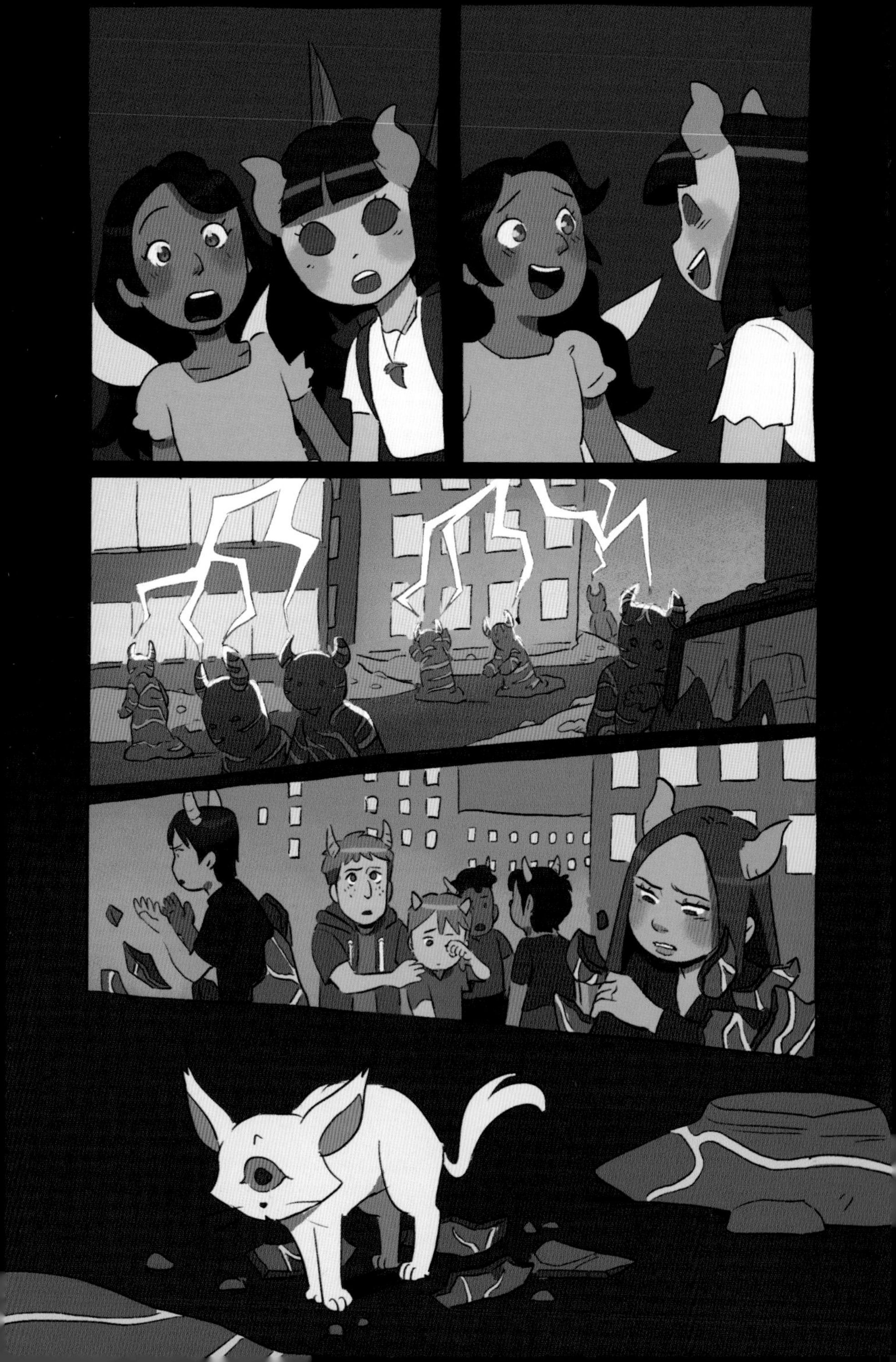

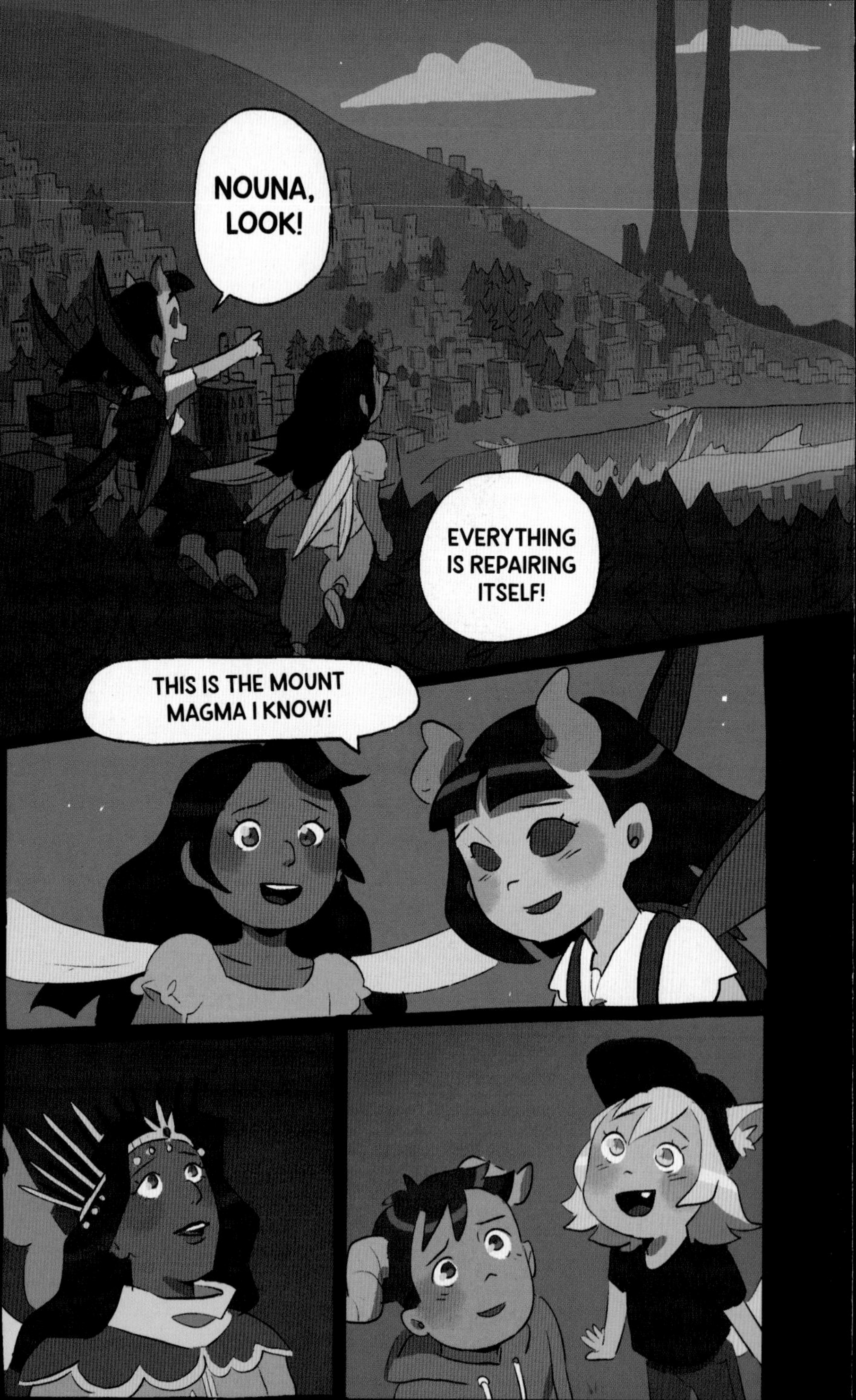
NOUNA, LOOK!
EVERYTHING IS REPAIRING ITSELF!
THIS IS THE MOUNT MAGMA I KNOW!

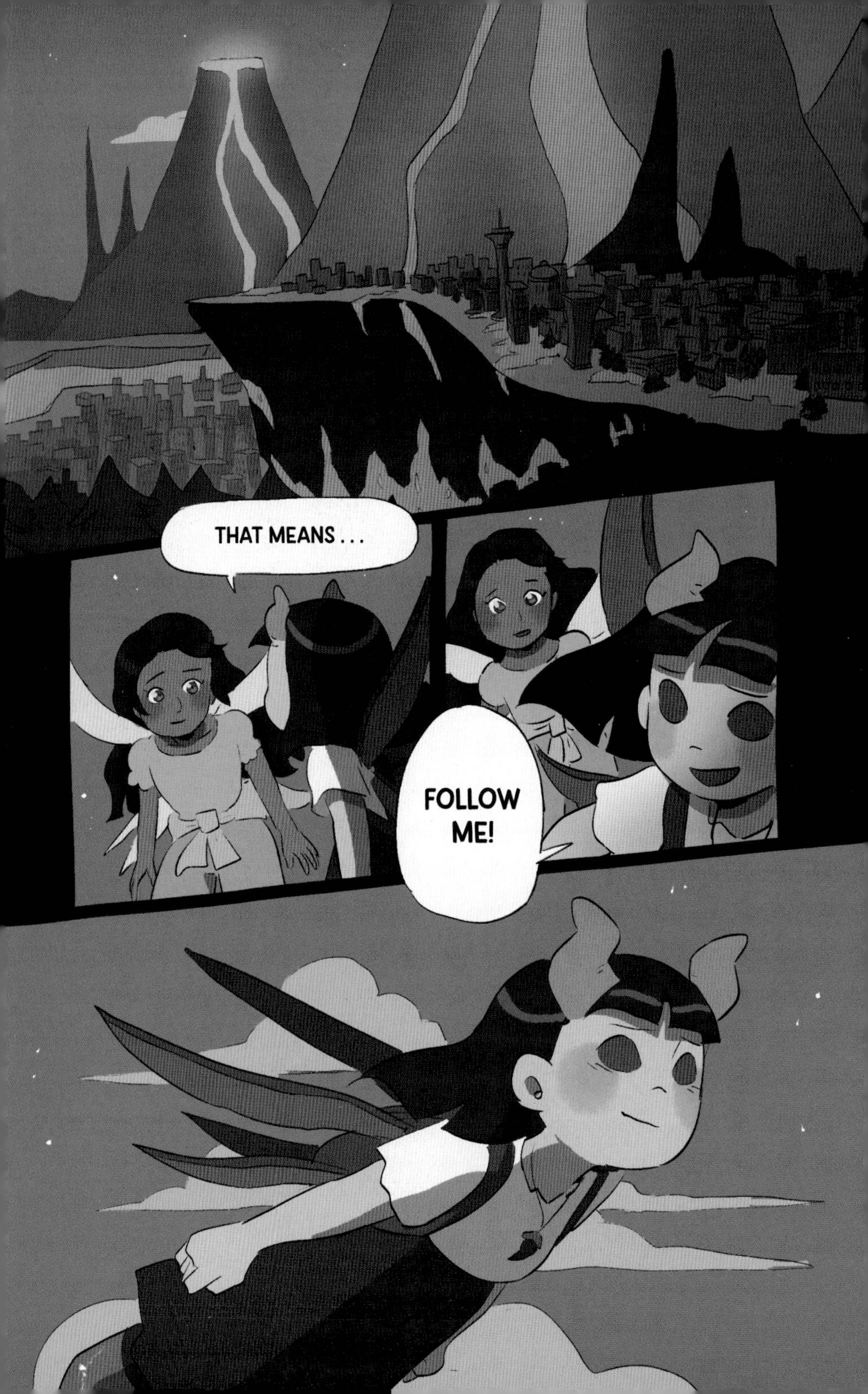
THAT MEANS . . .
FOLLOW ME!

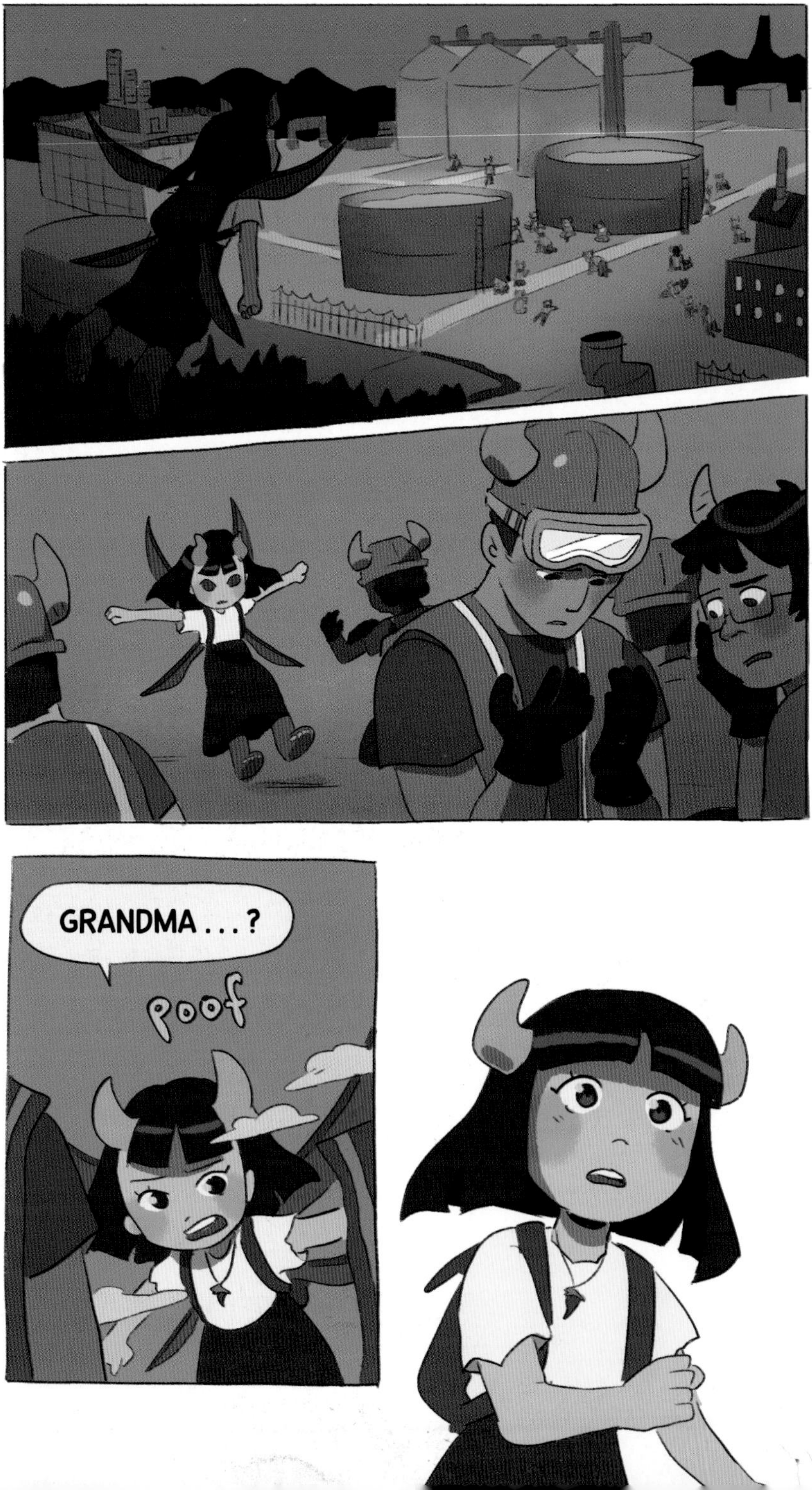
GRANDMA . . . ?
poof

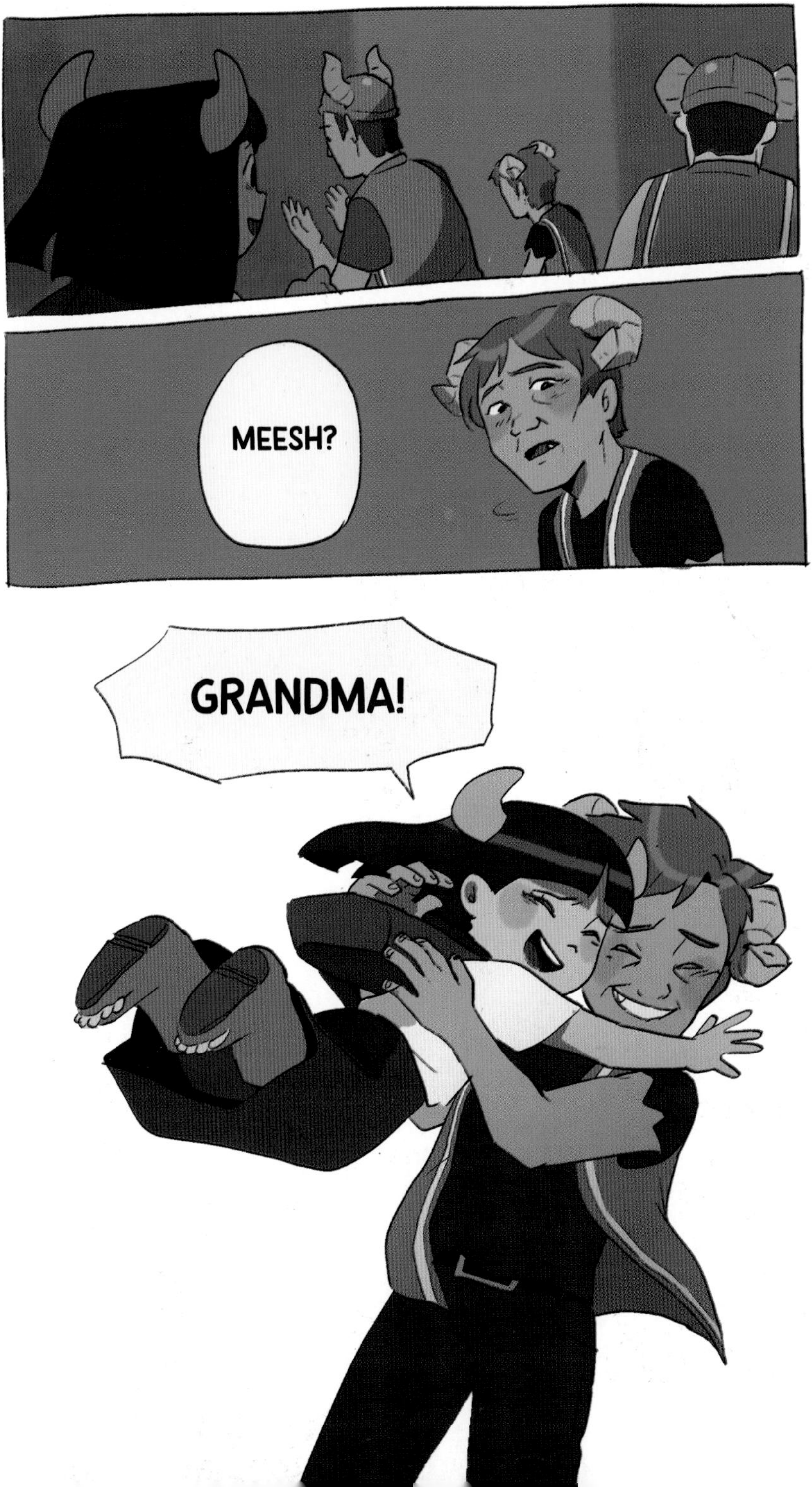
MEESH?
GRANDMA!

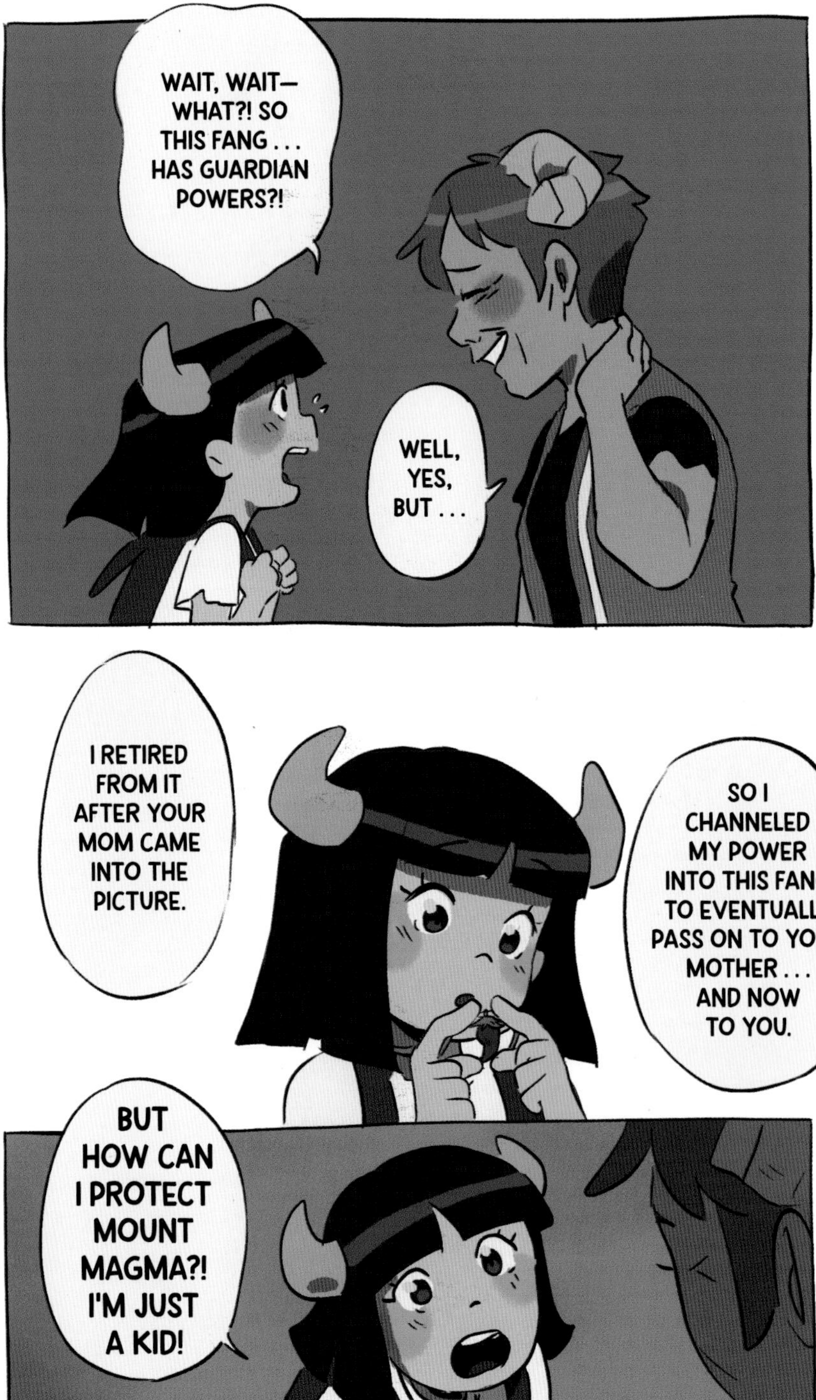
WAIT, WAIT— WHAT?! SO THIS FANG . . . HAS GUARDIAN POWERS?!
WELL, YES, BUT . . .
I RETIRED FROM IT AFTER YOUR MOM CAME INTO THE PICTURE.
SO I CHANNELED MY POWER INTO THIS FANG TO EVENTUALLY PASS ON TO YOUR MOTHER . . . AND NOW TO YOU.
BUT HOW CAN I PROTECT MOUNT MAGMA?! I'M JUST A KID!

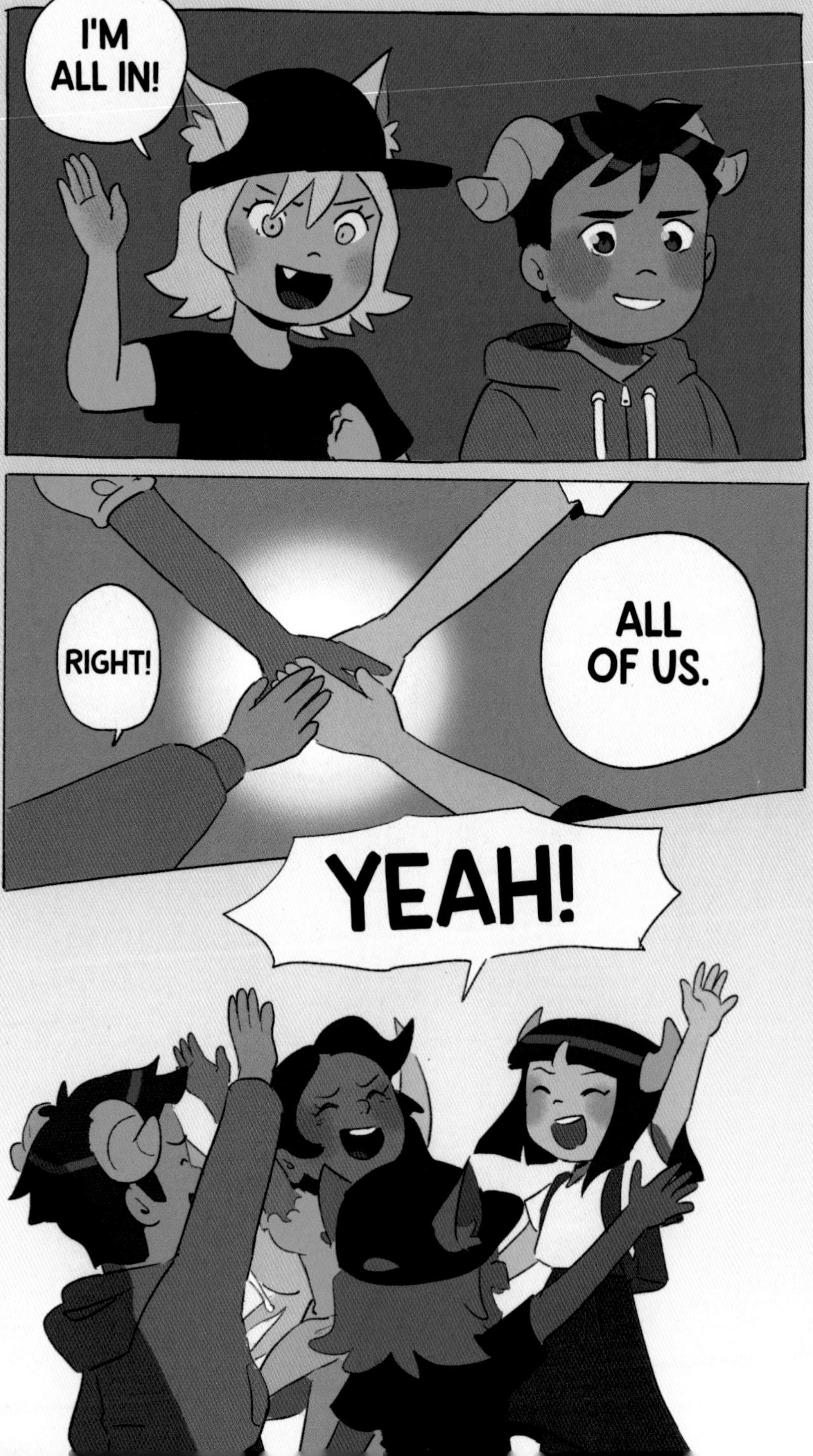
I'M ALL IN!
RIGHT!
ALL OF US.
YEAH!

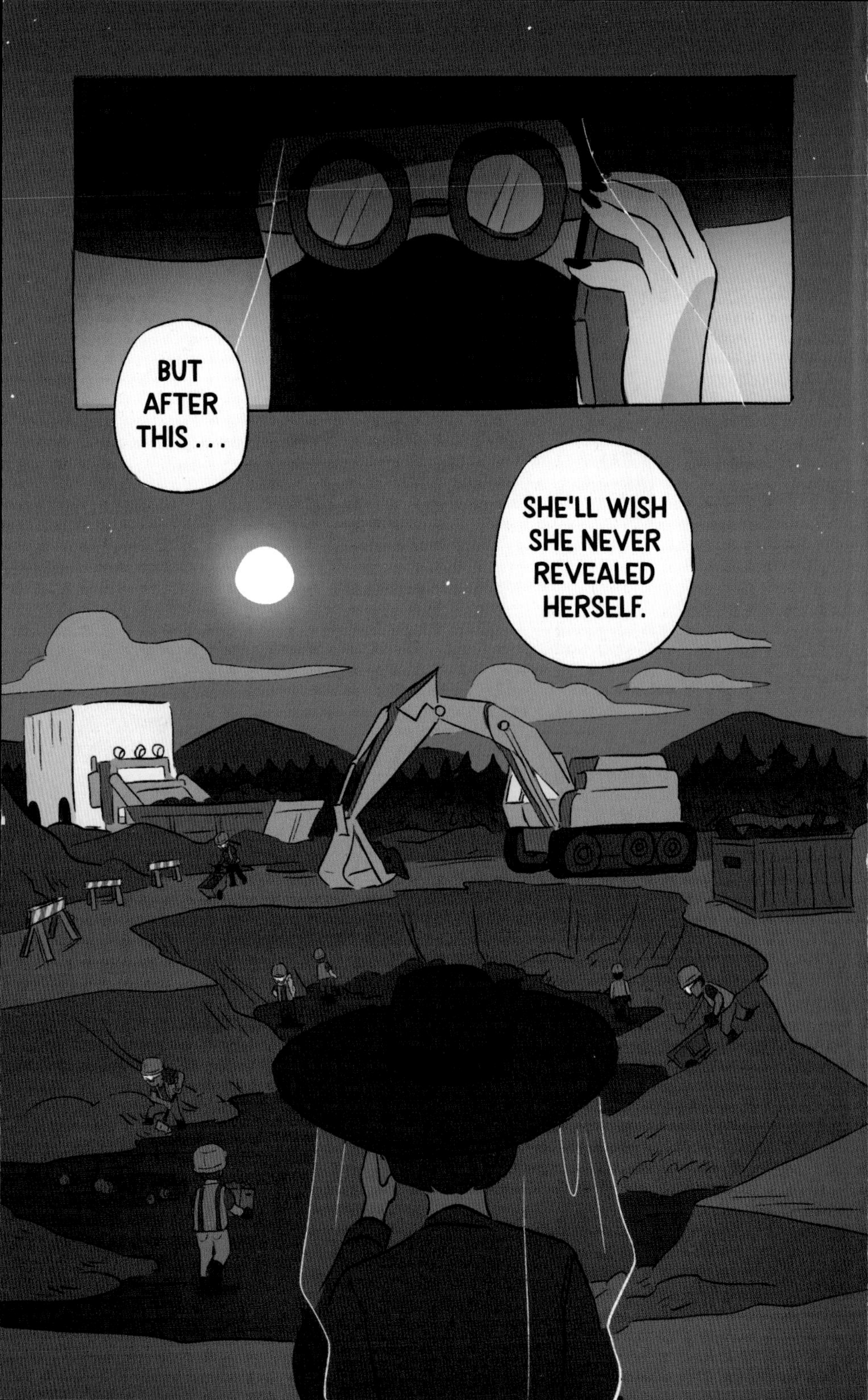
BUT AFTER THIS . . .
SHE'LL WISH SHE NEVER REVEALED HERSELF.